CONTENTS

Thou who didst dwell where Ruknabad once ran
Melodious beneath the Persian sky,
And watch with mind serene and steady eye
The tragic play that is the life of man;
And, seeing it was so since earth began
And shall continue after thou and I,
Being spent as swiftly as a lover's sigh,
Depart upon death's trackless caravan;
Out of dross sound by sovereign alchemy
Didst fashion melodies of liquid gold,
Creating riches of thy penury,
Transmuting death to immortality:
Accept these words that leave the whole untold,
And in fresh youth renew thy wisdom old.

INTRODUCTION

I

IT is two hundred years since the birth of Sir William Jones (1746–1794), the father of Persian studies in the west; one century and three-quarters since the publication of *A Persian Song*, his celebrated translation which introduced Ḥāfiẓ of Shīrāz to the literary world of London and Europe. The present is thus a peculiarly opportune time to review what his successors have done in furthering the study and interpretation of this, the greatest lyric poet of Persia; the more so since it has long been desirable to furnish students with a text-book appropriate to their needs as beginners in the appreciation of Persian lyrical poetry. The selection now presented has been made with the double object of exhibiting the various aspects of Ḥāfiẓ' style and thought, and of representing how English scholars have attempted to render his poetry in their own language. Lest it should be supposed that the work of two centuries has exhausted every aspect of the study of Ḥāfiẓ, and that the last word on his interpretation has been said, these introductory remarks will suggest fresh approaches to the subject, and propose a number of lines along which future research might with advantage be directed.

Ḥāfiẓ is by universal consent the supreme master of the art of the Persian *ghazal*—a literary form generally equated with the lyric; though perhaps the sonnet is in some respects a closer equivalent. When it is considered that literary critics of undoubted authority have estimated Persian poetry as an important contribution to the art of self-expression in metre and rhyme, and the Persian *ghazal* as a form unsurpassable of its kind, it may be readily conceded that Ḥāfiẓ is a poet eminently worth study; and it may without undue optimism be conjectured that as a master of a splendid art-form he can still teach useful lessons to all who are interested in the evolution of poetic expression. If it is added, as a personal opinion, that Ḥāfiẓ' technique can by modified imitation inspire new developments in western poetry, perhaps a claim so extravagant will not be rejected so summarily as similar claims less solidly founded; for Ḥāfiẓ is as highly esteemed by his countrymen as Shakespeare by us, and deserves as serious consideration.

The Persians were not greatly interested in the lives of their poets, and consequently we have little reliable information on which to construct a biography of Ḥāfiẓ; though modern scholars have displayed great learning and ingenuity in attempting to recover the salient facts of his career. The student is recommended to consult the charming preface to Gertrude Bell's *Poems from the Divan of Hafiz*; the section on Ḥāfiẓ in E. G. Browne's *Literary History of Persia*; the introduction to Ḥusain Pezhmān's edition of the *Dīvān*; and, above all, the voluminous and profound study of the poet by Dr Qāsim Ghanī (*Baḥth dar āthār u afkār u aḥvāl-i Ḥāfiẓ*) which is now appearing in Teheran. Not to duplicate what is readily accessible elsewhere, we confine ourselves here to the barest outline of the poet's life.

Shams al-Dīn Ḥāfiẓ of Shīrāz was born at the capital of the province of Fārs about the year 720/1320; some sixty years after the great catastrophe of Islamic history, Hūlāgū Khān's capture and sack of Baghdād; rather less than a century after the death of Muḥyī al-Dīn Ibn 'Arabī (d. 638/1240), the greatest theosophist of the Arabs; and fifty years after the death of Jalāl al-Dīn Rūmī (d. 672/1273), Persia's most original mystical poet. He grew up in an age when the finest Arabic literature had already been written, and in the shadow of the reputation of his distinguished fellow-citizen, Shaikh Sa'dī (d. 690/1291 or 691/1292). Persian poetry had thus reached its consummation in the romantic epic (Niẓāmī probably died in 599/1202), the mystical *mathnavī*, the *rubā'ī*, the *qaṣīda* (Anvarī died between 585/1189 and 587/1191), and gnomic verse; Ḥāfiẓ spent little time on the *qaṣīda* and *rubā'ī*, and none at all on the other classical forms, but elected to specialize in the *ghazal*, no doubt supposing—and not without

2

cause—that he had something to contribute to this most delicate of all poetic forms.

As a student, Ḥāfiẓ evidently learned the Qur'ān by heart (for so his name implies), and his poetry proves that, like other Persian poets, he acquired a competence in all the Muslim sciences taught in his day; for the Persian poet must have learning as much as original genius. It seems likely that he was a man of no great substance, especially if we admit the evidence of a manuscript of the *Khamsa* of Amīr Khusrau of Delhi (d. 725/1325) now preserved in the State Library of Tashkent which bears a colophon stating that it was written by "the humblest of God's creatures Muḥammad nicknamed Shams al-Ḥāfiẓ al-Shīrāzī" and completed on 24 Ṣafar 756/9 February 1355 (see A. A. Semenov's note in *Sukhan*, vol. II, pp. 95–6); for only a relatively poor man would seek his bread by transcribing other men's poems for pay. It remained for him therefore to develop and perfect his God-given genius for song, and by soliciting the favour of wealthy and powerful patrons to emulate in the fourteenth century those already legendary figures of the twelfth who had risen in the courts of princes to great eminence and abundant riches, and yet secured the highest prize of all, immortality in the hearts and on the lips of succeeding generations. Wealth, as it seems, was destined to elude Ḥāfiẓ' grasp, for the age in which he lived was an age of insecurity and sudden catastrophe; but he achieved in full measure the ampler portion of eternal fame, even in lands whose very names were unknown in his day and among peoples speaking a language cognate with his own, yet never imagined in his mind.

Shīrāz, "a large and flourishing town with many riches and many inhabitants" (as the anonymous author of the *Ḥudūd al-'ālam* called it, writing towards the end of the tenth century), capital of the province of Fārs from which Persia obtained her name in the West, at the time of Ḥāfiẓ' birth formed part of the dominions of Sharaf al-Dīn Maḥmūdshāh of the Injū dynasty, a fief of the Mongol overlord Uljāitū and his successor Abū Sa'īd.

3

The territories about the city were infested with robber bands, to prevent whose depradations formed no small part of the cares of the ruler. The death of Abū Saʿīd in 736/1335 provided the youthful Ḥāfiz with his first personal experience of the transient nature of human glory; for his follower Arpa Khān had Maḥmūdshāh immediately put to death. There followed a struggle for power between his four sons, Jalāl al-Dīn Masʿūdshāh, Ghiyāth al-Dīn Kaikhusrau, Shams al-Dīn Muḥammad and Abū Isḥāq Jamāl al-Dīn; Kaikhusrau was the first to pay the supreme penalty of unwise ambition (739/1339), to be followed to his grave the next year by Muḥammad. Meanwhile Shīrāz passed into the hands of Pīr Ḥusain, the Chupanid princeling with whom Muḥammad had conspired and who requited his confidence by slaying him; but the intruder had little joy of his filched possession; the infuriated populace drove him out, and when he would have returned the following year he fell out with a confederate and met his end. Masʿūdshāh, the eldest of Maḥmūdshāh's sons, fell victim to an imprudent intrigue in 743/1343; and after a further bout of violence the youngest of the brothers, Abū Isḥāq, at last succeeded in establishing his authority throughout Fārs. We have a fragment of Ḥāfiz (Brockhaus' edition of the *Dīvān*, no. 579), written many years after these events, in which the poet recalls the reign of "Shāh Shaikh Abū Isḥāq when five wonderful persons inhabited the kingdom of Fārs"—the Shāh himself, the chief judge of Shīrāz Majd al-Dīn Ismāʿīl b. Muḥammad b. Khudādād (for whom see no. 50 of this selection), a certain Shaikh Amīn al-Dīn, the eminent theologian and philosopher ʿAḍud al-Dīn ʿAbd al-Raḥmān b. Aḥmad al-Ījī (d. 756/1355), and Ḥājjī Qiwām al-Dīn Ḥasan, a favourite of the Shāh, whose death in 754/1353 Ḥāfiz celebrated with a necrology (Brockhaus no. 610).,

Abū Isḥāq was an ambitious man; having secured the mastery of Shīrāz and Fārs he sought to extend his dominion to embrace Yazd and Kirmān, and so brought himself into conflict with the neighbouring dynasty of the Muzaffarids. This house, founded by

4

Sharaf al-Dīn Muẓaffar (d. 713/1314) the fief successively of the Mongol Īlkhāns Arghūn, Ghāzān, and Uljāitū, had its capital at Maibudh near Yazd. Muẓaffar was succeeded by his son Mubāriz al-Dīn Muḥammad, at that time a lad of thirteen; he grew into a resolute and ruthless ruler, taking Yazd in 718/1318 or 719/1319 and holding his petty empire in the face of bloody rebellion; profiting by the chaos that resulted from the death of Abū Saʿīd, in 740/1340 he annexed Kirmān. Twice Abū Isḥāq essayed to wrest Kirmān from the grasp of its new master, and twice he failed; in 751/1350-1 he tried his hand against Yazd, but was speedily repulsed; a third attempt at Kirmān ended in a signal defeat (753/1352). Mubāriz al-Dīn, encouraged by this final verdict, now took the offensive into the enemy's camp, and in 754/1353 he captured Shīrāz; he pursued his triumph, took Iṣfahān, and put his stubborn foe to death in 757/1356 or 758/1357.

It appears that Shīrāz did not greatly enjoy its change of rulers, for Mubāriz al-Dīn was a Sunnī zealot; the story of the closing of the wine-taverns, and Ḥāfiẓ' supposed reference to the event, may be read in Browne (*Literary History of Persia*, vol. III, pp. 277-5). However, the conqueror did not long prevail in his new empire; for in 759/1358, while on a military expedition that had won for him the temporary possession of Tabrīz, he was made prisoner by his own son Shāh Shujāʿ and, after the barbarous fashion of those days, blinded; he died in 765/1364. Ḥāfiẓ does not appear to have esteemed it profitable to solicit the favour of the austere Mubāriz al-Dīn, though he has two poems in praise of his chief minister Burhān al-Dīn Fatḥ Allāh (Brockhaus, nos. 400, 571).

Shāh Shujāʿ enjoyed a relatively long reign, though he saw his share of fraternal envy and neighbourly rivalries. His brother Shāh Maḥmūd, who ruled over Abarqūh and Iṣfahān, in 764/1363 seized Yazd; to be in turn besieged in Iṣfahān until the two princes came to an understanding. The reconciliation was short-lived; the following year Maḥmūd allied himself to Uwais, the Jalāʾirid ruler of Baghdād since 756/1355, and after laying siege to Shīrāz for eleven months captured the city, only to lose it again in

767/1366. Shāh Maḥmūd died in 776/1375, and thereupon Shāh Shujāʿ possessed himself of Iṣfahān. Uwais succumbed suddenly in the same year; and the lord of Shīrāz thought the moment opportune to enlarge himself towards Ādharbāijān at the expense of Ḥusain, the new sovereign of Baghdād. However, what success Shāh Shujāʿ achieved was soon undone when he found his nephew Shāh Yaḥyā conspiring against him; he renounced his spoils, made peace with Ḥusain, and married his son Zain al-ʿĀbidīn to the Baghdādī's sister. This was far from the end of trouble between the two neighbours; and when Ḥusain was murdered by his brother Aḥmad in 783/1381 the latter, confronted by the inevitable succession of hopeful pretenders, was glad to solicit the friendly support of Shāh Shujāʿ, and to repudiate it as soon as his throne seemed secure. But meanwhile a cloud was gathering on the horizon that would presently grow into a storm sweeping all these petty conspiracies into ruin and oblivion. Tīmūr Lang, born at Kash in Transoxiana in 736/1336, had won his way through blood to the throne as "rightful heir" to Chaghatāi and true descendant of Chingiz; after ten years' wars of consolidation, he invaded Khurāsān in 782/1380-1, and within two years mastered Gurgān, Māzandarān and Seistān. Shāh Shujāʿ, recognizing the portents, bought the favour of the mighty conqueror with rich gifts and a daughter; death spared him further anxieties in 786/1384.

The reign of Shāh Shujāʿ saw the full blossoming of the flower of Ḥāfiẓ' genius. Being a man of more liberal views than his predecessor, he created the conditions indispensable to the free display of poetic talent; and though it is said that relations between the poet and his royal patron were at times lacking in cordiality (see Browne, *op. cit.* vol. III, pp. 280-2), Ḥāfiẓ immortalized him by name in four poems (cf. no. 28 of this collection and Brockhaus, nos. 327, 344, 346) and wrote a noble necrology for his epitaph (Brockhaus, no. 601); it is as certain as such conjectures can be that very many other poems in the *Dīvān*, though not naming Shāh Shujāʿ directly, were composed for him.

Future researchers may recover much from the obscure hints scattered up and down the poet's verses to shed new light on the dark history of these years in the chequered fortunes of Shīrāz.

Shāh Shujāʿ shortly before dying nominated his son Zain al-ʿĀbidīn ʿAlī to rule over Shīrāz, and his brother ʿImād al-Dīn Aḥmad to govern Kirmān. ʿAlī was immediately opposed by his cousin Shāh Yaḥyā b. Sharaf al-Dīn Muẓaffar (Ḥāfiẓ courted him by name in five poems) who although subsequently reconciled lost his command of Iṣfahān and fled to Yazd. In 789/1387 ʿAlī, learning that his nominee at Iṣfahān, Muẓaffar-i Kāshī, had yielded before the approach of Tīmūr, abandoned Shīrāz for Baghdād and left it to Shāh Yaḥyā to make what terms he could with the formidable invader. The people of Iṣfahān were so imprudent as to kill Tīmūr's envoys, and expiated their rashness in a fearful massacre. Tīmūr declared Sulṭān Aḥmad the governor of Fārs, as well as Kirmān; then followed a bewildering series of events, characteristic of the kaleidoscopic nature of the destinies of those times. Zain al-ʿĀbidīn ʿAlī on quitting Shīrāz had secured the friendship of his cousin Shāh Manṣūr b. Sharaf al-Dīn Muẓaffar at Shūshtar, but was almost immediately attacked and imprisoned by him. Shāh Manṣūr (whom Ḥāfiẓ complimented in a number of poems, including, according to some manuscripts, no. 37 of this selection) now walked into undefended Shīrāz; and when ʿAlī, released by his jailers, made common cause with Shāh Yaḥyā and Sulṭān Aḥmad against him, Manṣūr defeated the coalition and occupied all ʿIrāq. ʿAlī fled, but was captured by the governor of Raiy and handed over to Shāh Manṣūr, who ordered him to be blinded. Flushed with these successes, Manṣūr thought to match his fortunes against the dread Tīmūr's. It was an unlucky speculation. The mighty conqueror marched to the gates of Shīrāz, and there, after a desperate resistance, Manṣūr fell. The rest of the Muẓaffarids immediately declared their submission to Tīmūr; but their tardy realism secured them only a week's further lease of life, and in Rajab 795/March 1393 they were all executed.

7

Ḥāfiẓ had not lived to see the final ruin of the house that had patronized his genius and been immortalized in his songs. In the year 791/1389 (or, according to some authorities, 792/1390) he passed to the mercy of God, and discovered at last the solution to the baffling riddle of human life. His death took place in the beloved city that had given him birth; he lies buried in the rose-bower of Muṣallā, on the banks of the Ruknābād, so often celebrated in his poems; his grave is marked by a tablet inscribed with two of his songs.

Such, in brief outline, were the main events of fourteenth-century Fārs, so far as they affected Ḥāfiẓ' life. The legends of his relations with distant rulers, of his intended journey to India, of his debate with Tīmūr Lang, may be read in Gertrude Bell and the other biographers, for what they are worth; it is sufficient to say that we have no contemporary evidence for them, and that they rest in all likelihood upon no securer basis than the intelligent speculation of his readers in after times; modern criticism is perhaps entitled to make its own guesses with equal measure of certainty and uncertainty. What is indisputable is that these were the times in which the poet lived, and these the verses (or as much of them as are genuine, of which more hereafter) in which he expressed his reactions to the world about him. Being a near and interested witness of many transactions of great violence, and the incalculable destinies of kings and princes, he might well sing:

> "Again the times are out of joint; and again
>   For wine and the loved one's languid glance I am fain.
> The wheel of fortune's sphere is a marvellous thing:
>   What next proud head to the lowly dust will it bring?
> Or if my Magian elder kindle the light,
>   Whose lantern, pray, will blaze aflame and be bright?
> 'Tis a famous tale, the deceitfulness of earth;
>   The night is pregnant: what will dawn bring to birth?
> Tumult and bloody battle rage in the plain:
>   Bring blood-red wine, and fill the goblet again!"

2

It is said that in the year 770/1368-9 Ḥāfiẓ prepared a definitive edition of his poems. What truth there is in this tradition it is impossible now to decide; in any case we possess no manuscripts based upon this archetype; for all our transcriptions—they must surely run into many thousands scattered all over the world—probably go back ultimately to the edition put out after the poet's death by his friend Muḥammad Gulandām with a florid but singularly uninformative preface. Unless therefore the unexpected should happen, and beyond all reasonable hopes a manuscript or manuscripts turn up representing a tradition anterior to Gulandām's edition, we cannot get any nearer to the poems as Ḥāfiẓ himself wrote them than the text authorized after his death by a friend whose piety is unquestionable, but concerning whose scholarship and accuracy we are not in a position to form any judgement. The only other slight chance of escaping from this impasse, a slender one indeed, is to examine all the commentaries on the *Dīvān* (four in Persian and three in Turkish are known), every *takhmīs* or *tasdīs* (poems incorporating an ode of Ḥāfiẓ) composed by later poets,[1] and every *jung* (commonplace book) and *tadhkira* (biographies) in which Ḥāfiẓ is quoted, as well as every poem written since his time in which his verses are introduced by the figure known as *taḍmīn*; and it might well be found, at the end of all these labours, that we had still not progressed far beyond Gulandām.

Certainly well over a hundred printed or lithographed texts of Ḥāfiẓ have appeared, since the *editio princeps* issued by Upjohn's Calcutta press in 1791. Of these all but a very few represent a completely uncritical approach to the task of editorship. The best

1 A *takhmīs* by Jamāl-i Lubnānī, a contemporary of Ḥāfiẓ, containing Brockhaus no. 59, was published by M. Minovi in *Rūzgār-i Nau*, vol. III, pt. i, pp. 43-4, using a British Museum manuscript dated 813-4/1410-1; the text there given has some remarkable variants not found in any copy of the *Dīvān*.

European edition is no doubt that of H. Brockhaus (Leipzig, 1854–63) which is based on the recension of the Turkish commentator Sūdī (d. 1006/1598) and includes a considerable part of his commentary. Several critical texts have been prepared in recent years by Persian scholars; of these the most reliable is that published at Teheran in 1320/1941 under the editorship of Mīrzā Muḥammad Qazvīnī, E. G. Browne's friend and the *doyen* of modern Persian studies, and Dr Qāsim Ghanī, whose valuable and comprehensive monograph on the life and times of Ḥāfiẓ has already been mentioned. The most serious drawback to this otherwise admirable and beautiful text—it is a reproduction of an excellent original written in calligraphic *nastaʿlīq*—is its deficient critical apparatus. As this text—referred to hereafter as MQ—is based on a comparison of no fewer than seventeen manuscripts, several of them exceedingly old, and has been made by two of the most eminent Persian scholars now living, I have not hesitated to use it in editing these selections. At the same time I have mentioned in the notes such textual variants as are to be found in the editions of Brockhaus (B), V. R. von Rosenzweig-Schwannau (3 vols., Vienna, 1858–64), called hereafter RS, Ḥusain Pezhmān (=P, Teheran, 1318/1939), and (for a few poems, all so far published by this editor), Masʿūd Farzād (=F).

The first and most fundamental problem attending the task of editing Ḥāfiẓ is to decide which of the poems attributed to him in the various manuscripts are genuine products of his pen. An indication of the complexity of this problem is provided by the following figures. The Calcutta 1791 edition contains 725 poems; Brockhaus printed 692; Pezhmān has 994 items, many of them marked as doubtful or definitely spurious. The editors of MQ have admitted 495 *ghazals* as unquestionably genuine, beside 3 *qaṣīdas*, 2 *mathnavīs*, 34 occasional pieces (*muqaṭṭaʿāt*) and 42 *rubāʿīs*—a total of 573 poems. Their austere editorship causes a number of popular favourites (popular rather in India and Europe than in Persia) to disappear, perhaps the best known of them being the jingle *tāza ba-tāza nau ba-nau* which

E. H. Palmer and Gertrude Bell made into pleasant English verses.

When the supposititious poems have been rejected, the next task is to determine what lines of each genuine poem are authentic; for very many of them have been inflated in the manuscripts, sometimes by as much as four or five couplets. This labour accomplished, it yet remains to establish the correct order of the lines of each poem—there is sometimes the wildest variation in this respect between the manuscripts. Finally, and in many ways most troublesome of all, we have to settle the innumerable problems of verbal variants.

There are a number of different reasons for this wide inconsistency between the manuscripts. To consider the spurious poems first: the explanation of this phenomenon is fairly simple; no doubt the prevailing cause is the desire of copyists at one stage or other of the transmission of the text to secure for their own inferior versifying an unmerited immortality by signing their products with Ḥāfiẓ' name. This is the conclusion reached by all scholars who have looked at the problem, and not only in connexion with Ḥāfiẓ; for it is a very prevalent malaise of Persian literature. But it seems reasonable to suppose that this does not tell the whole story. It may well be, in the first place, that other poets, possibly in Ḥāfiẓ' lifetime even, used the same pen-name as the great master; and that lyrics by them, quite innocently confounded with the poems of the supreme Ḥāfiẓ, have been diligently incorporated into the *Dīvān*. Again, it is not an impossible conjecture that, just as painters of great eminence in Persia are known to have signed the work of their pupils after making a few masterly retouches, so a celebrated poet would add to his income by teaching the craft to promising aspirants and would permit their "corrected" exercises to bear his name; he would be able during his lifetime to exclude such school specimens from the canon, but if they survived into later times there would be nothing but consummate literary taste to distinguish them from the poet's own work; and literary taste declined lamentably in the generations that followed Ḥāfiẓ, if indeed it ever existed to any marked extent among professional copyists. Lastly we have perhaps to reckon with a third group of spuria: poems written by Ḥāfiẓ himself—juvenilia and such-like—but rejected by him in the fastidiousness of his mature judgement. It would interest the scribe who worked for pay, especially if he had in prospect a wealthy but ill-educated patron, by dint of drawing on all these subsidiary sources to impress and please his master with "the largest and completest copy of Ḥāfiẓ' poems yet assembled"; and so the evil tradition of an inflated text, once securely founded, would continue into later times and ultimately gain the deceptive respectability of age.

The phenomenon of obtrusive lines calls for a rather different diagnosis. The chief causes of this blemish seem to be twofold. First, we may conjecture that men of parts, while reading a good and uninflated manuscript of Ḥāfiẓ, might amuse themselves by noting in the margin verses of other poets, in the same metre and rhyme, which seemed to them comparable and apposite; these annotations would of course be incorporated by a later scribe into the body of the text. Secondly, it is highly likely—and there are numerous passages in the *Dīvān* which lend support to this supposition—that a considerable number of these extra lines go back to Ḥāfiẓ himself, and represent stages in his workmanship.

Verbal variants have their own variety of causes. Primarily there is the well-known carelessness of scribes, and, what is perhaps even more deplorable, their dishonesty; failing to understand a word or a phrase, they sometimes did not hesitate to bring their archetype within the range of their own limited comprehension. In the second place, these variants in many instances doubtless perpetuate the poet's first, second, third, or even fourth thoughts.

The foregoing analysis is not, the reader must believe, mere speculation; it is based upon a wide experience of manuscripts and a considerable apprenticeship in the trade of editing oriental texts; and chapter and verse could readily be quoted to illustrate every variety of contrariety and corruption. But this book is not the place to assemble materials of that nature; and we will leave the subject with a recommendation that future editors of Ḥāfiẓ should exercise their scholarship, not unprofitably, by classifying according to their causes the outstanding variants in the codices.

It will be useful to conclude this section of the preface by giving a few notes on the more important of the manuscripts used in the edition of MQ, and described fully in the introductory remarks of Mīrzā Muḥammad. From these details it may be easier for the future editor of Ḥāfiẓ, when he comes to collate the best copies in Europe, to compare their merits with those of the finest manuscripts in Persia.

KH. MS. belonging to Saiyid ʿAbd al-Raḥīm Khalkhālī, of Teheran. Dated 827/1424. Reproduced (with numerous errors) in Khalkhālī's edition of 1306/1927. Contains 495 *ghazals*; no preface or *qaṣīdas*. (Note: This is the oldest dated copy of the *Dīvān* hitherto reported. The next oldest are B = Bodleian copy dated 843/1439 and CB = Chester Beatty copy dated 853/1449. The British Museum has a *jung* dated 813–4/1410–1 which is reported by M. Minovi to contain about 110 *ghazals* of Ḥāfiẓ.)

NKH. MS. belonging formerly to Ḥājj Muḥammad Aqā-yi Nakhjawānī of Ādharbāijān, presented by him to Dr Qāsim Ghanī. Undated, ca. 850/1446. Contains 495 *ghazals*; no preface or *qaṣīdas*.

R. MS. belonging formerly to Aqā-yi Ismāʿīl Mirʾāt, presented by him to Dr Qāsim Ghanī. Undated, "very near the time of Ḥāfiẓ". No preface or *qaṣīdas*.

[Note. Other old MSS. include the following. TM¹ = copy dated 854/1450 in Majlis Library, Teheran. BM = British Museum copy dated 855/1451. BN = Bibliothèque Nationale, Paris, copy dated 857/1453. TM² = Majlis Library, Teheran, copy dated 858/1454.]

3

"I am very conscious that my appreciation of the poet is that of the Western. Exactly on what grounds he is appreciated in the East it is difficult to determine, and what his compatriots make of his teaching it is perhaps impossible to understand." So, fifty years ago, wrote Gertrude Bell, Ḥāfiẓ' most felicitous translator; and nothing has appeared in print in the West since to give a clearer picture to the inquirer. It is unfortunately true that in classical Persian literature, literary criticism never progressed beyond a certain stage; and while we have some admirable analyses of the tropes and figures that are accounted elegant in Persian poetry, and intricate accounts of the numerous metres, of appreciation in the Western sense we possess practically nothing. When it comes to assessing the respective merits of the poets, and explaining in what their particular virtues consist, the *tadhkira*-writers, our principal informants, are all too prone to indulge in a mixture of fulsome applause and verbal nebulosity, and that naturally does not take us very far.

Modern Persian writers have, however, gone a good way towards supplying the deficiencies of their predecessors; they have essayed to apply the canons of Western criticism to their national poets, so far as these can be applied; and we know now at least what Ḥāfiẓ' compatriots six centuries after think of his poetry. To help forward this aspect of our study within the limits proper to our present purpose, we offer a translation of extracts from the writings of two contemporary scholars, of undoubted authority, and thoroughly representative of the best modern Persian criticism.

(1) Riḍā-zāda Shafaq, *Tārīkh-i adabīyāt-i Īrān* (Tehran, 1321/ 1942), pp. 332–6.

"With the fine sensitivity and acute susceptibility which irradiate the Khwāja's poetry, it is remarkable how this liberal-hearted poet preserved the strength and serenity of his poetic imagination in the face of the bloody events of his time. All Persia was in the throes of insurrection and conflict; Fārs, and Shīrāz itself, did not escape this battle; and Ḥāfiẓ with his own eyes witnessed the slaying of kings, the devastation of houses, the wars of pretenders, even the quarrels between members of a single family, such as for instance the Muzaffarids; yet he seems to have regarded these events from some spiritual eminence as if they were the little waves of an ocean; his gaze was rather fixed on the unity of the ocean of nature, the meaning and purpose of the world. It is true that on occasion his mind rebelled, and in deep emotion he would say:

'What is this anarchy that I see in the lunatic sphere? I see all horizons full of strife and sedition.'

But he always returned to his mental composure, and sought for tranquillity of heart in a world tumultuous beneath the wings of his broad, celestial thoughts.

"This mystical steadfastness of Ḥāfiẓ is apparent even in his *qaṣīdas*; he belongs to that class of poets who rarely indulged in panegyric, was never guilty of hyperbole. He was not the man to flatter for flattery's sake; he never surrendered his steadfastness of purpose. Though every prince in his turn was powerful and all-conquering, Ḥāfiẓ never debased his language, nor transgressed the bounds of legitimate applause. He did not hesitate on occasion to proffer counsel, reminding them in penetrating and moving verses of the truth that every man in the end gets his deserts, that fate rewards and punishes every act, and reckons king and beggar equal and alike.

"Ḥāfiẓ' spiritual greatness and mental power proceeded from that mystical consciousness which in him attained perfection. That path of life of which Sanā'ī, 'Aṭṭār, Jalāl al-Dīn and Sa'dī had spoken each in turn and in his own way, was by Ḥāfiẓ described in language that plumbs the depths of feeling and soars to the heights of expression. Subjects of which others had spoken in detail, in his choice, brief lyrics found better and sweeter

15

treatment. So deeply immersed was he in the mystic unity, that in every ode and lyric, whatever its formal subject, he included one or more verses expressive of this lofty theme. This indeed is perhaps the greatest individual feature of Ḥāfiẓ' poetry; and it was by reason of this very immersion in the Unity that he had no time for the world's plurality, for differences of faith, and all vain disputes and enquiries:

'Excuse the war of all the seventy-two sects; as they have not seen the truth, they have plundered on the highway of legend.'

"Because he loved truth, sincerity and unity, Ḥāfiẓ railed against every manner of conflict and discord. He was especially pained and distressed by trifling quarrels and superficial differences, by the hypocrisy and imposture of false ascetics. He criticized bitterly those hypocritical Ṣūfīs who claimed to be following his own path but were in reality worldly men, parading their rags and making a display of their poverty. He had no desire to be numbered among them:

'The fire of deceit and hypocrisy will consume the barn of religion; Ḥāfiẓ, cast off this woollen cloak, and be gone!'

Perhaps in this respect, namely in detestation and revolt against hypocrisy and imposture, no other Persian poet has equalled Ḥāfiẓ.

"His true mastery is in the lyric (*ghazal*). In Ḥāfiẓ' hands the mystical lyric on the one hand reached the summit of eloquence and beauty, and on the other manifested a simplicity all its own. As we have already said, in short words he stated ideas mighty and subtle. Quite apart from the sweetness, simplicity and conciseness which are apparent in every lyric of Ḥāfiẓ, a spirit of genuine sincerity pervades every line. It is evident that the master's lyrics come straight from the heart; each poem is a subtle expression of the poet's innermost thoughts. It was by virtue of this same faith that the poet turned away and shrank from every kind of superficiality, that he rent to pieces the snare of trickery and deceit, and rejected the outward ornaments of the faiths and sects, upbraiding in his verses all hypocrites—shaikhs, ascetics and Ṣūfīs alike.

"Especially in his lyrics, Ḥāfiẓ in addition to the spark he borrowed from the fire of the *ghazals* of 'Aṭṭār and Rūmī, also took something from the style of his own age. In this respect he shewed himself a disciple particularly of the style of such predecessors and contemporaries as Sa'dī, Khwājū, Salmān-i Sāvajī, Auḥadī and 'Imād-i Faqīh; many of the master's verses and lyrics are parallel to theirs. [The author here quotes a few examples of such parallelisms.] Yet for all this Ḥāfiẓ was by no means content to be a mere imitator: he had his own style, and imparted a new lustre to the words. If his poetry is more often quoted than that of Khwājū and Salmān, this is due not solely to his spirituality, his greatness and his mystical influence; its celebrity is explained in part by the sweetness of his melody and the fluency and firmness of his verse. The poet himself, with that fine talent, that subtlety of taste and gift of revelation which he indisputably possessed, was well aware of the merit of his own composition, and it was in full and sure belief that he said:

'O Ḥāfiẓ, I have not seen anything lovelier than thy poetry;
(I swear it) by the Qur'ān thou hast in thy bosom.'

Indeed Ḥāfiẓ, with that high talent, spiritual subtlety, natural gift of language, minute meditation, mystical experience and passionate gnosis which were vouchsafed to him, evolved such a construction of words and a mingling of varied expressions and ideas that he created an independent style and characteristic form of mystical lyric; so much so that connoisseurs of Persian literature can immediately recognize his poetry and identify his accent.

"In addition to his inventive gift of weaving words together and giving ideas expression, Ḥāfiẓ used special words and technical terms which he himself innovated, or which, if already used by others, find ampler display in his vocabulary. Examples of these are the words *ṭāmāt* (idle talk), *kharābāt* (taverns), *mughān* (Magians), *mughbachche* (young Magian), *khirqa* (mystic's cloak),

17

salūs (hypocrite), *pīr* (elder), *hātif* (heavenly voice), *pīr-i mughān* (Magian elder), *girānān* (weighty ones), *raṭl-i girān* (bumper), *zannār* (girdle), *ṣaumaʿa* (monastery), *zāhid* (ascetic), *shāhid* (beauty), *tilasmāt* (talismans), *dair* (abbey, tavern), *kinisht* (church).

"In composing his poetry Ḥāfiẓ used various rhetorical figures such as *īhām* (amphibology), *murāʿāt-i naẓīr* (parallelism), *tajnīs* (play on words), *tashbīh* (simile) and the like, though he had a special partiality for *īhām*. [Some examples are quoted.] He borrowed some of the similes common to the poets, such as comparing the hair with unbelief, a chain, a hyacinth, a snare, a noose, a snake; the brow with a bow; the stature with a cypress; the face with a lamp, a rose, the moon; the mouth with a rosebud, a pistachio. But this kind of obvious artifice has not lessened the natural effect of his words. It is also possible to find in Ḥāfiẓ' compositions allusions and proverbs derived from the popular language; for example, 'beating the drum under the blanket' as an allusion to hiding something which cannot be concealed, as in the following verse:

'My heart is weary of hypocrisy and the drum under the blanket; O happy moment, when I hoist the standard at the wine-tavern.'"

(2) Mīrzā Muḥammad Qazvīnī, preface to Qāsim Ghanī, *Baḥth dar āthār u afkār u aḥvāl-i Ḥāfiẓ*, vol. I (Tehran, 1321/1942), pp. iv–ix.

"I remember one day we were talking about the poets of Persia, and Dr Ghanī asked me whom I considered to be the greatest of them. 'As is well known', I replied, 'poetry is made up of two elements—words, and meaning. The true poet and skilled artificer maintains a proper balance between the two factors of words and meaning, and does not exceed or fall short in respect of either. That is, he does not devote himself more than is necessary to beautifying his words and ornamenting his expressions, by employing elegant verbal artifices such as *tajnīs* (play on words), *ishtiqāq* (prosonomasia), *shibh-i ishtiqāq* (quasi-prosonomasia), *tarṣīʿ* (correspondence), *takrīr* (repetition), *qalb* (anagram), *taṣḥīf* (change of points), *taushīḥ* (acrostic), *siyāqat al-a'dād* (proposition of multiples), *luzūm mā lā yalzam* (double rhyme), letters *'uṭl* (unpointed) and *manqūṭ* (pointed), *muttaṣil* (joined) and *munfaṣil* (unjoined), and similar devices that are more like children's pastimes than rules governing elegant prose and poetry for serious men. Neither does the true poet so concern himself with refining his meaning by indulging in fine-spun fancies, involved ideas, highly abstruse similes and unintelligible references as to complicate his language and obscure his intention, making it necessary for the hearer to think hard guessing what he is driving at—such for example as characterizes the so-called 'Indian' poets. Moreover, he does not exaggerate the employment of such elegant artifices as *murā'āt al-naẓīr* (parallelism), *ṭibāq* (matching), *īhām* (amphibology), *ibhām* (ambiguity), *tafrī'* (evolution), *istiṭrād* (feigning), *talmīḥ* (allusion), *jam'* (combination), *taqsīm* (discrimination) and the like, to the point of overloading his expression and fatiguing the hearer.[1] It is obvious of course that the skilful use of any of these artifices, either singly or in combination with one or two others, contributes definitely to elegance of style; but when these devices are multiplied to excess, and above all when a number of them are crowded together in a single verse, or in close proximity, they produce an exceedingly artificial appearance and are in fact an affront to the very art of poetry; and they will end by wearying and exhausting the audience.

"'If we study the works of all the Persian poets of the first class, attentively, it will become clear that every one of them, in addition to his own inborn faculty and God-given genius, has paid scrupulous observance to this point, namely, the maintenance of a balance between words and meanings, and the avoiding of excess or deficiency in either respect. Nevertheless one can divide them into two quite distinct and different groups.

"'The first group consists of those poets whose style is quite simple and natural, free of all formal ornament and verbal

1 For an explanation of these terms see E. G. Browne, *Literary History of Persia*, vol. II, pp. 47–82.

decoration, devoid of every kind of artificiality and extravagance....Prominent representatives of this school are, first, Firdausī, Khaiyām and Jalāl al-Dīn Rūmī; and secondly, most of the very old poets of the Ṣaffārid, Sāmānid and early Ghaznavid periods, such as Ḥanẓala, Bādghīsī, Fīrūz-i Mashriqī, Abū 'l-Mu'ayyad-i Balkhī, Shahīd-i Balkhī, Rūdakī, Abū Shukūr-i Balkhī, Daqīqī, Rābi'a-i Qizdarī-i Balkhī, Abū Ṭāhir-i Khisravānī, Shākir-i Bukhārī, Labībī, Zainatī-i 'Alavī, 'Imāra-i Marvazī, Manṭiqī-i Rāzī, Kisā'ī-i Marvazī, and the like. Unhappily most of the poetry of these has been lost, but from what is preserved in the biographies and dictionaries and certain histories it is very clearly possible to conjecture that they were all very great poets of the first class....

"'Most of the first class Persian poets from the fifth and sixth (11–12th) centuries down to the present day—such as Farrukhī, 'Asjadī, 'Unṣurī, Ghaḍā'irī, Minūchihrī, Mukhtārī, Lāmi'ī-i Gurgānī, Mas'ūd-i-Sa'd-i Salmān, Sanā'ī, Mu'izzī, Adīb-i Ṣābir, Abū'l-Faraj-i Rūnī, Anvarī, Saiyid Ḥasan-i Ghaznavī, 'Am'aq-i Bukhārī, Khāqānī, Ẓāhir-i Fāryābī, Sharaf al-Dīn-i Shafurva, Jamāl al-Dīn Muḥammad ibn 'Abd al-Razzāq-i Iṣfahānī, his son Kamāl al-Dīn Ismā'īl, Athīr-i Akhsikatī, Athīr-i Ūmānī, Shaikh 'Aṭṭār, Sa'dī, Ḥāfiẓ and Jāmī—are all of the same class of poets, different at most more or less in the degree to which they have observed the aforementioned points.'

"After this statement, Dr Ghanī asked, 'Suppose for instance we now wish to choose from among all these masters of the first class, including every variety and group, moderns and ancients alike, and suppose we intend to exhibit before the world the greatest of them all—whom would you choose?'

"This was my answer. 'The reply to this question has been generally agreed on for centuries, and the problem has been finally disposed of. Despite all differences of individual inclination and preference, despite the general divergence of opinion entertained by people on most matters, practically all are agreed on this one question; that the greatest poets of the Persian language since the coming of Islam to the present time (each one in his special variety) are the six following—Firdausī, Khaiyām, Anvarī, Rūmī, Sa'dī, Ḥāfiẓ. In my view, one can confidently add to these six the great philosopher Nāṣir-i Khusrau, since all the characteristic merits and artistic qualities that have established these six in the front rank of Persian poets are completely and in every respect present in the person of Nāṣir-i Khusrau....In my opinion Nāṣir-i Khusrau yields the palm to none of the six masters mentioned, with perhaps the possible exception of Ḥāfiẓ.'

"Again Dr Ghanī persisted in his inquisition. 'If,' he said, 'for the sake of example, some foreign country, say England, proposed to us that it was desired to erect a statue—in Hyde Park maybe—to the greatest poets of every nation on earth—the greatest, that is, by the general consensus of his compatriots—and that only one poet, and no more, was to be chosen by each nation; which of these six would you personally select as being in your view, and that of most men, the most truly poetical of the poets of Persia?'

"'In my view,' I answered, 'and I think this view coincides with the opinion held by the great majority of Persian scholars, as well as by non-Persians who have either known Persian or become acquainted with Ḥāfiẓ through the medium of translations, it may be that out of all the Persian poets of the first class—I have already named a great number of them to my good friend, and I leave you to find the names of the rest in the biographies and anthologies—without any exception whatsoever, the man whose poems embrace and contain every beauty alike of language and meaning to be found in poetry, every quality of image and reality that exists in fine speech, and who is at the same time the most eloquent and melodious writer of every age, ancient and modern included, the man who, compared with all the poetic stars of the first magnitude, is as a shining sun—without any doubt or hesitation that man is Khwāja Shams al-Ḥaqq wa'l-Milla wa'l-Dīn Muḥammad Ḥāfiẓ-i Shīrāzī, may God sanctify his great soul! As another great poet, Jāmī, who was also almost his contemporary, declares in his *Bahāristān*, his poetry, with all its sweetness, delicacy, freshness, ease, elegance, flow, agreeableness and unaffectedness, is something very near a miracle; it is a just object of pride not only for Persians, it is a source of glory for all mankind.'"

4

The origin of the art-form chosen by Ḥāfiẓ to be his particular medium is wrapped in the obscurity of age; it remains a fascinating problem for the researcher to discover what exact process of evolution led ultimately to the perfect type familiar to us in his poems. One theory points to the "erotic prelude" (*nasīb*) which forms a constituent part of the characteristic ode of ancient Arabia, and suggests that in time this element was isolated into an independent unit, thus creating the *ghazal*. Alternatively it is argued that the *ghazal* is descended from some kind of lyrical poetry current in the courts of pre-Islamic Persia; but as no specimen of any such verse has been preserved this conjecture, attractive as it is, cannot command unconditional consent. What seems tolerably certain is that this form of poetry was always associated with music, that in fact it was designed to be sung; and it is natural to suppose that this very circumstance to a great extent determined the shape of the verses. It would be dangerous to place too much reliance on the references in classical Persian poetry to the sung poem at the palace of the old Persian kings, such for instance as the well-known passage in the *Khusrau u Shīrīn* of Niẓāmī where Bārbad is credited with composing to thirty varieties of melody whose names are given; but it would be equally dangerous to dismiss these references entirely as pure fiction. Perhaps we have in fact to deal here with multiple origins; the Persian *ghazal* may be a product of that cross-fertilization of Iranian genius by the imported culture of Arabia which produced so many remarkable manifestations of the human spirit.

Whatever the truth of this matter may be, we are on solid

ground when we examine the Arabic lyrics of the 'Abbāsid age
and declare that these are the models used, and improved upon,
by the later Persian poets. Leaving aside the suggestion that this
poetic form even in Arabic was introduced by Persian minstrels
reviving at the court of the Caliphs a tradition founded by their
ancestors at the court of the Chosroes, we do not lack for parallels
in the poetry of the school of Abū Nuwās to the simple, unmystical
lyric of the early Persian poets. The reader familiar with the
Persian lyric would be hard put to it to say whether the originals
of the following poems were written in Persian or Arabic; they
were in fact all Arabic.

THE SOLITARY TOPER

I sat alone with the wine-cup lip to lip,
We whispered together, and made us mighty free:
Right merry a fellow is wine, when a man would sip
And there is none that will bear him company.
Oh, I quaffed and quaffed the cup to my heart's delight.
Myself the saki, myself the toper, and all;
And I swear that never did eye behold a sight
One half so charming, and so fair withal.
And all the while, lest the evil eye should see,
I breathed in the beaker magic and sorcery.

(ABŪ NUWĀS)

NIGHTS OF JOY

Ah, many the long night thou and I
Have passed at ease with the wine-crowned cup,
Till the red dawn gleamed in the night-dim sky
And the stars of morn in the east rose up,
And along the west the stars of night
Like defeated armies pressed their flight.

Then the brightest of joys were ours to gain.
With never a care in the world to cloud,
And pleasure untouched by the hand of pain,
Were delight with eternal life endowed:
But alas! that even the fairest boon
Is doomed, like night, to be spent too soon.

(IBN ZAIDŪN)

WINE AND ROSES

"Bring wine!" I said;
But she that sped
Bore wine and roses beautiful.
Now from her lip
Sweet wine I sip,
And from her cheeks red roses cull.

(IBN ZAIDŪN)

FOUR THINGS

Four things there be that life impart
To soul, to body and to heart:—
A running stream, a flowered glade,
A jar of wine, a lovely maid.

(ABŪ NUWĀS)

THE FIRST KISS

I begged for a kiss, and she gave it me,
But with long refusal, and urging on.
Then I said, "Tormentor, generous be—
One more kiss, and my thirst is gone!"

She smiled, and spake me a proverb wise
Every Persian knows is true:
"Yield not one kiss to the young man's sighs:
For the next he will plague and pester you!"

(ABŪ NUWĀS)

A PRETTY JADE

'Tis a tender, pretty jade,
  And my heart would fain possess her;
Never lovelier form was made—
  Ask of them that can assess her!
God created her to be
A bane for poor mortality.

Pearls upon the air she flings
  When her ruby lips are singing;
See her fingers on the strings,
  Hear the rebec proudly ringing!
Cautiously I veil my sight
Lest her radiance blind me quite.

All my heart's desire is she:
O, that she might care for me!

(ABŪ NUWĀS)

These were the songs Rūdakī and his contemporaries knew
when they fashioned the *ghazal* that was to become a peculiarly
Persian form of poetry, and thereafter to exercise a profound
influence on the poetry of Turkey and Muslim India. Unfortunately all but a few scattered quotations of these early Persian
lyrics perished in the holocaust of the Mongol invasion, and what
remains is far too insufficient to enable us to trace in detail the
evolution of this art-form. We cannot say for certain when and
by whom the convention of the *takhallus* (pen-name and signature)
was created; Sanā'ī (d. *c.* 545/1150) used it freely, but not in-
variably; Farīd al-Dīn 'Aṭṭār (d. 627/1230) has it in all his lyrics
(he signs himself sometimes 'Aṭṭār and sometimes Farīd); by the
time of Saʿdī (d. 690–1/1291–2) the practice is thoroughly established. Similarly we cannot now determine the origins of the
various conventional images of the Persian lyric—rose and
nightingale, candle and moth, etc., etc.—and of all the familiar

similes repeated with variations a thousand times by the classical poets. Here are subjects eminently suitable for further research; the researcher will need to extend his studies over the whole of Arabic as well as Persian lyrical poetry if he is to achieve anything like finality in his conclusions.

A further topic urgently requiring investigation—and this theme is particularly vital for the understanding and appraisal of Ḥāfiẓ' use of the lyric—is the development of the mystical connotation of the conventional figures. The tradition was certainly ancient in Ḥāfiẓ' time, and there are plentiful traces of it in the old Ṣūfī poetry in Arabic; while the celebrated Ibn al-Fāriḍ (d. 632/1235) uses a fully developed system, as of course does Ibn 'Arabī (d. 638/1240) in his poetry. In Persian we find the convention firmly established already in the lyrics of Sanā'ī, as the following examples shew.

LOVE'S PRISONER

Thy beauty is my being's breath,
Thy majesty my fond pride's death;
Where'er thou art, my sweetest fair,
All life's felicity is there.

Loving thy loveliness divine,
Thy smile more potent far than wine,
All languid as thy slumb'rous eye
Intoxicated here I lie.

Ah, but thy finger-tips to kiss—
That were a more than earthly bliss,
Which to achieve were greater gain
Than monarch o'er both worlds to reign.

Anguished I yearn thy lips to touch;
Was ever heart's distraction such?—
A heart held firm and motionless
A prisoner of thy scented tress.

Thy mouth, the huntsman of my mind,
Plots with thy locks my heart to bind;
And how shall time unspring the snare
That keeps me fast and fettered there?

ROSES BLOOM

The nightingale hath no repose
For joy that ruby blooms the rose;
Long time it is that Philomel
Hath loved like me the rosy dell.

'Tis sure no wonder if I sing
Both night and day my fair sweeting:
Let me be slave to that bird's tongue
Who late the rose's praise hath sung.

O saki, when the days commence
Of ruby roses, abstinence
By none is charged: then pour me wine
Like yonder rose incarnadine.

LOVE'S OCEAN

Moslems all! I love that idol
    With a true and jealous zeal;
Not for dalliance, but bewildered
    In amazement here I kneel.

What is Love? A mighty ocean,
    And of flame its waters are,
Waters that are very mountains,
    Black as night, and swarming far.

Dragons fierce and full of terror
    Crouch upon its waveswept rim,
While a myriad sharks of judgement
    In its swelling billows swim.

Grief the barque that sails those waters,
  Fortitude its anchor is,
And its mast is bent and tossing
  To the gale's catastrophes.

Me they cast in sudden transport
  Into that unfathomed sea
Like a man of noble spirit
  Garmented in sanctity.

I was dead; the waters drowned me;
  Lo, the marvel, now I live
And have found a gem more precious
  Than the treasured worlds can give.

It is beyond the scope of this fragmentary study to trace the
development of the mystical *ghazal* in the writings of 'Aṭṭār,
Rūmī, Saʿdī, 'Irāqī and the rest of Ḥāfiz' predecessors; and we
must regretfully leave the full investigation of this fascinating
subject to another occasion, or another inquirer.

5

Ḥāfiz found in the *ghazal* a well-developed art-form; it had been
an instrument of many famous poets, each of whom had contributed in his turn something towards its evolution. Limited by
circumstance and tradition to a comparatively short length con-
venient for singing, it had begun its life as a poem of love and
wine; the Ṣūfīs had exploited its libertine reputation in their quest
for worldly shame, until the allegory had come finally to dominate
the simple reality. This new treatment of the form, that must have
seemed startlingly novel at first, was not long in fossilizing into
a hard convention; the miraculous facility of Saʿdī's style might
well have rendered further development impossible. The problem

Ḥāfiẓ faced was similar in its own way to that which confronted Beethoven—how to improve upon the apparently perfect and final; Ḥāfiẓ' solution was no less brilliantly original than Beethoven's.

Just as Beethoven's earliest compositions strikingly resemble the mature Haydn, so Ḥāfiẓ in his first period is perfect Saʿdī. It is only natural to suppose that the young poet was captivated by the legend of the most famous singer Shīrāz had ever produced; he must have been eager to learn every detail of his fame from the lips of those still living who had seen and heard him; to his youthful spirit it may well have seemed the acme of ambition to imitate his flawless style. Though his editor Gulandām, by following the tradition of arranging his poems alphabetically according to rhyme, destroyed all vestiges of a chronological sequence, it is still possible within certain limits to assign the *ghazals* to definite periods in the poet's life; further research will doubtless establish a more exact precision in this respect than we have yet achieved.

The outstanding characteristic of the poems of Ḥāfiẓ' first period is that each deals with a single theme. This theme is elaborated to the poet's content and satisfaction; but he does not introduce—as he always did later—a second or a third theme to combine with the first; much less (as we find increasingly in the last period) does he make brief and fragmentary references to themes (for it was only after his fame had been established and his style become known that he could afford such refinements and be confident of remaining intelligible). A second point to note in the early poems is the complete absence of that distinctive philosophy which is the invariable accompaniment of his mature compositions: what may be epitomized as the doctrine of un-reason, the poet's final answer to the inscrutability of fate, the utter incapacity of man to master the riddle of the universe. Thirdly, and as a natural corollary of the preceding point, we find in these products of early manhood very little of the Ṣūfī allegory—love in them is human love, wine is the red wine of the grape. In the present selection this early period seems to be represented by nos. 10, 16, 26, 27, 30, 49.

Ḥāfiẓ' second or middle period is marked by two important developments, the one relating to "words" and the other to "meaning" (to borrow the terminology of the Persian critics). The poet has found the escape for which he had been looking to rescue him from the impasse of Saʿdī's technical perfection. Hitherto the *ghazal* had treated only one theme at a time, and had measured perfection in relation to the variations composed upon that single subject. In the works of many of the older poets (and Saʿdī himself is not wholly exempt from this fault), the interest and ingenuity of the variations tended often to overshadow the significance of the theme itself; as a result the poem would cease to be an artistic unity; it would grow longer and longer; and there would be little difficulty for the critic actually to improve upon the poet's performance by pruning away the luxuriance of his imagination. Even in his younger days Ḥāfiẓ had always possessed too fine a critical sense to sacrifice unity on the altar of virtuosity; the new technique which he now invented depended wholly for success upon a rigid artistic discipline and an overwhelming feeling for shape and form.

The development in "words" (or, as we should say, poetic technique) invented by Ḥāfiẓ was the wholly revolutionary idea that a *ghazal* may treat of two or more themes, and yet retain its unity; the method he discovered might be described (to borrow a term from another art) as contrapuntal. The themes could be wholly unrelated to each other, even apparently incongruous; their alternating treatment would be designed to resolve the discords into a final satisfying harmony. As the poet acquired more and more experience of his new technique he was able to introduce further exciting innovations. It was not necessary to develop a theme to its logical conclusion at all; fragments of themes could be worked into the composition without damage to the resulting unity. It was the more easy to accomplish these experiments because convention had produced a regular repertory of themes—to which Ḥāfiẓ added a few of his own creation—and the audience would immediately recognize a familiar subject from the barest reference to it.

This brings us to Ḥāfiẓ' second development, that in "meaning". We have referred already (and shall refer frequently in the notes) to what we have called his philosophy of unreason, which constitutes the central core of the poet's message. It is not of course suggested that Ḥāfiẓ was the first Persian to discover, or to teach, that life is an insoluble mystery; the doctrine is implicit in the pessimism of 'Umar Khaiyām, the mysticism of Rūmī, even the pragmatism of Sa'dī; its roots are deeply grounded in both Neoplatonism and the transcendental theism of the Qur'ān, those twain fountain-heads of Ṣūfī theosophy. What Ḥāfiẓ did was rather to isolate this element from the mass of related and unrelated matter in which he found it embedded, and to put it forward as the focal point from which all theory, and all experience too, radiated. It was his justification for rejecting alike philosophy and theology, mosque and cloister, legalistic righteousness and organized mysticism; it enabled him to profess his solidarity with the "intoxicated" Ṣūfīṣ like martyred Ḥallāj, and to revive the dangerous antinomianism of the Malāmatīs; but above all it provided him with a spiritual stronghold out of which he could view with serene equanimity, if not with indifference, the utterly confused and irrational world in which it was his destiny to live. Indeed it is scarcely surprising that Ḥāfiẓ should have found his only comfort in this doctrine, for the events he witnessed, and still more the events of which he must have heard all too much in his childhood—the Mongol devastations and massacres—were sufficient to shatter all belief in a reasonable universe, and to encourage the most pessimistic estimate of the significance of the individual life. We who have witnessed two world-wide wars, and have survived into what the journalists so appositely call the atomic age, are well placed to understand Ḥāfiẓ, and to appreciate the motives underlying his doctrine of intellectual nihilism. We can even understand how profoundly his philosophy differs from

31

the hearty hedonism with which it has sometimes been confounded; the world's tragedy is too profound to be forgotten in unthinking mirth; and man for all his littleness and incapacity need not be unequal to the burden of sorrow and perplexity he is called upon to shoulder. Indeed, by abandoning the frail defences of intellectual reason and yielding himself wholly to the overwhelming forces of the spirit that surround him, by giving up the stubborn, intervening "I" in absolute surrender to the infinite "thou", man will out of his abject weakness rise to strength unmeasured; in the precious moments of unveiled vision he will perceive the truth that resolves all vexing problems, and win a memory to sustain him when the inevitable shadows close about him once more.

The middle period of Ḥāfiẓ' artistic life—the period of his greatest productivity—was devoted to the working out of these two developments and their exploitation in a wide variety of forms. It should be remembered that all the time the poet was under the necessity of earning a livelihood; and this aspect of his poetry should not be neglected in any broad review. The praise of patrons, and the poet's own self-applause, are readily explained by the hard circumstances of his life, even if to Western taste they form the least attractive features of his work. In any case, as Persian critics have justly remarked, patron-flattery plays a far smaller part in Ḥāfiẓ' poetry than in that of any other court-minstrel, and his panegyric has little of the extravagance that characterizes so much of Persian literature.

The salient feature of the third and last period of Ḥāfiẓ' work is an increasing austerity of style, coupled with a growing tendency towards obscurity and allusiveness. It is as though the poet was growing weary, or perhaps feeling a distaste for the display of virtuosity; and having established his philosophy and perfected his technique, he was now experimenting in a sort of surrealist treatment of the *ghazal*. The poems of this period are comparatively few in number, but they are in many ways the poet's most interesting productions; they will repay extended study, for they are quite unique in Persian literature, and have perhaps never been fully understood and appreciated; certainly no later poet seems to have attempted to continue these final experiments of the master craftsman. In this selection the third period is probably represented by nos. 15, 20, 33, 42, 46, 47.

6

If the analysis of Ḥāfiẓ' style given in the preceding section is anywhere near the truth—and the reader must be advised that no such reconstruction has, so far as the writer is aware, previously appeared in print—it necessarily follows that future translators of the poet will need an entirely fresh approach to their task from that which seems to have satisfied all his previous interpreters. To give an account of the methods followed by these interpreters, and of how they qualified for their undertaking, would expand these prefatory remarks unduly; their products, or typical specimens of them, may be studied here side by side with the originals; for the rest, the enquirer may if he desires consult three short articles contributed by the writer to the Persian periodical *Rūzgār-i Nau* (vol. IV, pt. 1, pp. 82–7; pt. 2, pp. 52–5; pt. 3, pp. 41–5), as well as a monograph published in *Islamic Culture* (April–July, 1946).

In the new versions offered here for the first time the attempt has been made to apply the new approach to Ḥāfiẓ to the task of translation. These versions are in the nature of an experiment, and are by no means uniform in design; it is hoped that they may serve their purpose of stimulating further trials. From what has been said it will be apparent that Ḥāfiẓ presents unusually difficult, if not insoluble, problems to the translator; these problems have not deterred the bold in the past, and they will assuredly not discourage the adventurous in the future.

There is one form of translation which appears to have written its own epitaph: this is the attempt, first made by Walter Leaf in twenty-eight versions, and then applied with indomitable industry by John Payne to the whole *Dīvān*, to imitate both the mono-rhyme and the complicated metrical schemes of the original Persian. It is abundantly obvious now—and should have been before the experiment was ever made—that Persian rhymes and rhythms are entirely inimitable in English; and that it is doing the poet a grave disservice to use his masterly works as a laboratory for the display of perverse ingenuity. *Sic pereant omnes!*

A list follows of the books from which the translations here reproduced are culled; and acknowledgments are hereby made, and grateful thanks expressed, alike to translators and publishers who first put them into print. Ḥāfiẓ has had many admiring interpreters in English, more than any other Persian poet; perhaps from his abode of everlasting bliss he will look down kindly upon the islands of the western seas, so remote from his beloved home-land, and be pleased that the two peoples who have given finer lyrics to the world than any other should in him (as in others of his tongue) find a common bond of interest and of friendship.

1771. William Jones, *A Grammar of the Persian Language.*
1774. John Richardson, *A Specimen of Persian Poetry.*
1785. Thomas Law in *Asiatick Miscellany*, vol. I. Calcutta.
1786. H. H. in *Asiatick Miscellany*, vol. II. Calcutta.
1787. John Nott, *Select Odes from the Persian poet Hafez.*
1800. John Haddon Hindley, *Persian Lyrics; or, scattered poems from the Diwan-i-Hafiz.*
1875. Hermann Bicknell, *Ḥáfiẓ of Shíráẓ.*
1877. Edward Henry Palmer, *The Song of the Reed and Other Pieces.*
1897. Gertrude Lowthian Bell, *Poems from the Divan of Hafiz.* (William Heinemann, Ltd.)
1898. Walter Leaf, *Versions from Hafiz,* an essay in Persian metre. (Alexander Moring, Ltd.)
1901. John Payne, *The Poems of Shemseddin Mohammed Hafiz of Shiraz.* (Villon Society: for private circulation only.)
1905. Richard Le Gallienne, *Odes from the Divan of Hafiz.* (L. C. Page & Co., Boston, U.S.A.)
1921. Elizabeth Bridges (Elizabeth Daryush), *Sonnets from Hafez and other Verses.* (O.U.P.)
1923. Reuben Levy, *Persian Literature, an introduction.* (O.U.P.)

TEXTS

۱   عشق آسان نمود اوّل

الا یا اَیّها السّاقی اُدرکاساً وناولها
کـه عشق آسان نمود اول ولی افتـاد مشکلها

ببـوی نـافـهٔ کآخر صبا زان طـرّه بگشـایـد
ز تاب جعد مشکینش چه خون افتاد در دلها

مرا در منزل جانان چه امن عیش چون هر دم
جـرس فـریـاد مـیـدارد کـه بربندید محملها

بمی سجّاده رنگین کن گرت پیر مغان گـویـد
کـه سـالك بیخبر نبـود ز راه و رسم منزلها

شب تـاریك و بیم موج و گردابی چنین هایل
کجا دانند حال ما سبکبـاران سـاحـلها

همه کارم ز خـودکامی بـبدنامی کشیـد آخر
نهان کی مـاند آن رازی کـزو سازنـد محفلها

حضوری گر همیخواهی ازو غایب مشو حافظ
متی ما تلق من تهوی دع الدّنیا وأهملها

37

صلاح کار کجا و من خراب کجا
ببین تفاوت ره کز کجاست تا بکجا

دل ز صومعه بگرفت و خرقهٔ سالوس
کجاست دیر مغان و شراب ناب کجا

چه نسبتست برندی صلاح و تقوی‌را
سماع وعظ کجا نغمهٔ رباب کجا

ز روی دوست دل دشمنان چه دریابد
چراغ مرده کجا شمع آفتاب کجا

چو کحل بینش ما خاک آستان شماست
کجا رویم بفرما ازین جناب کجا

مبین بسیب زنخدان که چاه در راهست
کجا همی‌روی ایدل بدین شتاب کجا

بشد که یاد خوشش باد روزگار وصال
خود آن کرشمه کجا رفت و آن عتاب کجا

قرار و خواب ز حافظ طمع مدار ایدوست
قرار چیست صبوری کدام و خواب کجا

38

اگـر آن ترك شیرازی بـدست آرد دل مـارا

بخال هنـدویش بخشم سمرقنـد و بخارارا

بده ساقی می باق کـه در جنّت نخواهی یافت

کنـار آب رکنـابـاد و گلگشت مـصـلّارا

فغـان کاین لولیان شوخ شیرین کار شهرآشوب

چنان بردند صبر از دل کـه تـرکـان خوان یغمارا

ز عشق نـاتمـام مـا جمال یـار مستغنی است

بآب و رنگ و خال و خط چه حاجت روی زیبارا

من از آن حسن روزافزون که یوسف داشت دانستم

کـه عشق از پردهٔ عصمت برون آرد زلیخارا

اگـر دشنـام فرمائی و گر نفرین دعا گویم

جـواب تـلخ میزیبد لـب لـعل شکرخارا

نصیحت گوش کن جانا که از جان دوستتر دارند

جـوانـان سعادتمنـد پنـد پیر دانـارا

حـدیث از مطرب و می گـو و راز دهـر کتر جو

کـه کس نگشود و نگشاید بحکمت این معمّارا

غـزل گفتی و در سفتی بیا و خـوش بخوان حافظ

کـه بر نظم تـو افشانـد فلك عقد ثریّارا

39

٤   صبا بلطف بگو

صبا بلطف بگو آن غزال رعنا را
که سر بکوه و بیابان تو داده‌ٔ ما را

شکر فروش که عمرش دراز باد چرا
تفقّدی نکند طوطی شکرخا را

غرور حسنت اجازت مگر نداد ای گل
که پرسشی نکنی عندلیب شیدا را

بخلق و لطف توان کرد صید اهل نظر
ببند و دام نگیرند مرغ دانا را

ندانم از چه سبب رنگ آشنائی نیست
سهی قدان سیه چشم ماه سیما را

چو با حبیب نشینی و باده پیمائی
بیاد دار محبّان باد پیما را

جز این قدر نتوان گفت در جمال تو عیب
که وضع مهر و وفا نیست روی زیبا را

در آسمان نه عجب گر بگفته‌ٔ حافظ
سرود زهره برقص آورد مسیحا را

٥ عهد شباب

رونـق عـهـد شبـابست دگـر بـستـان را
میرسد مژدهٔ گل بلبل خوش الحان را

ای صبا گر بجوانان چمن بـاز رسی
خدمت ما برسان سرو و گل و ریحان را

گر چنین جلوه کند مغبچهٔ باده فروش
خاکروب در میخانه کنم مژگان را

ای که بر مه کشی از عنبر سارا چوگان
مضطرب حال مگردان من سرگردان را

ترسم این قوم که بر دردکشان میخندند
در سـر کار خرابات کـنـنـد ایمان را

یار مـردان خدا باش که در کشتی نوح
هست خاکی که بآبی نخرد طوفان را

برو از خانهٔ گردون بدر و نان مطلب
کان سیه کاسه در آخر بکشد مهمان را

هر کـرا خوابگه آخر مشتی خاکست
گو چه حاجت که بافلاک کشی ایوان را

مـاه کنعانی مـن مسنـد مصر آن تو شد
وقت آنست که بدرود کنی زندان را

حافظا می خور و رندی کن و خوش باش ولی
دام تزویر مکن چـون دگران قرآن را

٦   قصر امل

بیا که قصر امل سخت سست بنیادست
بیار باده که بنیاد عمر بر بادست

غلام همّت آنم که زیر چرخ کبود
ز هر چه رنگ تعلّق پذیرد آزادست

چگویمت که بمیخانه دوش مست و خراب
سروش عالم غیبم چه مژدها دادست

که ای بلند نظر شاهباز سدره نشین
نشیمن تو نه این کنج محنت آبادست

ترا ز کنگرهٔ عرش میزنند صفیر
ندانمت که در این دامگه چه افتادست

نصیحتی کنمت یاد گیر و در عمل آر
که این حدیث ز پیر طریقتم یادست

غم جهان مخور و پند من مبر از یاد
که این لطیفهٔ عشقم ز رهروی یادست

رضا بداده بده وز جبین گره بگشای
که بر من و تو در اختیار نگشادست

مجو درستی عهد از جهان سست نهاد
که این عجوز عروس هزار دامادست

نشان عهد و وفا نیست در تبسّم گل
بنال بلبل بیدل که جای فریادست

حسد چه میبری ای سست نظم بر حافظ
قبول خاطر و لطف سخن خدادادست

42

زلف آشفته و خوی کرده و خندان لب و مست
پیرهن چاک و غزلخوان و صراحی در دست

نرگسش عربده جوی و لبش افسوس کنان
نیم شب دوش ببالین من آمد بنشست

سر فرا گوش من آورد بآواز حزین
گفت ای عاشق دیرینهٔ من خوابت هست

عاشقی را که چنین بادهٔ شبگیر دهند
کافر عشق بود گر نبود باده پرست

برو ای زاهد و بر درد کشان خرده مگیر
که ندادند جز این تحفه بما روز الست

آنچه او ریخت به پیمانهٔ ما نوشیدیم
اگر از خمر بهشتست و گر بادهٔ مست

خندهٔ جام می و زلف گره گیر نگار
ای بسا توبه که چون توبهٔ حافظ بشکست

شکفته شد گل حرا و گشت بلبل مست
صلای سرخوشی ای صوفیان باده پرست

اساس توبه که در محکمی چو سنگ نمود
ببین که جام زجاجی چه طرفه‌اش بشکست

بیار باده که در بارگاه استغنا
چه پاسبان و چه سلطان چه هوشیار و چه مست

ازین رباط دو در چون ضرورتست رحیل
رواق و طاق معیشت چه سر بلند و چه پست

مقام عیش میسّر نمیشود بی رنج
بلی بحکم بلا بسته‌اند عهد الست

بهست و نیست مرنجان ضمیر و خوش میباش
که نیستیست سرانجام هر کمال که هست

شکوه آصفی و اسب باد و منطق طیر
بباد رفت و ازو خواجه هیچ طرف نبست

ببال و پر مرو از ره که تیر پرتابی
هوا گرفت زمانی ولی بخاك نشست

زبان کلك تو حافظ چه شکر آن گوید
که گفتهٔ سخنت میبرند دست بدست

گل در بر و می بر کف و معشوق بکام‌ست
سلطان جهانم بچنین روز غلام‌ست

گو شمع میارید درین جمع که امشب
در مجلس ما ماه رخ دوست تمام‌ست

در مذهب ما باده حلال‌ست ولیکن
بی روی تو ای سرو گل اندام حرام‌ست

گوشم همه بر قول نی و نغمهٔ چنگ‌ست
چشم همه بر لعل لب و گردش جام‌ست

در مجلس ما عطر میامیز که ما را
هر لحظه ز گیسوی تو خوشبوی مشام‌ست

از چاشنی قند مگو هیچ وز شکّر
زآنرو که مرا از لب شیرین تو کام‌ست

تا گنج غمت در دل ویرانه مقیم‌ست
همواره مرا کوی خرابات مقام‌ست

از ننگ چه گوئی که مرا نام ز ننگ‌ست
وز نام چه پرسی که مرا ننگ ز نام‌ست

میخواره و سرگشته و رندیم و نظرباز
وانکس که چو ما نیست درین شهر کدام‌ست

با محتسم عیب مگوئید که او نیز
پیوسته چو ما در طلب عیش مدام‌ست

حافظ منشین بی می و معشوق زمانی
کایّام گل و یاسمن و عید صیام‌ست

۱۰   صبا اگر گذری

صبا اگر گذری افتدت بکشور دوست

بیار نفحهٔ از گیسوی معنبر دوست

بجان او که بشکرانه جان بر افشانم

اگر بسوی من آری پیامی از بر دوست

وگر چنانکه دران حضرتت نباشد بار

برای دیده بیاور غباری از در دوست

من گدا و تمنّای وصل او هیهات

مگر بخواب ببینم خیال منظر دوست

دل صنوبریم همچو بید لرزانست

ز حسرت قد و بالای چون صنوبر دوست

اگرچه دوست بچیزی نمیخرد مارا

بعالمی نفروشیم موئی از سر دوست

چه باشد ار شود از بند غم دلش آزاد

چو هست حافظ مسکین غلام و چاکر دوست

صبحدم مرغ چمن با گل نوخاسته گفت
ناز کم کن که درین باغ بسی چون تو شکفت

گل بخندید که از راست نرنجیم ولی
هیچ عاشق سخن سخت بمعشوق نگفت

گر طمع داری از آن جام مرصّع می لعل
ای بسا دُر که بنوک مژهات باید سفت

تا ابد بوی محبّت بمشامش نرسد
هر که خاک در میخانه برخساره نرفت

در گلستان ارم دوش چو از لطف هوا
زلف سنبل بنسیم سحری می‌آشفت

گفتم ای مسند جم جام جهان بینت کو
گفت افسوس که آن دولت بیدار بخفت

سخن عشق نه آنست که آید بزبان
ساقیا می ده و کوتاه کن این گفت و شنفت

اشک حافظ خرد و صبر بدریا انداخت
چکند سوز غم عشق نیارست نهفت

ای هدهد صبا بسبا میفرستمت
بنگر که از کجا بکجا میفرستمت

حیفست طایری چو تو در خاکدان غم
زاینجا بآشیان وفا میفرستمت

در راه عشق مرحلهٔ قرب و بعد نیست
میبینمت عیان و دعا میفرستمت

هر صبح و شام قافلهٔ از دعای خیر
در صحبت شمال و صبا میفرستمت

تا لشکر غمت نکند ملك دل خراب
جان عزیز خود بنوا میفرستمت

ای غایب از نظر که شدی همنشین دل
میگویمت دعا و ثنا میفرستمت

در روی خود تفرّج صنع خدای کن
کآیینهٔ خدای نما میفرستمت

تا مطربان ز شوق منت آگهی دهند
قول و غزل بساز و نوا میفرستمت

ساقی بیا که هاتف غیبم بمژده گفت
با درد صبر کن که دوا میفرستمت

حافظ سرود مجلس ما ذکر خیر تست
بشتاب هان که اسب و قبا میفرستمت

شراب و عیش نهان چیست کار بی بنیاد
زدیم بر صف رندان و هرچه بادا باد

گره ز دل بگشا وز سپهر یاد مکن
که فکر هیچ مهندس چنین گره نگشاد

ز انقلاب زمانه عجب مدار که چرخ
ازین فسانه هزاران هزار دارد یاد

قدح بشرط ادب گیر زانکه ترکیبش
ز کاسهٔ سر جمشید و بهمنست و قباد

که آگهست که کاوس و کی کجا رفتند
که واقفست که چون رفت تخت جم بر باد

ز حسرت لب شیرین هنوز می‌بینم
که لاله میدمد از خون دیدهٔ فرهاد

مگر که لاله بدانست بیوفائی دهر
که تا بزاد و بشد جام می ز کف ننهاد

بیا بیا که زمانی ز می خراب شویم
مگر رسیم بگنجی در این خراب آباد

نمیدهند اجازت مرا بسیر سفر
نسیم باد مصلّا و آب رکناباد

قدح مگیر چو حافظ مگر بنالهٔ چنگ
که بسته‌اند بر ابریشم طرب دل شاد

روز وصل دوستداران یاد باد   یاد باد آن روزگاران یاد باد

کام از تلخیِّ غم چون زهر گشت   بانگِ نوش شاد خواران یاد باد

گرچه یاران فارغند از یاد مـن   از من ایشانرا هزاران یاد باد

مبتـلا گشتم درین بنـد و بلا   کوشش آن حق گزاران یاد باد

گرچه صد رودست درچشم مدام   زنـده رود باغ کاران یاد باد

راز حافظ بعد ازین ناگفته ماند   ای دریغا رازداران یاد باد

سالها دل طلب جام جم از ما میکرد

وانچه خود داشت ز بیگانه تمنّا میکرد

گوهری کز صدف کون و مکان بیرونست

طلب از گم شدگان لب دریا میکرد

مشکل خویش بر پیر مغان بردم دوش

کو بتأیید نظر حلّ معمّا میکرد

دیدمش خرّم و خندان قدح باده بدست

واندران آینه صد گونه تماشا میکرد

گفتم این جام جهان بین بتو کی داد حکیم

گفت آنروز که این گنبد مینا میکرد

بیدلی در همه احوال خدا با او بود

او نمیدیدش و از دور خدارا میکرد

این همه شعبدهٔ خویش که میکرد اینجا

سامری پیش عصا و ید بیضا میکرد

گفت آن یار کزو گشت سر دار بلند

جرمش این بود که اسرار هویدا میکرد

فیض روح القدس ار باز مدد فرماید

دیگران هم بکنند آنچه مسیحا میکرد

گفتمش سلسلهٔ زلف بتان از پی چیست

گفت حافظ گلهٔ از دل شیدا میکرد

بازار بتان شکست گیرد	یارم چو قدح بدست گیرد
کو محتسبی که مست گیرد	هرکس که بدید چشم او گفت
تا یار مرا بشست گیرد	در بحر فتاده‌ام چو ماهی
آیا بود آنکه دست گیرد	در پاش فتاده‌ام بزاری
جای ز می الست گیرد	خرّم دل آنکه همچو حافظ

۱۷   دمی با غم بسر بردن

دمی با غم بسر بردن جهان یکسر نمی‌ارزد

بمی بفروش دلق ما کزین بهتر نمی‌ارزد

بکوی می فروشانش بجای بر نمیگیرند

زهی سجادهٔ تقوی که یک ساغر نمی‌ارزد

رقیب سرزنشها کرد کز این باب رخ بر تاب

چه افتاد این سر مارا که خاک در نمی‌ارزد

شکوه تاج سلطانی که بیم جان درو درجست

کلاهی دلکش است امّا بترک سر نمی‌ارزد

چه آسان می‌نمود اقل غم دریا ببوی سود

غلط کردم که این طوفان بصد گوهر نمی‌ارزد

ترا آن به که روی خود ز مشتاقان بپوشانی

که شادیّ جهانگیری غم لشکر نمی‌ارزد

چو حافظ در قناعت کوش و از دنییّ دون بگذر

که یک منّت ز دونان بصد من زر نمی‌ارزد

غلام نرگس مست تو تاجدارانند
خراب بادهٔ لعل تو هوشیارانند

ترا صبا و مرا آب دیده شد غمّاز
و گر نه عاشق و معشوق رازدارانند

ز زیر زلف دوتا چون گذر کنی بنگر
که از یمین و یسارت چه سوکوارانند

گذار کن چو صبا بر بنفشه‌زار و ببین
که از تطاول زلفت چه بیقرارانند

نصیب ماست بهشت ای خداشناس برو
که مستحقّ کرامت گناه‌کارانند

نه من بر آن گل عارض غزل سرایم و بس
که عندلیب تو از هر طرف هزارانند

تو دستگیر شو ای خضر پی خجسته که من
پیاده میروم و همرهان سوارانند

بیا بمیکده و چهره ارغوانی کن
مرو بصومعه کانجا سیاه‌کارانند

خلاص حافظ از آن زلف تابدار مباد
که بستگان کند تو رستگارانند

دوش دیدم که ملائک در میخانه زدند

کل آدم بسرشتند و به پیمانه زدند

ساکنان حرم ستر و عفاف ملکوت

با من راه نشین بادهٔ مستانه زدند

آسمان بار امانت نتوانست کشید

قرعهٔ کار بنام من دیوانه زدند

جنگ هفتاد و دو ملّت همه را عذر بنه

چون بدیدند حقیقت ره افسانه زدند

شکر ایزد که میان من و او صلح افتاد

صوفیان رقص کنان ساغر شکرانه زدند

آتش آن نیست که بر شعلهٔ آن خندد شمع

آتش آنست که در خرمن پروانه زدند

کس چو حافظ نگشاد از رخ اندیشه نقاب

تا سر زلف سخن را بقلم شانه زدند

گفتم کیم دهان و لبت کامران کنند
گفتا بچشم هر چه تو گوئی چنان کنند

گفتم خراج مصر طلب میکند لبت
گفتا درین معامله کمتر زیان کنند

گفتم بنقطهٔ دهنت خود که برد راه
گفت این حکایتیست که با نکته دان کنند

گفتم صنم پرست مشو با صمد نشین
گفتا به کوی عشق همین و همان کنند

گفتم هوای میکده غم میبرد ز دل
گفتا خوش آن کسان که دلی شادمان کنند

گفتم شراب و خرقه نه آیین مذهبست
گفت این عمل بمذهب پیر مغان کنند

گفتم ز لعل نوش لبان پیر را چه سود
گفتا ببوسهٔ شکرینش جوان کنند

گفتم که خواجه کی بسر حجله میرود
گفت آنزمان که مشتری و مه قران کنند

گفتم دعای دولت او ورد حافظ است
گفت این دعا ملایک هفت آسمان کنند

ساقی حدیث سرو و گل و لاله میرود
وین بحث با ثلاثهٔ غسّاله میرود

می ده که نو عروس چمن حدّ حسن یافت
کار این زمان ز صنعت دلّاله میرود

شکّرشکن شوند همه طوطیان هند
زین قند پارسی که به بنگاله میرود

طیّ مکان ببین و زمان در سلوك شعر
کاین طفل یکشبه ره یکساله میرود

آن چشم جادوانهٔ عابد فریب بین
کش کاروان سحر ز دنبـاله میرود

از ره مرو بعشوهٔ دنیا که این عجوز
مکّاره مینشیند و محتاله میرود

باد بهـار میوزد از گلستان شـاه
وز ژاله باده در قدح لاله میرود

حافظ ز شوق مجلس سلطان غیاث دین
غافل مشو که کار تو از ناله میرود

کنون که در چمن آمد گل از عدم بوجود
بنفشه در قدم او نهاد سر بسجود

بنوش جام صبوحی بنالهٔ دف و چنگ
ببوس غبغب ساقی بنغمهٔ نی و عود

بدور گل منشین بی شراب و شاهد و چنگ
که همچو روز بقا هفتهٔ بود معدود

شد از خروج ریاحین چو آسمان روشن
زمین باختر میمون و طالع مسعود

ز دست شاهد نازک عذار عیسی دم
شراب نوش و رها کن حدیث عاد و ثمود

جهان چو خلد برین شد بدور سوسن و گل
ولی چه سود که در وی نه ممکنست خلود

چو گل سوار شود بر هوا سلیمان وار
سحر که مرغ درآید بنغمهٔ داود

بباغ تازه کن آیین دین زردشتی
کنون که لاله برافروخت آتش نمرود

بخواه جام صبوحی بیاد آصف عهد
وزیر ملک سلیمان عماد دین محمود

بود که مجلس حافظ بیمن تربیتش
هر آنچه می‌طلبد جمله باشدش موجود

چـو آفتـاب مى از مشرق پیـالـه بر آید

ز بـاغ عـارض سـاق هـزار لالـه بر آید

نسیم در سر گل بـشکنـد كلالهٔ سـنبـل

چـو از میـان چمن بـوی آن كلاه بر آید

حكایت شب هجران نـه آن حكایت حالیست

كـه شمّهٔ ز بیانش بـصد رسـالـه بر آید

ز گرد خوان نگـون فلك طمع نتوان داشت

كه بى ملالت صد غصّه یك نوالـه بر آید

بسعى خود نتوان برد پى بگـوهر مقصود

خیـال بـاشد كاین كار بى حـوالـه بر آید

گرت چو نوح نبى صبر هست در غم طوفان

بلا بـگردد و كام هـزار سـالـه بر آید

نسیم زلف تو چون بگـذرد بتربت حافظ

ز خاك كالبدش صد هزار لاله بر آید

دست از طلب ندارم تا کام من برآید
یا تن رسد بجانان یا جان ز تن برآید

بگشای تربتم را بعد از وفات و بنگر
کز آتش درونم دود از کفن برآید

بنمای رخ که خلقی واله شوند و حیران
بگشای لب که فریاد از مرد و زن برآید

جان بر لبست و حسرت در دل که از لبانش
نگرفته هیچ کامی جان از بدن برآید

از حسرت دهانش آمد بتنگ جانم
خود کام تنگدستان کی زان دهن برآید

گویند ذکر خیرش در خیل عشقبازان
هرجا که نام حافظ در انجمن برآید

دیگر ز شاخ سرو سهی بلبل صبور

گلبانگ زد که چشم بد از روی گل بدور

ای گل بشکر آنکه توئی پادشاه حسن

با بلبلان بیدل شیدا مکن غرور

از دست غیبت تو شکایت نمیکنم

تا نیست غیبتی نبود لذّت حضور

گر دیگران بعیش و طرب خرّمند و شاد

مارا غم نگار بود مایهٔ سرور

زاهد اگر بحور و قصورست امیدوار

مارا شرابخانه قصورست و یار حور

می خور بیانگ چنگ و مخور غصّه ور کسی

گوید ترا که باده مخور گو هو الغفور

حافظ شکایت از غم هجران چه میکنی

در هجر وصل باشد و در ظلمتست نور

زهر هجری چشیدهام که مپرس	درد عشقی کشیدهام که مپرس
دلبری بر گزیدهام که مپرس	گشتهام در جهان و آخر کار
میرود آب دیدهام که مپرس	آنچنان در هوای خاک درش
سخنانی شنیدهام که مپرس	من بگوش خود از دهانت دوش
لب لعلی گزیدهام که مپرس	سوی من لب چه میگزی که مگر
رنجهائی کشیدهام که مپرس	بی تو در کلبهٔ گدائی خویش
بمقامی رسیدهام که مپرس	همچو حافظ غریب در ره عشق

خوشا شیراز و وضع بی مثالش   خداوندا نگه‌دار از زوالش

ز رکناباد ما صد لوحش الله   که عمر خضر می‌بخشد زلالش

میان جعفرآباد و مصلّی   عبیرآمیز می‌آید شمالش

بشیراز آی و فیض روح قدسی   بجوی از مردم صاحب کمالش

که نام قند مصری برد آنجا   که شیرینان ندادند انفعالش

صبا زان لولی شنگول سرمست   چه داری آگهی چونست حالش

گر آن شیرین پسر خونم بریزد   دلا چون شیر مادر کن حلالش

مکن از خواب بیدارم خدارا   که دارم خلوتی خوش با خیالش

چرا حافظ چو می‌ترسیدی از هجر   نکردی شکر ایّام وصالش

هاتفی از گوشهٔ میخانه دوش   گفت ببخشند گنه می بنوش

لطف الهی بکند کار خویش   مژدهٔ رحمت برساند سروش

این خرد خام بمیخانه بر   تا می لعل آوردش خون بجوش

گرچه وصالش نه بکوشش دهند   هر قدر ای دل که توانی بکوش

لطف خدا بیشتر از جرم ماست   نکتهٔ سربسته چه گوئی خموش

گوش من و حلقهٔ گیسوی یار   روی من و خاک در میفروش

رندی حافظ نه گناهیست صعب   با کرم پادشه عیب پوش

داور دین شاه شجاع آنکه کرد   روح قدس حلقهٔ امرش بگوش

ای ملک العرش مرادش بده   وز خطر چشم بدش دار گوش

سحر ببـوی گلستان دمی شــدم در بـاغ
که تا چو بلبل بیدل کنم علاج کم دماغ

بجلوهٔ گل سـوری نگاه مـیکـردم
که بود در شب تیره بروشنی چو چراغ

چنـان بحسن و جوانیّ خویشتن مغرور
که داشت از دل بلبل هزار گونه فراغ

گشاده نرگس رعنـا ز حسرت آب از چشم
نهاده لاله ز سودا بجان و دل صد داغ

زبان کشیده چو تیغی بسرزنش سوسن
دهان گشاده شقایق چو مـردم ایغـاغ

یکی چـو بـاده پرستان صراحی انـدر دست
یکی چـو ساقی مستان بکف گرفته ایاغ

نشاط و عیش و جوانی چو گل غنیمت دان
کـه حافظا نبود بر رسول غیر بـلاغ

هـزار دشمنم ار میـکنـنـد قصد هـلاك

گرم تـو دوستی از دشمنـان نـدارم بـاك

سـرا امیـد وصـال تو زنده مـیدارد

و گـر نـه هـر دم از هجر تست بیم هلاك

نفس نفس اگر از باد نشنـوم بـویش

زمـان زمـان چو گل از غم کنم گریبان چاك

رود بخواب دو چشم از خیال تو هیهات

بـود صبـور دل انـدر فراق تـو حاشاك

اگـر تـو زخم زنی بـه کـه دیگری مرهم

و گـر تـو زهر دهی بـه کـه دیگری تریاك

بـضرب سیفـك قتلی حیاتنـا ابدا

لأنّ روحی قد طاب أن یکـون فداك

عنـان مپیـچ که گـر میزنی بشمشیرم

سپر کنم سر و دستت نـدارم از قتراك

تـرا چنانکه توئی هـر نظر کجا بیند

بقدر دانش خود هـر کسی کـند ادراك

بچشم خـلـق عزیز جهان شـود حافظ

کـه بر در تو نـهـد روی مسکنت بر خاك

عشقبازیّ و جوانّ و شراب لعل فام

مجلس انس و حریف همدم و شرب مدام

ساقی شکّردهان و مطرب شیرین‌سخن

همنشینی نیک کردار و ندیمی نیک‌نام

شاهدی از لطف و پاکی رشک آب زندگی

دلبری در حسن و خوبی غیرت ماه تمام

بزمگاهی دلنشان چون قصر فردوس برین

گلشنی پیرامنش چون روضهٔ دار السّلام

صف نشینان نیک‌خواه و پیشکاران با ادب

دوستداران صاحب اسرار و حریفان دوستکام

بادهٔ گلرنگ تلخ تیز خوشخوار سبک

نُقلش از لعل نگار و نقلش از یاقوت خام

غمزهٔ ساقی بیغمای خرد آهسته تیغ

زلف جانان از برای صید دل گسترده دام

نکته دانی بذله گو چون حافظ شیرین سخن

بخشش آموزی جهان افروز چون حاجی قوام

هر که این عشرت نخواهد خوشدلی بر وی تباه

وانکه این مجلس نجوید زندگی بر وی حرام

مژدهٔ وصل تو کو کز سر جان برخیزم
طایر قدسم و از دام جهان برخیزم

بولای تو که گر بندهٔ خویشم خوانی
از سر خواجگی کون و مکان برخیزم

یا رب از ابر هدایت برسان بارانی
پیشتر زانکه چو گردی ز میان برخیزم

بر سر تربت من با می و مطرب بنشین
تا ببویت ز لحد رقص کنان برخیزم

خیز و بالا بنما ای بت شیرین حرکت
کز سر جان و جهان دست فشان برخیزم

گر چه پیرم تو شبی تنگ در آغوشم کش
تا سحرگه ز کنار تو جوان برخیزم

روز مرگم نفسی مهلت دیدار بده
تا چو حافظ ز سر جان و جهان برخیزم

در خرابات مغان نور خدا می‌بینم

این عجب بین که چو نوری ز کجا می‌بینم

جلوه بر من مفروش ای ملك الحاج که تو

خانه می‌بینی و من خانه خدا می‌بینم

خواهم از زلف بتان نافه گشائی کردن

فکر دورست همانا که خطا می‌بینم

سوز دل اشك روان آه سحر نالهٔ شب

این همه از نظر لطف شما می‌بینم

هر دم از روی تو نقشی زندم راه خیال

با که گویم که درین پرده چها می‌بینم

کس ندیدست ز مشك ختن و نافهٔ چین

آنچه من هر سحر از باد صبا می‌بینم

دوستان عیب نظربازی حافظ مکنید

که من اورا ز محبّان شما می‌بینم

بگذار تا ز شارع میخانه بگذریم
کز بهر جرعهٔ همه محتاج این دریم

روز نخست چون دم رندی زدیم و عشق
شرط آن بود که جز ره آن شیوه نسپریم

جائی که تخت و مسند جم میرود بباد
گر غم خوریم خوش نبود به که می خوریم

تا بو که دست در کمر او توان زدن
در خون دل نشسته چو یاقوت احمریم

واعظ مکن نصیحت شوریدگان که ما
با خاك کوی دوست بفردوس ننگریم

چون صوفیان بحالت و رقصند مقتدا
ما نیز هم بشعبده دستی برآوریم

از جرعهٔ تو خاك زمین درّ و لعل یافت
بیچاره ما که پیش تو از خاك کمتریم

حافظ چو ره بکنگرهٔ کاخ وصل نیست
با خاك آستانهٔ این در بسر بریم

دوستان وقت گل آن به که به عشرت کوشیم
سخن اهل دلست این و بجان بنیوشیم

نیست در کس کرم و وقت طرب میگذرد
چاره آنست که سجّاده بمی بفروشیم

خوش هوائیست فرح بخش خدایا بفرست
نازنینی که برویش می گلگون نوشیم

ارغنون ساز فلک رهزن اهل هنرست
چون ازین غصّه ننالیم و چرا خروشیم

گل بجوش آمد و از می نزدیمش آبی
لاجرم زاتش حرمان و هوس میجوشیم

می کشیم از قدح لاله شرابی موهوم
چشم بد دور که بی مطرب و می مدهوشیم

حافظ این حال عجب با که توان گفت که ما
بلبلانیم که در موسم گل خاموشیم

شاه شمشاد قدان خسرو شیرین دهنان
که بمژگان شکند قلب همه صف شکنان

مست بگذشت و نظر بر من درویش انداخت
گفت ای چشم و چراغ همه شیرین سخنان

تا کی از سیم و زرت کیسه تهی خواهد بود
بندهٔ من شو و بر خور ز همه سیم تنان

کمتر از ذرّه نه‌ای پست مشو مهر بورز
تا بخلوتگه خورشید رسی چرخ زنان

بر جهان تکیه مکن ور قدحی می داری
شادی زهره جبینان خور و نازك بدنان

پیر پیمانه کش من که روانش خوش باد
گفت پرهیز کن از صحبت پیمان شکنان

دامن دوست بدست آر و ز دشمن بگسل
مرد یزدان شو و فارغ گذر از اهرمنان

با صبا در چمن لاله سحر میگفتم
که شهیدان که اند این همه خونین کفنان

گفت حافظ من و تو محرم این راز نه ایم
از می لعل حکایت کن و شیرین دهنان

دانی کـه چیست دولت دیـدار یار دیدن

در کـوی او گدائی بر خسروی گزیدن

از جـان طـمع بریدن آسـان بـود ولیـکن

از دوستان جانی مشکل تـوان بریدن

خواهم شدن بستان بستان چون غنچه با دل تنگ

وانجا به نیك نامی پیراهنی دریدن

گه چـون نسیم بـا گل راز نهـفتـه گفتن

گه سرّ عشقبازی از بلبلان شنیدن

بوسیدن لـب یـار اقل ز دست مگذار

کاخر ملول گردی از دست و لب گزیدن

فرصت شمار صحبت کـز این دو راهه منزل

چون بگذریم دیگر نتـوان بهم رسیدن

گوئی برفت حـافظ از یـاد شـاه یحیی

یا رب بیادش آور درویش پروریدن

صبحست ساقیا قدحی پر شراب کن
دور فلك درنگ ندارد شتـاب کـن

زان پیشتر کـه عالم فانی شود خراب
مـارا ز جام بادهٔ گلگون خراب کن

خورشید می ز مشرق ساغر طلوع کرد
گر برگ عیش می‌طلبی ترك خواب کن

روزی که چرخ از گل ما کوزها کند
زنهار کاسهٔ سر ما پر شراب کـن

مـا مـرد زهد و توبه و طامات نیستیم
با مـا بجام بادهٔ صافی خطاب کن

کار صـواب باده پرستیست حافـظا
بر خیر و عـزم جـزم بکار صواب کن

۷۱

مزرع سبز فلك دیدم و داس مه نو
یادم از کشتهٔ خویش آمد و هنگام درو

گفتم ای بخت بخفتیدی و خورشید دمید
گفت با این همه از سابقه نومید مشو

گر روی پاك و مجرّد چو مسیحا بفلك
از چراغ تو بخورشید رسد صد پرتو

تکیه بر اختر شب دزد مکن كاین عیّار
تاج كاووس ببرد و كمر كیخسرو

گوشوار زر و لعل ارچه گران دارد گوش
دور خوبی گذرانست نصیحت بشنو

چشم بد دور ز خال تو كه در عرصهٔ حسن
بیدق راند كه برد از مه و خورشید گرو

آسمان گو مفروش این عظمت كاندر عشق
خرمن مه بجوی خوشهٔ پروین بدو جو

آتش زهد و ریا خرمن دین خواهد سوخت
حافظ این خرقهٔ پشمینه بینداز و برو

٤٠ عیش

کارم بکاست الحمد لله

گه جام زرکش گه لعل دلخواه

پیران جاهل شیخان گمراه

وز فعل عابد استغفر الله

چشمیّ و صد نم جانّ و صد آه

از قامتت سرو از عارضت ماه

درس شبانه ورد سحرگه

عیشم مدامست از لعل دلخواه

ای بخت سرکش تنگش بر کش

مارا برندی افسانه کردند

از دست زاهد کردیم توبه

جانا چه گویم شرح فراقت

کافر مبیناد این غم که دیدست

شوق لبت برد از یاد حافظ

٤١ وجود ما معمائیست

گرفتم باده با چنگ و چغانه

ز شهر هستیش کردم روانه

که ایمن گشتم از مکر زمانه

که ای تیر ملامترا نشانه

اگر خودرا ببینی در میانه

که عنقارا بلندست آشیانه

که با خود عشق بازد جاودانه

خیال آب و گل در ره بهانه

ازین دریای ناپیدا کرانه

که تحقیقش فسونست و فسانه

سحرگاهان که مخمور شبانه

نهادم عقل را ره توشه از می

نگار می فروشم عشوهٔ داد

ز ساقّ کمان ابرو شنیدم

نبندی زان میان طرف کمروار

برو این دام بر مرغی دگر نه

که بندد طرف وصل از حسن شاهی

ندیم و مطرب و ساق همه اوست

بده کشتیّ می تا خوش برانیم

وجود ما معمّائیست حافظ

73

بیا با ما مورز این کینه داری ** که حقّ صحبت دیرینه داری
نصیحت گوش کن کاین دُر بسی به ** از آن گوهر که در گنجینه داری
ولیکن کی نمائی رخ برندان ** توکز خورشید و مه آیینه داری
بد رندان مگو ای شیخ و هش دار ** که با حکم خدائی کینه داری
نمی‌ترسی ز آه آتشینم ** تو دانی خرقهٔ پشمینه داری
بفریاد خمار مفلسان رس ** خدارا گر می دوشینه داری
ندیدم خوشتر از شعر تو حافظ ** بقرآنی که اندر سینه داری

ای که دایم بخویش مغروری ** گر ترا عشق نیست معذوری
گرد دیوانگان عشق مگرد ** که بعقل عقیله مشهوری
مستی عشق نیست در سر تو ** رو که تو مست آب انگوری
روی زردست و آه درد آلود ** عاشقانرا دوای رنجوری
بگذر از نام و ننگ خود حافظ ** ساغر می طلب که مخموری

رفتم بباغ صبحدمی تا چنم گلی
آمد بگوش ناگهم آواز بلبلی

مسکین چو من بعشق گلی گشته مبتلا
واندر چمن فکنده ز فریاد غلغلی

میگشتم اندر آن چمن و باغ دمبدم
میکردم اندر آن گل و بلبل تأملی

گل یار حسن گشته و بلبل قرین عشق
آنرا تفضّلی نه و اینرا تبدّلی

چون کرد در دلم اثر آواز عندلیب
گشتم چنانکه هیچ نماندم تحمّلی

بس گل شکفته میشود این باغ را ولی
کس بی بلای خار نچیدست ازو گلی

حافظ مدار امید فرج از مدار چرخ
دارد هزار عیب و ندارد تفضّلی

نسیم صبح سعادت بدان نشان که تو دانی

گذر بکوی فلان کن در آن زمان که تو دانی

تو پیك خلوت رازیّ و دیده بر سر راهت

بمردی نه بفرمان چنان بران که تو دانی

بگو که جان عزیزم زدست رفت خدارا

ز لعل روح فزایش ببخش آن که تو دانی

من این حروف نوشتم چنانکه غیر ندانست

تو هم ز روی کرامت چنان بخوان که تو دانی

خیال تیغ تو با ما حدیث تشنه و آبست

اسیر خویش گرفتی بکش چنان که تو دانی

امید در کمر زرکشت چگونه ببندم

دقیقه‌ایست نگارا در آن میان که تو دانی

یکیست ترکی و تازی درین معامله حافظ

حدیث عشق بیان کن بدان زبان که تو دانی

٤٦   ساقینامه

بیا ساق آن می که حال آورد

به من ده که بس بیدل افتاده‌ام

کرامت فزاید کمال آورد

وز این هر دو بیحاصل افتاده‌ام

بیا ساق آن می کز او جام جم

به من ده که گردم به تأیید جام

زند لاف بینائی اندر عدم

چو جم آگه از سرّ عالم تمام

76

بیا ساق آن کیمیای فتوح　　که با گنج قارون دهد عمر نوح

بده تا به رویت گشایند باز　　در کامرانیّ و عمر دراز

بیا ساق آن می که عکسش ز جام　　به کیخسرو و جم فرستد سلام

بده تا بگویم به آواز نی　　که جمشید کی بود و کاووس کی

دم از سیر این دیر دیرینه زن　　صلائی به شاهان پیشینه زن

همان مرحله است این بیابان دور　　که گم شد در او لشکر سلم و تور

همان منزل است این جهان خراب　　که دیده‌است ایوان افراسیاب

کجا رفت پیران لشگر کششی　　کجا شیده آن ترک خنجر کشش

بیا ساقی آن بکر مستور مست　　که اندر خرابات دارد نشست

به من ده که بدنام خواهم شدن　　خراب می و جام خواهم شدن

بیا ساقی آن آب اندیشه سوز　　که گر شیر نوشد شود بیشه سوز

بده تا روم بر فلک شیرگیر　　به هم بردرم دام این گرگ پیر

بیا ساقی آن می که حور بهشت　　عبیر ملایک در آن می سرشت

بده تا بخوری در آتش کنم　　دماغ خرد تا ابد خوش کنم

بیا ساقی آن می که شاهی دهد　　به پاکیّ او دل گواهی دهد

به من ده مگر گردم از عیب پاك　　برآرم به عشرت سر از این مغاك

چو شد باغ روحانیان مسکنم　　در اینجا چرا تخته‌بند تنم

شرابم ده و روی دولت ببین　　خرابم کن و گنج حکمت ببین

من آنم که چون جام گیرم به دست　　ببینم در آن آینه هرچه هست

به مستی دم از پارسائی زنم　　در خسروی در گدائی زنم

که حافظ چو مستانه سازد سرود　　ز چرخش دهد رود زهره درود

الا ای آهـوی وحشـی، کجائی؟   مـرا بـا تـوست بسـیار آشنائی
دو تنهارو، دو سرگردان بیکس   دو راه است و کین از پیش و از پس
بیـا تـا حـال یـکـدیـگـر بدانیم   مـراد هم بجوئیم ار تـوانـیم
که میبینم که این دشت مشوش   چراگهی ندارد ایمن و خوش

که خواهد شد، بگوئید، ای حبیبان   رفیق بیکسان، یار غریبان
مگر خضر مبارک پی در آید   ز یمن همّتش این ره سر آید

نکرد آن همـدم دیرین مـدارا   مسلمانان، مسلمانان، خدارا !
چنین بیرحم زد زخم جدائی   که گوئی خود نبوده‌است آشنائی
برفت و طبع خوشباشم حزین کرد   برادر بـا برادر کی چنین کـرد؟
مگر خضر مبارک پی تـوانـد   که این تنها بدان تنها رساند

مـگـر وقت عـطـا پروردن آمـد   که فـالم لا تذرنی فـرداً آمـد
کـه روزی رهـروی در سرزمینی   به لطفش گفت رند رهنشینی
که «ای سالک، چه در انبانه داری؟   بیا دامی بنه گر دانه داری »
جوابش داد و گفـتـا «دانـه دارم   ولی سیمرغ میبایـد شکارم »
بگفتا « چون به دست آری نشانش؟   کـه از مـا بینشان است آشیانش
نیـاز مـا چه وزن آرد بدین ساز؟   که خورشید غنی شد کیسه پرداز!»

چـو آن سرو سـهـی شـد کاروانی   ز بـال سرو مـیـکـن دیدبانی
لب سر چشمه‌ئی و طرف جوئی   نم اشگئیّ و بـا خـود گفتگوئی
بـه یـاد رفتگـان و دوسـتـداران   مـوافـق گـرد بـا ابر بـهـاران
چو نالان آیدت آب روان پیش   مـدد بخشش ز آب دیدهٔ خویش

مده جام می و پای گل از دست   ولی غافل مباش از دهر بدمست

رفیقان، قدر یکدیگر بدانید   چو معلوم است شرح، از بر بخوانید

مقالات نصیحتگو همین است   که حکم انداز هجران در کمین است

چو ماهی کلك آرم به تقریر   تو از نون والقلم مپرس تفسیر

روان را با خرد درهم سرشتم   وازآن، تخمی که حاصل بود، کشتم

فرحبخشی در این ترکیب پیداست   که مغز شعر نغزش جان اجزاست

یا وز نکهت این طیب امید   مشام جان معطّر ساز جاوید

که این نافه ز چین جیب حور است   نه زآن آهوکه از مردم نفور است!

۴۸ فتنهٔ روزگار

سر فتنه دارد دگر روزگار   من و مستی و فتنهٔ چشم یار

همیدارم از دور گردون شگفت   ندانم که‌را خاك خواهد گرفت

وگر پیر مغ آتشی میزند   ندانم چراغ که برمیکند

فریب جهان قصهٔ روشن است   سحر تا چه زاید شب آبستن است

در این خونفشان عرصهٔ رستخیز   تو خون صراحی به ساغر بریز

بر سر بازار جانبازان منادی میزنید
بشنوید ای ساکنان کوی رندی بشنوید

دختر رز چند روزی شد که از ما گم شدست
رفت تا گیرد سر خود هان و هان حاضر شوید

جامهٔ دارد ز لعل و نیم تاجی از حباب
عقل و دانش برد و شد تا ایمن از وی نغنوید

هر که آن تلخ دهد حلوا بها جانش دهم
ور بود پوشیده و پنهان بدوزخ در روید

دختری شبگرد تند تلخ گلرنگست و مست
گر بیابیدش بسوی خانهٔ حافظ برید

٥٠   اسمعیل

مجد دین سرور و سلطان قضات اسمعیل
که زدی کلک زبان آورش از شرع نطق

ناف هفته بد و از ماه رجب کاف و الف
که برون رفت ازین خانهٔ بی نظم و نسق

کنف رحمت حق منزل او دان وانگه
سال تاریخ وفاتش طلب از رحمت حق

TRANSLATIONS

1 LOVE'S AWAKENING

1

Ho, saki, haste, the beaker bring,
Fill up, and pass it round the ring;
Love seemed at first an easy thing—
But ah! the hard awakening.

2

So sweet perfume the morning air
Did lately from her tresses bear,
Her twisted, musk-diffusing hair—
What heart's calamity was there!

Within life's caravanserai
What brief security have I,
When momently the bell doth cry,
"Bind on your loads; the hour is nigh!"

3

Let wine upon the prayer-mat flow,
An if the taverner bids so;
Whose wont is on this road to go
Its ways and manners well doth know.

4

Mark now the mad career of me,
From wilfulness to infamy;
Yet how conceal that mystery
Whereof men make festivity?

A mountain sea, moon clouded o'er,
And nigh the whirlpool's awful roar—
How can they know our labour sore
Who pass light-burthened on the shore?

5

Hafiz, if thou wouldst win her grace,
Be never absent from thy place;
When thou dost see the well-loved face,
Be lost at last to time and space.

A. J. A.

2 WHERE IS THE PIOUS DOER?

Where is the pious doer? and I the estray'd one, where?
Behold how far the distance, from his safe home to here!

Dark is the stony desert, trackless and vast and dim,
Where is hope's guiding lantern? Where is faith's star so fair?

My heart fled from the cloister, and chant of monkish hymn,
What can avail me sainthood, fasting and punctual prayer?

What is the truth shall light me to heaven's strait thoroughfare?
Whither, O heart, thou hastest? Arrest thee, and beware!

See what a lone adventure is thine unending quest!
Fraught with what deadly danger! Set with what unseen snare!

Say not, O friend, to Hafez, "Quiet thee now and rest!"
Calm and content, what are they? Patience and peace, O where?

ELIZABETH BRIDGES (ELIZABETH DARYUSH)

Sweet maid, if thou would'st charm my sight,
And bid these arms thy neck infold;
That rosy cheek, that lily hand,
Would give thy poet more delight
Than all Bocara's vaunted gold,
Than all the gems of Samarcand.

Boy, let yon liquid ruby flow,
And bid thy pensive heart be glad,
Whate'er the frowning zealots say:
Tell them, their Eden cannot show
A stream so clear as Rocnabad,
A bower so sweet as Mosellay.

O! when these fair perfidious maids,
Whose eyes our secret haunts infest,
Their dear destructive charms display;
Each glance my tender breast invades,
And robs my wounded soul of rest,
As Tartars seize their destin'd prey.

In vain with love our bosoms glow:
Can all our tears, can all our sighs,
New lustre to those charms impart?
Can cheeks, where living roses blow,
Where nature spreads her richest dyes,
Require the borrow'd gloss of art?

Speak not of fate: ah! change the theme,
And talk of odours, talk of wine,
Talk of the flowers that round us bloom:
'Tis all a cloud, 'tis all a dream;
To love and joy thy thoughts confine,
Nor hope to pierce the sacred gloom.

Beauty has such resistless power,
Than even the chaste Egyptian dame
Sigh'd for the blooming Hebrew boy:
For her how fatal was the hour,
When to the banks of Nilus came
A youth so lovely and so coy!

But ah! sweet maid, my counsel hear
(Youth should attend when those advise
Whom long experience renders sage):
While music charms the ravish'd ear;
While sparkling cups delight our eyes,
Be gay; and scorn the frowns of age.

What cruel answer have I heard!
And yet, by heaven, I love thee still:
Can aught be cruel from thy lip?
Yet say, how fell that bitter word
From lips which streams of sweetness fill,
Which nought but drops of honey sip?

Go boldly forth, my simple lay,
Whose accents flow with artless ease,
Like orient pearls at random strung:
Thy notes are sweet, the damsels say;
But O! far sweeter, if they please
The nymph for whom these notes are sung.

SIR WILLIAM JONES

4 FRIENDLY ZEPHYR

Go, friendly Zephyr! whisp'ring greet
Yon gentle fawn with slender feet;
Say that in quest of her I rove
The dangerous steeps, the wilds of love.

Thou merchant who dost sweetness vend
(Long may kind heav'n thy life defend!)
Ah, why unfriendly thus forget
Thy am'rous sweet-billed parroquet?

Is it, O rose! thy beauty's pride
That casts affection far aside,
Forbidding thee to court the tale
Of thy fond mate, the nightingale?

I know not why 'tis rare to see
The colour of sincerity
In nymphs who boast majestic grace,
Dark eyes, and silver-beaming face.

What tho' that face be angel fair,
One fault does all its beauty marr;
Nor faith, nor constancy adorn
Thy charms, which else might shame the morn.

By gentle manners we control
The wise, the sense-illumin'd soul:
No idle lure, no glitt'ring bait
Th' experienc'd bird will captivate.

What wonder, Hafez, that thy strain,
Whose sounds inchant th' etherial plain,
Should tempt each graver star to move
In dances with the star of love?

J. NOTT

5 SPRING SONG

With sullen pace stern winter leaves the plain,
　　And blooming spring trips gaily o'er the meads,
Sweet Philomel now swells her plaintive strain,
　　And her lov'd rose his blushing beauties spreads.

O Zephyr, whilst you waft your gentle gale,
  Fraught with the fragrance of Arabia's groves,
Breathe my soft wishes through yon blooming vale,
  Tell charming Leila how her poet loves!

O! for one heavenly glance from that dear maid,
  How would my raptur'd heart with joy rebound;
Down to her feet I'd lowly bend my head,
  And with my eyebrows sweep the hallow'd ground.

Could those stern fools who steal religion's mask,
  And rail against the sweet delights of love,
Fair Leila see, no paradise they'd ask,
  But for her smiles renounce the joys above.

Trust not in fortune, vain deluded charm!
  Whom wise men shun, and only fools adore.
Oft, whilst she smiles, Fate sounds the dread alarm,
  Round flies her wheel; you sink to rise no more.

Ye rich and great, why rear those princely domes?
  Those heaven-aspiring towers why proudly raise?
Lo! whilst triumphant all around you blooms,
  Death's aweful angel numbers out your days.

Sweet tyrant, longer in that flinty breast
  Lock not thy heart, my bosom is its throne;
There let the charming flutt'rer gently rest;
  Here feast on joys to vulgar souls unknown.

But ah! what means that fiercely-rolling eye,
  Those pointed locks which scent the ambient air;
Now my fond hopes in wild disorder fly,
  Low droops my love, a prey to black despair.

Those charming brows, arch'd like the heavenly bow,
  Arm not, O gentle maid, with such disdain;
Drive not a wretch, already sunk full low,
  Hopeless to mourn his never-ceasing pain.

But to the fair no longer be a slave;
   Drink, Hafez! revel, all your cares unbend,
And boldly scorn the mean dissembling knave
   Who makes religion every vice defend!

J. RICHARDSON

6 THE HOUSE OF HOPE

The house of hope is built on sand,
And life's foundations rest on air;
Then come, give wine into my hand,
That we may make an end of care.

Let me be slave to that man's will
Who 'neath high heaven's turquoise bowl
Hath won and winneth freedom still
From all entanglement of soul;

Save that the mind entangled be
With her whose radiant loveliness
Provoking love and loyalty
Relieves the mind of all distress.

Last night as toping I had been
In tavern, shall I tell to thee
What message from the world unseen
A heavenly angel brought to me?

"Falcon of sovereign renown,
High-nesting bird of lofty gaze,
This corner of affliction town
Befits thee ill, to pass thy days.

"Hearest thou not the whistle's call
From heaven's rampart shrills for thee?
What chanced I cannot guess at all
This snare should now thy prison be."

Heed now the counsel that I give,
And be it to thy acts applied;
For these are words I did receive
From him that was my ancient guide.

"Be pleased with what the fates bestow,
Nor let thy brow be furrowed thus;
The gate to freedom here below
Stands not ajar to such as us."

Look not to find fidelity
Within a world so weakly stayed;
This ancient crone, ere flouting thee,
A thousand bridegrooms had betrayed.

Take not for sign of true intent
Nor think the rose's smile sincere;
Sweet, loving nightingale, lament:
There is much cause for weeping here.

What envying of Hafiz' ease,
Poor poetaster, dost thou moan?
To make sweet music, and to please,
That is a gift of God alone.

A. J. A.

7 WILD OF MIEN

Wild of mien, chanting a love-song, cup in hand, locks disarrayed,
Cheek beflushed, wine-overcome, vesture awry, breast displayed.

With a challenge in that eye's glance, with a love-charm on the lip,
Came my love, sat by my bedside in the dim midnight shade:

O'er my ear bending, my love spake in a sad voice and a low,
"Is it thus, spite of the old years, lover mine, slumber-bewrayed?"

To the wise comes there a cup, fired of the night, pressed to the lip;
An he bow not to the Wine Creed, be he writ Love's renegade.

Go thy way, saint of the cell, flout not the dreg-drainer again;
In the first hour of the world's birth was the high hest on us laid.

Whatsoe'er potion His hand pours in the bowl, that will we quaff,
Heady ferment of the Soul-world, or the grape-must unallayed.

Ah, how oft, e'en as with HAFIZ, hath the red smile of the vine
And the curled ringlet on Love's cheek a repentance unmade!

WALTER LEAF

8 RED ROSE

The rose has flushed red, the bud has burst,
And drunk with joy is the nightingale—
Hail, Sufis! lovers of wine, all hail!
For wine is proclaimed to a world athirst.
Like a rock your repentance seemed to you;
Behold the marvel! of what avail
Was your rock, for a goblet has cleft it in two!

Bring wine for the king and the slave at the gate
Alike for all is the banquet spread,
And drunk and sober are warmed and fed.
When the feast is done and the night grows late,
And the second door of the tavern gapes wide,
The low and the mighty must bow the head
'Neath the archway of Life, to meet what...outside?

Except thy road through affliction pass,
None may reach the halting-station of mirth;
God's treaty: Am I not Lord of the earth?
Man sealed with a sigh: Ah yes, alas!
Nor with Is nor Is Not let thy mind contend;
Rest assured all perfection of mortal birth
In the great Is Not at the last shall end.

For Assaf's pomp, and the steeds of the wind,
And the speech of birds, down the wind have fled,
And he that was lord of them all is dead;
Of his mastery nothing remains behind.
Shoot not thy feathered arrow astray!
A bow-shot's length through the air it has sped,
And then...dropped down in the dusty way.

But to thee, oh Hafiz, to thee, oh Tongue
That speaks through the mouth of the slender reed,
What thanks to thee when thy verses speed
From lip to lip, and the song thou hast sung?

GERTRUDE BELL

9 MY BOSOM GRAC'D

My bosom grac'd with each gay flow'r,
　I grasp the bowl, my nymph in glee;
The monarch of the world this hour,
　Is but a slave compar'd to me.

Intrude not with the taper's light,
　My social friends, with beaming eyes;
Trundle around a starry night,
　And lo! my nymph the moon supplies.

Away, thy sprinkling odours spare,
　Be not officiously thus kind;
The waving ringlets of my Fair,
　Shed perfume to the fainting wind.

My ears th' enlivening notes inspire,
　As lute or harp alternate sound;
My eyes those ruby lips admire,
　Or catch the glasses sparkling round.

Then let no moments steal away,
　Without thy mistress and thy wine;
The spring flowers blossom to decay,
　And youth but glows to own decline.

THOMAS LAW

Zephyr, should'st thou chance to rove
By the mansion of my love,
From her locks ambrosial bring
Choicest odours on thy wing.

Could'st thou waft me from her breast
Tender sighs to say I'm blest,
As she lives! my soul would be
Sprinkl'd o'er with ecstasy.

But if Heav'n the boon deny,
Round her stately footsteps fly,
With the dust that thence may rise,
Stop the tears which bathe these eyes.

Lost, poor mendicant! I roam
Begging, craving she would come:
Where shall I thy phantom see,
Where, dear nymph, a glimpse of thee?

Like the wind-tost reed my breast
Fann'd with hope is ne'er at rest,
Throbbing, longing to excess
Her fair figure to caress.

Yes, my charmer, tho' I see
Thy heart courts no love with me,
Not for worlds, could they be mine,
Would I give a hair of thine.

Why, O care! shall I in vain
Strive to shun thy galling chain,
When these strains still fail to save,
And make Hafiz more a slave.

J. H. HINDLEY

Thus spoke at dawn the field-bird to the newly wakened rose:
"Be kind, for many a bloom like you in this meadow grows."
The rose laughed: "You will find that we at truth show no
　　distress,
But never did a lover with harsh words his love so press.
If ruby wine from jewelled cup it is your wish to drink,
Then pearls and corals pierced with eyelash you must strive to link.
Love's savour to his nostrils to entice he ne'er can seek,
Who on the tavern's earthy floor has not swept dusty cheek."

In Iram's garden yesternight, when, in the grateful air,
The breeze of coming day stirred the tress of hyacinth fair,
I asked: "Throne of Jamshid, where is thy world-revealing cup?"
It sighed: "That waking fortune deep in sleep lies muffled up."
They are not always words of love that from the tongue descend:
Come, bring me wine, O taverner, and to this talk put end.
His wit and patience to the waves are cast by Hafiz' tears.
What can he do, that may not hide how love his being sears?

R. LEVY

12 LAPWING

Wind from the east, oh Lapwing of the day,
I send thee to my Lady, though the way
Is far to Saba, where I bid thee fly;
Lest in the dust thy tameless wings should lie,
Broken with grief, I send thee to thy nest,
　　　　　Fidelity.

Or far or near there is no halting-place
Upon Love's road—absent, I see thy face,
And in thine ear my wind-blown greetings sound,
North winds and east waft them where they are bound,
Each morn and eve convoys of greeting fair
　　　　　I send to thee.

Unto mine eyes a stranger, thou that art
A comrade ever-present to my heart,
What whispered prayers and what full meed of praise
          I send to thee.

Lest Sorrow's army waste thy heart's domain,
I send my life to bring thee peace again,
Dear life thy ransom! From thy singers learn
How one that longs for thee may weep and burn;
Sonnets and broken words, sweet notes and songs
          I send to thee.

Give me the cup! a voice rings in mine ears
Crying: "Bear patiently the bitter years!
For all thine ills, I send thee heavenly grace.
God the Creator mirrored in thy face
Thine eyes shall see, God's image in the glass
          I send to thee.

"Hafiz, thy praise alone my comrades sing;
Hasten to us, thou that art sorrowing!
A robe of honour and a harnessed steed
          I send to thee."

GERTRUDE BELL

13 SECRET DRAUGHT

The secret draught of wine and love repressed
Are joys foundationless—then come whate'er
May come, slave to the grape I stand confessed!
Unloose, oh friend, the knot of thy heart's care,
Despite the warning that the Heavens reveal!
For all his thought, never astronomer
That loosed the knot of Fate those Heavens conceal!

Not all the changes that thy days unfold
Shall rouse thy wonder; Time's revolving sphere
Over a thousand lives like thine has rolled.
That cup within thy fingers, dost not hear
The voices of dead kings speak through the clay
Kobad, Bahman, Djemshid, their dust is here,
"Gently upon me set thy lips!" they say.

What man can tell where Kaus and Kai have gone?
Who knows where even now the restless wind
Scatters the dust of Djem's imperial throne?
And where the tulip, following close behind
The feet of Spring, her scarlet chalice rears,
There Ferhad for the love of Shirin pined,
Dyeing the desert red with his heart's tears.

Bring, bring the cup! drink we while yet we may
To our soul's ruin the forbidden draught;
Perhaps a treasure-trove is hid away
Among those ruins where the wine has laughed!—
Perhaps the tulip knows the fickleness
Of Fortune's smile, for on her stalk's green shaft
She bears a wine-cup through the wilderness.

The murmuring stream of Ruknabad, the breeze
That blows from out Mosalla's fair pleasaunce,
Summon me back when I would seek heart's ease,
Travelling afar; what though Love's countenance
Be turned full harsh and sorrowful on me,
I care not so that Time's unfriendly glance
Still from my Lady's beauty turned be.

Like Hafiz, drain the goblet cheerfully
While minstrels touch the lute and sweetly sing,
For all that makes thy heart rejoice in thee
Hangs of Life's single, slender, silken string.

GERTRUDE BELL

That day of friendship when we met—Recall;
Recall those days of fond regret,

                                    Recall.

As bitter poison grief my palate sours:
The sound: "Be it sweet!" at feasts of ours

                                    Recall.

My friends, it may be, have forgotten long;
But I a thousand times that throng

                                    Recall;

And now while fettered by misfortune's chain,
All those who grateful sought my gain

                                    Recall.

Though thousand rivers from my eyes descend,
I Zindarud, where gard'ners tend,

                                    Recall;

And crushed by sorrow that finds no relief,
Those who brought solace to my grief

                                    Recall.

No more from ḤÁFIẒ' lips shall secrets pass:
Those who once kept them, I, alas!

                                    Recall.

                                    H. BICKNELL

15 A MAD HEART

I

Long years my heart had made request
Of me, a stranger, hopefully
(Not knowing that itself possessed
The treasure that it sought of me),
That Jamshid's chalice I should win
And it would see the world therein.

That is a pearl by far too rare
To be contained within the shell
Of time and space; lost vagrants there
Upon the ocean's margin, well
We know it is a vain surmise
That we should hold so great a prize.

II

There was a man that loved God well;
In every motion of his mind
God dwelt; and yet he could not tell
That God was in him, being blind:
Wherefore as if afar he stood
And cried, "Have mercy, O my God!"

III

This problem that had vexed me long
Last night unto the taverner
I carried; for my hope was strong
His judgement sure, that could not err,
Might swiftly solve infallibly
The riddle that had baffled me.

I saw him standing in his place,
A goblet in his grasp, a smile
Of right good cheer upon his face,
As in the glass he gazed awhile
And seemed to view in vision clear
A hundred truths reflected there.

IV

"That friend who, being raised sublime
Upon the gallows, glorified
The tree that slew him for his crime,
This was the sin for which he died,
That, having secrets in his charge,
He told them to the world at large."

So spake he; adding, "But the heart
That has the truth within its hold
And, practising the rosebud's art,
Conceals a mystery in each fold,
That heart hath well this comment lined
Upon the margin of the mind.

"When Moses unto Pharaoh stood,
The men of magic strove in vain
Against his miracle of wood;
So every subtlety of brain
Must surely fail and feeble be
Before the soul's supremacy.

"And if the Holy Ghost descend
In grace and power infinite
His comfort in these days to lend
To them that humbly wait on it,
Theirs too the wondrous works can be
That Jesus wrought in Galilee."

V

"What season did the Spirit wise
This all-revealing cup assign
Within thy keeping?" "When the skies
Were painted by the Hand Divine
And heaven's mighty void was spanned,
Then gave He this into my hand."

"Yon twisted coil, yon chain of hair
Why doth the lovely Idol spread
To keep me fast and fettered there?"
"Ah, Hafiz!", so the wise man said,
"'Tis a mad heart, and needs restraint
That speaks within thee this complaint."

A. J. A.

16 CUP IN HAND

When my Beloved the cup in hand taketh
The market of lovely ones slack demand taketh.

I, like a fish, in the ocean am fallen,
Till me with the hook yonder Friend to land taketh.

Every one saith, who her tipsy eye seëth,
"Where is a shrieve, that this fair firebrand taketh?"

Lo, at her feet in lament am I fallen,
Till the Beloved me by the hand taketh.

Happy his heart who, like Hafiz, a goblet
Of wine of the Prime Fore-eternal's brand taketh.

J. PAYNE

17 NOT ALL THE SUM OF EARTHLY HAPPINESS

Not all the sum of earthly happiness
Is worth the bowed head of a moment's pain,
And if I sell for wine my dervish dress,
Worth more than what I sell is what I gain!
Land where my Lady dwells, thou holdest me
Enchained; else Fars were but a barren soil,
Not worth the journey over land and sea,
Not worth the toil!

Down in the quarter where they sell red wine,
My holy carpet scarce would fetch a cup—
How brave a pledge of piety is mine,
Which is not worth a goblet foaming up!
Mine enemy heaped scorn on me and said:
"Forth from the tavern gate!" Why am I thrust
From off the threshold? is my fallen head
Not worth the dust?

Wash white that travel-stained sad robe of thine!
Where word and deed alike one colour bear,
The grape's fair purple garment shall outshine
Thy many-coloured rags and tattered gear.
Full easy seemed the sorrow of the sea
Lightened by hope of gain—hope flew too fast!
A hundred pearls were poor indemnity,
                              Not worth the blast.

The Sultan's crown, with priceless jewels set,
Encircles fear of death and constant dread;
It is a head-dress much desired—and yet
Art sure 'tis worth the danger to the head?
'Twere best for thee to hide thy face from those
That long for thee; the Conqueror's reward
Is never worth the army's long-drawn woes,
                              Worth fire and sword.

Ah, seek the treasure of a mind at rest
And store it in the treasury of Ease;
Not worth a loyal heart, a tranquil breast,
Were all the riches of thy lands and seas!
Ah, scorn, like Hafiz, the delights of earth,
Ask not one grain of favour from the base,
Two hundred sacks of jewels were not worth
                              Thy soul's disgrace!

                              GERTRUDE BELL

18 SLAVES

Slaves of thy shining eyes are even those
That diadems of might and empire bear;
Drunk with the wine that from thy red lip flows,
Are they that e'en the grape's delight forswear.
Drift, like the wind across a violet bed,
Before thy many lovers, weeping low,
And clad like violets in blue robes of woe,
Who feel thy wind-blown hair and bow the head.

Thy messenger the breath of dawn, and mine
A stream of tears, since lover and beloved
Keep not their secret; through my verses shine,
Though other lays my flower's grace have proved
And countless nightingales have sung thy praise.
When veiled beneath thy curls thou passest, see,
To right and leftward those that welcome thee
Have bartered peace and rest on thee to gaze!

But thou that knowest God by heart, away!
Wine-drunk, love-drunk, we inherit Paradise,
His mercy is for sinners; hence and pray
Where wine thy cheek red as red erghwan dyes,
And leave the cell to faces sinister.
Oh Khizr, whose happy feet bathed in life's fount,
Help one who toils afoot—the horsemen mount
And hasten on their way; I scarce can stir.

Ah, loose me not! ah, set not Hafiz free
From out the bondage of thy gleaming hair!
Safe only those, safe, and at liberty,
That fast enchained in thy linked ringlets are.
But from the image of his dusty cheek
Learn this from Hafiz: proudest heads shall bend,
And dwellers on the threshold of a friend
Be crownèd with the dust that crowns the meek.

GERTRUDE BELL

19 LAST NIGHT I DREAMED

Last night I dreamed that angels stood without
The tavern door, and knocked in vain, and wept;
They took the clay of Adam, and, methought,
Moulded a cup therewith while all men slept.
Oh dwellers in the halls of Chastity!
You brought Love's passionate red wine to me,
Down to the dust I am, your bright feet stept.

102

For Heaven's self was all too weak to bear
The burden of His love God laid on it,
He turned to seek a messenger elsewhere,
And in the Book of Fate my name was writ.
Between my Lord and me such concord lies
As makes the Huris glad in Paradise,
With songs of praise through the green glades they flit.

A hundred dreams of Fancy's garnered store
Assail me—Father Adam went astray
Tempted by one poor grain of corn! Wherefore
Absolve and pardon him that turns away
Though the soft breath of Truth reaches his ears,
For two-and-seventy jangling creeds he hears,
And loud-voiced Fable calls him ceaselessly.

That, that is not the flame of Love's true fire
Which makes the torchlight shadows dance in rings,
But where the radiance draws the moth's desire
And sends him forth with scorched and drooping wings.
The heart of one who dwells retired shall break,
Rememb'ring a black mole and a red cheek,
And his life ebb, sapped at its secret springs.

Yet since the earliest time that man has sought
To comb the locks of Speech, his goodly bride,
Not one, like Hafiz, from the face of Thought
Has torn the veil of Ignorance aside.

GERTRUDE BELL

20 CONVERSATION

"Ah, when shall I to thy mouth and lips attain?"
"'Fore God, but speak, for thy word is sovereign."
"'Tis Egypt's tribute thy lips require for fee."
"In such transaction the less the loss shall be."

103

"What lip is worthy the tip of thy mouth to hold?"
"To none but initiates may this tale be told."
"Adore not idols, but sit with the One, the True!"
"In the street of Love it is lawful both to do."

"The tavern's breath is balm to the spirit's smart."
"And blessed are they that comfort the lonely heart."

"No part of faith is the dervish cloak and the wine."
"Yet both are found in this Magian faith of mine."
"What gain can coral lips to an old man bring?"
"A honeyed kiss, and his youth's recovering."

"And when shall bridegroom come to the couch of the bride?"
"The morn that Moon and Jupiter stand allied."
"Still Hafiz prays for thy yet ascending might."
"So pray and praise the angels in heaven's height."

A. J. A.

21 SPRING

Cypress and Tulip and sweet Eglantine,
Of these the tale from lip to lip is sent;
Washed by three cups, oh Saki, of thy wine,
My song shall turn upon this argument.
Spring, bride of all the meadows, rises up,
Clothed in her ripest beauty: fill the cup!
Of Spring's handmaidens runs this song of mine.

The sugar-loving birds of distant Ind,
Except a Persian sweetmeat that was brought
To fair Bengal, have found nought to their mind.
See how my song, that in one night was wrought,
Defies the limits set by space and time!
O'er plains and mountain-tops my fearless rhyme,
Child of a night, its year-long road shall find.

And thou whose sense is dimmed with piety,
Thou too shalt learn the magic of her eyes;
Forth comes the caravan of sorcery
When from those gates the blue-veined curtains rise.
And when she walks the flowery meadows through,
Upon the jasmine's shamèd cheek the dew
Gathers like sweat, she is so fair to see!

Ah, swerve not from the path of righteousness
Though the world lure thee! like a wrinkled crone,
Hiding beneath her robe lasciviousness,
She plunders them that pause and heed her moan.
From Sinai Moses brings thee wealth untold;
Bow not thine head before the calf of gold
Like Samir, following after wickedness.

From the Shah's garden blows the wind of Spring,
The tulip in her lifted chalice bears
A dewy wine of Heaven's minist'ring;
Until Ghiyasuddin, the Sultan, hears,
Sing, Hafiz, of thy longing for his face.
The breezes whispering round thy dwelling-place
Shall carry thy lament unto the King.

GERTRUDE BELL

22　THE ROSE RETURNS

Returns again to the pleasaunce the rose, alive from the dead;
Before her feet in obeisance is bowed the violet's head.

The earth is gemmed as the skies are, the buds a zodiac band,
For signs in happy ascendant and sweet conjunction spread.

Now kiss the cheek of the Saki to sound of tabor and pipe,
To voice of viol and harp-string the wine of dawntide wed.

The rose's season bereave not of wine and music and love,
For as the days of a man's life her little week is fled.

The faith of old Zoroaster renews the garden again,
For lo, the tulip is kindled with fire of Nimrod red.

The earth is even as Eden, this hour of lily and rose;
This hour, alas! Not an Eden's eternal dwelling-stead!

The rose with Solomon rides, borne aloft on wings of the wind;
The bulbul's anthem at dawn like the voice of David is shed.

Fill high the bowl to our lord's name, 'Imād-ud-Din Mahmūd;
Behold King Solomon's Asaph in him incarnated.

Beyond eternity's bounds stretch the gracious shade of his might;
Beneath that shadow, O HAFIZ, be thine eternity sped.

WALTER LEAF

23 TULIPS

When from the goblet's eastern brim shall rise
    The gladd'ning sun-beams of our sparkling wine;
To grace the maid, tulips of richest dyes
    Shall on her cheek's empurpled garden shine.

The gale shall spread yon hyacinthine wreaths
    O'er the warm bosom of the blushing rose;
When, scented by those locks, it softly breathes
    From the sweet maze where many a flow'ret blows.

The night that parts a lover from his love,
    Is fraught with such distress, such tender wail;
That scanty would an hundred volumes prove,
    To register the fond, the mournful tale.

Be thine the steady patience, that sustain'd
    The prophet Noah, when the deluge rose;
Then shall the wish of countless years be gain'd,
    And joyful terminate thy lengthen'd woes.

The fav'rite hope, long foster'd in thy breast,
  Thy single effort never will obtain:
The wish'd success on various aids must rest;
  Without those aids thy own attempts are vain.

O, let not avarice tempt thy wild desires
  To toil for wealth in fortune's glitt'ring mine!
Small is the pittance mortal man requires,
  And trifling labour makes that pittance thine.

Should the sweet gales, as o'er thy tomb they play,
  The fragraunce of the nymph's lov'd tresses bring;
Then, Haufez, shall new life inspire thy clay,
  And ceaseless notes of rapture shalt thou sing.

J. NOTT

24   I CEASE NOT FROM DESIRE

I cease not from desire till my desire
Is satisfied; or let my mouth attain
My love's red mouth, or let my soul expire,
Sighed from those lips that sought her lips in vain.
Others may find another love as fair;
Upon her threshold I have laid my head,
The dust shall cover me, still lying there,
When from my body life and love have fled.

My soul is on my lips ready to fly,
But grief beats in my heart and will not cease,
Because not once, not once before I die,
Will her sweet lips give all my longing peace.
My breath is narrowed down to one long sigh
For a red mouth that burns my thoughts like fire;
When will that mouth draw near and make reply
To one whose life is straitened with desire?

When I am dead, open my grave and see
The cloud of smoke that rises round thy feet:
In my dead heart the fire still burns for thee;
Yea, the smoke rises from my winding-sheet!
Ah, come, Beloved! for the meadows wait
Thy coming, and the thorn bears flowers instead
Of thorns, the cypress fruit, and desolate
Bare winter from before thy steps has fled.

Hoping within some garden ground to find
A red rose soft and sweet as thy soft cheek,
Through every meadow blows the western wind,
Through every garden he is fain to seek.
Reveal thy face! that the whole world may be
Bewildered by thy radiant loveliness;
The cry of man and woman comes to thee,
Open thy lips and comfort their distress!

Each curling lock of thy luxuriant hair
Breaks into barbèd hooks to catch my heart,
My broken heart is wounded everywhere
With countless wounds from which the red drops start.
Yet when sad lovers meet and tell their sighs,
Not without praise shall Hafiz' name be said,
Not without tears, in those pale companies
Where joy has been forgot and hope has fled.

GERTRUDE BELL

25 LIGHT IN DARKNESS

High-nesting in the stately fir,
The enduring nightingale again
Unto the rose in passionate strain
Singeth: "All ill be far from her!

"In gratitude for this, O rose,
That thou the Queen of Beauty art,
Pity the nightingales' mad heart,
Be not contemptuous of those."

I do not rail against my fate
When thou dost hide thy face from me;
Joy wells not of propinquity
Save in the heart once desolate.

If other men are gay and glad
That life is joy and festival,
I do exult and glory all
Because her beauty makes me sad.

And if for maids of Paradise
And heavenly halls the monk aspires,
The Friend fulfils my heart's desires,
The Tavern will for heaven suffice.

Drink wine, and let the lute vibrate;
Grieve not; if any tell to thee,
"Wine is a great iniquity",
Say, "Allah is compassionate!"

Why, Hafiz, art thou sorrowing,
Why is thy heart in absence rent?
Union may come of banishment,
And in the darkness light doth spring.

A. J. A.

26 O ASK NOT

O love, how have I felt thy pain!
    Ask me not how—
O absence, how I drank thy bane!
    Ask me not how—

In quest, throughout the world I err'd,
And whom, at last, have I preferr'd?
    O ask not whom—

In hope her threshold's dust to spy,
How streamed down my longing eye!
    O ask not how—

Why bite my friends their lips, displeas'd?
Know they what ruby lip I seiz'd?
    O ask not when—

But yester-night, this very ear
Such language from her mouth did hear—
    O ask not what—

Like Hafiz, in love's mazy round,
My feet, at length, their goal have found,
    O ask not where.

H. H.

27 SHIRAZ

Shiraz, city of the heart,
    God preserve thee!
Pearl of capitals thou art,
    Ah! to serve thee.

Ruknabad, of thee I dream,
    Fairy river:
Whoso drinks thy running stream
    Lives for ever.

Wind that blows from Ispahan,
    Whence thy sweetness?
Flowers ran with thee as thou ran
    With such fleetness.

Flowers from Jafarabad,
    Made of flowers;
Thou for half-way house hast had
    Musella's bowers.

Right through Shiraz the path goes
    Of perfection;
Anyone in Shiraz knows
    Its direction.

Spend not on Egyptian sweets
    Shiraz money;
Sweet enough in Shiraz streets
    Shiraz honey.

East Wind, hast thou aught to tell
    Of my gipsy?
Was she happy? Was she well?
    Was she tipsy?

Wake me not, I pray thee, friend,
    From my sleeping;
Soon my little dream must end;
    Waking's weeping.

Hafiz, though his blood she spill,
    Right he thinks it;
Like mother's milk 'tis his will
    That she drinks it.

R. LE GALLIENNE

28 RANG THROUGH THE DIM TAVERN

Rang through the dim tavern a voice yesterday,
"Pardon for sins! Drinkers of wine, drink! Ye may!"

Such was the word; hear the good news, Angel-borne;
Mercy divine still to the end holds its way.

Great are our sins; greater is God's grace than all;
Deep are his hid counsels, and who says them nay?

Bear her away, Reason the Dull, tavernwards,
There shall the red wine set her pale veins a-play.

Union with Him strife or essay forceth not;
Yet, O my heart, e'en to the full, strive, essay.

Still is my ear ringed of His locks ringleted,
Still on the wine-threshold my face prone I lay.

HAFIZ, awake! Toping no more counts for sin,
Now that our Lord Royal hath put sins away.

WALTER LEAF

'Twas morning, and the Lord of day
  Had shed his light o'er Shiraz' towers,
Where bulbuls trill their love-lorn lay
  To serenade the maiden flowers.

Like them, oppressed by love's sweet pain,
  I wander in a garden fair;
And there, to cool my throbbing brain,
  I woo the perfumed morning air.

The damask rose with beauty gleams,
  Its face all bathed in ruddy light,
And shines like some bright star that beams
  From out the sombre veil of night.

The very bulbul, as the glow
  Of pride and passion warms its breast,
Forgets awhile its former woe
  In pride that conquers love's unrest.

The sweet narcissus opes its eye,
  A teardrop glistening on the lash,
As though 'twere gazing piteously
  Upon the tulip's bleeding gash.

The lily seemed to menace me,
  And showed its curved and quivering blade,
While every frail anemone
  A gossip's open mouth displayed.

And here and there a graceful group
  Of flowers, like men who worship wine,
Each raising up his little stoup
  To catch the dewdrop's draught divine.

And others yet like Hebes stand,
    Their dripping vases downward turned,
As if dispensing to the band
    The wine for which their hearts had burned.

This moral it is mine to sing:
    Go learn a lesson of the flowers;
Joy's season is in life's young spring,
    Then seize, like them, the fleeting hours.

                                        E. H. PALMER

30 HOPE

What though a thousand enemies propose
        To slay me,
With thee my loving friend, how shall my foes
        Affray me?

This is my hope of life, to hold thee nigh
        To cherish;
Absent, it is my constant fear that I
        Must perish.

(Each breath the breeze brings not to me her scent
        I languish,
E'en as the mournful rose, whose robe is rent
        In anguish.)

Shall slumber drowse my senses, and mine eyes
        Not view thee?
Or, being far, my heart not agonize
        To woo thee?

Better than others' balm, thy blade to endure
        Doth please me;
Thy mortal poison, than another's cure
        To ease me.

Slain by thy sword, eternal life is mine
      To inherit;
To die for thee, were benison divine
      Of spirit.

Swerve not thy steed; spare not thy lance's tip
      Nor falter;
My head shall be thy mark, my hand yet grip
      Thy halter.

(Yet how shall every sight attain to thy
      True being?
For as the mind doth know, so much the eye
      Hath seeing.)

All men shall say that Hafiz hath renown
      Immortal,
Whene'er his head gaineth its dusty crown,
      Thy portal.

A. J. A.

31 GIVE

Give, O Give love's sportful joys;
Youth, and all that youth employs;
Wine like rubies bright, and red;
And the board with dainties spread;
Gay associates, fond to join
In the cup of circling wine!

Give the handmaid's lip divine,
Blushing deeper than her wine;
Minstrels vers'd in tuneful art;
And the friend that's next our heart;
With the valued, chearful soul,
Drainer of the brim-full bowl!

Give the nymph, that's tender, kind,
Pure in heart, and pure in mind,

As th' unsullied fount that laves
Eden's banks with blissful waves,
And whose beauty sweetly bright
Shames the clear moon's full-orb'd light!

Give the festive hall, that vies
With our boasted Paradise;
Round it, breathing rich perfume,
Let refreshing roses bloom;
Such as, with unfading grace,
Deck the blest abode of peace!

Give companions, who unite
In one wish, and one delight;
Brisk attendants, who improve
All the joys of wine and love;
Friends who hold our secrets dear,
And the friend who loves good chear!

Give the juice of rosy hue,
Briskly sparkling to the view,
Richly bitter, richly sweet,
Such as will exhilarate:
While the fair-one's rubi'd lip
Flavours ev'ry cup we sip.

Give the girl, whose sword-like eye
Bids the understanding die,
Tempting mortals to their fate
With the goblet's smiling bait;
Damsels give with flowing hair,
Guileful as the hunter's snare!

Give, to spend the classic hour,
One deep-read in learned lore,
One, whose merry, tuneful vein
Flows like our gay poet's strain,
And whose open generous mind
Blesses and improves mankind!

Mortals, wilfully unwise,
Who these mirthful gifts despise,
Entertain no pleasing sense
Of voluptuous elegance:
Scarce of such can it be said,
That they differ from the dead.

J. NOTT

32 WHERE ARE THE TIDINGS OF UNION?

Where are the tidings of union? that I may arise—
Forth from the dust I will rise up to welcome thee!
My soul, like a homing bird, yearning for Paradise,
Shall arise and soar, from the snares of the world set free.
When the voice of thy love shall call me to be thy slave,
I shall rise to a greater far than the mastery
Of life and the living, time and the mortal span:
Pour down, oh Lord! from the clouds of thy guiding grace
The rain of a mercy that quickeneth on my grave,
Before, like dust that the wind bears from place to place,
I arise and flee beyond the knowledge of man.
When to my grave thou turnest thy blessed feet,
Wine and the lute thou shalt bring in thine hand to me,
Thy voice shall ring through the folds of my winding-sheet,
And I will arise and dance to thy minstrelsy.
Though I be old, clasp me one night to thy breast,
And I, when the dawn shall come to awaken me.
With the flush of youth on my cheek from thy bosom will rise.
Rise up! let mine eyes delight in thy stately grace!
Thou art the goal to which all men's endeavour has pressed,
And thou the idol of Hafiz' worship; thy face
From the world and life shall bid him come forth and arise!

GERTRUDE BELL

1

Within the Magian tavern
  The light of God I see;
In such a place, O wonder!
  Shines out such radiancy.

Boast not, O king of pilgrims,
  The privilege of thee:
Thou viewest God's own Temple;
  God shews Himself to me.

2

Combed from the fair ones' tresses
  I win sweet musk to-day,
But ah! the distant fancy
  That I should gain Cathay.

3

A fiery heart, tears flowing,
  Night's sorrow, dawn's lament—
All this to me dispenses
  Your glance benevolent.

4

My fancy's way thine image
  Arresteth momently;
Whom shall I tell, what marvels
  Within this veil I see?

Not all the musk of China,
  The scents of Tartary,
Excel those subtle odours
  The dawn breeze wafts to me.

If Hafiz plays at glances,
  Friends, be not critical:
For truly, as I know him,
  He truly loves you all.

A. J. A

34 DUST

Come, let us pass this pathway o'er
  That to the tavern leads;
There waits the wine, and there the door
  That every traveller needs.

On that first day, when we did swear
  To tipple and to kiss,
It was our oath, that we would fare
  No other way but this.

Where Jamshid's crown and royal throne
  Go sweeping down the wind,
'Tis little comfort we should moan:
  In wine is joy to find.

Because we hope that we may bring
  Her waist to our embrace,
Lo, in our life-blood issuing
  We linger in this place.

Preacher, our frenzy is complete:
  Waste not thy sage advice;—
We stand in the Beloved's street,
  And seek not Paradise.

Let Sufis wheel in mystic dance
  And shout for ecstasy;
We, too, have our exuberance,
  We, too, ecstatics be.

The earth with pearls and rubies gleams
    Where thou hast poured thy wine;
Less than the dust are we, it seems,
    Beneath thy foot divine.

Hafiz, since we may never soar
    To ramparts of the sky,
Here at the threshold of this door
    Forever let us lie.

A. J. A.

35   SEASON OF THE ROSE

The season comes, that breathes of joy,
    In rosy garment drest;
Let mirth, my friends, your care employ;
    O, hail the smiling guest!
Old-age now warns us to improve
The vernal hours with wine and love.

To the fond wishes of the heart
    How few are gen'rous found!
And the sweet hours, which bliss impart,
    Pass on in hasty round:
Then, for the wine I love so well,
My sacred carpet I will sell.

The gale, that smells of spring, is sweet;
    But sweeter, should the fair,
With winning elegance replete,
    Its grateful freshness share:
By her gay presence chear'd, we pass
With brisker glee the rosy glass.

Soft sweep the lyre of trembling strings;
    'Twill fate's black rage suppress;
Fate o'er the child of merit flings
    The mantle of distress:
Then let loud sorrow's wailing cry
Be drown'd in floods of melody.

With boiling passion's eager haste,
    Comes forth the blushing rose;
Shall we not wine like water waste,
    Soft dashing as it flows?
Now that our throbbing bosoms prove
The wild desires of hope, and love.

O Haufez! thy delightful lay,
    That on the wild wind floats,
Resembles much, our poets say,
    The nightingale's rich notes;
What wonder then, thy music flows
In the sweet season of the rose.

                                   J. NOTT

36 MYSTERY

I

Monarch of firs that stately rise,
Of honeyed lips sole emperor,
The arrows of whose flashing eyes
Transfix the bravest conqueror—

Lately in wine as passing by
This lowly beggar he espied,
"O thou", he said, "the lamp and eye
Of such as make sweet words their pride!

"How long of silver and of gold
Shall thy poor purse undowered be?
Be thou my slave, and then, behold!
All silver limbs shall cherish thee.

"Art thou a mote, my little one?
Be not so humble: play at love!
And thou shalt whisper to the sun,
Whirling within its sphere above.

"Put not thy trust in this world's vows;
But if thou canst a goblet get,
Enjoy the arched and lovely brows,
The bodies soft and delicate!"

2

Then spake my elder of the bowl
(Peace to his spirit Allah grant!):
"Entrust not thy immortal soul
To such as break their covenant.

"Leave enemies to go their road;
Lay hold upon the Loved One's hem;
As thou wouldst be a man of God,
Such men are devils: heed not them."

3

I walked where tulips blossomed red,
And whispered to the morning breeze:
"Who are yon martyrs cold and dead,
Whose bloody winding-sheets are these?"

"Hafiz", he answered, "'tis not mine
Or thine to know this mystery;
Let all thy tale of ruby wine,
And sugar lips, and kisses be!"

A. J. A.

37 RAPTURE'S VISION

Say, where is rapture's vision? Eyes on the Loved One bending,
More high than kingly splendour, Love's fane as bedesman
    tending.

Light 'twere, desire to sever forth from the soul, but natheless
Soul-friends depart asunder—there, there the pain transcending!

Fain in the garden budlike close-wrapped were I, thereafter
Frail reputation's vestment bloomlike asunder rending;

Now like the zephyr breathing love-tales in roses' hearing,
Now from the yearning bulbul love's myst'ry apprehending.

While yet the hand availeth, sweet lips to kiss delay not;
Else lip and hand thou bitest too late, when comes the ending.

Waste not the hour of friendship; outside this House of Two
    Doors
Friends soon shall part asunder, no more together wending.

Clean out of mind of Sultan Mansūr hath HAFIZ wandered;
Lord, bring him back the olden kind heart, the poor befriending.

WALTER LEAF

38 WINE WORSHIP

Saki, the dawn is breaking;
    Fill up the glass with wine.
Heaven's wheel no delay is making—
    Haste, haste, while the day is thine!

Ere to our final ruin
    Space and the world speed by,
Let wine be our great undoing,
    Red wine, let us drink and die!

See, on the bowl's horizon
    Wine, the red sun, doth rise:
Here's glory to feast the eyes on—
    Drive sleep from thy languid eyes!

When Fate on his wheel is moulding
    Jars from this clay of mine,
Let this be the cup thou'rt holding
    And fill up my head with wine!

Never was I a shrinker,
    No hypocrite monk am I;
Let wine, the pure wine of the drinker
    Be the talk men address me by.

Wine is the sole salvation,
    Its worship and works sublime;
Be firm thy determination,
    Hafiz—be saved in time!

A. J. A.

39 HARVEST

In the green sky I saw the new moon reaping,
    And minded was I of my own life's field:
    What harvest wilt thou to the sickle yield
When through thy fields the moon-shaped knife goes sweeping?

In other fields the sunlit blade is growing,
    But still thou sleepest on and takest no heed;
    The sun is up, yet idle is thy seed:
Thou sowest not, though all the world is sowing.

Back laughed I at myself: All this thou'rt telling
    Of seed-time! The whole harvest of the sky
    Love for a single barley-corn can buy,
The Pleiads at two barley-corns are selling.

Thieves of the starry night with plunder shining,
    I trust you not, for who was it but you
    Stole Kawou's crown, and robbed great Kaikhosru
Of his king's girdle—thieves, for all your shining!

Once on the starry chess-board stretched out yonder
    The sun and moon played chess with her I love,
    And, when it came round to her turn to move,
She played her mole—and won—and can you wonder?

Ear-rings suit better thy small ears than reason,
    Yet in their pink shells wear these words to-day:
    "HAFIZ has warned me all must pass away—
Even my beauty is but for a season."

R. LE GALLIENNE

123

All my pleasure is to sip
Wine from my beloved's lip;
I have gained the utmost bliss—
God alone be praised for this.

Fate, my old and stubborn foe,
Never let my darling go:
Give my mouth the golden wine
And her lips incarnadine.

(Clerics bigoted for God,
Elders who have lost the road—
These have made a tale of us
"Drunken sots and bibulous."

Let th' ascetic's life be dim,
I will nothing have of him;
If the monk will pious be,
God forgive his piety!)

Darling, what have I to say
Of my grief, with thee away,
Save with tears and scalding eyes
And a hundred burning sighs?

Let no infidel behold
All the bitterness untold
Cypress knows to see thy grace,
Jealous moon to view thy face.

It is yearning for thy kiss
That hath wrought in Hafiz this,
That no more he hath in care
Nightly lecture, matin prayer.

A. J. A.

124

With last night's wine still singing in my head,
I sought the tavern at the break of day,
Though half the world was still asleep in bed;
The harp and flute were up and in full swing,
And a most pleasant morning sound made they;
Already was the wine-cup on the wing.
"Reason", said I, "'tis past the time to start,
If you would reach your daily destination,
The holy city of intoxication."
So did I pack him off, and he depart
With a stout flask for fellow-traveller.

Left to myself, the tavern-wench I spied,
And sought to win her love by speaking fair;
Alas! she turned upon me, scornful-eyed,
And mocked my foolish hopes of winning her.
Said she, her arching eyebrows like a bow:
"Thou mark for all the shafts of evil tongues!
Thou shalt not round my middle clasp me so,
Like my good girdle—not for all thy songs!—
So long as thou in all created things
Seest but thyself the centre and the end.
Go spread thy dainty nets for other wings—
Too high the Anca's nest for thee, my friend."

Then took I shelter from that stormy sea
In the good ark of wine; yet, woe is me!
Saki and comrade and minstrel all by turns,
She is of maidens the compendium
Who my poor heart in such a fashion spurns.
Self, HAFIZ, self! That must thou overcome!
Hearken the wisdom of the tavern-daughter!

Vain little baggage—well, upon my word!
Thou fairy figment made of clay and water,
As busy with thy beauty as a bird.

Well, HAFIZ, Life's a riddle—give it up:
There is no answer to it but this cup.

R. LE GALLIENNE

42 THE DRUNKARD

Come, vex me not with this eternal spite;
For old companionship demands its right.
Heed then my counsel, costlier and more rare
Than all the jewels in thy casket there.
Yet how to drunkards shall thy face be shown
That holds a mirror to the sun and moon?

Chide not the drunkard, greybeard; peace, be still;
Or wouldst thou quarrel with the Heavenly will?
Fearest thou not the fiery breath of me
Shall burn the woollen cassock circling thee?

Pour me the wine of yesternight again
To ease the throbbing of a bankrupt's brain.

Hafiz, thy songs of songs are loveliest;
I swear it, by the Scriptures in thy breast!

A. J. A.

43 MAN OF SELF

Man of Self, lifted up with endless pride,
We forgive thee—for Love to thee is denied.

Hover not round the raving lovers' haunts;
Take thy "Reason Supreme" for goal and guide!

What of Love's drunken frenzy knows that brain
That the grape's earthly juice alone hath plied?

Get a Moon-love, and teach thy heart to strive,
Though thy fame, like a sun, be spread world-wide.

'Tis the white face, the anguish-burdened sigh,
Tell the secrets the heart of love would hide.

Let the bowl clear the fumes that rack thy brain;
HAFIZ, drink deep, and name and fame be defied.

WALTER LEAF

44 ROSE AND NIGHTINGALE

I walked within a garden fair
At dawn, to gather roses there;
When suddenly sounded in the dale
The singing of a nightingale.

Alas, he loved a rose, like me,
And he, too, loved in agony;
Tumbling upon the mead he sent
The cataract of his lament.

With sad and meditative pace
I wandered in that flowery place,
And thought upon the tragic tale
Of love, and rose, and nightingale.

The rose was lovely, as I tell;
The nightingale he loved her well;
He with no other love could live,
And she no kindly word would give.

It moved me strangely, as I heard
The singing of that passionate bird;
So much it moved me, I could not
Endure the burden of his throat.

Full many a fair and fragrant rose
Within the garden freshly blows,
Yet not a bloom was ever torn
Without the wounding of the thorn.

Think not, O Hafiz, any cheer
To gain of Fortune's wheeling sphere;
Fate has a thousand turns of ill,
And never a tremor of good will.

A. J. A.

45 LOVE'S LANGUAGE

Breeze of the morning, at the hour thou knowest,
The way thou knowest, and to her thou knowest,
   Of lovely secrets trusty messenger,
I beg thee carry this despatch for me;
   Command I may not: this is but a prayer
Making appeal unto thy courtesy.

Speak thus, when thou upon my errand goest:
   "My soul slips from my hand, so weak am I;
Unless thou heal it by the way thou knowest,
   Balm of a certain ruby, I must die."

Say further, sweetheart wind, when thus thou blowest:
   "What but thy little girdle of woven gold
   Should the firm centre of my hopes enfold?
   Thy legendary waist doth it not hold,
And mystic treasures which thou only knowest?"

Say too: "Thy captive begs that thou bestowest
   The boon of thy swift falchion in his heart;
   As men for water thirst he to depart
By the most speedy way of death thou knowest.

"I beg thee that to no one else thou showest
   These words I send—in such a hidden way
   That none but thou may cipher what I say;
Read them in some safe place as best thou knowest."

When in her heart these words of mine thou sowest
For HAFIZ, speak in any tongue thou knowest;
Turkish and Arabic in love are one—
Love speaks all languages beneath the sun.

R. LE GALLIENNE

46 SAKI SONG

I

Come, saki, come, your wine ecstatic bring,
Augmenting grace, the soul's perfectioning;
Fill up my glass, for I am desperate—
Lo, bankrupt of both parts is my estate.

Bring, saki, bring your wine, and Jamshid's bowl
Shall therewith bear to view the vast void whole;
Pour on, that with this bowl to fortify
I may, like Jamshid, every secret spy.

Bring, saki, bring your alchemy divine
Where Korah's wealth and Noah's years combine;
Pour on, and there shall open forth to thee
The gates of fame and immortality.

Bring wine, O saki, and its image there
To Jamshid and Chosroes shall greeting bear;
Pour on, and to the pipe's note I shall say
How Jamshid fared, and Ka'us, in their day.

   Sing of this old world's ways, and with your strings
   Make proclamation to those ancient kings.
   Still spreads the same far desert to be crossed
   Where Salm and Tur their mighty armies lost;
   Still stands the selfsame crumbling hostelry
   Afrasiyab took his palace for to be.
   Where now the captains that his armies led,
   And where the sword-swift champion at their head?
   High was his palace; ruin is its doom;
   Lost now to memory his very tomb.

Bring, saki, bring your virgin chastely veiled,
Your tavern-dweller drunkenly regaled;
Fill up, for I am avid of ill fame,
And seek in wine and bowl my utmost shame.

Bring, saki, bring such brain-enflaming juice
As lions drink, and let wide havoc loose;
Pour on, and lion-like I'll break the snare
Of this old world, and rise to rule the air.

Bring wine, O saki, that the houris spice
With angel fragrance out of Paradise;
Pour on, and putting incense to the fire
The mind's eternal pleasure I'll acquire.

Bring, saki, bring your throne-bestowing wine:
My heart bears witness it is pure and fine;
Pour on, that, shriven in the tide of it,
I may arise triumphant from the pit.

Why must I yet the body's captive be,
When spiritual gardens call to me?
Give me to drink, till I am full of wine,
Then mark what wisdom and what power are mine;
Into my keeping let your goblet pass,
And I will view the world within that glass;
Intoxicate, of saintliness I'll sing,
And in my beggar's rags I'll play the king.
When Hafiz lifts his voice in drunken cheer,
Venus applauds his anthem from her sphere.

A. J. A.

1

Whither fled, wild deer?
I knew thee well in days gone by,
When we were fast friends, thou and I;
Two solitary travellers now,
Bewildered, friendless, I and thou,
We go our separate ways, where fear
    Lurks ambushed, front and rear.

Come, let us now enquire
How each is faring; let us gain
(If gain we may, upon this plain
Of trouble vast, where pastures pure
        From fear secure
Are not to find) the spirit's far desire.

2

Beloved friends, declare:
    What manner of man is there
That shall the lonely heart befriend,
That shall the desolate attend?
    Khizer, the heavenly guide,
He of the footfall sanctified,
Perchance he cometh, and shall bring
In purpose deep and mercy wide
An end of all my wayfaring.

3

'Twas little courtesy
That ancient comrade shewed to me.
Moslems, in Allah's name I cry!
The pitiless blow he struck me by,

So pitiless, to strike apart
The cords that bound us heart to heart,
    To strike as if it were
    No love was ever there.

He went; and I that was so gay
To grief convert; was such the way
Brother should act with brother? Yea,
    Khizer, the heavenly guide,
    He of the footfall sanctified,
Haply the shadow of his gracious wing
    Lone soul to lonely soul shall bring.

4

But surely this the season is
When of the bounty that is His
Allah dispenses; for I took
Lately this omen from the Book:
"Leave me not issueless!" the Prophet cried.

It happened on a day one sat beside
The road, a rare bold fellow; when there went
Upon that way a traveller intent
To gain the goal. Gently the other spake:
"What in thy scrip, Sir traveller, dost thou take?
If it be truly grain, come, set thy snare."
The traveller answered, "Grain indeed I bear;
But, mark this well, the quarry I would win
Shall be the Phoenix." "Certes, then how begin
The quest?" the other asked. "What sign has thou
To lead thee to his eyrie? Not till now
Have we discovered any mark to guide
Upon that quest. By what weight fortified
Shall our dire need those scales essay to hold
Wherein the sun hath cast his purse of gold?"

Since that cypress tall and straight
Joined the parting camel-train,
By the cypress sit, and wait
Watchful till he come again.
Here, beside the bubbling spring
Where the limpid river runs,
Softly weep, remembering
Those beloved departed ones.
As each pallid ghost appears,
Speak the epic of thy pain,
While the shower of thy tears
Mingles with the summer rain.
And the river at thy feet
Sadly slow, and full of sighs,
Tributaries new shall meet
From the fountains of thine eyes.

6

Give never the wine-bowl from thy hand,
Nor loose thy grasp on the rose's stem;
'Tis a mad, bad world that the Fates have planned—
Match wit with their every stratagem!

Comrades, know each other's worth;
And when ye have this comment lined
Upon the margin of the mind,
Recite the text by heart:
So say the moralists of this earth;
For lo, the archer ambushed waits,
Th' unerring archer of the Fates,
To strike old friends apart.

7

When I take pen in hand to write
And thus my marshalled thoughts indite,
By the Eternal Pen,
What magic numbers then

Flow from my fingers, what divine
And holy words are mine!
For I have mingled Soul with Mind,
Whereof the issuing seed I have consigned
To music's fruitful earth;
Which compound brings to birth
(As having for its quintessential part
Of poesy the purest art)
Most gladsome mirth.

Then come, I bid thee; let this fragrant scent
Of fairest hope, and soft content,
Bear to thy soul delight eternal:
For verily the musk's sweet blandishment
Was sprinkled from the robe of sprites supernal;
It was not wafted here
From that wild, man-forsaking deer!

A. J. A.

48 THE TIMES ARE OUT OF JOINT

Again the times are out of joint; and again
For wine and the loved one's languid glance I am fain.
The wheel of fortune's sphere is a marvellous thing:
What next proud head to the lowly dust will it bring?
Or if my Magian elder kindle the light,
Whose lantern, pray, will blaze aflame and be bright?
'Tis a famous tale, the deceitfulness of earth;
The night is pregnant: what will dawn bring to birth?
Tumult and bloody battle rage in the plain:
Bring blood-red wine, and fill the goblet again!

A. J. A.

49 THE CRIER

Send the criers round the market, call the royst'rers' band to hear,
Crying, "O yes! All ye good folk through the Loved One's
    realm, give ear!

"Lost, a handmaid! Strayed a while since! Lost, the Vine's wild
    daughter, lost!
Raise the hue and cry to seize her! Danger lurks where she is
    near.

"Round her head she wears a foam-crown; all her garb glows
    ruby-hued;
Thief of wits is she; detain her, lest ye dare not sleep for fear.

"Whoso brings me back the tart maid, take for sweetmeat all
    my soul!
Though the deepest hell conceal her, go ye down, go hale her
    here.

"She's a wastrel, she's a wanton, shame-abandoned, rosy-red;
If ye find her, send her forthright back to
                                      HAFIZ, Balladier."
                                         WALTER LEAF

50 ISMAIL

Ismail is dead, of men and cadis best:
His pen, like its great master, takes its rest.

Much wrote he of God's law, and lived it too—
Would I could say as much for me and you!

The middle of the week he went away—
The month of Rajab it was, and the eighth day.

In this uncertain dwelling ill at ease,
To a more ordered house he went for peace.

His home is now with God, and if you write
"The mercy of God", interpreting aright

The mystic letters standing side by side,
You then shall read the year when Ismail died.

R. LE GALLIENNE

NOTES

MQ 1, B 1, RS 1, F 1, P 1.

Metre: هزج مثمّن سالم ∪ – – – | ∪ – – – | ∪ – – – | ∪ – – –.

Order of lines: B + RS 1 2 4 3 5 6 7. F 1 2 3 4 6 5 7. P as MQ.

1. First hemistich was stated by the Turkish commentator Sūdī (d. 1006/1598) to be a quotation (*taḍmīn*) from the Umayyad caliph-poet Yazīd b. Muʿāwiya (d. 64/683); and this statement has been accepted by most modern editors without question. But Mīrzā Muḥammad Qazvīnī in an article contributed to the Tehran periodical *Yādgār* (vol. 1, no. 9, pp. 69–78) argues cogently in rejection of the attribution.

2. For جعد F reads زلف. For the alternative interpretations of ببوی see WC, 1, 2.

3. For منزل F reads مجلس. For امن RS + P read جای. The poet compares this world with the alighting-place (*manzil*) of a caravan-train; every moment the bell of a camel departing from the caravanserai warns all other travellers that their lodgment there is only temporary, and that they too must soon be quitting this life.

4. The پیر مغان ("Magian elder") is the symbol of the man intimate with all the secrets of life; he knows by experience that reason is powerless to solve the ultimate riddle of the universe (cf. 3⁸), and that it is only the wine of unreason that makes life in this world a tolerable burden. For a fuller treatment of this theme, see no. 15. The terms *sālik* and *manāzil* belong to the technical vocabulary of the Ṣūfīs, see R. A. Nicholson, *The Mystics of Islam*, p. 28.

5. A fine description of the "dark night of the soul"; the imagery of the sea is more common in Persian mystical poetry than might have been expected of a people little given to sea-faring. WC, 1, 3 gives the usual interpretations of "the light-

burthened ones of the shores"; it seems more probable, however, that the poet is here referring, as so often, to the orthodox worshipper (whether ritualist or Ṣūfī) whose feet are firmly planted on his faith so that he has no comprehension of the agonies of the insatiably inquisitive soul.

6. For كزو P reads كز آن. It is the eternal affliction of the lover of God that he is constrained by the ecstasy of his emotion to reveal the secret that should remain hidden; so did Ḥallāj, who paid for his indiscretion upon the gallows, see 15 [8]. The biography of the poet 'Irāqī offers an excellent illustration of this theme, see my *Song of Lovers*, pp. xv–xvi.

7. The pattern of the poem is completed by rounding it off, as it was begun, with a hemistich in Arabic.

AJA translates 1 2 3 4 6 5 7.

Other verse-translations by GB, JP, HB, RAN, JR, RG.

2

MQ 2, B 12, RS 12, P 5.

Metre: مجتثّ مثمّن مخبون محذوف ∪−∪−|∪∪−−|∪−∪−|‾∪∪−.

Order of lines: B + RS 1 3 2 7 4 5 6 8. P 1 3 2 4 5 6 7 8.

1. By *ṣalāḥ* the poet clearly intends formal righteousness; he has abandoned the safe piety of the ritualist for the dissolute intoxication of unreason; so l. 3 expands the theme.

2. The cloister and penitential robes of the Ṣūfī are as unsatisfying and hypocritical to the true lover as the formal religion of the orthodox theologian and lawyer.

3. Listening to music was condemned by the orthodox as an unlawful pleasure, and many Ṣūfī sects agreed with this prohibition; cf. Tale 20 in chapter 2 of Sa'dī's *Gulistān* (my *Kings and Beggars*, pp. 84–6). The hearing of sermons on certain days was on the other hand a well-approved exercise, and many Ṣūfī books, e.g. the *Kitāb sittīn majālis* of 'Abd al-Qādir al-Jīlānī (d. 561/1166) are collections of such addresses.

4. The hearts of the enemies of God (the ritualists) are like
extinguished candles, they do not blaze with the flame of love
kindled by the contemplation of the Divine beauty. Cf. R. A.
Nicholson's translation (*Eastern Poetry and Prose*, p. 173) of a
fragment from Ḥāfiẓ:

> "Of this fierce glow that Love and You
> Within my breast inspire,
> The Sun is but a spark that flew
> And set the heavens afire!"

5. For بفرما P reads بفرياد. "The dust which collects on the
tomb (of a saint) and the railing is considered to be sacred....It
is carefully swept up and sold in small quantities to pilgrims, and
when they are making the circumambulation of the tomb, those
who have sore eyes will put their fingers through the railing, to
get a bit of this dust and rub it on their eyes. It is used also to
cure burns, or other wounds, and swellings; it is thought to
possess the power to raise the dead and is often given to one in
a swoon." B. A. Donaldson, *The Wild Rue*, p. 67.

6. The dimple in the chin of the Beloved is a pitfall for the
unwary traveller; yet the desolation of unrequited love is a
necessary condition of the pilgrim's progress.

7. "Love seemed at first an easy thing"; but the early rapture
of discovery, the delirious joy of the Beloved's mocking glances and
playful reproofs, was soon followed by the long sorrow of exile.

8. For خواب و خواب P reads خواب.

EB translates (or rather paraphrases) 1 4 2–3 5 6 8. Other
verse-translations by GB, JP, HB.

3

MQ 3, B 8, RS 8, F 2, P 6.

Metre: هزج مثمّن سالم ∪−−−|∪−−−|∪−−−|∪−−−.
Order of lines: B+RS 1 2 3 4 8 5 6 7 9. F 1 2 3 5 4 6 7 8 9.
P as MQ.

For a detailed discussion of this poem, see my article "Orient Pearls at Random Strung" in BSOAS, xi, 4 (1946).

1. The Shīrāzī Turk is a symbol of fair-skinned, youthful beauty; the Hindu (black mole) is in apposite contrast. Samarkand and Bokhara are the most famous cities of ancient Turkestan —an appropriate dowry for the Turk migrant to Persian Shiraz, for Ḥāfiẓ forever the loveliest of cities.

2. The blue waters of the Ruknābād and the red roses of the Muṣallā complete (with the ruby wine) the poet's colour-scheme, as do their melodious names his word-picture.

3. For *lūlīs* (gipsy singers) and the "Feast of Plunder", see GB, p. 151.

4. Self-sufficiency (*istighnā*) is the characteristic of the Divine beauty; God does not require our love, yet it is our overpowering need that we should love Him.

5. The story of Joseph and Potiphar's wife is a favourite symbol with the Persian poets of the mystic love; the foundation of the legend in the Qur'ān is found in Sūra XII, 23-54. Love for the Divine beauty lures the true lover from the chastity of formal faith to the infamy of helpless unreason.

6. For the first hemistich as given in the text, B + RS + F read بدم گفتی و خرسندم عفاك الله نکو گفتی, which is a *taḍmīn* from Sa'dī. It seems probable that the variants represent the poet's own changes of mind, rather than any copyist's error.

7. The poet is addressing himself, rather than (as WJ and GB make out) the Shīrāzī Turk; the "wise old man" is the usual Magian elder. It is probably unsafe to conjecture from the mention of "happy youths" that this poem belongs to Ḥāfiẓ' early period; the phrase is used to balance the reference to the *pīr*; and the poem has all the marks of maturity.

8. An excellent statement of the poet's philosophy of unreason; *ḥikmat* is the key-word—the intellect is powerless to fathom the mystery of life: in this particular context, the paradox of the cruel

self-sufficiency of beauty, drawing the lover out of the peace and safety of his formal faith and leading him onward through the wilderness of boundless suffering. Hence, his only consolation is to be found in the ecstasy of the experience of spiritual love.

9. Has this splendid close a *double entendre*—an appeal to the generosity of the hoped-for patron?

WJ translates 1 2 3 4 8 5 7 6 9.

Other verse-translations by GB, JP, HB, WL, RG, EGB, AJA.

4

MQ 4, B 9, RS 9, P 9.

Metre: محذوف مخبون مثمّن مجتثّ ∪−∪−|∪∪−−|∪−∪−|$\overline{∪∪}$−.

Order of lines: B + RS 1 2 6 3 4 5 7 * 8. P as MQ.

1. For a full treatment of the Wild Deer theme, see no. 47. For عشق کوه P reads سر بکوه.

2. The "sugar-cracking parrot" is of course the poet.

3. For حسنت B + RS + P read حسن. The rose is here (as frequently, cf. 44) a symbol of self-sufficient beauty; the nightingale of the helpless lover.

4. For بحسن خلق و لطف B + RS read بخلق و لطف.

5. Cf. 47[8].

7. The first hemistich is a *taḍmīn* from Sa'dī:

جز این قدر نتوان گفت بر جمال تو عیب

که مهربانی از آن طبع و خو نمی آید

B + RS add a line after this verse:

بشکر صحبت اصحاب و آشنائی بخت   بیاد دار غریبان دشت و صحرارا

This, however, is merely an inferior doublet of verse 6.

8. For نه B + RS + P read چه. For سرود B + RS + P read سماع.

TL translates 1 2 3 5 7 4 8.

Other verse-translations by JP, HB, RG.

5

MQ 9, B 7, RS 7, P 8.

Metre: ‮رمل مثمّن مخبون محذوف‬ ⏑⏑−−|⏑⏑−−|⏑⏑−−|⎯⎯−.
Order of lines: B + RS 1 2 3 4 5 6 8 7 9 * 10. P as MQ.

4. The "moon" is, of course, the face of the young beloved; the "polo-stick of pure ambergris", the curved black love-lock, sometimes compared with a dark cloud obscuring the radiant effulgence of the beloved's beauty; so, as here, bringing the lover to a distraction of grief and bewilderment.

5. For ‮این‬ P reads ‮آن‬. For ‮سرکار‬ B+P read ‮سر و کار‬. HB translates:

"I fear that tribe of mockers who topers' ways impeach,
    Will part with their religion the tavern's goal to reach."

6. This obscure line (which the commentators explain variously) is omitted by JR. HB translates:

"To men of God be friendly: in Noah's ark was earth
    Which deemed not all the deluge one drop of water worth."

He adds the note: "By 'earth' is to be understood Noah himself. Although he was a mortal, his sanctity caused him to be preserved from the Flood." RS explains similarly, adding that Noah did not fear the flood at all. Indian commentators see in *khākī* a reference to the doctrine of Muḥammad the Logos (*vide* R. A. Nicholson, *Studies in Islamic Mysticism*, p. 87), but this is surely far-fetched. The obscurity arises from the poet's desire to use the elegance of the two elements (earth and water) in a single line; for the mention of all four elements in two lines, see E. G. Browne, *Chahár Maqála* (transl.), p. 47. Taking the line in its context, the poet appears to be referring to himself: though the troubled world without threatens to engulf every living thing in a flood of calamities, here is one man safely lodged in the ark of his defiant faith of unreason who fears not the uttermost catastrophe; therefore, O lovely one, befriend him, recalling that all the earth's

riches are but perishing dross, and come forth from your hiding-
place; shake off the black lock that conceals your beauty, and
look upon your lover with favour. But see Mīrzā Muḥammad
in *Yādgār*, vol. I, pt. 8, pp. 61–3.

9. The "moon of Canaan" is Joseph, the prototype of perfect
beauty; see the note on 3⁵ and the Qur'ānic passage there referred
to. The poet offers his Joseph the "throne of Egypt"—his own
heart. After this line B + RS add another:

در سر زلف ندانم که چه سودا داری
باز بر هم زدهٔ گیسوی مشك افشان را

This, however, seems to be a doublet of verse 4, possibly a
copyist's quotation glossing it.

JR translates 1 2 3 5 7 8 9 * 4 10.
Other verse-translations by JP, JN, HB.

6

MQ 37, B 32, RS 13, F 5, Q 16.
Metre: مجتثّ مثمّن مخبون مقصور: ∪–∪– | ∪∪–– | ∪–∪– | ∪̄∪̄–.
Order of lines: B + RS 1 2 3 4 5 6 9 7 8 10 11. F 1 2 * 3 4 5 6 8
9 10 11. P 1 2 * 6 9 3 4 5 7 8 10 11.

2. *Ta'alluq* sc. attachment to other than the Divine beloved,
i.e. to this perishing castle of hope, the world. After this line
F + P add:

مگر تعلّق خاطر بماه رخساری   که خاطر از همه غمها بمهر او شادست

This addition certainly improves the sequence.

3. For مست و خراب B + RS read مست خراب.

4. The *sidra* is a tree standing at the farthest boundary of
paradise, where Muḥammad had his second vision of Gabriel,
see Qur'ān LIII, 13–17. The poet thus compares his own revelation
in the tavern with that vouchsafed to the Prophet; and in l. 11

claims divine inspiration for his poetry—a claim repeated several times elsewhere, as in 47[28].

5. It is only in the intoxication of the vision of unreason that man rises to his original home in heaven, cf. 46[20-1], and contrast 34[8].

6. The pun on the word *ḥadīth* (= tale, Prophetic tradition) is clearly deliberate; the taverner has his own Traditions to recount, and the poet is acting as his *rāwī*; as we learn from the next verse, the taverner is here himself merely a transmitter, and states his *isnād* direct; if indeed this line (7) is not merely a doublet of 6, as the repeated rhyme strongly suggests.

9. The second hemistich is a *taḍmīn* from Auḥadī (d. 738/1337):

مده بشاهد دنیا عنان دل زنهار   که این عجوزه عروس هزار دامادست

The poem in which this line occurs was obviously studied by Ḥāfiẓ closely when writing the present lyric, for our poet quotes from it several times:

زروی خوب وفا جوی کاهل معنی را

دل از تعلّق این صوت و صورت آزادست

نمودهٔ که دگر عهد می‌کند با ما

مکن حکایت عهدش که سست بنیادست

نصیحتی کنمت یاد گیر و بعد از من

بگوی راست که اینم ز اوحدی یادست

10. For بیدل B + RS + F + P read عاشق.
AJA translates 1 2 * 3 4 5 6 8 9 10 11.
Other verse-translations by JP, HB, RG.

7

MQ 26, B 44, RS, 25 P 70.

Metre: رمل مثمّن مخبون مقصور $\cup\cup--|\cup\cup--|\cup\cup--|\overline{\cup\cup}-$.
Order of lines unvaried.

1-3. The poet appears here (as elsewhere often) to describe

an actual incident that occurred to him, and then to use it as a text for his meditations.

4. For عاشق B + RS read عارف, which is clearly inferior.

5. The *rūz-i alast* is the day of man's creation, when God said *Alastu bi-Rabbikum?* (Am I not your Lord?) and man replied *Balā* (Yes); see GB's note on p. 153 and cf. 8⁵; the Qur'ānic sanction is Sūra VII, 171.

6. For آنچه B + RS read زآنچه.

7. Cf. 8².

WL translates 1 2 3 4 5 6 7.

Other verse-translations by JP, HB, RG.

8

MQ 25, B 43, RS 24, P 67.

Metre: مجتثّ مثمّن مخبون مقصور ∪−∪−|∪∪−−|∪−∪−|∪∪−.
Order of lines unvaried.

3. For *istighnā* see note on 3⁴. The Qur'ānic sanction appears to be Sūra LXIV, 6: "The messengers (of God) were ever coming to them with clear tidings, and they said, Shall a man be our guide? And they disbelieved, and turned away. And God was independent (*wa-'staghnā 'llāhu*); and God is absolute (*ghanī*), worthy of praise."

4. The "double-door of the world" is clearly birth and death, see WL, p. 69, and cf. 1³, 37⁶.

5. The poet puns *balā* (yes) and *balā* (sorrow), suggesting that it was the cup of sorrow man agreed to drink on creation's day (see note on 7⁵); the fact of coming into existence meant separation from the Divine beloved, and life is a perpetual grief of separation relieved only from time to time by the ecstatic God-given vision of union, ever to be followed in turn by the renewal of the dark night of the soul.

7. Āṣaf (Asaph) was Solomon's minister; the wind was his

steed (cf. Qur'ān XXXVIII, 37; XXXIV, 12); and he understood the language of the birds (cf. Qur'ān XXVII, 16). For طرف B + RS read طرفه, manifestly in error.

8. The sequence is perfect: it is idle to lift oneself up to worldly renown and glory, for all worldly honours are nothing worth—the arrow soars merely to fall in the dust.

9. For سخت B + RS read سخنش.

GB translates 1 2 3 4 5 6 7 8 9.

Other verse-translations by JP, HB, WL.

9

MQ 46, B 34, RS 15, P 52.

Metre: هزج مثمّن اخرب مكفوف مقصور

$$--\cup\,|\,\cup--\cup\,|\,\cup--\cup\,|\,\cup--.$$

Order of lines: B + RS 1 2 3 5 4 6 7 8 9 10 11.   P 1 2 4 3 6 5 7 8 9 10 11.

1. For معشوق B + RS + P read معشوقه; but cf. l. 11.

2. The beautiful face of the beloved is as often compared with the full moon.

3. P reads بی نرگس مخمور تو ایدوست حرامست.

4. For چشم P reads من. For نی P reads گوش. For گوشم P reads چشم. For لب B + RS read تو.

5. For مارا B + RS + P read جانرا. For هر لحظه زگیسوی B + RS + P read هر دم ز سر زلف.

6. For ز شکر P reads وزشکر. For ای چاشنی P reads از چاشنی. For از لب B + RS read با لب; P reads در لب.

7. For کوی B + RS + P read کنج. It is a common poetic legend that treasures lie concealed in ruins; the poet here gives a most elegant turn to the conceit.

8. The poet here summarizes the doctrine of the Malāmatī sect of the Ṣūfīs, who held that salvation lies in courting the

148

condemnation of mankind, and acted accordingly; a theory admirable enough in itself which in later times occasioned grave scandals fatal to the repute of Islamic mysticism.

9. For سرگشته P reads آشفته.

10. For the functions of the *muḥtasib* see R. Levy in *Encyclopaedia of Islam*, vol. III, pp. 702–3. For عیش B + RS + P read شرب.

11. The "festival of the fast" is the *'īd al-fiṭr*, celebrated on 1 Shauwāl to mark the end of Ramaḍān; and perhaps this poem was actually written for such an occasion; though it is more likely that it marks the return of an absent friend, or the renewed favour of a beloved.

TL translates 1 2 5 4 11.
Other verse-translations by JP, HB, RG.

10

MQ 61, B 31, RS 12, P 37.

Metre: مجتثّ مثمّن مخبون مقصور ∪–∪–|∪∪– –|∪–∪–|‾∪∪–.
Order of lines: P 1 2 3 4 6 5 7. B + RS as MQ.

3. For بار B reads باد. For the conceit, see note on 2⁵.

5. For قد و بالای RS reads قد بالای. The heart is called *ṣanaubarī* because its shape resembles a fir-cone; the adjective is used in modern Persian for the pituitary or pineal gland.

JHH translates 1 2 3 4 5 6 7.
Other verse-translations by JP, HB.

11

MQ 81, B 77, RS 58, P 48.

Metre: رمل مثمّن مخبون مقصور ∪∪– –|∪∪– –|∪∪– –|‾∪∪–.
Order of lines: B + RS 1 2 4 3 5 6 7 8. P as MQ.

5. The garden of Iram is said to have been planted in the sandy deserts near Aden by the legendary king Shaddād, grandson

of Iram; according to the Qur'ān (Sūra LXXXIX, 6–8) and its
commentators, it was destroyed by God in a great flood (cf. Sūra
XXXIV, 16) together with its builders. Sūdī in his annotation to
this verse says that the poet composed it in the Bāgh-i Iram of
Shāh Shujāʿ, ruler over extensive territories in Persia (d. 786/1384);
it is certain that Ḥāfiẓ lived for some time at his court: he men-
tions him in several lyrics (see 287) and wrote a chronogram on
his death.

6. The heroic king of ancient Persia, Jamshīd, is said to have
had a magic cup in which the whole world could be seen;
similarly Alexander is credited with the possession of a mirror
having identical properties. The poet meditates as always on the
transitory nature of earthly glory; love is the only immortal, too
great a mystery to be mouthed by man (verse 7: RL and GB have
erred), too great a grief withal to be concealed (verse 8).

RL translates 1 2 3 4 5 6 7 8.
Other verse-translations by GB, JP.

12

MQ 90, B 82, RS 63, P 36.

Metre: مضارع مثمّن اخرب مكفوف محذوف

$$- - \cup\, |\, - \cup - \cup\, |\, \cup - - \cup\, |\, - \cup -.$$

Order of lines: B + RS 1 2 3 4 6 5 8 9 7 10. P as MQ.

1. King Solomon is said to have sent the hoopoe as his
messenger to Bilqīs, the Queen of Sheba; for the full story see
GB, pp. 148–9; the Qur'ānic sanction is Sūra XXVII, 20–38.

3. From this to verse 8 (excluding verse 7) is surely to be
taken as the message sent by Ḥāfiẓ on the "wings of the morning
breeze" to his faithful absent friend; the translators do not
appear to have seen this.

7. This verse best follows verse 9 (as in B + RS) and is the
completion of the heavenly message; the poet compares the wine-
cup (the symbol of unreason) with the all-revealing mirror of

Alexander. For this idea, cf. 15⁵. For the significance of the heavenly messenger (verse 9), cf. 6³.

9. The poet changes his theme with his mood; love is the supreme sorrow, and the wine-cup of unreason its only solace.

10. This is surely a broad hint from the poet to his patron for a royal gift, cf. GB, p. 150, and the story of Farrukhí in E. G. Browne, *Chahár maqála* (transl.), p. 44: "He also ordered Farrukhí to be given a horse and equipment suitable to a man of rank, as well as two tents, three mules, five slaves, wearing apparel and carpets."

GB translates 1 2 3 4 6 5 8 9 7 10.
Other verse-translations by JP, HB.

13

MQ 101, B 199, RS 83, P 175.

Metre: مجتثّ مثمّن مخبون مقصور ∪ − ∪ − | ∪ ∪ − − | ∪ − ∪ − | ∪∪ −.
Order of lines: B + RS 1 2 3 4 5 6 8 7 9 * 10. P as MQ.

1. The poet rejects as void the solitary joys of the anchorite (the solitary, cell-dwelling Ṣūfí, cf. 2²) in favour of the convivial joys of the tavern (the ecstatics' circle). The translators miss this point.

2. For the sentiment cf. 3⁸ and note.

4. HB takes the point better: "With reverence grasp the goblet." The idea of the wine-cup being made of the clay of the dead, or of dead kings is a commonplace in Persian poetry; cf. FitzGerald's *Rubá'iyát*, xxxvii; Jamshíd, Bahman, [Kai]-kubád, [Kai]-ká'ús and Kai-[khusrau] are ancient Persian kings; see GB, p. 165. For the catalogue of names, cf. 46⁷⁻⁸.

6. For the romance of Shírín and Farhád (incorporated by Niẓámí into his *Khusrau u Shírín*), see GB, pp. 165–6.

7. One of the loveliest lines in Ḥāfiẓ, epitomizing his philosophy of unreason as the only solution to the riddle of the world's impermanence.

8. For the conceit of the treasure in the ruins, see note on 9[7].

9. For Muṣallā and Ruknābād—the beauty-spots of Shiraz—see 3[2], 27[2-3]. The poem was perhaps written in answer to an invitation to visit a patron abroad. After this line B + RS add:

رسید در غم عشقش بجانم آنچه رسید   که چشم زخم زمانه بجان او مرساد

10. GB takes the alternative explanation offered by the commentators on the second hemistich; it seems more probable, however, that the poet meant by *abrīsham-i ṭarab* the silken string of music, balancing the allusion to the harp in the first hemistich. For the combination wine + music, cf. 3[8], 22[2].

GB translates 1 2 3 4 5 6 8 7 9 * 10.
Other verse-translations by JP, HB.

14

MQ 103, B 253, RS 139, P 180.
Metre رمل مسدّس مقصور ‏. –‿–.| –‿– –| –‿– –|
Order of lines: B + RS 1 2 3 4 5 * 6. P 1 § 2 3 4 5 6.

1. After this line P adds:

اینزمان در کس وفاداری نماند   ز آن وفاداران و یاران یاد باد

But it is frigid and worthless.

2. For شاد B + RS read باده. HB glosses, "'Be it sweet!'—an expression used at drinking parties"; apparently reading نوش باد خوانان which breaks the rhyme. The reference is of course to the sweet singing of the revellers.

4. For بند و بلا B + RS read بند بلا. Does the poet intend this line ironically?

5. The Zinda-rūd is a famous river at Isfahan, see GB, p. 171; Ḥāfiẓ says in another place:

اگرچه زنده رود آب حیاتست   ولی شیراز ما از اصفهان به

The poet evidently recalls a visit to Isfahan and a patron there who now neglects him. After this line B + RS add:

نیك در تدبیر غم در ماندہام   چارہ آن غمگساران یاد باد

This, however, is merely an inferior doublet of verse 4.

6. For دریغا B + RS read دریغ آن.

HB translates 1 2 3 4 5 * 6.

Other verse-translations by JP, RG, GB.

15

MQ 142, B 123, RS 9, F sep., P 111.

Metre: رمل, مثمّن مخبون مقصور ᵕᵕ––|ᵕᵕ––|ᵕᵕ––|‾ᵕᵕ‾–.

Order of lines: B + RS 1 2 3 4 5 8 6 7 9 10.   F 1 2 6 3 4 8 * 7 9 5 10.   P 1 2 3 4 8 * 5 7 9 6 10.

1. This is one of the finest poems of Ḥāfiẓ; at the same time its text exhibits remarkable variants, especially in the order of the lines. AJA in his translation follows the edition of F in his pamphlet *Dil-i shaidā-yi Ḥāfiẓ*, which may be studied with advantage as representing a vigorously new approach to the criticism of the poem. For the cup of Jamshīd, see note on 11[6]; for the heart as a mirror of the world, cf. 12[7]. The *ḥadīth* beloved of the Ṣūfīs no doubt underlies the train of thought: من عرف نفسه فقد عرف ربّه " Who knows himself knows his Lord."

2. For لب. گوهریرا که بهر داشت صدف در همه عمر P reads P + F read رو. The poet seems to refer in the second hemistich to those "light-burthened ones of the shore", the formal Muslims (see note on 15) who will not venture upon the ocean of unreason in quest of the pearl of Divine cognition.

3. By *naẓar* is meant the mystic's intuitive vision, see L. Massignon, *La Passion d'al-Hallaj*, p. 853. For the riddle, cf. 14 and note, 3[8].

4. See note on 12⁷.

5. Can any doubt remain after this verse that Ḥāfiẓ intends by the imagery of the wine-cup the ecstatic's rapt vision? Note the word *ḥakīm*: God is the only philosopher; man's own man-made *ḥikmat* is unworthy of the name (cf. 3⁸). The name *ḥakīm* is frequently given to God in the Qur'ān.

6. For دور P reads درد. For او B + RS + P read و او. For خدارا F + P read خدایا.

7. For این B + RS + F + P read آن. For خویش B + RS + F + P read عقل. For شعبدهٔ F reads شعبده‌ها. The Sāmirī is a magician who made a calf "of saffron hue" for the Israelites to worship, see Qur'ān, Sūra xx, 85 ff. The "staff" and "white hand" were symbols of Moses' divine wizardry, see Sūra xx, 18 ff.

8. The reference is to Ḥusain b. Manṣūr al-Ḥallāj, "martyr-mystic of Islam" (d. 309/921), who was gibbeted on the charge of uttering blasphemy, notably the phrase انا الحقّ "I am the truth". The poet explains his crime as being that of revealing the unutterable mystery of the love of God in the ecstasy of his emotion; cf. 10⁷. After this line P + F add:

و آنکه چون غنچه دلش راز حقیقت بنهفت

ورق خاطر از این نکته محشّا میکرد

[For و آنکه P reads آنکه. For دلش P reads لبش. For خاطر P reads خاطر. For نکته P reads نسخه. For نکته P reads دفتر.]

10. For زلف B + RS read زلف چو زنجیر. The ringlets of the beloved which veil the effulgent beauty of his face (cf. 5⁴ and note) are also a chain to keep the lover's mad heart under restraint, else he must wholly lose his reason.

AJA translates 1 2 6 3 4 8 * 7 9 5 10.
Other verse-translations by JP, HB, WL.

16

MQ 148, B 151, RS 37, P 193.

Metre: هزج مسدّس اخرب مقبوض محذوف — ∪ — — | ∪ — ∪ — | ∪ — —.

Order of lines: B + RS 1 3 2 4 5. P as MQ.

5. See note on 7⁵. This line gives a mystical meaning to what is otherwise the simplest and lightest of Ḥāfiẓ' lyrics, highly reminiscent in style of the early lyrics of Sanā'ī.

JP translates 1 3 2 4 5.

Other verse-translations by HB, WL.

17

MQ 151, B 142, RS 28, P 206.

Metre: هزج مثمّن سالم ∪ — — — | ∪ — — — | ∪ — — — | ∪ — — —.

Order of lines: B + RS 1 * 2 3 § 5 4 6 7. P as MQ.

1. For the second hemistich cf. 14. After this line B (in parentheses) + RS add:

دیار یار مردمرا مقیّد میکند ور نه

چه جای فارس که این محنت جهان یکسر نمی ارزد

[RS omits جهان breaking the metre; B reads کین for این که.] This line, however, breaks the sequence and is rightly rejected.

3. After this line B + RS add:

بشوی این دلق دلتنگی که در بازار یکرنگی

مرقّعهای گوناگون می احمر نمی ارزد

[B reads حمرا for احمر.] This line again breaks the sequence, and is perhaps a doublet of verse 1.

5. For چه B + RS + P read بس. For این طوفان (for the phrase and its significance see 5⁶ with note) P reads یك موجش. Contrast 1¹, 15²; here the poet is clearly speaking of the vanity of worldly ambition.

6. A splendid message to the present times!

7. For دنیّی B + RS + P read دنیای. The poem perhaps marks Ḥāfiz' reaction to a failure to win the favour of a patron; unless it is all to be taken mystically.

GB translates 1 * 2 3 § 5 4 6 7.
Other verse-translations by JP, RG.

18

MQ 195, B 137, RS 23, P 131.

Metre: مجتثّ مثمّن مخبون مقصور ⏑–⏑–|⏑⏑––|⏑–⏑–|‾‾⏑–.
Order of lines: B + RS 1 4 2 6 3 5 8 7 9 *. P 1 3 6 4 2 7 8 5 9.

2. GB has misunderstood غمّاز which here means "informer"; the scented breeze of morning and the flooding tears betray the secret of love otherwise well guarded. RS translates correctly:

> "Dich verrieth der Wind des Morgens,
> Mich des Auges Wasserfluth:
> Und doch wahren sonst Verliebte
> Ihr Geheimniss treu und gut."

3. For ز زیر P reads بزیر. For سوکواراند B + RS + P read بیقراراند which is obviously inferior; especially in the context of the next line, where the image of the violets tossing restlessly beneath the tyranny of the fair one's locks is a superb conceit. Perhaps, however, the following emendation improves:

ز زیر زلف دو تا چون گذر کنی بنگر

که از تطاول زلفت چه سوکواراند

گذار کن چو صبا بر بنفشه‌زار و بین

که از یمین و یسارت چه بیقراراند

Such a rearrangement gives far better balance (note the repetition of زلف) and is more in the character of the poet.

4. For سوکواراند B + RS + P read بیقراراند.

7. Cf. 47⁶˒¹⁰, a passage strikingly similar to the present. Khiḍr
is confounded in Muslim legend with Elias, and is said to have
guided Alexander in his quest of the Fountain of Life; see GB,
pp. 158–9. Ḥāfiẓ appears to represent himself as a neophyte of
these mysteries; his companions are intimate with them.

8. For يا B + RS + P read برو,, less elegantly; the poet calls
from the door of the tavern. The erghwan is the crimson Judas
tree.

9. Cf. 15¹⁰ for the sentiment; submission is the only salvation,
intellectual enquiry is profitless. After this line B (in parentheses)
+ RS read:

ز نقش چهرهٔ حافظ همی توان دانست   که ساکنان در دوست خاکساراند

A double signature would, however, be most unusual, and the
line introduces a theme extraneous to the poem.

GB translates 1 4 2 6 3 5 8 7 9 *.
Another verse-translation by JP.

19

MQ 184, B 222, RS 108, P 141.

Metre: رمل مثمّن مخبون مقصور: ∪∪ – – | ∪∪ – – | ∪∪ – – | ‾∪∪ –.
Order of lines: B + RS 1 2 3 5 * 4 6 § 7. P 1 2 5 3 6 * 4 7.

1. For the Muslim legend of creation, see GB, pp. 169–71.
This and the following line appear to describe an actual vision
of the poet, in which he saw himself being served with wine by
angels out of a cup fashioned of Adam's dust. In his spiritual
fervour he sees himself the sole heir of creation (verse 3), an idea
familiar enough to the "intoxicated" Ṣūfīs; cf. my Niffarī, pp.
30 (8), 193–5, 156 (18). GB has not understood the poem too
well.

2. For راه نشین B + RS read خاك نشین; cf. 47¹² and note. The
second hemistich means "they sprinkled the wine of drunkenness
over me".

3. God created man to be his vice-gerent; see Qur'ān, Sura II, 30; VI, 166. For the Ṣūfī doctrine, see R. A. Nicholson, *Studies in Islamic Mysticism*, pp. 113, 130, 156.

4. Cf. 'Umar Khaiyām:

می خور که ز تو قلّت و کثرت ببرد   واندیشهٔ هفتاد و دو ملّت ببرد

پرهیز مکن ز کیمیائی که از او   یك جرعهٔ هزار علّت ببرد

And Fitzgerald:

> "The Grape that can with Logic absolute
> The two-and-seventy jarring sects confute;
>   The sovereign Alchemist that in a trice
> Life's leaden metal into Gold transmute."

5. For ایزد P reads آنرا. This line is presumably to be taken in close conjunction with the following: the "concord" is that of complete submission, which consumes the human will as the moth is consumed by the flame. For صوفیان B + RS + P read حوریان.

After this line B + RS (and P after verse 6) add:

ما بصد خرمن پندار ز ره چون نرویم   چون ره آدم بیدار بیك دانه زدند

On the meaning, see GB, p. 171.

6. After this line B + RS add:

نقطهٔ عشق دل گوشه نشینان خون کرد

همچو آن خال که بر عارض جانانه زدند

7. For نگشاد B + RS + P read نکشید. For سخن را بقلم B + RS + P read عروسان سخن, but the text of MQ gives an excellent balance between سخن and اندیشه, نقاب and قلم.

GB translates 1 2 3 5 * 4 6 § 7.

Other verse-translations by GP, HB.

20

MQ 198, B 136, RS 22, F 6, P 135.

Metre: مضارع مثمّن اخرب مكفوف مقصور

$$- - \cup\ |\ - \cup - \cup\ |\ \cup - - \cup\ |\ - \cup -.$$

Order of lines: P 1 2 3 4 6 5 7 8 9. B + RS + F as MQ.

1. This is one of Ḥāfiẓ' few conversation-pieces: a curious and remarkable technique, reminiscent of the سؤال and جواب of the learned treatises, and, in particular, the shorter mystical tracts of Suhrawardī Maqtūl, e.g. the 'Aql-i surkh (ed. Mahdī Bayānī, Isfahan 1319/1940). The poet imagines a conversation between an old Ṣūfī and a beautiful boy who is the focus of his meditation.

2. The tribute of Egypt, Egypt being the wealthiest province of the Muslim empire.

3. For نكتهدان P reads خردهدان which destroys the elegant verbal play.

4. The elder seeks to draw the boy forth from the tavern to the temple; the boy replies that in his religion God is worshipped through the adoration of his image in material beauty—a fundamental doctrine of this school of Ṣūfīs, and a practice which led inevitably to grave scandals.

6. How can the wearer of the khirqa of renunciation be a wine-bibber? The Magian faith resolves this dilemma too.

8. RS following the commentators identifies khwāja with Ḥāfiẓ' patron Qiwām al-Dīn Ḥasan (the minister of Shāh Shujā'), involving a play on the words mushtarī and mah; but this seems rather far-fetched. For آنزمان F reads سحر.

9. For او B + RS + F + P read تو, which must surely be adopted unless the interpretation of RS is accepted, to the ruination of an otherwise perfect poem.

AJA translates 1 2 3 4 5 6 7 8 9.
Another verse-translation by JP.

21

MQ 225, B 158, RS 44, P 214.

Metre: مضارع مثمن اخرب مكفون محذوف

$$--\cup|-\cup-\cup|\cup--\cup|-\cup-.$$

Order of lines: B + RS 1 2 3 4 5 * 6 § 7 8. P as MQ.

1. For the circumstances alleged as attending the composition of this poem, see GB, p. 173: Cypress, Tulip and Rose are supposed to be the names of three handmaidens who nursed Ghiyāth al-Dīn Purābī of Bengal during a sickness. RS quoting Sūdī explains the three cups as referring to the practice of drinking three glasses of wine after a meal to fidelity; WC speaks of three morning cups to purge the body of ill-humours. I strongly suspect, however, that the poet is here referring to a discussion (baḥth) between commentators, probably of his day, on a tradition (ḥadīth) relating to the ritual washing of the dead; and that he intends a *double entendre*—winter is departed, let us lave its corpse with wine.

2. The *dallāla* is the marriage-broker whose task it is to exaggerate the beauty of the girl to the hoped-for husband; but spring is so beautiful that its beauty exceeds all that the broker could invent. GB does not appear to grasp the meaning; HB is better, albeit more pedestrian:

"Drink wine! our blooming bride, the meadow, shines forth in
        beauty's height;

No need of the Dallálah's practice while days like these delight."

3. GB: "The parrots of India are the court poets of Ghiya-suddin, and the Persian sweetmeat is the ode that Ḥāfiẓ sent to Bengal."

4. For يكساله P reads صدساله. The poem was presumably written in one night.

5. For آهوانهٔ آهو P reads جادوانهٔ عابد. After this line B + RS add:

خوی کرده می خرامد و بر عارض سخن   از شرم روی او غرق ژاله می رود

160

6. After this line B + RS add:

چون سامری مباش که زر دید و از خری

موسی بهشت و از پی روساله می رود

8. The commentators identify this Ghiyāth al-Dīn alternatively as the king of Bengal (acc. 769/1367), and the Prince of Herat Ghiyāth al-Dīn Pīr ʿAlī (ruled 772–92/1370–89). The name does not occur elsewhere in the *Dīvān*.

GB translates 1 2 3 4 5 * 6 § 7 8.

Other verse-translations by JP, HB.

22

MQ 219, B 121, RS 7, P 203.

Metre: مجتثّ مثمّن مخبون مقصور ∪ – ∪ – | ∪ ∪ – – | ∪ – ∪ – | $\overline{\cup\cup}$ –.

Order of lines: B + RS 1 2 3 4 8 5 6 7 9 * §.   P 1 2 3 4 5 6 7 8 9 §.

3. For روز B + RS + P read دور.

4. For خروج B + RS + P read بروج, which is rather a frigid metaphor: "clusters of sweet herbs, radiant as the zodiacal mansions of the sun" (HB).

5. The breath of Jesus in Muslim legend has power to raise the dead, cf. 15[8]. ʿĀd and Thamūd are named in the Qurʾān as unbelieving peoples who rejected the messengers sent to them by God and were in consequence utterly destroyed; see Qurʾān, Sūra VII, 65–79; XXVI, 123–59; XLI, 14–17.

6. Cf. 3[2]; the wine of unreason is the only consolation for the tragedy of evanescent beauty.

7. A splendid conceit; for Solomon riding the wind see note on 8[7].

8. The "faith of old Zoroaster" is of course intended here as the Magian wine-bibbing: a magnificent heresy for a Muslim to propound! For the story of Nimrod: "Nimrod, the king of the

day, caused Abraham to be cast into a great fire, which was
miraculously turned into a rose garden. Hence the fire of Nimrod
which enflames the tulip." (WL, p. 71.) The legend is related
in comment upon Qur'ān, Sūra XXXVII, 97.

9. For Āṣaf see note on 8[7]. 'Imād al-Dīn Maḥmūd was a
minister of Shāh Shaikh Abū Isḥāq (reigned 742–57/1341–56),
one of Ḥāfiẓ' patrons.

10. *Tarbiyat* is the technical word for the protection afforded
by a royal patron to a young poet, see Niẓāmī 'Arūḍī, *Chahār
maqāla*, p. 30[18]: تربيت را شاعر چنين كه است واجب پادشاه بر امّا و
كند تا در خدمت او پديدار آيد. For this line B + RS substitute
the following:

ز عيش كام ابد جو بدولتش حافظ   كه باد تا بابد ظلّ رأفتش ممدود

In P the following is given (in B + RS additional to the preceding,
B placing it in parentheses):

بيار باده كه حافظ مدامش استظهار

بفضل و رحمت عامست و غافر معهود

[The second hemistich in B + RS reads بفضل رحمت غفار بود و
خواهد بود.]

WL translates 1 4 2 3 8 6 7 9 *.
Other verse-translations by JP, HB, RG.

23

MQ 234, B 196, RS 82, P 212.
Metre: مجتثّ مثمّن مخبون $\cup - \cup - | \cup \cup - - | \cup - \cup - | \cup \cup - -$.
Order of lines: B + RS 1 2 4 3 6 5 7. P 1 2 3 4 6 5 7.

1. For مشرق RS reads شرق (a misprint). For the simile, see 38[3].

3. For حكايت B + RS read شكايت.

4. For B + RS read مکن ای دل . HB is more faithful: نتوان کرد

"From Heaven's inverted tray, O heart! expect not to obtain,
    Save by reproach and hundred pangs, one particle of gain."

5. For P reads ره . For پی B + RS + P read بود که این . For کاین باشد
For گوهر cf. 15². Personal suffering and divine grace are both
required for spiritual attainment.

6. For طوفان see note on 5⁶.

7. For B + RS read لطف , P reads وصل . Cf. 32⁴. For زلف لاله
(a repeated rhyme, see verse 1) B + RS + P read ناله, which is
surely superior, cf. 24².

JN translates 1 2 3 6 5 4 7.
Other verse-translations by JP, HB.

24

MQ 233, B 249, RS 135, P 202.

Metre: مضارع مثمّن اخرب – – ∪ – | ∪ – – | – – ∪ | – ∪ – – .
Order of lines: B + RS 1 * 4 5 2 § ‡ 3 ‖ 6. P 1 2 3 4 5 ‡ 6.

1. This is one of Ḥāfiẓ' finest and most interpolated lyrics.
After this line B + RS add:

هر دم چو بی وفایان نتوان گرفت یاری

مائیم و خاك كویش تا جان ز تن برآید

The immediate repetition of the rhyme suggests that this line is
merely a copyist's quotation.

2. Smoke is a common metaphor in Persian poetry for a
burning sigh. After this line B + RS add:

بر خیز تا چمن را از قامت و قیامت

هم سرو در بر آید هم نارون برآید

بر بوی آنکه در باغ یابد گلی چو رویت

آید نسیم و هر دم گرد چمن برآید

P adds the second of these lines after verse 5.

3. For رخ B + RS read رو .

After this line B + RS add:

هر يك شكست زلفت پنجاه شست دارد

چون اين دل شكسته با آن شكن برآيد

which is extremely frigid.

5. Note the contrast between جان and دست ; the beloved will not satisfy the material needs of the poor, much less the spiritual aspirations of the lover.

GB translates 1 * 4 5 2 § ‡ 3 ‖ 6.

Other verse-translations by JP, RG.

25

MQ 254, B 292, RS 11, P 255.

Metre: مضارع مثّمن اخرب مكفوف مقصور

$$--\cup\,|\,-\cup-\cup\,|\,\cup--\cup\,|\,-\cup-.$$

Order of lines: B + RS 1 2 3 5 6 4 7. P as MQ.

2. For بيدل B + RS read عاشق . RS does not take this verse as part of the nightingale's lament; HB follows him in this.

3. The poem is evidently addressed to an absent friend, cf. verse 7.

5. A reminiscence of Qur'ān, Sūra LV, 72: حُورٌ مَقْصُورَاتٌ فِى

ٱلْخِيَامِ .

6. هُوَ ٱلْغَفُورُ is a common Qur'ānic phrase, see Sūra x, 107; XII, 99; XXVIII, 15; XXXIX, 54; XLII, 3; XLVI, 7; LXXXV, 14.

AJA translates 1 2 3 4 5 6 7.

Other verse-translations by JP, GB.

26

MQ 270, B 313, RS 4, P 279.

Metre: خفيف مخبون مقصور ‎ ⏑⏑−−|⏑−⏑−|⏑⏑−.

Order of lines unvaried.

3. See 2⁵ and note.

7. It would appear from the form of the signature that this poem, like some others, was written by Ḥāfiẓ for singing by a famous minstrel; hence the poet's reference to himself in the third person. The lyric clearly belongs to the poet's early life, and is perhaps the simplest in the *Dīvān*.

HH translates 1 2 3 5 4 7.

Other verse-translations by JP, Derozio (in *Calcutta Review* for September 2, 1827).

27

MQ 279, B 322, RS 7, P 291.

Metre: هزج مسدّس محذوف ‎ ⏑−−−|⏑−−−|⏑−−.

Order of lines: B+RS 1 2 3 4 5 6 8 9 7. P as MQ.

2. For Ruknābād and Muṣallā see 3², 13⁹. لوحش الله ‎ "beware, God forbid" is an abbreviation of the Arabic لا أوحش الله ‎ "may God not desolate". For Khiḍr, see note on 187.

3. Jaʿfarābād has now completely disappeared; see GB, p. 167, HB, p. 177.

4. For بجوی ‎ B+RS read بخواه‎. For روح قدسی ‎ see Qur'ān, Sūra II, 81, 254; V, 109; XVI, 104; and see GB, p. 167; cf. 15⁹.

5. Egyptian sugar was (as it still is) famous for sweetness; so Ḥāfiẓ says elsewhere:

دهان شهد تو داده رواج آب خضر

لب چو قند تو برد از نبات مصر رواج

For the "sweetmakers" of Shiraz, cf. 3³.

6. For *lūlī* see note on 3³. This poem and 3 are clearly closely related.

RG translates 1 2 3 4 5 6 8 7.

Other verse-translations by JP, GB, HB.

28

MQ 284, B 333, RS 18, P 296.

Metre: سریع مطویّ موقوف :−∪−.|−∪∪−|−∪∪−.

Order of lines: B + RS 1 2 5 3 4 6 7 8 9. P 1 2 3 5 4 6 7 8 9.

2. For لطف B + RS read عفو. For سروش cf. 6³.

3. خام "raw" is a metaphor for "inexperienced", and is contrasted with پخته "cooked", "experienced"; in this case the "cooking" is to take place with the "fire" of the wine. Elsewhere Ḥāfiẓ says:

ز تاب آتش سودای عشقش   بسان دیگ دایم میزنم جوش

5. For دانی B + RS read گوئی. WL has misunderstood the second hemistich; RS is better:

> "Grösser ist die Gnade Gottes
> Als die Fülle uns'rer Schuld;
> Schweige! Kennst du denn die Gründe,
> Die verborgenen, der Huld?"

8. For Shāh Shujāʿ see note on 11⁵. The three-line close is unusual, but explained by the panegyrical tone of the poem.

WL translates 1 2 5 3 4 6 7.

Another verse-translation by JP.

29

MQ 295, B 348, RS 1, P 303.

Metre: مجتثّ مثمّن مخبون مقصور :∪−∪−|∪∪−−|∪−∪−|‾∪‾−.

Order of lines: P 1 2 3 5 4 6 7. B + RS as MQ.

1. For the conventional scene, cf. 44¹⁻².

2. For بجلوه B + RS read بچهرهٔ . For تیره B + RS + P read
تاری .

3. Cf. 25². EHP mistranslates.

5. For دهان گشاده P reads سپر گرفته . For ایغاغ B + RS read
ایغاغ ; but ایغاغ (ایقاق) is said to be a Turki word meaning
"fault-finder, critic", see Mīrzā Muḥammad, *Ta'ríkh-i-Jahán-gushá* (vol. III, London 1937), pp. 298–9.

6. For یکی B + RS read گهی (twice).

7. A reference to Qur'ān, Sūra v, 99 مَا عَلَى ٱلرَّسُولِ إِلَّا ٱلْبَلَٰغُ .
EHP translates 1 2 3 4 5 6 7.
Other verse-translations by JP, HB (two verses only).

30

MQ 300, B 355, RS 2, P 309.

Metre: مجتثّ مثمّن مخبون مقصور $\cup - \cup - | \cup \cup - - | \cup - \cup - | \overline{\cup \cup} -$.
Order of lines: P 1 2 4 5 3 6 7 8 9. B + RS as MQ.

2. The first hemistich is a *taḍmīn* from Ẓahīr Fāryābī (d.
598/1201–2):

مرا امید وصال تو زنده میدارد   وگر نه بی تو نه جانم بماند نه اثرم

For صد رهم B + RS read هر دم . For دم هر.

3. For بویش B + RS + P read بویت .

5. For دیگری P reads دیگران (twice).

6. For لأنّ P reads بأنّ .

7. فتراك literally "saddle-strap" by which game was secured.

8. For دانش B + RS read بینش .

AJA translates 1 2 3 4 5 6 7 8 9.
Other verse-translations by JP, HB.

MQ 309, B 412, RS 47, R 319.

Metre: رمل مثمّن مقصور ‎ $- \cup - - | - \cup - - | - \cup - - | - \cup -.$

Order of lines unvaried.

2. For همنشین...ندیمی B + RS read ندیم...همنشینی.

4. For دلنشان B + RS read دلستان.

6. For تلخ تیز B has تیز تلخ, RS has تلخ و تیز (then و خوشخوار و سبك).

8. For نکته دانی cf. 20³. Ḥājjī Qiwām al-Dīn, minister of Sulṭān Uwais of Baghdad (reigned 756–76/1355–74), is said to have founded a college for Ḥāfiẓ in Shiraz; the poet praises him elsewhere. So GB, p. 154; but MQ identifies with Qiwām al-Dīn Ḥasan, minister of Abū Isḥāq Injū, see p. 162 above; and K. Süssheim (*Encyclopaedia of Islam*, vol. II, p. 211) with Qiwām al-Dīn Muḥammad, minister of Shāh Shujāʿ.

9. For عشرت B + RS read صحبت. For مجلس B + RS read عشرت JN translates 1 2 3 4 5 6 7 8 9.

Other verse-translations by JP, HB.

MQ 336, B 439, RS 74, P 380.

Metre: رمل مثمّن مخبون محذوف ‎ $\cup \cup - - | \cup \cup - - | \cup \cup - - | \overline{\cup \cup} -.$

Order of lines: B + RS 1 2 3 4 6 5. P as MQ.

1. This famous poem is inscribed on Ḥāfiẓ' tomb. Cf. 46²¹⁻².

2. بولای تو "by thy love I swear".

3. For پیشتر B reads بیشتر (misprint).

5. B + RS end the poem with half this line and half of l. 7:

خیز و بالا بنمای ای بت شیرین حرکات

که چو حافظ ز سر جان و جهان بر خیزم

6. For the idea, cf. 20⁷.

7. B + RS omit the first hemistich, and the second hemistich of l. 5; the repetition of the phrase سر جان و جهان suggests a doublet, and the rhyme جهان is already used in l. 1. Perhaps we should emend:

خیز و بالا بنما ای بت شیرین حرکات

تا چو حافظ ز جهان دست فشان بر خیزم

The "shaking of the sleeves" is often mentioned as a gesture of world-forsaking in the Ṣūfī dance, and the phrase here balances well the idea شیرین حرکات. The poem seems to have been written for recitation at the Ṣūfī *dhikr*; for Ḥāfiẓ in the third person, see note on 267.

GB translates 1 2 3 4 6 5.
Other verse-translations by JP, HB.

33

MQ 357, B 392, RS 27, P 385.

Metre: رمل مثمّن مخبون محذوف ∪∪−−|∪∪−−|∪∪−−|‾∪∪−.
Order of lines: B + RS 1 * § 2 6 ‡ 3 4 5 7. P as MQ.

1. This remarkable poem is considerably interpolated. For نورست و کجا، B + RS read نوری ز کجا. The tavern is the darkness in which the Divine light rises, cf. 25⁷. After this verse B + RS add:

کیست دردی کش این میکده یارب که درش

قبلۀ حاجت و محراب دعا می‌بینم

منصب عاشقی و رندی و شاهدبازی

همه از تربیت لطف شما می‌بینم

2. For the immediate repetition of the rhyme (خدا...خدا می‌بینم), cf. 30¹⁻²; 40¹⁻². The poet Sanā'ī seems to have been particularly partial to this device. The "king of pilgrims" is the

commander of the annual pilgrim train to Mecca. The "house of God" is the "ancient house" at Mecca, the Ka'ba.

3. Cf. 1². Cathay was the famous country for musk, won from the pod of the musk-deer. The poet puns here: خطا می‌بینم can also mean "I see the error", i.e. of supposing that I can attain the musk-strewing locks of the beloved.

4. B + RS read نالهٔ شب آه سحر.

6. After this line B + RS add:

$$نیست در دائرهٔ جز نقطهٔ وحدت کم و بیش$$

$$که من این مسئله بی چون و چرا می‌بینم$$

[RS omits جز by error.]

AJA translates 1 2 3 4 5 6 7.

Other verse-translations by JP, HB.

34

MQ 372, B 367, RS 2, P 329.

Metre: مضارع مثمّن اخرب مکفوف مقصور

$$--\cup|-\cup-\cup|\cup--\cup|-\cup-.$$

Order of lines: B + RS 1 2 3 4 5 6 7 * 8. P 1 3 2 4 5 7 6 8.

1. For ز شارع B + RS read بشارع.

2. Cf 7⁵ and note.

4. بو is a shortened form of بود. The translator has omitted the conceit of the red onyx.

6. B + RS read بحالت رقصند. The Mevlevi (whirling) dervishes raise their arms during their gyrations. The poet puns here on the double meaning of دست بر آوردن, which also signifies "to supplicate", i.e. for a draught of wine.

7. For درّ و B + RS + P read قدر. After this line B + RS add:

$$زان پیشتر که عمر گرانمایه بگذرد \qquad بگذار تا مقابل روی تو بگذریم$$

BUTTING IN

"They're doing *what?*" Drum McLean shouted, and it was a few seconds before he realized that Harley couldn't talk, what with McLean's fingers digging into his neck. He released the chubby little man, and let him fall, red-faced and gasping, to the polished clay tiles of his office floor.

"The gals is leavin'!" Harley finally managed. "All of 'em. They was just pullin' out from in front of Jamaica's Pleasure Barge when I seen 'em," Harley offered in a strangled little voice.

"And one a the men kicked me right smack in the chest!" he cried.

McLean ground his teeth. "What men? Who was with them?"

"Ain't never seen him afore. About six-one, six-two, green eyes—they practically drill holes in you. He's a real tough-lookin' hombre." McLean knew who that tough-looking sonofabitch had been—Slocum. He didn't quickly forget some no-name drifter who had told him off in his own town!

JAKE LOGAN

SLOCUM AND THE HELPLESS HARLOTS

JOVE BOOKS, NEW YORK

This is a work of fiction. Names, characters, places, and incidents are
either the product of the author's imagination or are used fictitiously,
and any resemblance to actual persons, living or dead, business
establishments, events, or locales is entirely coincidental.

SLOCUM AND THE HELPLESS HARLOTS

A Jove Book / published by arrangement with
the author

PRINTING HISTORY
Jove edition / July 2001

The Penguin Putnam Inc. World Wide Web site address is
www.penguinputnam.com

ISBN: 0-515-13136-9

A JOVE BOOK®
Jove Books are published by The Berkley Publishing Group,
a division of Penguin Putnam Inc.,
375 Hudson Street, New York, New York 10014.
JOVE and the "J" design
are trademarks belonging to Penguin Putnam Inc.

PRINTED IN THE UNITED STATES OF AMERICA

10 9 8 7 6 5 4 3 2 1

1

Slocum rode through an Arizona desert that was, for an all-too-short moment, lush with spring. He barely noticed the balmy weather, however, and the tiny purple and orange and yellow flowers that his horse's hooves crushed underfoot as he ambled along all went unobserved. Neither did he notice the birdsong that filled the air, nor the families of quail that bobbed along from the cover of one bushy hillock to the next, or that the sky above was a clear and seamless blue-white.

All he could think about, as he made his way toward Twin Buttes, was that book.

That damn book!

He still had a worn and tattered copy of it stuck in his back pocket. It wasn't tattered because of its age, for it had only been published three months ago. It was tattered because he'd thrown it against walls—and trees, and rocks—so many times.

He tugged it out of his pocket once more and stared at the scuffed cover, half-thinking that if he looked at it just one more time, the title would change. But it didn't. It still read, in clear black type, *John Slocum: The Dealer of Death.*

He growled under his breath, and his Appy gelding, Chaco, took this as a command to speed up his jog. Slocum had to rein him back in before he looked at the book again.

The cover was just the same. The title, then a picture of a cold, cruel-looking, squat-faced, obsidian-eyed hombre—not like him at all!—who stood alone in the middle of a dusty Western street, guns blazing. The sonofabitch on the cover looked like he ate babies for breakfast.

Slocum growled at the picture, then opened the front cover. For the twentieth time, he read what was printed on the flyleaf: *If you like this book, be sure to read* John Slocum: Death Rides a Spotted Stallion *by the exciting new author Dusty Rhodes! Coming soon to a fine retailer near you!*

He cocked back his arm, as if to hurl the book at the nearest saguaro, then stopped himself. He'd just have to go retrieve it again, wouldn't he?

He'd like to get his hands on this Dusty Rhodes character, that's what he'd like to do! It beat him how some jackass he'd never met could write so many things about him that were downright lies, yet pen so much that was right on the money, blow for blow, even if the style was past flowery.

He'd read this first book after some kid had cornered him in Bent Elbow, Nevada, begging for him to sign his damn name on a copy. He'd gone right over to Jessup's Mercantile and bought one for himself. Once he'd gotten over the shock of it (then thrown it away at least a dozen times), he'd made himself sit down and read it.

It was him, all right, or it was supposed to be. He barely recognized some of the exploits that the author attributed to him, and could see others as they happened, although he'd be damned if he remembered saving any orphaned kids from a flash flood or any widows from a burning building. Or shooting Ry Cantrell's horse out from under him back in Broken Tree. Of course, the writer hadn't called Cantrell by his right name. Richard Chesley, they'd called him in the book. Not much imagination. Even used the same initials. He wished they'd just used *his* initials!

What he couldn't figure out was how in the hell somebody had written about that little skunk-up with Ry. Why, Slocum had only butted heads with Ry— and turned him over to the authorities—about eight or nine months back, and he sure as hell didn't remember any scribblers being around!

Wouldn't a fellow notice something like that? Wouldn't he notice some little candy-assed, four-eyed, back East note-taker, for that was the way he imagined this little sonofabitch Dusty Rhodes. But he couldn't remember a soul that fit that description, not out of the entire populace of Broken Tree, California. Hell, he doubted that more than two or three of the residents could even read!

"Aw, shit," he grumbled, and shoved the book down in one of his front pockets.

Chaco took this for another command, and swung into a slow lope. "Easy, boy," Slocum said softly, and reined him back down to a jog.

The gelding was young, only four, and eager as

hell. Slocum had picked him up back in Nevada after his good leopard mare, Cheyenne, had been lamed sliding down a cliff face that Slocum hadn't exactly intended her to slide down. She'd be all right, but it was going to take a while.

He'd left her in the care of the best horse wrangler he knew, Esteban Vargas, and borrowed this little dandy of an Appy gelding to ride in the meantime. Chaco had a bottle brush tail, two white socks behind and one in front, and a white blaze down his face. He also had a ticked and speckled white blanket that dusted his croup like late spring snow settled on the breast of a red clay hill, and his temperament was just as hot as that sorrel color of his.

Slocum was pleased with the gelding, and he'd be sorry to give him up once he got back up to Nevada. He figured that ought to be sometime next month, if all went well in Twin Buttes with Tom Malloy. But he couldn't ride two horses, as nice as Chaco was, and his Cheyenne mare—a sweet little leopard, spattered from head to tail with ebony spots the size of a man's fist, and the best reining horse he'd ever owned—was special.

Thinking about horses had taken his mind off the book, but he remembered it again when his hand brushed his pocket on the way to his watch, which he read with a frown left over from the book.

Three-fifteen. He should make Twin Buttes along about nightfall. And if he ever got his hands on this sniveling little Dusty Rhodes character—a summer name if ever he heard one!—he'd *really* give him something to write about!

• • •

It was just coming dusk when he rode into Twin Buttes. The town was like many in central Arizona Territory. It had grown up around first one mine, then two, then three, and was still a going concern. It ran twenty-four hours a day, and the darkening streets bustled with miners just coming off shift, more miners headed for a night's work underground, gamblers on the scout for a good game (or maybe coming off one), and cowhands seeking comfort or the next whiskey.

Comfort abounded in Twin Buttes. The streets were thick with women, bad women. Or good women, depending on how you defined it. Tired whores in tattered dresses leaned against porch posts, strolled lewdly along the walkways, lurked in the mouths of alleys. As far as he could tell, the soiled doves of Twin Buttes were no prettier or uglier than those of any other city, but they sure looked a lot more bedraggled, not to mention ill-tempered. There wasn't a smiling face in the bunch.

Odd.

He didn't give it further thought, though. By the time he got Chaco settled in at Dunphey's Livery and found the hotel that Mad Hat Crockett had recommended, it was fully night and chilly as all get-out. He left the hotel, worming his way through the milling crowds. He followed the line of new and shiny gaslights up the street until at last he came to the Lazy Ace Café. This too had been recommended by Mad Hat. He found a table at the back, and ordered a steak and all the trimmings.

Now, Mad Hat—the reason Slocum was in Twin Buttes in the first place—was a half-crazy old miner who'd struck it rich, years back, out in California. Not in gold, but in silver, a mountain of it. He'd bought himself a mansion in San Francisco and lived there a total of four whole years before the bright-metal fever came on him again, and for the past fifteen years he'd been a nomad, breaking rocks and living in the wild. His wife and his daughter stayed behind in the big house in San Francisco, wanting for nothing—except, perhaps, Mad Hat's company.

Slocum had run into Mad Hat while his mare was lamed up in Bent Elbow. They'd got to talking in the saloon one night, and all the next day, and before Slocum knew it, Mad Hat had settled the princely sum of 250 dollars—with 250 more promised once the job was completed—on Slocum to deliver an envelope.

"Why me?" Slocum had asked, fingering the gold pieces suspiciously.

Mad Hat had shrugged his grimy shoulders and tugged at his ragged mustache and said, "Why not? 'Sides, I heard'a you more'n once. Figure you to be trustworthy. More'n I can say for most'a these other yahoos."

Looking around the crude barroom in which he and Mad Hat had been seated—and seeing the haggard and shifty faces of the crowd—Slocum had had to agree with him.

"You take that to Tom Malloy in Twin Buttes in the Arizona Territory," Mad Hat had said while he twirled a boiled egg from the bar between gnarled fingers. "Put it in his hand by May the fifteenth. You do that, and you get paid the other two-fifty. His hand and no other, got that?"

Slocum had nodded. He'd figured that Mad Hat was aptly named, but he wasn't going to judge him, not when there was five hundred dollars involved. Still, he couldn't help asking, "What's so important you can't trust it to the U.S. Mail?"

Mad Hat had just stared at him through pale blue eyes and said, "You want the job or not, Slocum?"

Which was why he had left his mare in Bent Elbow, why he had borrowed the Appy colt from Esteban Vargas, and why he was presently sitting in this café in Twin Buttes, Arizona, watching a hatchet-faced waiter carry a steak toward his table.

The steak was bigger and some better than he had expected—at least, it was someplace between still moving and charred to a crisp—although it was helped immensely by a smothering of ketchup. As he ate, he figured that he had plenty of time to find this Tom Malloy. It was only the twelfth of May. Tomorrow would be the thirteenth. He'd start asking around then. After all, Twin Buttes wasn't that big a town. Likely the first or second person he asked could steer him to Malloy.

Hell, he could probably be on his way by tomorrow night!

Well, maybe not tomorrow night. He'd passed several gaming houses—and a whole lot of whores— on his way to the café. Maybe he'd while away tomorrow night in the arms of one of Twin Buttes' many doves. Maybe he could put a smile on one or two of their faces.

He brightened. Maybe he'd have a look-see tonight.

He dug into his steak.

Miranda Richards lugged her suitcases through the front door of the U-Bet Hotel and leaned against a wall, trying to catch her breath. It had been a stroke of luck, seeing him head into this place, but then, the last eight months had been marked by an astonishing streak of luck on her part.

It had been a miracle that she'd overheard Esteban Vargas remark that he was tending to Slocum's mare when she was just on her way out of that little town in Nevada, bedraggled and disappointed, and about to give up and go home. A pure miracle. If she hadn't been in the general store just then, and if Vargas hadn't stopped outside to talk to a friend at that exact moment, if he hadn't mentioned that Slocum had business in Twin Buttes, Arizona, she would have lost him for good. Or for a few months anyway.

She had given this lucky streak a good deal of thought while she was riding the stage down from Nevada. Perhaps she was meant to have more than a biographer's relationship with John Slocum. After all, that made three times she'd nearly lost him completely, then found him again through astounding circumstances.

They seemed amazing to her, at any rate. What else would you call stumbling over a drunk that kept repeating Slocum's name? What else would you call a ranting gunman standing spread-legged in the middle of a Colorado street, angrily firing his pistol into the air because Slocum had ridden out before he could take a shot at him?

Miranda sniffed. As if John Slocum would stay around to shoot it out with some braggart of a cowhand who fancied himself a shootist! Slocum was far too gallant and fine a human being for that.

"Miss?"

Drat. Daydreaming again. She looked over at the desk clerk, who was eyeing her, brows lifted. She smiled and said, "Sorry. I'd like a room, please."

He took her money and gave her a key, and then went back to his newspaper, content to let her find her own room. Her suitcases in tow, she struggled up the stairs, found Room 12, locked the door behind her, and began to unpack.

Ah, Slocum, she thought dreamily as she lifted out her latest manuscript. There wasn't much yet, but she was confident that there were a thousand stories in this paladin of the plains. She had already written four, only the first of which had been published. The second was due out any day now. She'd heard the first story by chance, and after the fact, and it was then that she began to follow him, keeping herself low and in the background and out of his sight, and scribbling like a madwoman.

He had such a rugged presence! She had read her editor, John Cubbersworth, the riot act when she saw the first book's cover.

"Slocum is a handsome man," she wrote in her

letter to Cubby, "not some toad-faced wanton killer! Don't you read the books you publish?"

She'd reminded him that Slocum was six-foot-one, not five-foot-six, as the so-called illustrator had imagined; that his eyes were the most incredible sea-green, not the muddy black-brown on the cover; that his jaw was square, not weak; and his hair was black as anthracite.

Well, at least they'd gotten his hair right.

Miranda had wanted to add that he had the most marvelous twinkle in his eyes when he was amused, and the most breathtaking look when he was angry or intent, and that when she had written that he was rugged, she'd meant it in the most flattering way possible. Honestly, it just made a girl's insides turn all to squish!

But she didn't say any of that, of course. Cubby wouldn't understand. After all, she'd practically grown up with him. His father and her father were chums. Or had been, until her father's death, twelve years past. There had been a brief moment when she might have entertained thoughts of marriage with Cubby. However, by the time he got around to asking her, she was twenty-five and writing for the *Examiner*. She had tasted a life of freedom, and had no wish to tangle herself in the constrictive bonds of matrimony—particularly to a man of whom she was very fond, but nothing more.

Penny dreadfuls, dime novels, half-dimers—she'd leapt at the chance to write one when Cubby offered. Cubbersworth & Son published dozens every month. She supposed Cubby had felt sorry for her after the little shake-up at the *Examiner* that left her jobless. She supposed he thought she could just hole up in her rooms and confabulate stories about fragile heroines touring the continent and finding love in the arms of rakish noblemen or foreign princes.

Miranda had different ideas, though. She'd set out on a pilgrimage, and she'd stumbled across John Slocum. Blind luck, wonderful blind luck, to find a man as adventurous, as bold, as handsome and stalwart as he! Oh, he was going to keep food on her table for a very long time. He was going to turn her pen name, Dusty Rhodes, into a household word.

Staying in the same hotel with Slocum was a bold move, but she thought she might be able to get a more personal sense of the man if she lived in his bailiwick. At least, that's what she told herself as she set the last empty suitcase on the pine-plank floor and shoved it under the bed.

She'd talked to him just once in all the time she'd been following him around the West, and that had been a furtive "Excuse me!" when she'd accidentally bumped into him on a railway platform in Denver.

She had pulled her bonnet low. She didn't believe he'd seen her face.

She wondered which room he was in. Oh, wouldn't it be fabulous if he were in the next room? She could put a glass to the wall and actually hear him moving around, perhaps hear him involved in an actual conversation! Surely that would add authenticity to her books! She wondered if she could catch the correct cadence of his speech, and then wondered if it would be right to change it smack dab in the middle of the series.

Miranda sat on the edge of her mattress, debating the merits of artistic license versus realism, as the occupants of the next room returned rather noisily. At first she thought it was a man and his wife, but it soon became apparent that there was not a marital bond between the two, who had very obviously been drinking. After a great deal of female giggling and rumbling male speech, not a word of which she could make out—not that she wanted to, for heaven's sake—the conversation ceased and the bedsprings began to creak.

Their headboard must have been against Miranda's wall, because pretty soon the bureau began to move a little, and then the china bowl and pitcher set began to shiver rhythmically, and poor Miranda, red-faced and full of umbrage, stood up and stiffly put her bonnet back on. Maybe it hadn't been such a wise idea to change from the Sugarfoot Hotel to the U-Bet.

Well, she'd be an adult about it. She'd go for a walk to pass the time. She'd walk, and she'd think about the next plot point in the new Slocum book she was writing. After all, they couldn't keep at it all night. These things took just a few minutes, didn't they?

As she locked her door behind her and tiptoed down the hall to the sound of complaining bedsprings, she thought that at least John Slocum wasn't in there, doing Lord knows what with that harlot.

John Slocum was a gentleman!

2

Slocum groaned mightily with his orgasm at the same time that Flossie yelped long and loud in delight, and then shivered down into a happy limpness. He eased off her and lay back against the pillows in exhaustion. It had been two weeks since he'd been with a woman, and he intended to spend a good bit of money with Flossie tonight.

"Christ Almighty, gal," he muttered with a smile. He reached for his fixings and began to roll himself a quirlie. "That yell of yours could peel paint!"

Flossie, a pretty, round, bleached-blond strumpet that he'd picked up outside Hoolihan's Frivolities, giggled and curled against his side. She looked a lot less bedraggled once he'd gotten the clothes off her.

"I was just surprised, that's all," she whispered dreamily. "Ain't nobody diddled me that good—leastwise, ain't nobody made me come—for going on two years now." With a finger, she followed the line of a scar down his chest. "Usually gotta diddle myself for that." Her finger left the first scar and found another, which she began to follow lower.

Slocum grinned. "Well, if you can just hold your horses for a few minutes, Floss, I'll diddle you again."

"You ain't gonna go to sleep?"

"Not hardly, Floss."

Her hand slid under the covers, and she took hold of him. He didn't tell her to let go. He lit the quirlie, took a drag, and asked, "You ever heard of a man named Tom Malloy?"

"Sure," she said distractedly. She was kissing his chest.

He supposed he ought to participate, and craned an arm back to encircle her shoulders. His hand came to rest on one plump, pillowy breast, and he began to play with the nipple, twisting it idly.

He figured he'd better talk fast, as he could feel himself responding to her touch below the line of covers. He said, "Don't suppose you'd know where I could find him, do you?"

For a moment, she raised her head from his chest. "Oh, he's always around, I reckon. Why you lookin' for Big Tom?"

Slocum cocked a brow. Big Tom? He suddenly hoped this letter he was carrying for Mad Hat didn't contain bad news. But Flossie's hand was working wonders beneath the covers, and thickly, he said, "Got business with him, that's all."

"Accordin' to my hand on your Mr. Johnson," she said, smiling slyly, "you got more urgent business with me, Slocum."

He didn't argue. He stubbed out the quirlie, then took her in his arms again.

Miranda Richards stood on the walk in front of the hotel, teeth chattering with cold. Obviously she should have brought a wrap, but those disgusting noises coming from the other side of her wall had rushed her outside before she'd thought to bring one. She hugged herself and tried not to think about it.

Twin Buttes bustled around her. It was after nine in the evening, but the gas jets along the sidewalks cast their soft glow over miners and cowboys and cardsharps and businessmen, white and Mexican and Chinese and Negro alike, all busy going someplace, and the faces of uncharacteristically grim prostitutes, waiting—or trolling—for their next customers.

It was just occurring to her that she'd best not stand there long or someone would take her for a lady of the evening, when a Chinese man, in the grimy clothing of a miner just off duty, jingled some coins in her face and took hold of her arm.

"No!" she shrieked in surprise. "No, no!" While he prattled in a language she couldn't understand, she waved her hands at him and backed away, finally losing sight of him in the throng. Flustered and blushing, she quickly set off up the street, brushing at her sleeve, as if she could wipe away his touch. Of all the gall! She'd find a quiet restaurant and have a cup of tea, that's what she'd do.

Except that she soon learned that there was no such thing as a quiet restaurant in Twin Buttes. With the exception of a few mercantiles and specialty stores, most everything ran twenty-four hours a day. People banged in and out of doors as if it were high noon, with the exception being that nearly all the traffic—male and female alike—was drunk, or well on their way to it.

She settled for the Lazy Ace Café, that being the place she was closest to when an inebriated cowboy made a sloppy pass at her. She ducked inside, and found a small table along the side wall.

"Tea," she said when the waiter came. "Earl Grey." Fastidiously, she peeled off her gloves.

The waiter cocked an insulant brow. "Never heard'a no Earl Whatshisname, and we ain't got no tea. Got coffee and beer."

"Coffee then," she said, but the waiter just kept standing there. "Coffee, *please,*" she said again.

"Gotta order somethin' to eat," he said, and poked his thumb back toward a small sign on the far wall that read EAT HERE, DRINK SOMEPLACE ELSE.

With a sigh, Miranda scanned the chalkboard menu, and said, "Apple pie, no cheese." It was the least expensive item on the list, other than the pickle plate.

The waiter disappeared.

While she waited, she took a lead pencil and a slim notebook from her bag, and began making notes. It was her habit to record the minutiae of every store, restaurant, hotel, and stage stop in which she had the fortune to spend any length of time. These written descriptions came in quite handy later on.

She was just making note of the many crudely painted signs haphazardly tacked along the walls when a shadow fell over her, a shadow much too large and looming to be the waiter's. She hurriedly closed her notebook and looked up into a most handsome male face. The man smiled at her.

He was nearly six feet tall, she noticed immediately, with dark brown hair that was silvered at the temples, and eyes the color of those dark little river pebbles that Western children called Apache tears. His face was narrow yet pleasing, his nose was strong, and an impossibly thick but well-groomed graying mustache all but covered his upper lip. Best of all, he was almost impossibly clean—she could smell the soap from where she sat—and his clothes were neatly pressed and brushed. Not a fleck of dust in sight.

He had the look of a dashing hero, and the wheels and gears in her brain suddenly went into double time. Perhaps she could use him as Slocum's sidekick. Maybe as a sheriff, or a rancher in trouble. Maybe she could spin him off into a whole new series!

"Evening, miss," he said, and tipped his hat. He had a deep baritone voice too. All the better! "You new to our fair city?"

"I came in on the morning stage," she replied as the waiter slid her pie and coffee onto the table. The pie looked soggy, and the coffee looked far too strong for anybody to drink at nine-thirty in the evening.

"I'll take the same, Joe," the stranger said without taking his eyes from Miranda's, and pulled out a chair. Almost as an afterthought, he said, "Mind?"

She opened her mouth to welcome him, but thankfully, common sense took hold of her. She raised her hand, palm held forward, and said, "I don't believe we've been introduced, sir."

He straightened, but he didn't push the chair back under the table. Smile never breaking, he swept off his hat. His hair was neatly and recently cut. How refreshing! She was liking him more with every passing second.

"Drummond McLean, ma'am," he said. "Of the Daisy Cutter Mine. Also own the paper and a couple of other things around town."

She'd only been in Twin Buttes for a day, but she recognized the name. She'd seen it plastered over half the town. McLean Mercantile, McLean Fine Firearms, McLean Feed & Grain, and McLean All-Family Outfitters, among others. Then, of course, there was the *Twin Buttes Sentinel.* That had been the first place she'd walked past on her way up from the stage depot. "Drummond McLean, Owner & Publisher" had been stenciled on the front door in large gold letters, edged with black.

"And you are . . . ?" he coaxed.

She felt heat rising into her cheeks, and quickly said, "Miranda Richards." She stuck out her hand, and McLean shook it solemnly. "Pleased, Mr. McLean. Do sit down," she added.

He settled his hat back on his head and sat. "My friends call me Drum," he said as the waiter brought his order.

"Drum," she repeated.

He grinned at her and forked an enormous bite of pie into his mouth, at which point any schoolgirl fantasies Miranda had been entertaining flew straight out the window. He chewed with his mouth open.

She dropped her eyes, keeping them on the coffee cup, which she raised to her lips. She had just taken the first scorching sip of the vile stuff when, his mouth full of half-chewed pie, McLean said, "So, Miranda. Will you be working at Jamaica's or Rose's place?"

She swallowed with a too-hot and too-big gulp, and choking, managed to get out, "I beg your pardon?" She'd never heard of this Jamaica, but she'd seen Rose's place, all right. It was a fancy-fronted, pink and gold and baby-blue bawdy house a bit farther down the street, with a big ornate sign that read:

ROSE'S ALL-NIGHT ALL-DAY
24-HOUR COMFORT AND ENTERTAINMENT

Matter-of-factly, Drummond McLean said, "Well, those are the two best houses, and you're one high-class filly. If you're wanting to freelance, I've gotta tell you right now that this isn't the town for it. The street whores are on their way out, and a pretty little gal like you has to watch out for her interests. We keep a tight rein on our sporting gals here in Twin Buttes. For their own protection, you understand. Rose runs a fine house, real high-class. You'd have your own room, no sharing."

Miranda's entire face went hot. She stood straight up, jarring the table slightly and upsetting both McLean's and her own coffee. "Mr. McLean!" she exclaimed, and snatched up her bag.

He had the audacity to smile at her. "That's Drum," he said.

"Mr. McLean," she repeated through clenched teeth, "I am certainly not in . . . not in *that* line of work. I will have you know that I'm a journalist!"

His smile never broke. "Well, I'm right sorry. You could'a fooled me. That's a compliment. You've got a real nice figure. And you were standin' out in front of that hotel for quite a long time, Miranda."

He'd been watching her! He'd followed her up the blessed street!

"You are very rude, Mr. McLean, and extremely presumptuous," she snapped, tucking her bag under her arm with a little *snap.* "And I'm *Miss Richards* to the likes of you!"

She heard him laughing as she stormed out of the café.

She marched straight up the street, knocking an unfortunate miner flat when he flashed a dime at her and gave her what she could only describe as a lascivious look. She strode straight into the lobby of the U-Bet Hotel, past the startled clerk, up the stairs, and directly to her room, where she locked the door behind her.

"That . . . that *pig!*" she said under her breath. She felt along the bureau for matches and struck one, then held it to the wick. Her hands were shaking. "Of all the brass-plated gall!"

The lamp lit at last, she shook out the match. "I do *not* look like a common strumpet!" she said firmly. And then, her brow wrinkling, she added, "At least, I don't think that I do."

Whatever had given McLean—and those two
other men who'd accosted her—the idea that she
was?

She turned toward the mirror and regarded herself. Her honey-blond hair was neatly done up, with
no elaborate curls. Very businesslike, she was sure
of it. Her face was the same old oval: pretty features,
she supposed, but no rouge on her lips or cheeks to
give anyone the idea she was cheap. Certainly not!
Brown eyes stared back at her. Calf eyes, Cubby had
called them the one night, long ago, when they
had . . .

Now what had made her think of that? She peered
closer into the mirror. Did it show, after all these
years? Had McLean somehow sensed that she
wasn't precisely "pure"?

"Don't be ridiculous, Miranda Richards!" she
muttered to her own reflection. "You'd think there
was a big red A pinned to your chest!"

She was still flustered, though, and to take her
mind off it she continued taking inventory. McLean
had said she had a fine figure, and she had to grant
that he was a keen observer—on that point anyway.
She was proud of her figure. Full bust, tiny waist,
ripe hips, all covered demurely in a proper businesslike dress of deep sage green, buttoned right up
to the chin.

She liked to think that she was possessed of a
rather stunning pair of legs too, although no one ever
saw them. At least, no one had seen them since
Cubby, and he'd been so anxious that he hadn't even
noticed. For the thousandth time since she'd acqui-

esced and spent the night with him, she found herself wondering why God had given men and women such powerful urges when the outcome was so disappointing.

Not that it hadn't been satisfying for Cubby. He'd taken her three times, grunting happily when each episode was finished. He'd seemed so enthusiastic about it!

Frankly, Miranda had been stumped. Men took your clothes off and climbed aboard, pumped like minks for a minute or two, then groaned and rolled off. Why, she'd barely gotten a warm feeling from it! And then, after the third time, when Cubby was finally sated, he'd pecked her on the cheek, rolled over, and gone straight to sleep.

She'd been ruined, and she hadn't even had any fun.

Well, she hadn't made that mistake again. She was well aware that she'd go to her grave a soiled woman. But if she had anything to do with it, she'd die a famous writer. Ruined but acclaimed. She knew it was her destiny. Perhaps one thing would outweigh the other.

In the next room, those horrible people started up again. Her bureau began to jiggle, and the things on it started to shiver in time to the bump and squeak of a bed rocking and a headboard banging.

They wouldn't chase her out this time. She moved to the side of the bureau and began to pound on the wall with her fist.

"Stop it!" she shouted. "Stop it, you rank hedonists!"

They didn't stop. She pounded once again, then sat down on the edge of her bed, her arms crossed and her back stiff. Her unseen neighbors kept up their bouncing and jiggling for nearly twenty minutes before it grew quiet again, and she found herself wondering. Twenty minutes? What woman on earth could put up with *that* for twenty minutes?

The man must not be very good at it, that was all Miranda could think, and the woman must surely be a prostitute. Miranda couldn't imagine any woman gritting her teeth for twenty minutes with her own husband. She assumed a woman could tell her own husband to get off her and leave her alone, for heaven's sake.

But still, listening to the activities in the next room had made Miranda feel a little funny in the pit of her stomach. She found that her breasts had grown so tight that the bodice of her dress seemed too confining. And when she stood up, the feeling in her stomach moved directly down a notch, centering between her legs.

She sat down again, but it didn't go away. If anything, it was worse. She leaned back on the bed, squirming and wondering if she was dying, but it only made the fire between her legs worse.

Should she have the clerk send for a doctor? Heavens, no! In her present weak-kneed and jelly-legged condition, she thought it would be extreme folly to try to walk down the stairs—or to try to walk anywhere at all, for that matter.

She supposed she could shout down to him from the top of the steps. But once the doctor arrived, whatever could she say to him? That her nipples felt like they had been clamped in vises, and that her belly had taken on a life of its own?

Certainly not!

From the next room came the rumbling, wordless sound of male speech, followed by the milky tones of a woman. It was the male voice that plucked a chord in Miranda, however, and she closed her eyes, wishing for it to go away.

Her breasts were no better, and lying there, she unbuttoned her bodice. Perhaps a little breathing room would be in order. But when she loosened her clothing there was no improvement, and when she accidentally touched one tightly drawn nipple through the thin fabric of her camisole, she opened her mouth and gasped. That one small touch sent shivers racing through her torso, down to that aching, liquid space between her legs and back up again, as if the two parts of her body were connected by a taut silver wire.

"Good Lord," she moaned, and threw her arms wide so as not to be tempted again. She knew what it was, and she didn't need a doctor for it. It was the fire that was never quenched, that's what it was. It was God's cruel joke on women the world over. It was just that the feeling was so strong this time, almost stronger than she could bear! She'd ask to have her room changed in the morning, that's what she'd do.

And she lay there a long time, reciting Lincoln's Gettysburg Address over and over until she felt normal enough to get up and dress for bed.

3

Tom Malloy couldn't sleep. Shielded from the chill in an old sheepskin jacket and crouched on his heels, his rifle across his knees, he sat a short distance from the entrance to the Bum Nugget Mine, alternately staring up at the stars or out across the still, night-silvered desert. Even at night, even through the cold, he could still smell spring in the air.

"Crimmeny, Tom!" said a sleepy voice from behind him. "Ain't you got no blasted sense? It's practically mornin'!"

Grinning, Tom stood up and turned. There was Skunky, wrapped in a shabby blanket and yawning wide. His gap-toothed mouth shone like an unkempt picket fence in the bright moonlight, and ragged white hair glistened where it stuck out from beneath his battered hat.

"It's only half past eleven," Tom said good-naturedly. "Go back to sleep, you old coot."

"Cain't," Skunky grouched. "The sound'a you prowlin' around out here woke my sleepin' parts up for good an' all. And stop callin' me an old coot or I'll tan your hide."

Skunky was practically old enough to be Tom's

25

grandfather and just about the toughest old buzzard he'd ever had the privilege to meet, but since Skunky was more than a foot shorter than Tom, he didn't see much peril in the threat.

"All right," Tom said, looking down from the lofty height of six feet, five inches. "All right, you old geezer."

Skunky sat down on a rock, muttering, "One'a these days I'm gonna swat you to kingdom come. . . ."

"You keep on promising," Tom said with a grin, "but you never come through."

Skunky looked up and cast a long, searching look out through the moonlit desert. "Where's Riggs?"

Tom shrugged. "Run off."

Skunky slapped his knee and spat. "Hellfire and damnation! Another one? Now, don't that beat everything! That mangy little cayuse! First Tomlin, then Boyce, then Whatshisname—"

"Hartemyer," said Tom.

"Then Hartemyer, and now Riggs." Skunky paused and squinted. "You sure he run off? Maybe Drum McLean's men did him dirty!"

Tom shook his head. "His bedroll and his horse are gone. If the McLean outfit got him, I don't reckon they would have tidied up after him so good."

Skunky sighed. "Dang it anyhow! That's the third guard we've had what's run off in the nighttime! You reckon McLean's threatenin' to kill their mamas or somethin'?"

"Something like," Tom said philosophically.

Tom had been working the Bum Nugget for the past year, ever since he'd claimed the land. Everybody had told him that he was too far out from the core of the strike, and that he'd be more likely to find water out here than silver, by which they meant that he wasn't going to find anything at all.

But he'd found traces of ore, traces that told his instincts there was much more if only he could find it! He'd promised Clementine that the next time he saw her, he'd be a rich man. He couldn't go back on that promise. After all, how could a poor man hope to win the hand of Clementine Crockett, the one and only daughter of Mad Hat Crockett, the seventh richest man in California?

The funny thing was that after a year away, he could hardly remember Clementine's face without refreshing his memory. He'd worn the little ivory frame that carried her picture down to a nub from looking at it ten or twelve times a day. Anyway, it was like looking into the face of a stranger. He couldn't for the life of him remember the sound of her voice.

But now he had bigger fish to fry, for McLean was after his claim. That, more than anything else, told him there was silver in this land, and a lot of it. McLean was no penny-ante operator. He owned a good quarter of the town, and his mine, the Daisy Cutter, brought up more ore in one day than Tom had seen come out of the Bum Nugget in the last year.

Of course, it helped that McLean had thirty men

working his mine. Here at the Bum Nugget, it was just Tom and Skunky.

McLean had offered to buy Tom out at first. The offers, always refused, got bigger and bigger, and then stopped. That was when McLean started trying to scare him off. First, somebody poisoned the little well that he and Skunky had dug. Thank God the first casualty had been one of the pack mules and not Skunky or himself! Two days after they had finished digging a new well—and were rejoicing over having accidentally hit an underground spring—the timbers in the shaft had mysteriously burned, and half the mine had collapsed. Spontaneous combustion, the sheriff had said.

"Spontaneous, my ass!" Tom had railed. "Spontaneous combustion doesn't leave behind kerosene jugs!"

But Sheriff Doolin was in Drum McLean's pocket, all right, and after the fire, Tom never again left the mine alone. This meant that either he or Skunky had to go into town for supplies alone. On his last sojourn into Twin Buttes, Skunky had been grazed along the temple—"stray slug," Sheriff Doolin had said with a dismissive shrug—and Tom had started hiring men.

He could scarcely afford it. He and Skunky were already living off rattlesnake and jackrabbit. But since the men he hired had a tendency to run off in the middle of the night without bothering to stop and ask for their wages, it evened out.

He stretched his long arms wide. "Suppose I'll have to go into town pretty soon. Hire a new fella."

"Better hire a whole dad-blamed crew," Skunky muttered. He was half asleep, his head nodding on his chest. He snugged his blanket around his shoulders, and added, "Any time now, McLean's gonna give up on them potshots he's been takin', and we's gonna find ourselves massacred by a batch of fake Apache."

"It won't come to that," Tom said, but he had his doubts. It would be just like McLean to send a gang of men out here to kill them, carve up their bodies a little, and plant a few Apache arrows around. There hadn't been any Indians in this area for at least five years, but that didn't stop them from being blamed for half the thievery and mayhem in the county.

Skunky looked up from the shroud of his blanket. "Can we go back to sleep now?"

"You go," Tom said. "I'll stand guard till two."

Skunky rose creakily, muttering, "And then you'll wake me. I just hates it when them fellers run off! Bunch'a heartless cowards, that's what they are, makin' an old man give up his sleep to do their job . . ."

Skunky mumbled and groused his way up the hill to the little campsite, which was directly in front of the Bum Nugget's mouth, and settled back down into his bedroll.

Tom turned toward the desert again. Somewhere in the distance a coyote gave voice, and was rapidly joined in song by a second coyote, then a third. Tom would watch and listen, and he would wait. And tomorrow or the next day, he'd go into town to try to find some new fool to hire.

He wasn't looking forward to it.

Flossie, tired but happy, tugged on her last shoe and stood up. Slocum was asleep, and a peek at his watch told Flossie that it was after two in the morning. Once again, she dug fingers into her purse to count the money he'd given her by the light of the moon. Ten whole silver cartwheels!

Her smile turned to a frown, though. There was still Tiger Forbush to deal with. By the time he got done, that ten dollars in silver would turn to a dollar's worth of nickels and dimes and two-bit pieces.

Carefully—and feeling someplace between exhilarated and guilty—she took eight silver dollars from her purse and tucked them inside the waistband of her dress in a little silver row. Tiger would believe Slocum had only paid her two, she told herself. Maybe she didn't have to tell him about Slocum at all. And tonight, after she met him and paid him off, she'd have money for kerosene and fuel to light and warm her crib over on Fourth Street, and in the morning she could have a real meal. With meat. And she'd still have a couple of dollars to save under the corner of the bedpost.

She went to the bed and brushed a last kiss over Slocum's forehead, then stepped lightly to the door. Her hand on the knob, she turned and whispered, "You know what, Slocum? If I'd'a knowed you was gonna be so gosh-darn good at it, I would'a done you for free." She tipped her head. "Well, almost."

She turned again and slipped silently from the room.

At four in the morning, Jamaica Vance eased her tired body into bed. Alone. Again. Jamaica never slept with the customers, unless it was someone she really took a fancy to. Nobody had taken her fancy in a month of Sundays, though, and it was beginning to make her as nervous as a cat in a roomful of rocking chairs. A woman shouldn't have to go so long without manly comfort. It wasn't natural.

But then, who was there to choose from? Jamaica'd had her fill of grubby miners years ago, back when she was working for Sally. And Lulu. And Deacon. And before that, on her own. Now she was on her own again, but she owned this house.

Besides Drum McLean—and she wouldn't touch that rattlesnake with a ten-foot pole!—there was only a handful of attractive men in town. Those were all happily married or at least disinterested, or were too cheap to pay house prices and took their pleasures with the street whores. And she had a sneaking suspicion that Mr. Keilor Kent and Mr. Burt Jenkins, without a doubt the two snappiest dressers and best-looking fellows in town, were seeing each other on the sly.

Such things didn't bother her. To each his own, she figured.

The sound of bedsprings squeaking and squealing came through the walls on either side of her room, and she smiled. Money in the bank, but not as much money as there used to be. These days, on her busiest nights, the income from the house was barely keeping her even.

Drum McLean was cutting in deeper and deeper every day, taking little razor-sized nips out of her profits that, at the present time, had added up to a large, bleeding gash. And he didn't show any signs of stopping the whittling. She had protected the girls as long as she could—protected their salaries anyway—but Drum had been carving at her so long that two weeks ago, she'd had to fess up to the girls or lose the house entirely.

The girls were wonderful about it, and although she overheard a few of them discussing ingenious ways to kill Drummond McLean (or at least get him tarred and feathered), so far it was nothing but talk. And they were all still at work, albeit at half wages.

Jamaica turned toward the window. Moonlight streamed in over her long russet hair, which she'd taken down from its pins for the night, and she pulled away an errant tress before she nestled deep into her covers. Still, she couldn't sleep. She heard the sounds of laughter drifting up to her from inside the house and outside, down on the street. Miners' laughter, that is. She didn't believe she'd heard a whore laugh for a very long time.

Drum McLean had taken away any reasons for laughter, and he'd taken it from the street gals a long time ago. At least she still owned the house. At least her girls could still manage a laugh when they were paid for it, and an occasional smile on their own time.

But McLean was tightening the clamps on that

little meat grinder he was slowly feeding her through. Jamaica didn't know how much longer she could hang on.

Flossie, after turning three more tricks—two in the alley over by the Painted Pony Saloon and another in a disused back stall at Millinger's Livery—was just heading wearily home when Tiger Forbush suddenly appeared before her. The slimy little slug had been waiting in ambush, in the shadows of the Long Tanks Bar.

Her first thought was that there'd be no kerosene or firewood for her tonight. It would be just like Tiger to prowl around back by the cribs, waiting to see if any of them went out and bought anything with money he thought was his. Or that of his boss, Drummond McLean.

"Hello, Tiger," Flossie said, and reached for her purse automatically.

Tiger, who was a shortish, weasel-like little man with a face only a mother could love—if that mother was nearsighted and half-drunk—snatched the little purse from her hands before she had a chance to twist open the clasp. He pulled out the coins and weighed them in his hand. "How many'd you turn, Floss?"

There was never much variety in their conversations. All business, that was Tiger.

"Seven," she said, figuring that would be enough to cover the money in her purse.

Tiger counted the coins once, then counted them

again. Without looking up, he asked, "Where'd you take 'em?"

She shrugged. "The usual. Couple'a alleys. Millinger's. The toolshed out back of Dray's."

He looked up. "And that was all?" His face was shadowed, and she couldn't read it.

"Sure," she said a little tremulously.

"And all them places are inside the U-Bet Hotel?"

Flossie felt her spine turn to ice. Tiger had been watching her. Had he seen her go in or come out? Maybe both. She'd spent five hours with Slocum.

Quickly, she said, "Oh, yeah. And at the hotel. Feller wouldn't let me leave, and then I fell asleep."

Tiger just looked at her.

"Well, I did!"

"Them out-of-town fellers pay you gals a good bit better than locals, don't they, Floss?" he asked in a low tone. "Don't seem to me you got enough money here to account for an out-of-town trick. Not five hours' worth."

Floss was good and scared now. She'd seen some awful things come about as a result of Tiger's displeasure with this girl or that. Blue Betty now had a purpling scar down the length of one side of her face, and he'd nearly cut Elvira Jones's right tittie clean off. Back Alley Sue had disappeared completely only three months ago.

Flossie swallowed and tittered out what she hoped was a self-deprecating giggle. She slapped her forehead. "Well, I near clean forgot!" She dug fingers into her waistband, scooped out two of the precious silver dollars, and handed them to Tiger. "Didn't dare carry 'em in my bag."

Suddenly Tiger's knife was out and pressed against her belly.

Flossie gasped in horrified surprise, and Tiger, far too close to her, said, "How much more, Floss?"

"That's all, Tiger," she breathed thinly, her eyes darting from the blade to his eyes, then back again to the blade. "I swear!"

And then Tiger's bony little hand felt along her waistband. He began plucking coins out, and Flossie shivered in terror.

"One, two, three . . . six more," he said. "Eight bucks you was tryin' to cheat me out of!"

The knife pressed harder against her belly. She heard the faint tear as it sliced slowly through the fabric of her dress, then felt a sharp, bright pain as its point dug into her skin.

"I swear, Tiger," she said weakly as she began to sob. "I swear on my mama's grave, I wasn't tryin' to cheat—"

That was as far as she got, because Tiger's blade suddenly ripped into her. She was aware of a hard, dull thud as the blade skittered off a rib, then drove through and slammed into her backbone.

She was down on the ground by then, although she had no memory of falling, and he just kept on stabbing her.

Finally, he wiped his blade on her skirts, then stood up. Through motionless, glassy eyes, she watched him resheath the knife and heard him say, as if from a great distance, "Guess that'll teach you."

4

Slocum stretched his arms and yawned before he reached for his watch. With a sleepy grin, he noted that the hands read nearly nine o'clock. Sleeping in like this could get to be a habit with him, particularly if he had somebody like Flossie keeping him up till all hours. He supposed Flossie had cut out sometime during the night. He couldn't blame her. A gal in her line of work couldn't spend much time napping on the job.

Whistling, he snagged his hat off the bedpost and settled it on his head, then stood up and tugged on his britches and boots.

Ten minutes later he was downstairs, intending to get himself some breakfast, then find the nearest bathhouse and barber. He ought to be cleaned up and on the scout for this Tom Malloy character by 10:30. Not that he needed to be cleaned up and shaved to find Malloy, and not that Flossie had complained the night before. But he was getting so rank that even *he* was wrinkling his nose!

Besides, it did a man good to have somebody else shave him once in a while, and Slocum could afford it. He'd only spent thirteen dollars—all right, twenty-three, counting Flossie—of that 250-dollar payment that Mad Hat had given him.

He had just picked up a newspaper at the front desk, and was reaching for the knob on the hotel's front door, when it suddenly swung in—and nearly smacked him in the head.

"Watch out, goddammit!" he snarled before he realized the person on the other side of the door was a woman. A very attractive woman, in fact.

She stood in the doorway, her pretty mouth open and her eyes blinking in surprise. Quickly, he took measure of her: honey-blond hair, about five-foot-six, brown eyes, better-than-nice figure. A whole lot better than nice. She looked to be in her mid-to-late twenties, and there was no ring on her finger. Either a whore or a professional woman of another kind.

He took her for the latter. She didn't have a whore's taste in clothes, for her plain green dress was buttoned right up to her chin and she wore no doodads. Maybe she was a lady drummer, selling buttons or trinkets or geegaws to stores around the territory. More women were doing that these days, he supposed.

But her fingertips were faintly stained a purplish black with ink. A schoolteacher perhaps? He supposed Twin Buttes must have a few kids, although he hadn't yet seen a one.

The surprise on her face quickly turned to annoyance, though, and before it could turn to something ranker, he took off his hat and hurriedly said, "I'm right sorry about the cussin', miss. Didn't see you."

She colored a bit. She stammered, "My fault entirely, Mr. Slocum," and pushed past him.

Shrugging, he went out into the morning and started up the street to the café. He was halfway there before he realized she'd known his name.

Miranda stood in the privacy of her hotel room, slowly and methodically banging her head against the wall. Of all the idiot things! She'd called him Mr. Slocum right to his face! Not only that, but he'd gotten a good look at her, hadn't he? How was she going to follow him when she could no longer melt into the background?

She sat on the edge of the bed, mournfully staring out the window. This wouldn't do, it just wouldn't do at all. She'd have to start all over, start a brand-new series with a brand-new hero. It wasn't fair!

She was the one who'd done it, though. Of all the addlepated stunts! She should have prepared herself better, that was all. To be near him was the reason she'd changed hotels, and she should have known she'd run into him sooner or later. She *had* known it.

Why, oh, why couldn't she just have said "sir" instead of calling him by name? Why had she opened her mouth at all? A simple nod with her head down would surely have placated him.

She realized she was weeping, albeit silently, and daubed her eyes with a hankie. Through the window, she caught a glimpse of him down below as he crossed the street, then disappeared again beneath the long covered sidewalk that fronted the next row of buildings.

"Stupid," she muttered under her breath, and then more sternly, "You're a fool, Miranda Richards."

She stood up and dried her tears, steeled herself, and marched to the door. "You're a journalist, don't forget that," she said to herself sternly as she pulled on her gloves. "This may be the last Slocum book you'll ever write, you gold-plated little idiot, but you will, by gosh and by golly, write it!"

She would follow John Slocum and get her story. She'd make one up if she had to. Cubby was counting on her. She was counting on herself! Stepping purposefully from her room, she made her way down the stairs and out the door, and started up the street after him.

Tom Malloy was nearly to town when somebody took a shot at him. The hat flew off his head before he heard the distant blast of the rifle. He dived off his horse, grabbed his worn Henry from the boot, and threw himself behind a small outcrop of boulders.

He waited, hatless, cursing under his breath, for a good five minutes before he saw signs of movement. The dust trail of a galloping horse and rider rose in the hills to the south, moving swiftly away.

Swearing, he stood up and brushed powdery dust from his knees. "Coward," he spat. "If just one of you cur dogs would get close enough to fight fair, I'd blast you into next week!" He waved his rifle at the retreating sniper for good measure.

The truth of it was that if there was anyone who could blast that fellow into kingdom come, it was

Tom Malloy. He hadn't served in the Army, but he'd been by far the best shot in his class at military school. It had broken his father's heart when he hadn't joined up after graduation.

But Tom Malloy had bigger things on his mind than endlessly drilling or fighting Indians, which, it seemed, was nearly all the Army did anymore. He had no taste for a last supper of arrows and scalping knives. Neither did he fancy a soft desk job back East, which was what his father had wanted for him.

No, he wanted to leave Illinois behind for once and for all and go West. Not in a blue uniform on a cavalry horse, but in his own clothes, and under his own power. He'd wanted adventures of his own making.

But after a few years of rattling around, he'd met Miss Clementine Crockett, the belle of San Francisco, and that was the end of his aimless wandering. He took one look at those blond ringlets, that delicate oval face, those pampered hands and tiny waspwaist, and he was a goner. It had been love at first sight.

"I hope you know what I'm going through for you, Clementine," he said as he stuck the rifle back in his boot and began to search for his hat.

Actually, he was beginning to wonder if she even remembered him. She hadn't written in months, even though he'd certainly been a loyal correspondent. He wrote a letter every week, come dust storm or flood or heat wave. Before he claimed the mine, he'd even tracked down her father to ask for permission to marry her.

Tom was old-fashioned that way.

He'd finally found Mad Hat, who was something of a legend with San Francisco folks, up in northern California. The older San Franciscans, the ones who had dug their money out of the ground or made it to the top laying rails—overseeing those who laid them, that is—had a certain fondness for Mad Hat. The young ones, like Clementine, pretended he didn't exist. She had said very little about her father, and what she had said hadn't been very enthusiastic. Or complimentary.

Personally, Tom had developed a genuine liking for the old coot, and couldn't for the life of him figure why Clementine and her mother looked down their noses at him. Mad Hat was surely an eccentric old cuss, but to Tom's mind, you couldn't help but admire him. Tom had stayed with him for a fortnight, cooking beans over a campfire and breaking rocks. And Mad Hat had developed a fondness for him too. By the time Tom left, Mad Hat was calling him "son." It tickled Tom no end.

Of course, it remained to ask Clementine if she'd have him, but Tom felt a good bit better about the whole thing once he had her daddy's permission.

He'd left that out of the letters he'd written to Clementine, both the finding of Mad Hat and the asking for permission. He hadn't even asked her to marry him yet. It wasn't the sort of thing you just wrote down and sent off, and then hoped somebody didn't rob the mail. That would be agony.

No, he'd make his money the honest way, he'd decided, then ask her in person once he was rich.

Not rich like Mad Hat—that was impossible!—but rich enough. That was, if some scrofulous sonofabitch hired by that dog Drummond McLean didn't shoot him first.

He found his hat hanging from a prickly pear and disengaged it carefully. Two holes, one entry and one exit, punctuated the crown.

"Damn!" he breathed as he stuck his fingers through them. A quarter-inch lower and he would have been playing a harp for sure.

He pulled out a stray cactus spine, then clamped the hat back on his head and went to his horse. He'd need more than one man, he realized. By the time this thing was over, he was going to need an army.

It was just past eleven—and far, far, too early for such things—when Sassafras came pounding on Jamaica's door.

"Go away!" she shouted, and pulled the feather pillow over her head.

But Sassafras wouldn't go away. She pounded again, much to Jamaica's displeasure, and cried, "Wake up, Jamaica! Didn't you hear me? They found a dead girl down by the cribs! Wake up, wake up!"

Slowly, Jamaica pulled the pillow away. "I'm coming," she said. He'd stopped carving them up, she realized. This time he'd killed one of them. McLean wouldn't have done it himself, of course. It would have been one of those odious henchmen of his, probably Tiger, if she didn't miss her guess. For the last few months they had been terrorizing the street girls, stripping them of their money for "protection."

If you asked Jamaica—or any other sane person—they would have said that the only things those girls needed protection from were McLean's minions.

She stood up, accidentally knocking to the floor the book she'd been reading over the past few days. *John Slocum: The Dealer of Death* was its title, and she quickly picked it up and jammed it under her pillow. This was no time to be dreaming about the past, dreaming about lost loves and better times. The current situation demanded her full attention.

After hurriedly throwing on a wrapper, she made her way downstairs to the kitchen. The girls were already gathered, and it took her a few minutes to get everyone calmed down so that they could hear her.

"All right, one at a time." Jamaica turned toward a pale, teary-eyed blonde who was swathed in a green ostrich-trimmed negligee. "Abra?"

"Somebody killed her, Miss Jamaica," she sniffed. "They cut her up somethin' terrible."

"Killed who?" Jamaica prodded. "Which girl was murdered?"

"Flossie Carmichael," offered Cindy. Cindy was one of the girls Jamaica had taken in from the streets when the troubles started. She would have taken more, but the house was jammed to the rafters, with girls living two and three to a room even up in the attic. The house was big enough to accommodate ten comfortably, but she suddenly found herself with thirty mouths to feed!

"I knowed her when I was . . ." Cindy shuddered, and poked a finger toward the street. "When I was out there. She was a real nice gal, Miss Jamaica, real kind. She'd always stand you a cup'a coffee if'n it was a bad night and you was cold." Cindy dissolved into tears then, and one of the other girls comforted her.

Mrs. Arnot, the cook, planted flour-dusted fists the size of small hams on her wide hips, and announced, "You gals ain't got nothin' to fret over. You're safe as long as you're in this house."

"But for how long?" Sassafras asked, waving an unlit cigarillo. Sassafras was a dark, sleek, rawboned yet elegant girl whose parents had come from the islands, and who—with her jangling gold earrings and bright turbans—lent a touch of the exotic to the house's roster. "How do we know they ain't gonna work their way in here? First they'll get rid of the girls on the streets, and then it'll be us!"

"I think it's more complicated than that, Sass," Jamaica said with a sigh. "However, if any of you want to leave, there'll be no hard feelings. In fact, I'll cheer for you. You're wiser than I am. And you'll sure as hell be safer."

Little Abra looked up, blinking. "But you're gonna stay, aren't you, Miss Jamaica?"

Jamaica, trying to appear more resolute than she felt at the moment, drew herself erect. "This is my house. I'm not budging."

"Then I'll stay too, Miss Jamaica," Abra said, wiping at her tears with a pink-nailed forefinger. "You been the nicest to me of anybody."

"I'm ain't goin' nowhere," said Connie, a tall strawberry blonde. She raised her chin and crossed her arms stubbornly.

"Me neither," echoed Susan, a cherubic brunette whose honey-brown hair fell nearly to her knees. "They're not chasing me out!"

"Oh, hell," groaned Sassafras, bending to light her cheroot on the stove lid. "I'll stay with you idiots," she said, blowing smoke through her nostrils.

"Me too!" chirped another voice.

But several of the girls expressed plans to move on, and as soon as possible. In the flurry of conversation and argument that ensued, Jamaica eased her way out of the kitchen. No one noticed.

She walked up the hall and into the parlor, picking up a stray scarf here, emptying an ashtray there, straightening slip covers and moving chairs back into place out of habit. Vance Sitwell, her piano player, was asleep on the big red-plush sofa, as usual. He was still fully dressed, right down to his sleeve garters and his boots, with his bowler hat pulled low over his eyes and his soft snores rising toward the ceiling. She let him sleep. Since their sudden influx of fugitive whores, the parlor sofa had become his bedroom.

She went to the bar in the corner, unlocked it, and poured herself a bourbon. Booze before breakfast coffee was a cardinal sin in her house, but she broke her own commandment without thinking. The first bourbon she slugged back for purely medicinal purposes. Then she poured herself another. She carried the glass to the front windows and looked out over the town, arms crossed over her ample bosom.

She'd come here when the town was just starting
to boom, when the house was a good distance from
the town, and all she could see through these front
windows was a mercantile, a livery, and two saloons
in the distance. Now she saw a busy street right
outside her door: a thriving city, its sidewalks filled
with the jostling bodies of men—tall men, short
men, fat men, men in desperate need of home cooking, men of every shape and size and color—nearly
all of whom needed the services she supplied.

It was her town. Well, Rose's too, if you were
to ask the old bat up the street, but nobody had.
Jamaica wasn't going to let anybody run her out of
it. She knew that now.

And then her eye came to rest on a certain somebody out there across the street, a man with a particularly self-assured way of walking, a familiar way
of striking a lucifer. A man whose stance and slim
hips and wide shoulders, even with his broad back
turned toward her, was unforgettable after all these
years and still sent a shiver up her spine. And when
he turned slightly to toss away the match, showing
his profile, she gave in fully to happiness, and to
hope.

There was salvation after all. And salvation
looked absolutely nothing like the cover on his
book.

She left her bourbon glass skidding and sloshing
on the hall table and raced past the satin bellpulls,
past the gracefully curving front stairs, and to the
stained-glass front door. She threw it wide and, bare-

footed and still in her nightclothes, raced outside and onto the walk.

"Slocum!" she shouted gleefully through cupped hands. "Hey, Slocum!"

5

Tiger Forbush yelped and landed against the wall of McLean's inner office with a satisfying *crack*. He slithered to the floor.

"You stupid idiot," Drum McLean hissed, and rubbed his knuckles. Tiger, a skinny little varmint if ever he'd seen one, had been harder to the fist than he'd suspected. Must be all those bones so close to the surface. "You could have just beat her."

Tiger stayed slumped against the wall, holding a skeletal hand to his cheek and wincing. "Sorry, Boss," he muttered, then worked his jaw from side to side.

"Yeah, you're sorry, all right," McLean spat. "You're one sorry sonofabitch. Get up."

Tiger slowly worked his thin frame off the floor, but he still cowered against the wall. "You done hittin'?" he asked nervously.

McLean glared at him. "You're lucky I'm in a good mood this morning, elsewise McGee would be hauling you up out of his well come tomorrow."

Tiger gulped.

"Give me your knife."

"What?"

"Give me that pigsticker of yours," McLean repeated.

Slowly, Tiger reached to the back of his belt, unsheathed his blade, and stepped tentatively forward to hand it over. McLean snatched it from Tiger's shaking hand and dropped it into his desk drawer.

"Now the money," he said.

Tiger dug into a pocket and produced a purse, which he handed to McLean.

McLean emptied it onto the desk and tossed it back, empty. "Well?" he barked. "Sit down!"

Tiger slid nervously into the chair opposite him, his back to the door whose glass read *D. McLean, Publisher*. Behind him, McLean could make out the distorted forms of bodies going about their business in the outer offices, and hear the loud *clunk* and *whoosh* of the presses. Nobody out there could hear a damn thing that went on in his private office, not while Joe and Pete were running the presses.

McLean made a show of counting the coins and let Tiger sweat it out. Tiger and his crony, Harley Hobbs—who sat quietly in the corner, twisting his hat in his fat, sweaty hands—came every morning at this time to turn over the money they'd taken from the street hookers. This morning's take was about average.

The boys were supposed to confiscate half the money the whores took in, in return for the supposed "protection" they provided, which in truth was nonexistent. But McLean knew they were taking more and pocketing the difference, and slapping the girls around in the process.

He pretended ignorance most of the time. Let them get the girls good and scared, he figured. The more of them that left town—the ugly ones, the older ones, the ones on the street—the better. And it was all right with him if Tiger and Harley skimmed the take. It kept the two of them interested and on the job.

McLean had bigger fish to fry.

"All right," he said, looking up at last. Tiger's narrow shoulders relaxed visibly.

McLean swept the coins into a small cash box with the side of his hand, and sat back. "From now on, Tiger, use your fists. And hit 'em where it doesn't show till they take their clothes off. And Harley?"

In the shadows of the corner, Harley jumped a little. "Boss?" he said, the pink rising into his chubby cheeks.

"If I hear one more time that you corn-holed some whore so she could keep some of her money, they're gonna find you outside of town in the bottom of an arroyo. That's sick, you hear me? I won't have it in my town."

"But Drum," Harley started in, he face bright red, "I didn't do no such a thing! If Wilma told you that, she's lyin'!"

"Wilma too?" McLean said, arching his brows. "She wasn't the one who told me, Harley."

"Shit," Harley muttered, and stared at the floor.

"Ha-ha," brayed Tiger.

"Shut up, the both of you," McLean said, and slammed his desk drawer for punctuation. Idiots. He

was surrounded by idiots. "Well, what are you waiting for? Get out!"

The two men, one bony, pale, and furtive, and the
other chubby-cheeked and a sick little son of a bitch
if McLean had ever known one, scuttled out the
back door and into the alley.

They were luckier than they knew, because despite everything, Drum McLean was in a very good
mood that morning. Whistling, he stood up, settled
his hat on his head, and walked out into the main
newspaper office and out onto the street.

"Slow down!" Slocum shouted. "One at a goddamn
time!"

He was a hairsbreadth away from pulling his Colt
and shooting at the ceiling, just to silence all this
female racket. There must have been thirty whores
crowded into the parlor, all dripping with feathers
and silk and spangles and bright gauzy stuff, and
smelling of perfume. He wouldn't have minded exactly—there wasn't anything near a dog in the
whole batch of them—but they were making one
hell of a racket, and crowding into him so close that
they'd already nearly toppled him over the couch.

He jumped up on a chair. "Enough!" he thundered
again, and this time, they all shut up.

"Come on," Jamaica said, and reached through
the crowd to take his hand. Once he'd hopped down
and they were both clear of the throng, she turned
and announced, "I'm gonna finish telling this to Slocum. Alone. I mean it," she added, and unceremo-
niously tugged him up the stairs.

He hadn't seen Jamaica for nearly ten years, but he had to admit that the time had very worn well on her, nicely seasoning her with an air of sophistication, rather than aging her. Of course, she'd been only eighteen then, and at twenty-eight she was just coming into her prime. She'd come a long way from that mining camp, by the looks of it.

She was just as beautiful—and just as sleek-hipped and red-haired and green-eyed and flamboyant—as he remembered. It had been up in Durango that they'd first met. He'd spent a week and a half with her while he was taking care of some business, and when it had concluded he'd hauled her to Denver with him.

She'd left in the middle of the night, leaving only a note that said, "You've got to roam, and I've got to find work. I'll always remember you, darlin'."

It was signed "Mudge," for that was the name she was going by at the time. He didn't know that Jamaica fit her any better, but it was better for a whore than Mudge. Sounded foreign, he thought, and he reckoned that was always a boost for business.

She led him into a bedroom he took to be hers. It was large, with three big windows looking down on the street. They were framed by forest-green curtains. The bed drapes and the furnishings—two chairs flanking a fireplace, and a fainting couch at the foot of the bed—were in varying shades of green too, as were the silk sheets and comforter. And her negligee. Green was always her color.

"Slocum?"

He looked up. His eyes had been riveted to the

deep V between her breasts. "Sorry," he said with just a hint of a libidinous grin. "What the hell's the deal with those gals? I mean, why'd they come stormin' at me that way?"

She walked to the bed and pushed aside the bed-clothes to pick up a well-worn book. She waved it at him. One glimpse at the cover, and he groaned.

"Everybody's reading it, Slocum," she said. Her bow-shaped mouth curved up at the corners, and she shrugged. "I guess they heard me shouting your name at the top of my lungs. And they all know that I know you. Knew you," she corrected herself.

He sat down in a yellowish-green upholstered chair and leaned back, groaning in disgust while he absently toyed with the tassels on its arms. "Explains the mob scene downstairs, I reckon. If I ever get my hands on that Dusty Rhodes hombre . . ."

Jamaica sat opposite him, on the damask-upholstered fainting couch. "If it's any comfort, you're quite a popular fellow around here. I'm guessing that my ladies are down in the kitchen right now, drawing straws to see who gets first crack at coaxing you into her bed." Her smile faded. "The ladies that are left anyway."

She paused, and Slocum sat, silently waiting. She had managed to tell him a good bit of the tale before they were swamped in whores in the parlor, and he thought he had the gist of it. Drum McLean was muscling in on the prostitutes of Twin Buttes for whatever reason, and he had killed—or his men had killed—some whore last night. Jamaica's girls blamed him for another girl's disappearance, and for the beating and mutilation of several others.

It was an old story. This Drum McLean was nothing more than an aspiring pimp, and a greedy one. Slocum had seen it happen countless times before in these wild towns, although never with a man who owned a newspaper. That was a new one. Slocum was as jaded as they come, but a fellow sort of expected the press to be, well, upstanding!

"Slocum," she said at last, "I wouldn't ask you, but I'm about at the end of my rope. You've got to help me. Help all of us. I'll pay you. It won't be much at first, but you know I'm good for it."

He closed his eyes for a moment. It was never easy, was it? He'd gotten directions out to Tom Malloy's mine while he was sitting in the barber's chair, and he had figured to ride out and deliver the letter today, and be off for Nevada—and the other half of his money—tomorrow. The last thing he needed was Jamaica—and the two-dozen-or-so other barely dressed women downstairs—depending on him. Probably every whore in town.

But he couldn't turn her down. They had a certain history together. And looking at her, still disheveled from her bed, all rosy-cheeked and Titian-haired— and falling out of her nightclothes—he couldn't say no. Still, he had Mad Hat Crockett's business to attend to first.

He blew air out through pursed lips and said, "All right. And you ain't hiring me, Mudge. I mean, Jamaica. I'll do what I can. But I've got to take care of something else first. And you'd best think about what it is exactly that you want me to do."

SLOCUM AND THE HELPLESS HARLOTS   55

Jamaica frowned, her delicate brows knotting as she bowed her head. A long curl of red hair toppled over her brow, and she blew it aside. He wanted to feel that long red hair against his chest in the worst way.

"Do?" she said, looking up. "Well, make it stop, of course! Make *him* stop!"

Slocum chuckled in spite of himself. As usual, she hadn't thought it through. But then, women that looked the way Jamaica did didn't have to think. He found himself wishing that her negligee would just slip off, and leave her naked. Had the years changed her? The girl he remembered was tiny-waisted and full-breasted, and as red-haired below as she was above. He wanted to get his arms around her and help that negligee get to falling, and as soon as possible.

"Lots of ways to make it stop, Mudge," he said a little thickly. "Sorry. Jamaica. Gonna take me a while to get used to that moniker of yours, I reckon."

She smiled. "You can call me Mudge if you want, darlin'. Just don't let anybody else hear you. Why, it'd ruin my reputation for sure!"

And then, as if she'd read his mind, she rose and walked over to him. She settled down in his lap and pressed herself against him, and he hugged her around the waist. It was not at all an unpleasant sensation.

She kissed his cheek, and then, serious once more, she whispered, "Just make it go away. All of them. Drum McLean and his little toadies. And what exactly," she asked, combing her fingers through his hair, "do you have to do first?"

Slocum let his hand wander up from her waist to cup one breast through the thin fabric of her negligee. Her breasts were still firm and high. The nipples were pale shell-pink and very large, as he recalled.

She pressed herself into his hand and unconsciously ground her hips into his lap. Slocum, who had been hard before she came over to him, cleared his throat before he said, "Mudge, why don't we talk about this later?" He slipped his hand inside her gown while he asked the question.

She closed her eyes for a moment, seeming to savor his touch, and he took advantage of the opportunity to slide the negligee off her shoulders and away from her torso. He'd remembered correctly. Her skin was milky white and flawless, and her breasts were plump and round and tipped in the palest pink. The nipples were already knotted and peaked, darkened and swollen with her excitement, and hard as rubies against his fingers.

Without thinking, he dipped his head and sucked one glorious nipple into his mouth. He slithered his tongue around the hard and swollen peak, bit gently into the aureole.

She growled, low in her throat, and whispered, "Slocum."

It didn't have the tone of "no" in it, and while he suckled her, he slid her gown's tie free with one hand and opened it, exposing her completely. He stroked her slowly from shoulder to knee, pausing at the indention of her waist and the gentle bell of her hip.

Breaking out in shivers, she squirmed against him. She made a little mewing sound, and opened her legs slightly.

"It's been so long, Slocum," she whispered as she cradled his head at her breast. "So long."

He slid his hand between her thighs then, and found her already drenched with moisture. He slipped one finger inside her, then two, while his mouth left her breast and found her lips. He kissed her long and deep, all the while stroking her below and gently playing with that little nub of flesh that brought women their greatest pleasure.

And then she was unbuckling his belt and tugging his britches down, and she was just as hungry as he was, and as eager. She knelt before him and took him into her mouth for a moment, licking and lapping at the head, sucking it as he had suckled her breast, and just when he was about to tell her that he couldn't stand it any longer, she straddled him.

She eased down upon him slowly, her eyes closed as if she wished to savor every moment of his entry, and his hands went to her waist to aid her. It was so tiny that his fingers overlapped, but he scarcely had the time—or the inclination—to think about this. He pulled her closer so that he could nip and kiss her breasts as her body slowly sheathed him in liquid fire.

When at last she was down all the way, impaled on his shaft, he drew her torso closer and whispered, "I've missed you, Mudge."

A green and tasseled easy chair in the bright morning light wasn't exactly the best place to make love, but they managed. She rode him slow and easy, then hard and fast, and she climaxed almost immediately and collapsed against his chest, panting.

But Slocum hadn't finished, not by a long shot. "We're not through yet, Mudge," he muttered.

She smiled dreamily and whispered, "I didn't think so, Slocum. Do me right. Do me good, like only you can." She kissed him and looked into his eyes. "Do me all over," she breathed.

He stood up and carried her to that big four-poster bed of hers, leaving her negligee in a puddle on the floor, and laid her on the rumpled satin sheets. Then he kicked free from his britches and boots, and shrugged out of his gunbelt and vest and shirt. He stretched out beside her then, drawing her near, stroking her, petting her, opening her legs again.

He was on the brink of entering her once more when she grinned up at him. "Your hat, Slocum?"

He took it off with a sheepish grin, and sailed it across the room.

6

Miranda sat in the Oak Leaf Coffee House, alternately drumming her fingers impatiently on the tabletop or nibbling on a stale sugar cookie—one of a plate of four that she'd had to buy just to sit down.

Through the big plate-glass window, she frowned in displeasure at Jamaica's Pleasure Barge, a large corner building of two and a half stories, gingerbread-trimmed and whimsically painted to resemble a paddle-wheel boat. The "wheel" made an arch that reached to the second floor, and there were bright blue waves and bubbly foam stenciled around the base of the building.

Miranda knew just what type of establishment Jamaica's was, all right, and Slocum had been in there for a very long time. Far too long for just a pleasant chat!

She was, for the first time, becoming disenchanted with her hero. To think that this man of iron, this paladin of the plains and paragon of virtue, would consort with a common trollop! She'd seen that red-headed strumpet holler at him from the porch, and she was a barely dressed strumpet at that!

An entire hour had gone by and there was still no

sight of Slocum, although Miranda's time hadn't been exactly wasted. She'd made copious notes on the interior of the Coffee House (chipped cups, stale baked goods, and all) and she'd overheard a few juicy tidbits. At this time of day anyway, it seemed that most of the customers were street prostitutes, and they were talking of nothing but last night's murder.

On this subject too, Miranda had taken pages of notes, gleaned from three separate sets of coffee drinkers over the past hour. The victim's name was Flossie—no one seemed to know her last name, although there were several guesses that it was something Irish—and she was either twenty-four or twenty-seven, depending on which conversation one was to believe. She had lived three blocks away in something called the cribs, which Miranda intended to visit later that day, just to make some color notes. Flossie's body had been found just steps away from this pitiful home, stabbed and slashed in a most gruesome and grisly manner.

Miranda had also learned that this incident was not the first. Prostitution seemed to be a dangerous profession in Twin Buttes, and several of the women upon whom she'd eavesdropped had made their intentions clear. They were getting out of town and moving on to greener—and less deadly—pastures.

She had begun to think that she might get a separate book out of the murder. That is, if Cubby wasn't too put off by the seamy nature of the subject.

She was about to signal the waiter for a fourth

refill of her mug when someone in the crowd caught her eye. It was that openmouthed masticator, Drummond McLean, the so-called gentleman who had taken her for a prostitute the night before. Standing across the street, on the walk right out in front of Jamaica's Pleasure Barge, he was engaged in a heated conversation with an extremely tall—she didn't believe she'd ever seen anyone so tall!—and good-looking fellow. A tad dusty and a little grimy around the edges, but good-looking. She found herself thinking that if he had a bath, he might just turn out to be deadly handsome.

Both men appeared to be agitated, however, and McLean's hands were balling into fists. The tall one stood his ground and angrily said something to Drummond McLean, then ripped off his hat and waved it in McLean's face.

"There's the double-dealin', slab-sided sonofabitch now, Emmaline," said an incensed—and very loud—soiled dove's voice from the next table. She was pointing to the two men across the street. "Why don't you just go on over and slit his throat? Get this damned thing over with!"

Miranda blinked. Who were they talking about, McLean or this other fellow? She hoped it was McLean.

And then the strangest thing happened! Slocum stepped out of Jamaica's, hatless and with his shirt unbuttoned and the tails flapping. That redheaded slattern was at his side. He placed himself between the two men, and while the redhead dragged the tall man back through the door, Slocum had a few rough words with McLean.

Whatever Slocum had said, McLean acted shocked. No, appalled! Miranda could see him feigning innocence clear across the street. And then Slocum said something else, and after a few brisk words in reply, McLean turned smartly on his heel and strode off down the sidewalk. Slocum stood there, looking after him angrily and fiddling for a moment with the butt of his holstered gun, and then he turned and followed the tall man back inside Jamaica's.

This was certainly a new development! She didn't know the plot yet, but she had a feeling there was a whole new book in it.

"Who was that feller?" she overheard one soiled dove ask another.

"I don't know, Meg, but I'd do him for free," came the sighed reply.

"Hell, Emmaline, the quality of gents you pull in, I'll wager that you'd pay *him* for the favor!"

To the sounds of coarse laughter, Miranda plucked a few coins from her purse, slid them onto the tabletop, walked out into the sunshine, and quickly crossed the street. Jamaica's Pleasure Barge sat on the corner of Fourth Street and Vine. Surely there'd be a side window at which she could listen.

"But goddamn it, Jamaica, look what McLean's boys did to my hat!" Tom Malloy was saying as Slocum came in the door. He waved his topper again, and nearly hit Slocum in the face with it.

Doors and hats alike seemed to be aiming directly for his nose this morning. Slocum couldn't win. The next thing he knew, somebody'd be flinging a horse at him.

However, after his interlude with Mudge—Jamaica, that is—he was feeling plumb generous. So instead of grabbing the hat and ripping it into pieces, he simply ducked.

"Oh. Sorry," said Tom, who seemed to suddenly realize where he was waving his arm.

"Jamaica tells me you're Tom Malloy, that right?" Slocum asked. This boy was sure a tall drink of water, all right. Slocum's eyes met Malloy's nose, square on.

"I am," Tom said, scowling. "I was just gettin' a good mad goin' when you stuck your beak into my business! What's it to you anyhow? And who the hell are you?"

"Slocum," Slocum answered curtly. The hat-swinging aside, he was delighted that Tom Malloy had just fallen in on him like this. It'd save him a ride out to the mine. What had Jamaica called it? The Bum Nugget, that was it. But he wished that Malloy would just calm the hell down. He added, "John Slocum. Mad Hat Crockett sent me to find you."

Slocum got his wish, because Tom's expression suddenly softened. "Mad Hat Crockett? Is he all right?" His brow creased with concern. "There's nothing wrong with the old coot, is there?"

"He's fine," Slocum said, and searched his pockets. He pulled out the envelope and handed it over. "Hired me to bring you this."

Tom took the envelope, but held it away from him as if it might bite him. "Why?"

Slocum snorted. "Hell, I don't know! Reckon the reason's inside."

Gingerly, Tom tore an end off the envelope and pulled out a grimy sheet of paper. When he opened it, Slocum caught a glimpse of the letterhead of the Select Hotel in Bent Elbow, Nevada. Slocum shook his head. That crazy Mad Hat, stealing stationery from a hotel! Too cheap to buy paper, and with all his money too.

But a glimpse was all that Slocum got, and he and Jamaica stood there while Tom read the letter, then read it again, his face draining of blood.

Finally, Jamaica said, "Well, Tom? What in the name of Bessie is it?"

Slowly, Tom folded the paper and put it back into its envelope, then tucked the whole business into a pocket. He shrugged. "Private."

It was all the same to Slocum, although it looked like whatever the message had been, it had hit this boy pretty damned hard. "Any reply?" he asked.

"Not one I can think of right now," Tom replied dismally, staring at his boots. "Damn it anyway," he muttered before he looked up at them again. "You going back to where Mad Hat is?"

Slocum nodded. "Going back whether you have an answer for him or not. Well, as soon as I get Jamaica's problem straightened out."

Jamaica took his arm and gave it a squeeze.

"Then I've got some time to think," Tom said softly.

Slocum nodded. "That you do."

Tom cocked his head. "Slocum. Say, you wouldn't by any chance be the same feller as the one in that book, would you?"

"He is," Jamaica said proudly before Slocum had a chance to open his mouth.

Tom dug into his hip pocket and held up a brand-new book. *John Slocum: Death Rides a Spotted Stallion* by Dusty Rhodes. "Got it from a feller just in from up north," he said. "Paid him double for it too. We don't get anything until it's a month old." He peered at the cover, then back at Slocum. "Doesn't look much more like you than the first one, does it?"

Slocum fairly ripped it from Tom's hands. Another one of the blasted things! "God*damn* it!" he spat, glaring at the cover. "If I ever get my hands on—"

"Don't tear it up!" cried a horrified Jamaica, and she wrenched it from his fingers. She handed it back to Tom, and in a whisper, confided, "He's a little touchy on the subject of literature."

Slocum growled, "Literature, my ass."

"There, there, honey," Jamaica said, patting his hand.

A Negress, slender and sleek and regally beautiful, stepped out of a doorway and into the foyer. "You gonna get dressed sometime today, Jamaica?" she demanded, hands on her lean hips.

Jamaica rolled her eyes, then felt at her hair. "Oh,

law!" she said. "Sassafras, see that these boys have whatever they want. And don't let anybody leave till I get back downstairs! Slocum, Tom told me something real interesting—or at least the beginning of it—while you were out front, playing at having a pissing contest with McLean."

She turned to go upstairs, then whirled back around and planted a kiss on the side of his jaw. "I'm so glad you're here," she whispered. "For more reasons than you can know. And don't you say a word, Tom Malloy, till I get back!" She fled up the stairs in a cloud of green.

"Follow me, gents," said Sassafras with a smile, and she led them down the long hall and into the kitchen, her earrings jangling.

Up at the Bum Nugget Mine, there hadn't been much to do that morning, at least not much that one man could do alone. Anyway, that was what Skunky told himself. He was presently sitting high atop the hill over the Bum Nugget, rifle across his knees, staring out over the distance and waiting for Tom to return. Hopefully, he'd come with several men, all of them armed to the teeth.

But it wouldn't be several. Skunky knew as well as anybody else that Tom couldn't afford a gang of miners, let alone hired guns, especially considering the bottomless pockets of the man they were up against. Tom would be lucky if he could talk one drunk into coming out here.

From Skunky's perch, he could see nearly 360 degrees. More hills like this one, with the road to town below, twisting through, and flatlands. Not a blessed tree in sight. He sort of missed the trees, being from Indiana, although Indiana was sure a long time ago. He'd like to get back there someday, he thought. Maybe look up his brother, see if old Mort was still alive. He probably was. He'd had the sense to stay put instead of coming west.

As Skunky watched, a fully loaded supply wagon came into view on the thin, unkempt track of what passed for a road, and it surely was barreling along. A few seconds later, he realized that the horses were out of control. The driver was alternately flapping his arms or hanging on for dear life.

Now, Skunky's eyes were getting a little old and kind of rheumy—though he'd never admit it—and he couldn't see too well at this distance, but his guess was that the driver had lost the reins. Maybe one had broken, or maybe the fellow had gotten lax and fallen asleep and just dropped them, but he sure as shooting had no control whatsoever over his team.

The team of chestnuts were racing, but so far they'd had sense enough to stay on the road, so Skunky stayed put to watch the show as the wagon barreled for town. He wished he'd brought his old binoculars, by God!

And then the freight wagon hit a rock, or at least he figured that was what happened, and bumped up high in the air, sailing forward close to fifteen or twenty feet before it landed again and continued on its way. By some miracle, the driver stayed on and the axle wasn't busted all to hell. But when it landed with a jouncing jolt that Skunky heard, even at this distance, a couple of crates bounced off the back.

This, at last, brought Skunky to his feet.

As the wagon crossed the valley and disappeared, jolting and thundering around the bend behind the far hills, Skunky started the long slide down to the mouth of the mine. Abandoned merchandise, that's what it was! He was going to get down there and lay claim to those crates before some other smart sonofabitch came along.

And who knows? There might be a whole case of preserves down there! Jam, jelly, he didn't care. His sweet tooth had been troubling him something awful for weeks, and Tom never remembered to pick him up any candy or the like while he was in town. Skunky reckoned he could pick a little busted glass out of peach or strawberry jam the same as anybody else. He wasn't proud, just hungering for something sugary.

Maybe there was a whole case of licorice or horehound drops down there!

Salivating in anticipation, he reached the bottom of the hill and the mouth of the Bum Nugget in slap time. He threw a saddle on Whisk, his mare. He grabbed a couple of extra ropes, just in case. And then he headed out toward his treasure, whistling.

Miranda stood pressed against the wall outside the curlicued kitchen window of Jamaica's Pleasure Barge, beneath the arch of the building's false paddle wheel. It was difficult to look nonchalant, as if she had an actual reason for being there, but at least

Vine Street wasn't too heavily traveled by pedestrians. Most of the foot traffic, and the horse traffic too, was on Fourth, which the Pleasure Barge faced. When the occasional fellow did pass by—or shot her a curious glance from across the way—she made a show of looking at her watch pin and then craning her head up and down the street, as if she were waiting for someone.

So far, it had worked.

Except that Slocum and this other fellow, this Tom Malloy, hadn't said much of anything since Sassafras—whom she took to be another of Jamaica's soiled doves—had brought them into the kitchen. All she'd learned was Tom Malloy's name and that he owned a mine, the Bum Nugget by name, and that Drummond McLean was giving him and his partner, a man with the rather unfortunate name of Skunky, a very hard time indeed. Just this morning, someone had shot a hole through Tom Malloy's hat and narrowly missed splitting his skull!

She made cursory notes of all this, figuring to expand them later. Tom Malloy was an interesting character, all right, but she was supposed to be writing about Slocum. How did he fit into all this anyway?

And she also learned that her second book was at last available somewhere, if not in Twin Buttes. This gave her a real thrill, and it was all she could do to stand there and wait for something to happen.

Slocum seemed none too happy about it, though, and this caused her distress. A person would think that a man would be grateful to be immortalized!

Why, out of all the shootists and gun-toters in the
West, she had chosen him, chosen Slocum out of all
of them! Yet there he was, drinking coffee and de-
claring angrily that if he ever caught up with "Dusty
Rhodes," he'd "wring the lyin' sonofabitch's neck."

She sniffed derisively. Ungrateful lout!

Her disillusionment with Slocum was rapidly
deepening. Trafficking with known slatterns, and in
the daytime too! Why, he'd come right out onto the
street half-dressed, practically advertising that he'd
been with one of those low women! This certainly
wasn't the wholesome image of a knight of the
plains that she'd portrayed in her novels.

Feet of clay, John Slocum, she wanted to shout.
Feet of clay!

She'd been so lost in her thoughts that she hadn't
seen the shabbily dressed man sidling up to her until
he was a scant three feet away. Leering, he jingled
a few coins in her face and said, "What you say,
honey? The alley?"

Without a word, she raised her arm and smacked
him smartly across the face with her bag.

His hand came up to rub at the reddening mark,
and he said, "All right, all right! I reckon we could
get us a room if'n you're set on it."

She raised the handbag to strike again, and he
backed off, grumbling, "No call to get so all-fired
uppity about it." He wandered off down the street.

And then, from inside the building, she heard
someone new enter the kitchen. She chanced a quick
peek.

"Jamaica," said Slocum. He scraped his chair

back to stand up, and Tom Malloy belatedly followed suit.

It was the red-haired guttersnipe that Miranda had seen Slocum with earlier, except now she looked, well, beautiful. Dressed in a low-cut, green satin gown, with her flame-colored hair elaborately piled atop her head, she would have looked at home in any of San Francisco's more expensive dining and dancing establishments. At eleven at night, though, and most certainly not at high noon.

"Hello, boys," Jamaica said as Sassafras poured her a cup of coffee. "And for heaven's sake, sit down, you two."

Miranda pulled back from the window, berating herself for daring to look for so long.

"Now, Tom," Jamaica continued. "What's the rest of this news you had to tell me? And start from the beginning. I think Slocum's going to be very interested in what you have to say."

7

Skunky unsaddled old Whisk and checked her tie rope before he walked back up the little path to the mine's mouth. Once at the campsite, he happily stood over his plunder. Four trips it had taken him, and he'd made sure to cover his tracks on the last trek up from the road. A smooth piece of wood drawn in a careful line had fixed the wheel tracks where his boots and the boxes had crossed them. A handful of brush whisked carefully over the dust and gravel at the site had taken care of his heel and toe marks. And at the last, a tumbleweed dragged behind the mare had obliterated her hoofprints.

It had done the trick, but then, he'd done this before. The stage, for instance, was always bumping off stray hat boxes or drummers' sales kits, but mostly, he just let those lay unless there was something worthwhile to be had. Sooner or later somebody official would ride out and pick up the ones still on the road, and scratch their heads over the ones that had "disappeared."

He was fairly certain that if anybody came looking for these particular crates, they'd ride right past the place where they'd bounced off the wagon, and

would never be the wiser. He'd even picked up
every last splinter of the broken box.

There hadn't been any sweets, and that was a rotten shame if you asked him. But there had been
something better—a whole crate full of brand-
spanking-new Winchesters, a crate filled with car-
tridges boxes, and one smaller, unmarked crate that
he hadn't seen from the distance. The crate with the
rifles had busted wide open, which had caused all
the trips. But the one with the ammunition had held.
He figured they could always use ammunition, what
with every mother's son in the territory taking potshots at them, and they could sell the rifles.

Drummond McLean wouldn't need them. *Didn't*
need them, more like. That was the gospel according
to Skunky. The crates had been addressed to Mr. D.
McLean at the Daisy Cutter Mine, and Skunky figured McLean and his bunch were trouble enough
without new Winchesters in their hands.

Squatting, he picked up the last splinters from the
Winchester crate and threw them on the fire, where
the others were being slowly consumed. He poured
himself another cup of coffee and sat all the way
down. He'd already put the rifles and the ammunition crate inside the mine, away from prying eyes,
but he wanted a look-see at what was in the third
box.

He stuck a pick between the box and the lid and
began to lever it off. The lip popped, and he put
down his pick and pulled it free bare-handed. Inside,
atop a mound of excelsior, was a folded sheet of
paper, which he pulled out and read.

"Dear Mr. McLean," it said, "I am enclosing a few 'frills' for the boys—at no extra charge to you— including the latest Dusty Rhodes, just out. I don't imagine that you have the second one there yet, but I have some connections with the publisher and thus have obtained a handful. I also have a friend with Peach Tree Canning, the evidence of which association is enclosed herein. Yours Very Sincerely, A. P. Musgrave, Esq."

Skunky squinted at the note, read it again, then tossed it too on the fire. He began to dig through the packing material.

Books. Goddamn books! The dime and half-dime kind, the big ones that a kid could fold in half and carry in his back pocket. There were a couple of Panhandle Slims, some Buffalo Bills, one Dead Eye and the Kid, and several John Slocums, those being three copies of *Death Rides a Spotted Stallion*.

Skunky scratched his head, but didn't give it much further thought. Instead, he kept digging. Books, books, and more books, and then he came to the mother lode.

Fruit! Tinned fruit! There were peaches and apples and candied plums, a dozen bright cans of them. The books forgotten and strewn about him in the dust, he reached into the crate with a gnarled hand and pulled out a tin of peaches, hefting its syrupy weight as it sloshed. He fumbled for his pocketknife, jabbed it into the lid, and began to saw happily, drooling all the while.

● ● ●

"He bought out Rose?" Jamaica said for the second time. Her eyes bugged out like a heifer that had just been poleaxed. It was not, Slocum thought, her most attractive expression. "Tom Malloy, you didn't tell me that!"

Big Tom shrugged his shoulders. "Didn't give me time, Jamaica. But stop yelling. I'm telling you now, aren't I?"

"Who's yelling!" Jamaica shouted. There was high color in her cheeks, and her nostrils were flared. Jamaica's Irish was getting the better of her, and Slocum figured he'd best speak up before she started throwing crockery. Sassafras, who was obviously wiser than either himself or Big Tom, had already slipped out the kitchen's swinging door.

"Calm down, Mudge," Slocum said softly, in a voice both comforting and firm.

Tom screwed up his face. "Who's Mudge?"

Slocum ignored him. He took Jamaica's arm and said, "Just hush and let Tom finish the story." When she opened her mouth to argue, he added, "It'll be all right. I'll take care of it."

He was lying, because he wasn't at all certain that it was anything he *could* take care of. But he guessed he'd said it convincingly enough, because she closed her mouth with a *click* and sat back, waiting.

"Now?" asked Tom, who had started and stopped so many times that Slocum figured he must be dizzy.

"Now," said Slocum.

"Like I said," Tom began again, "McLean bought

out Rose. Well, bought her out or elbowed her out, I'm not sure which."

Jamaica snorted.

"She's packing as we speak," Tom went on. "Hell, she might be gone by now. Half of her girls've already hit the road. She signed the place over last night or this morning, depending on whose story you listen to. He's got those two weasels of his scouring the streets for new girls to take the place of the ones that quit, and Tiger Forbush is going to run it for him."

Slocum noticed that Jamaica sniffed derisively at the mention of Tiger. She saw him eyeing her, and explained, "Tiger Forbush and Harley Hobbs. They're McLean's minions, and a couple of lower, more sniveling little butt-holes you're never likely to meet. Harley's a joke, but Tiger . . ." She paused thoughtfully, her brow creasing. "I've got a feelin' that Tiger's responsible for a lot of the trouble in town."

"I swan," Tom said, "McLean's bound and determined to own the whole damn town, my mine included. It'd serve the bastard right if he did end up with all of it, and the entire citizenry moved out just to spite him." He leaned back, his eyes twinkling. "I'd like to see that." He ran his thumb and index finger through the air, as if blocking a headline. "Drummond McLean, Emperor of Exactly Zip-Squat Nothin'."

Slocum, however, leaned forward. "And he's tryin' to get his hands on your mine too?"

Big Tom nodded. "The Bum Nugget. I'm pretty

sure there's ore down there—I mean, I'm already hitting hints of it—but since I've only got myself and Skunky to work it and McLean's got thirty men . . ." He scowled. "McLean owns the Daisy Cutter Mine, east of me, and I got a pretty fair idea that he's following that vein of his due west. Pretty soon he's gonna be smack under my claim, Slocum. Can't prove it, but like I said, I've got a strong feeling. His men have been taking potshots at Skunky and me, and they've driven off every man I've hired to help us out. That's why I came into town today. They ran off the last one during the night. They've tried to burn me out once, and I've got another strong feeling that they're gonna try again. Maybe not burning, but something—"

"Could we talk about *my* problem?" Jamaica cut in a little huffily.

"Seems to me you've both got the same problem," Slocum said thoughtfully. "Drummond McLean."

"And what are "we" going to do about it?" she asked, folding her arms across her bosom with a *swish* of silk.

Slocum didn't answer her, but turned instead to Big Tom. "You find anybody willin' to work your mine?"

Big Tom shook his head in disgust. "Even the damn drunks turned me down. They're all scared shitless of McLean. Why?"

Slocum turned back to Jamaica. "You reckon the town whores could band together for more than five minutes?"

Jamaica just stared at him.

Slocum said, "Mudge, I want you to send out your gals and have them round up every whore in town. The street gals, Rose's gals, every skirt and bustle that works this town. Can they all fit in here?"

With obvious misgivings, Jamaica said, "Maybe in the parlor and the hall if everybody stands up and packs in. But why, Slocum?"

"Stop askin' questions. How many altogether?"

"Fifty, maybe sixty. Subtracting the gals who've already left town or ended up at the undertakers."

Slocum turned to Big Tom. "You ever thought of issuing stock in that mine of yours?"

Big Tom tucked his chin and stared up from beneath his hat brim. "Huh?"

The kitchen door swung a few inches open and Sassafras stuck her head in. Grinning wide, she said, "I'll send the ladies out pronto. You're just as smart in the flesh as you are in that book of yours, John Slocum." Her head disappeared and the door swung closed.

"What in the blue blazes are you two *talking* about?" Jamaica demanded.

"I'm still tryin' to figure out who Mudge is," Big Tom muttered.

Miranda listened, scribbled frantically, while Slocum outlined his plan, and by the time Tom Malloy had agreed and left with a list in his hand—and a good-sized crowd of outrageously dressed women had begun to crowd into Jamaica's Pleasure Barge—her mind was made up.

She straightened, unbuttoned the few top buttons

at her neck, repinned her hat at what she hoped was a jaunty angle, and sauntered inside with the rest of them, trusting that she'd be lost in the crowd.

She was. Only one woman eyed her and asked, "New in town?"

"Sure am," she replied. "Name's Miranda." Then quickly, she added, "Miranda the Minx," as an afterthought.

"Slow Nell," said the other woman, a brassy blonde, and stuck out her hand. As Miranda shook it, she said, "You sure don't dress the part, Miranda. And you picked a helluva time to land in Twin Buttes."

"Guess so," Miranda replied. Her stomach was full of butterflies with their wings fully a-flap. Why, she'd never done anything so bold in her life! To think she was standing right here, in an actual house of ill repute, surrounded by a wild-colored sea of plumed and bobbing hats on the heads of Twin Buttes's soiled doves! And not fifteen feet away from Slocum, who was just stepping up to the second riser of the stairs and raising his hand for silence.

"Ladies!" he said. "Ladies, if I could have your attention?"

The room quieted. Miranda had lost count at fifty-three. By her estimation, there were well over sixty women packed into the parlor and hallway. Jamaica had vastly underestimated the number left in town.

"Everybody knows Drum McLean is out to take over the whoring trade in Twin Buttes," Slocum began, and suddenly the room was filled with angry shouts and the rattle of cheap jewelry, and fists waving above the plumed hats.

Slocum held up his hand once more, and the silence came again.

"Well, he's out to get Tom Malloy's mine too, and probably a lot of other places I just haven't heard about yet. If you ladies are willin', I've got a plan that I think will take care of McLean. It might just get you out of the sportin' trade too. Not that I got anything against whores, mind you," he added with a grin, and few of the women laughed.

Miranda's lips pursed, however. Honestly. Slocum was supposed to be above that sort of thing. At least, the fictional Slocum was. In just one short day, the chink between the real Slocum and the Slocum she'd made up had widened to a chasm.

The blonde next to her, Slow Nell, shouted, "Who are you, anyway, mister? Why should we believe anything you got to say?"

It was a good question. Miranda knew that Slocum had class and was an honest customer—she didn't believe she could have been mistaken about that too—and it seemed obvious that Jamaica knew it. But these women didn't know him from Adam.

"How do we know you ain't workin' for McLean?" called another prostitute, hidden from Miranda.

Miranda watched as Jamaica stepped up the stairs to stand beside Slocum. "Ladies!" Jamaica shouted over the growing rumble of discontent. "Ladies, please! This man is John Slocum. He's as honest as they come. I've known him for ten years, and I can vouch for him."

"Why, Jamaica!" called a woman from the corner. "You must'a knowed him when you was seven then!"

Laughter followed, and then somebody asked, "Hey! Would he be the same Slocum from that book?"

Miranda felt a bloom of pride, but on the stairs, Slocum colored angrily.

"The same," said Jamaica.

A new buzz and hum swept over the crowd.

"Quiet!" Slocum boomed.

The throng fell into silence immediately, and every eye in it was on him. "Now, it seems to me that Twin Buttes is a fair piece from any other civilized town. Far enough, anyway, that it'd take quite a while for word to get around that the town was in need of new soiled doves. Even longer for them to get here."

"Don't need no new whores!" shouted somebody in the back.

Slocum ignored the heckling. "Now, me and Big Tom and Jamaica here have come up with an idea. What we're proposin' is that you all leave town. Go on strike, sort of." Before the crowd had a chance to question the wisdom of this, he quickly added, "You ain't gonna go far, and you won't be gone long. Just long enough to give this town a taste of what it's like to be without the comfortin' arms of womenfolk. And you won't lose money on the deal either, in case you were gonna ask." He shot a look

at a brunette in the first row, and she closed her
mouth without asking her question.

Miranda, however, knew what Slocum was going
to propose—after all, she'd been standing outside
the window while they hatched the scheme—but she
had to admire the way Slocum was telling it to this
mob. Masterful control, that was what she'd call it
in her next book.

"Now, what we've got in mind is for y'all to go
out to Tom Malloy's mine, the Bum Nugget," Slocum continued. "Tom's roundin' up supplies right
now. You probably all know that Tom's had trouble
out at his mine."

Several of the women nodded, and Miranda heard
a woman murmur, "Poor Tom."

"McLean's after him too," Slocum said, "in case
I didn't already say that. It's got so that Big Tom
can't even hire anybody to work out there. Mc-
Lean's scared them all off. Well, Tom and I figure
that the sportin' ladies of Twin Buttes are a site
braver and stronger and steadier than all the hired
diggers in the world."

Slow Nell piped up again. "You askin' us to actually work that mine, Slocum? You tetched in the
head?"

"It's a really good idea, Nell!" Miranda whispered. "Just listen to him!"

But the crowd was growing restless again, and
Slocum had to signal for silence. It was a while before he got it.

"Nobody's forcin' you to work the mine," he said.
"But if you decide to, if we can help Big Tom tunnel

down to the mother lode, every woman who helps—
and I mean who really works and doesn't just carry
one rock up the shaft—will get a one-percent share
in the mine profits. In perpetuity. Well, for as long
as the mine pays out anyway. And one percent of a
rich strike is a whole helluva lot of money. Tom
tells me he and Skunky have already blasted a good
bit."

"Yeah?" shouted Slow Nell. "What if it don't pay
out nothin' at all?"

"Then at least you will have got McLean off your
backs," Slocum replied.

Miranda waited for someone to ask Slocum just
exactly how this would be accomplished. She
wanted him to explain it again, because she didn't
fully understand it herself. But nobody asked, and
she was loath to draw attention to herself by raising
the question.

"Come on, ladies," coaxed Jamaica. "We're all in,
or it's not going to work. Besides, any gal who's
still in town once we leave is bound to be worked
to death inside six hours. I say the smart money goes
with us—or else gets the hell out of town."

As one, the ladies in the crowd giggled and
laughed, and a woman in the back called, "Aw,
turds. I'm in."

"Me too," said another, and another.

"I broke rocks one year with my brother, 'fore he
got lynched," said a strawberry blonde in a bright
blue getup. "It ain't so hard."

"And it sure beats endin' up dead in a back alley,"
offered a dishwater blonde.

Miranda nodded. Despite herself, she was beginning to feel a real sense of camaraderie with these
women.

"Let's get a vote," said Slocum.

"All in favor?" said Jamaica.

A cheer of yeses and ayes and you bet, sugars
rose up.

"All opposed?" said Jamaica, once the crowd had
quieted.

There was absolute silence.

"The ayes have it then," Slocum said with a grin.
"Now, if anybody knows a gal that was, um, otherwise occupied while we were holdin' this little
meeting, round her up and tell her what's happening.
Everybody who's goin' meet back here at three
o'clock. We'll have buggies and wagons ready to
haul y'all out to the Bum Nugget. And bring what
you need, but bring as little as you can."

"That means no matched and monogrammed sets
of steamer trucks, Rose," Jamaica said, and arched
a brow at an extremely overweight blonde at the
front of the crowd. Miranda took her to be the in-
famous Rose—of Rose's Pleasure Palace—whom
McLean had just forced out of business.

Miranda wouldn't have wanted to run into Rose
in a dark alley. Heavily made up, she was barely
five feet tall and easily weighed over three hundred
pounds, with a deep frown line between her brows
that made it look as though she were scowling all
the time. She was older, but Miranda wouldn't have
hazarded a guess as to just how *much* older.

Rose carped, "Screw you, Jamaica," and crossed

her arms over a bosom the size of a newborn calf. She made no move to waddle out the door, though.

"All right, ladies," Jamaica said brightly. "Get crackin'!"

8

"They're doing what?" Drum McLean shouted, and it was a few seconds before he realized that Harley couldn't talk, what with McLean's fingers digging into his neck. He released the chubby little man, and let him fall, red-faced and gasping, to the polished clay tiles of his office floor.

"They're leavin'!" Harley finally managed raggedly. "All of 'em!" He was still down on all fours, like a dog. Well, he wasn't a very well-trained dog if he couldn't even handle a few whores!

McLean booted him in the backside, and he went sprawling. "Where the hell are they going?" McLean demanded. "There's no place to go, goddamn it! And where's Tiger?"

Harley scrambled across the office floor and cowered in a corner. "Don't know, Boss," he said, and when McLean raised a hand to his face, Harley ducked. Twelve feet away, and the fat little coward was still cringing! For not the first time, McLean thought that he should have hired actual men instead of these blithering idiots. Pliable was good, and these two fools were certainly that, but he should have considered backbone.

"They was just pullin' out from in front of Jamaica's place when I seen 'em," Harley offered in a strangled little voice. He rubbed at his neck. McLean could see his thumbprints all the way across the room. "About six or seven wagons' worth of 'em," Harley continued. "I tried to stop 'em."

McLean arched a brow. "How?"

Harley sat up a little straighter. "Why, I went up there and I said, 'You whores get back to business and stop this foolishness.' I was real firm."

"And?"

"And one'a the men kicked me right smack in the chest!" Harley answered indignantly, then grew thoughtful. "He was on his horse, elsewise I 'spect he would'a kicked me in the knee. . . ."

McLean ground his teeth. "What men? Who was with them?"

Harley picked up his hat and craned himself up from the floor, using a filing cabinet to steady himself. "Big Tom Malloy. And some other fella. Ain't never seen him afore. The stranger was the one what kicked me."

McLean walked to the coatrack and pulled down his hat. "This stranger. Was he tallish? About six-one, six-two? Green eyes?"

Harley nodded rapidly. "That's him. Them green eyes practically drill holes in you. He's a real tough-lookin' hombre, and ridin' a red Palouse horse."

McLean didn't recognize the horse, but he knew who that tough-looking sonofabitch had been. He didn't quickly forget some no-name drifter who had told him off in his own town!

He settled his hat on his head angrily and gave
Harley a shove. "C'mon," he commanded, and
opened the rear door.

"Where we goin'?" Harley asked meekly as he
stumbled through the door and into the alley.

McLean followed him out. "Rose's old place."

"But Rose was with 'em!" Harley peeped. Then
his cheeks bunched up with a mean little smile.
"That wagon was leanin' so far to the side it looked
like it was gonna flip right over. Crikey, she's a fat
'un!"

"Shut up, Harley."

McLean marched out of the alley and up the street
with Harley trotting behind. The town looked different. It was the distinct absence of the women that
did it. Normally, there'd be at least two whores on
every block of the main street. They were there, po-
sitioned like sentries, twenty-four hours a day,
lounging nonchalantly against the mouths of alleys
or strutting their wares in a more obvious fashion.
Now there were none.

The closer to Rose's place he got, the more Mc-
Lean felt an incensed heat rising up his neck. Tiger
had better be there, all right, and he'd better have
kept Rose's whores—now *his* whores—where they
belonged!

But when McLean pushed open the gaily painted
front door of Rose's place, there wasn't a soul in
evidence. He walked through, going quickly from
room to room with Harley at his heels. The air held
the lingering stench of cheap perfume. A still-warm
pot of coffee sat at the back of the kitchen stove,

and an African violet had been brushed to the floor in someone's hurry, its spilled soil still moist. Angrily, he ground the violet under his boot heel.

He took the stairs two at a time. The upstairs chifforobes were still half filled with clothing, but every room showed signs of swift packing, with items strewn about haphazardly. He couldn't find a single valise or carpetbag in the whole place.

In the middle of the upstairs hall, he stopped stockstill. "Harley!" he shouted.

Harley, who at least had the sense to keep his mouth shut during the inspection, said, "Yeah, Boss?"

"Where the hell's Tiger?"

Harley shrugged.

"Goddamn it!" McLean said through gritted teeth. "He was supposed to be here. He was supposed to be in charge!"

The day was going nothing like it should have. In fact, his future, quite suddenly, was looking nothing like he'd imagined, and he had an overpowering feeling that he had Big Tom Malloy and that stranger to thank for it. He should have put Malloy out of commission months ago. He shouldn't have fiddled around and tried to be nice about it. He should have taken sterner measures.

Well, he'd take care of it now, that was for certain sure. But first, he had to calm the hell down and find out where those whores had taken off to. And he had to find Tiger.

He straightened his shoulders, smoothed his vest, gave his coat a tug, and ran a finger over his mustache. "All right," he said, more to himself than Harley.

"What's that, Boss?" Harley asked. The fat little sonofabitch was just too goddamn eager for words, wasn't he?

McLean sighed. Slowly, he said, "Which way were they headed?"

"Who's that?"

McLean closed his eyes for a moment, lest he punch Harley into next week. At the moment, like it or not, he needed him.

"The whores, you idiot. And Tom Malloy. And the stranger."

Harley nodded. "Oh! South, on the road down to the mine."

The road down to the mine didn't mean much, because that road, ragged thing that it was, went past half the mines in Twin Buttes, then curved southwest on around to Hoople Flats. But Hoople Flats was nearly thirty miles away.

McLean figured the whores weren't going to stop at any mines. They'd have to go through Hoople Flats and on to Kingston, the first town of any size with a population big enough to support a few more prostitutes. With the load he imagined those six or seven wagons were carrying, they'd be lucky to make it to Hoople Flats in two days. He'd have plenty of time to catch them. And when he did, those whores would be handing out free favors to his men for weeks.

He'd even let Harley do with them what he

pleased. That'd teach those thankless slatterns to kite out on *his* town!

Without another word, he stepped forward and walked down the stairs, boots thudding on the carpeted risers, and turned into the front hall. And there, he heard a muffled sound.

"Harley," he said, pointing, and Harley opened the door of the house's sole closet.

Tiger tumbled out, naked as the day he was born and trussed like a Christmas goose. Except that instead of ropes of twine, he was bound up in tightly knotted, colorful scarves and a bright purple boa.

"Jesus," McLean muttered as Harley tugged the gag from Tiger's mouth and began to work on the knotted scarves.

"Explain," McLean said.

And Tiger Forbush, the brave killer of whores, the man with the ready blade—at least, up until this morning, when McLean had taken it away from him—actually sniffled. "It ain't my fault, Boss," he wailed as Harley worked at the knots. "I was upstairs with Janette when all of a damn sudden they came at me!"

"Who? Big Tom Malloy?"

"The whores!" yelped Tiger before he twisted sharply toward Harley and snapped, "Careful! You don't have to take my wrist off!"

McLean just waited. He was too blasted mad to say anything.

"They pounced on me, that's what they did," Tiger said as his hands came free. He started to work at the scarves binding his naked legs. "There must'a been a hundred of 'em—a thousand—and they was all hittin' me and latchin' on to my arms and legs, and they put a pillow over my face, and bit my ear, and—" He stopped suddenly and felt at his left earlobe, chin quivering. "It bleedin'?" he asked Harley.

McLean ground his teeth. "Get up," he said curtly.

"But my feet ain't—"

"Get up!"

Tiger, with Harley's assistance, rose to his feet, a movement somewhat impeded by his ankles, which were still bound together by a final silk scarf of peacock blue. He stood naked and weaving, covered in gooseflesh, with both his bony hands cupped over his crotch. "Yeah, Boss?"

McLean just stood there for a moment, unable to give voice to the anger he was feeling at the moment. He finally gave his head a terse shake. "Get dressed," he said curtly, then marched past them and out onto the street.

He kicked the first dog that crossed his path.

Once they were clear of the town and things had settled down to a dull roar, Slocum was finally able to get an accurate head count. In all, forty-one women had opted to go to the Bum Nugget and try their luck. He supposed the rest had hopped the stage—a frightening thought, and he sure hoped they hadn't all tried to cram into one coach!—or lit out on their own. He half-wished that Rose had chosen to flee as well. Not because he had anything against her, but because he had strong doubts that she could even waddle down into the mine, let alone work it, without having a heart seizure. She also took up a lot of room. The team pulling her wagon was already shining with sweat.

Goosing Chaco into a slow jog, he took inventory of the party as he rode to the front of the line. He had to admit that it was probably the most colorful crew that had ever hoped to work a claim. Scarlet and teal and bright purple and pink plumes jutted from hats and shivered with the jarring motion of the wagons, colorful parasols waved jauntily in the air, and beneath the hats and parasols were shawls and frocks of every loud color in the rainbow. Except for one, he noticed as he rode past.

He turned his head back for a second look. Plain, dull green, nearly gray, and buttoned right up to the chin. The wearer didn't look like any whore he'd ever seen before.

And then, after he'd ridden clear up to the front of the line, he suddenly remembered her. She was the gal he'd bumped into in the hotel lobby, the one who'd known his name.

Now, that was downright curious. First, that she was a whore. He'd had pegged her for a saleswoman. She seemed too prissy to even walk past a sporting house without averting her eyes or some damned thing, but there she was, plain as day, in a wagon load of cats! And how the hell had she known who he was?

He scratched the back of his head, and his hat wiggled a little. Well, maybe the desk clerk had said something to her.

He didn't mull it over any further, because just then Big Tom rode up beside him.

"I count forty-one," Big Tom said.

Slocum nodded. "Same here."

"I don't mind saying that I'm relieved."

"Why's that?"

Big Tom fiddled with his reins. "Because you said there were over sixty hens at the meeting! Why, if I gave each of them a one-percent interest, I'd be left with less than forty percent! They could band together and kick me off my own claim!"

Slocum smiled. "Couldn't kick you off it exactly."

"Well, they could tell me what to do!" Big Tom said a little indignantly. "Same damn thing."

Slocum let him stew, and trained his gaze on the horizon once again. He'd been checking ever since they left town, north, south, east, and west. There was no sign of anyone or anything, save for a few hawks riding the high wind currents and a coyote slinking through the brush in the distance, to the west. He just caught a glimpse of the tip of its tail.

"How much longer before we get to this mine of yours?" he asked.

Big Tom, who had been fingering the pocket into which he'd stuck that letter, looked up. "Maybe three hours, at this speed. I suppose we could get a trot out of 'em, but that team pulling Rose . . ."

"I know," said Slocum. He considered asking Big Tom just exactly what had been in that letter, what it was that had turned him white, but thought better of it. He didn't know Tom well enough. And even if he'd known him for years, there were some things that you just didn't ask. Still, curiosity gnawed at him.

Three hours was a long time to think about something and not be able to ask one simple question. Well, he'd better do something about getting them there faster, hadn't he?

"Aw, shit," he muttered before he held up his hand and shouted, "Whoa up!"

It took another five minutes before all the drivers understood that he meant them, and within that time they had two near-collisions. But they finally got stopped, and he loped back to the wagon in which Rose was perched in all her blue and orange satin glory, a tiny parasol held high over her bulk. She took up one bench seat all by herself, and her belly nearly brushed the back of the seat in front of her.

He tipped his hat to her, then turned to the three girls sitting on the seat in front of her. "Ladies, if two of you wouldn't mind switching wagons? This team is a little tired, and we want to make better time."

The girls grumbled, but they got down, leaving a little twig of a gal, dressed all in canary yellow, alone on the front seat to drive the team. Rose's face had gone bright red, and the furrow between her brows had deepened dramatically. "Are you sayin' I weigh too much, you cocksucker?"

Despite himself, Slocum flinched just a little. He had expected a lot of things from her, but not exactly that.

He smiled and leaned forward, balancing himself

on his saddle horn, and said softly, "No, ma'am, you're saying it, but I guess it's just as true either way."

The nastiest expression that he'd ever seen on a female face came over Rose's features. "I'll have you know that I still have a twenty-four-inch waist, you pig-screwer," she snarled.

He didn't answer. He simply reined his horse away, made certain that the three other girls were spread out among three other wagons, and then rode forward, shaking his head. He didn't even think to look at that little gal again, the one who had known his name.

A twenty-four-inch waist? Right. By that measuring tape, he was only two feet tall.

"The old bitch giving you trouble?" Big Tom asked once Slocum reached the front of the column.

"Wipe that smirk off your face," Slocum said, and signaled for the column to start forward again.

9

Miranda thought they would never reach the mine, and when they did, she wished that they hadn't. For some reason, she'd imagined that there would at least be some form of shelter. But no. Nothing but a hole cut into the side of a gentle, undulating hill. That and rocks, rocks, and more rocks. There wasn't even a scrawny tree to shade her from the sun.

"Dear, oh, dear," she muttered for perhaps the third time, but on this occasion she was overheard.

"Oh, it ain't so bad, Miss Minx," said a voice behind her. She turned to find her friend from the meeting, Slow Nell.

"But where will we sleep?" Miranda asked, hearing the pathetic quality in her own voice, but unable to hold it back. She had certainly ridden through a great deal of landscape like this while she was following Slocum, but there was a great deal of difference between riding past the Devil's own country and actually trying to sustain life in it.

Especially when that life was yours.

There were a million questions on her mind, things that she hadn't even considered when she was back in town, standing in Jamaica's parlor with those dozens of other women. Where would they bathe or cook? Where in heaven's name would they go to relieve themselves?

Well, they probably wouldn't have to relieve themselves, because she couldn't imagine that they'd hauled enough water with them to see to the needs of the horses, let alone themselves. What on earth had she gotten herself into?

Teetering on the edge of hysterics, she felt her knees begin to buckle.

A hand pulled her back up before she could sink more that a few inches, though.

"Look there," said Slow Nell, and pointed. "Slocum and Big Tom are already gettin' a handle on it."

Weakly, Miranda followed the line of Nell's finger down the gravelly brush-dotted slope. Slocum and Big Tom were indeed doing something, but she couldn't tell what.

When she looked blankly back at Slow Nell, the woman explained, "Tent stakes, honey. They're gonna rig up some tents for us. And Pansy says there's a spring on the other side of this hill, so we won't die of thirst."

She smiled warmly at Miranda, and Miranda felt hope returning. Of *course* there was a spring. Of *course* Slocum was building them shelter. She hadn't invented him entirely. He was a resourceful man, a clever man. He would take care of them.

"Hey, Skunky," Slow Nell said, rather shyly, to someone behind Miranda, and Miranda turned to look.

A little old man stood down below, a man as sun-baked as the land, with a thin shock of white hair poking from beneath his hat. He was paused in the middle of unharnessing their team, the buckle dangling from his hand.

He colored slightly, and doffed his shapeless hat. "Afternoon, Miss Nell. I'm right pleased to see you come up with the rest, even if it was sure a big surprise to me."

Slow Nell smiled for all the world like the Mona Lisa. "I just bet it was. You gonna be able to stand all us hens cluttering up your digs, Skunky?"

Miranda thought he looked as if he was actually in a state of shock over it—and who wouldn't be a little shocked to see nine crammed wagons coming right to your doorstep when you only expected one rider? But he said, "You won't be no trouble, Miss Nell. Tom, he explained it. Sorta. Although I'll be diddly-damned if . . . Excuse me, ma'am. I didn't mean to talk harsh."

Nell opened her mouth to say something in reply, but just then Big Tom shouted, "You about finished unhitching those teams, Skunky?"

"One more," he shouted back, then tipped his hat to Miranda and Slow Nell again. "Best be gettin' on with it." He leaned in toward Nell, and said softly, "Mayhap tonight, we can . . . I mean . . . the two of us can, um . . ."

"We'll see, Skunky," Slow Nell said with a little wink, and Skunky's face nearly split in two with a grin.

"Yes'm, that'd be fine, just fine," he said as he

slipped free the last harness buckle and led the team from their traces and away, across the long slope and past the place where Slocum and Big Tom— and now a handful of women—were driving stakes into the hard ground.

"Old friend?" asked Miranda, once he was out of earshot.

Surprisingly, Slow Nell blushed. "Oh, he's my sweetie-dumplin'."

Slocum tossed the canteen to Big Tom, wiped his mouth with the back of his hand, and said, "All right, ladies. Let's get this canvas up!"

It was getting to be late in the day, and they were working on the last of the makeshift shelters. Most of the women had pitched in, one way or another. Jamaica and her girls had helped with the first two tents, and then let a new crew spell them while they got settled in and started the cook fires going.

He gazed up again, memorizing the immediate terrain. The Bum Nugget was carved out of a series of hills that had probably once been the west wall of a wide canyon. To the east, a wide, flat stretch of desert led to a similar stretch of hills in the distance. Drum McLean's mine lay in the hills beyond.

But Slocum was more interested in the west, and the land he was standing on. He was roughly halfway up the incline, with the tents at his back, and the wagons and the picket line were clustered father down and to the south. There was a small ramada to shade the horses, although he thought he and Tom had best get busy building another one, however makeshift it might be.

Slightly uphill and also to the south was the entrance of the mine itself. The forces of nature had created this particular hill with lots of little nooks and crannies, and Tom and Skunky had started digging in a place where the hill actually made a bit of an L shape. They piled their diggings right outside it, so that the land was flat for at least ten feet or so. From the mine's mouth, Slocum would be able to survey most all of their camp, with the exception of the horses.

Up above him was desert—a combination of rock and earth, paloverde and scrub—that rose up a little like a layer cake. The women were building fires at a point roughly level with the mine. Further up, about halfway to the sawtoothed top, a rock formation snaked horizontally across the hill's surface like fancy frosting trim applied by a six-year-old. If Slocum didn't miss his guess, and he seldom did, that line of rocks—and more importantly, the soil behind it—had weathered enough that he could get the whole crew behind it and to safety, if necessary.

He gave a terse nod. If McLean decided to do something stupid, this was just about as good a place to be as any.

There were women everywhere. Big women, tiny women, fat women, skinny women. Except for Rose—who sat on the hillside, that silly little parasol shading her wide, scowling face—they all hauled water, made pallets on the hard desert floor beneath canvas props, prepared to bake bread, soaked beans, made coffee, and did a dozen other things. He supposed that they were so busy settling in that the full force of what they were doing hadn't had a chance to sink in.

A strike. That's what it was, pure and simple. He'd heard of miners' strikes and railroad strikes, but try though he might, he'd never heard of a strike by whores. Strikes sometimes turned into riots, sometimes ended up with a lot of people getting killed. That's why he'd moved the women out of town. Not that a whores' strike was of such great monetary importance, he supposed—unless it was to Drummond McLean—but it was certainly of more immediate importance to the men of Twin Buttes. He wasn't taking any chances.

"There, almost got it," he said, and snugged the last grommet to a spike in the ground.

"Finally!" breathed the brassy blonde beside him, and she brushed away a stray lock of hair. She was looking a mite disheveled, as were all the women by this time. "Thought we'd never get this sonofabitch up!" And then she stuck out her hand. "Slow Nell's my name."

He took it, and she gave him a firm handshake. She was somewhat older than the majority of the women, but was still hanging together just fine.

"You don't need to tell me who you are, Slocum," she added when he started to open his mouth. "I read all about you. It's an honor to be shepherded by such a celebrated man."

"Ma'am," he began, "I'm not—"

"Sure you are," she said, as if that closed the subject then and there. She shook out her skirts. "You're in books. I read it! Well, partway. You need us for anything else?"

Slocum shook his head.

"Fine then. I'm gonna go get myself cleaned up. Now, where's that Miranda got to?"

Followed by the four other women who had been helping with the tent, she wandered off toward the cook fires.

"Just checked the road again," Big Tom said. He had just walked up.

"And?"

"Still nothing. You meet Slow Nell?"

Slocum nodded. He was watching her. She'd gone past the fires and walked up to that gal in the dull green dress, who was seated on a rock and looked to be scribbling something on a pad. She was bent close to the paper to take advantage of the fading light.

"Skunky's sweet on her," said Tom.

"Sweet on who?" Slocum asked in surprise. He'd been thinking about the little honey blonde in green.

"Slow Nell! Who else did you think I meant? She's the only reason he didn't pitch a fit when we showed up with all these hens. I suppose I'll hear about it later, though," Big Tom added sheepishly.

"Where is the Skunky anyhow?" Slocum asked. He was still staring at that little blonde. She didn't belong here, not at all.

"Digging a privy." He pointed down the hill, to a point halfway between the remuda and the tents.

Sure enough, there was Skunky, his shovel busy and the pale dirt flying.

At last, Slocum looked over at Tom. "A what?"

"Well, we can't have all these women squatting in the brush, for God's sake! I told him to dig it down as deep as he could, and then take some scrap lumber from the timber pile and make a bench seat with a hole in the middle to set over it. We got any canvas left?"

Slocum pointed to one of the wagons down the hill. There was a small amount of canvas remaining, sewn into the shape of a pup tent, which he had planned to rig for himself. He figured he and Jamaica deserved a little privacy.

But Big Tom said, "Good! I'll see if I can't rig that around to make a modesty screen for the outhouse."

So much for that. Well, he and Jamaica could find another place. They would, if he had anything to say about it.

Big Tom turned to go and fetch his canvas, but before he could, Slocum caught his arm. "Who's that little gal Slow Nell's talkin' to?"

"Damned if I know," Big Tom replied. "She doesn't really . . . fit in, does she?"

Slocum remembered something his mother used to say about a petunia growing in an onion patch, but refrained from mentioning it. These other gals sure weren't onions, but the little blonde was an entirely different breed nonetheless.

"No, she doesn't belong," Slocum said at last. "You never saw her before?"

"Never. I would've remembered." Big Tom cast a glance toward the road below. "How soon do you think he'll come?"

"Tomorrow," said Slocum. "He'll come tomorrow."

Big Tom sat with his back against a rock, his stomach full of good food. It was quite a change from his usual fare, since neither he nor Skunky could cook worth a hill of beans. He very nearly hadn't gotten any supper at all, because the impressive Mrs. Arnot, Jamaica's cook, and Edna Merle, Rose's scrawny little cook, had gotten into a donnybrook over the ingredients for the stew.

He didn't know the actual cause of it, because there were women screaming, "More carrots, you cow!" and "Ain't you never heard of beef?" and "This ain't fit for a chamber pot, let alone the pig trough!" and he couldn't exactly remember who had been hollering what. But he'd managed to get them calmed down, and dinner, all in all, had turned out past fine.

Skunky had gotten over his mad at being asked to dig the privy, and was sitting off to the side of the group with Slow Nell, talking shyly. Slow Nell seemed to be talking shyly too. He didn't know why Skunky didn't just marry her. Sure, she was about thirty years younger than he was, but that was common out here. Men often went through three or four wives.

Tom snorted. Worked them to death, more like, he thought. Well, Skunky had it coming. He hadn't even gone through the first one yet, as far as Tom knew.

And neither had *he*. Once again, he stroked his pocket, the one that contained Mad Hat's letter. He didn't want to read it again. He'd memorized it on the first reading, back in town. The words had practically burned themselves into his soul.

"Dear Tom," the letter had said in dark blue ink, written in a careful hand. "I just heard that Clementine's getting herself hitched to some greenhorn yahoo, just come out there from New York City if you can believe that. You'd think there weren't no gals east of the Mississip. The wedding's on the twenty-fifth, so get back there and stop it and talk some sense into her if you can. If you still want her, that is. Wouldn't blame you if you just said the hell with it and her. I'm sending this with a jasper by the name of Slocum, and if you don't write back and he don't bring it, he don't get the rest of his money. Let me know what day you got this on. If he don't get this to you by the fifteenth, then he also don't get the rest of his money." The letter was signed, "Your friend and hope-to-be future father-in-law, Mad Hat Crockett."

Tom sighed heavily. Slocum had brought the letter to him a couple of days early, all right, and if he hopped a stage within the next few days, he could make it out to San Francisco in time. But in time to do what? Break up Clementine's marriage? Beat this New York fiancé into a bloody pulp? Walk right in on the wedding, and when the preacher got to the

objections part, march up to the altar with his guns
drawn and kidnap her?

He couldn't even hear the sound of her voice anymore.

She didn't write. She hadn't, not once.

If he hadn't had that ivory-framed picture to look
at . . .

"This place taken?"

He looked up into the face of the blond girl, the
out-of-place girl, the girl dressed in drab green. In
spite of himself, he gulped. Up close, she was downright beautiful.

"No, ma'am," he said, remembering himself.
"Pull up a rock." There was enough light from the
cook fires and the smaller fires the women had built
that he could see a small, dark smudge on her skirts
as she sat down, and dark stains on her fingertips.

"Thank you," she said once she was settled. She
smiled at him. Not a come-hither smile, just a
friendly one. That was odd.

He cleared his throat and stuck out a hand. "Tom
Malloy. Everybody calls me Big Tom."

She took his hand and gave it a surprisingly firm
shake. "I know. I'm Miranda."

He didn't let go of her hand. Instead, he turned it
palm up, inspecting the smudges. "Ink?"

She pulled back immediately and folded her
hands in her lap. "Yes," she said, staring not at him,
but at the ground. "My, um, diary."

He chuckled. "Reckon you had a good bit to put
in it today. This is quite a deal, isn't it?"

She looked up again. She had light eyes, although

he couldn't exactly tell what color. They were kind eyes, though, and all of a sudden he had a nearly uncontrollable urge to just tell her everything, tell her about Clementine and Mad Hat and the idiot suitor from New York, tell her of his frustration over the mine and life in general, to just open a vein and let all his troubles spill out like so much foul blood.

There was something about her, something that made a man feel he could tell her anything, that she'd listen and understand and soothe him. Nobody had soothed him for a long time.

But he didn't tell her. Only babies needed to be soothed.

She said, "I'd like to believe him, wouldn't you?"

It took him a second to figure out that she was talking about Slocum. Before supper, he'd called everyone to attention and had made a brief speech telling everybody what they were supposed to do, and why they were doing it. He'd also said that they expected a visit from Drum McLean, although he had reassured everyone that there would be no violence.

Tom didn't believe that for one minute, and he had a feeling Slocum didn't either. He hadn't had a chance to talk to Slocum since, as Slocum had disappeared with Jamaica directly afterward.

And now that they were all out here, he didn't exactly know what he'd do if things came to violence. There were women here, for God's sake!

"You can believe him," Tom said steadily as he looked up into those eyes that said, *Tell me, tell me everything, tell Mama*. He corrected himself. "Well,

Drum McLean might threaten. He's good at that. But I don't think he'll really *do* anything."

Of this, he was suddenly fairly certain. Why, a man would have to be an idiot to murder forty-one women and three men. He'd have to be an idiot to even try to intimidate them. But then, that was what they expected McLean to do, wasn't it?

Miranda was far too well spoken for a crib girl, and too demurely dressed to be a sporting gal period. Even a fancy one. *Especially* a fancy one. But he couldn't just ask what her story was, and so he said, "Where you from, Miranda?"

"San Francisco," she replied matter-of-factly, and his heart sank. Here he'd almost forgotten about Clementine, at least for the moment, and she'd reminded him! When he didn't reply, she added, "Have you ever been there?"

"Once," he said glumly. "Once, a long time ago."

Drummond McLean sat on an empty powder keg in the opening of the Daisy Cutter Mine, his lead men grouped around him. The rest lounged outside, warming their hands at the fires or resting their weary bones.

"But Boss, these here are just rock-breakers mostly!" Tiger Forbush was saying.

From his attitude, McLean thought in disgust, *you'd never know I found him stark naked and tied with scarves in a closet this afternoon.*

He said, "They're bodies, Tiger. Now shut up and listen to your betters. Mordecai," he said, turning to the middle-aged but tough-looking gent beside Tiger, "is everybody armed with a new rifle? I need to make a good show."

He imagined thirty men riding after those ungrateful little harlots, thirty men each armed with a gleaming new Winchester. He pictured each and every man pressing the rifle butt to his thigh, and the barrels glinting in the sun. His own private army. That ought to scare the living shit out of those whores!

Mordecai thumbed back his hat, exposing pale hair, blond shot through with gray. "About them rifles, Mr. McLean. Josh brought that shipment in today, 'cept it was a few crates short. Them Winchesters we was supposed to get was most of the part that was missin'."

McLean's hands balled into fists. "What?"

Mordecai didn't flinch. "They were there when he loaded up. Josh had some trouble with the team, and he thinks the crates must'a got bumped off. I was gonna send a man to ride back up over the Hoople Flats road tomorrow."

McLean forced himself to relax, although it was difficult. He'd been there only a few hours, and already he felt gritty, as if the grime of the mine had wriggled its way into his clothing like a living thing. That was bad enough, but now to find out that the rifles were missing? If he was going to take out his anger on somebody, Mordecai Jones was not the man to pick. Standing beside Mordecai, Tiger smirked almost imperceptively, and McLean made a mental note to take it out on *him*. Later.

McLean said, "All right, Mordecai. Just find them. How are we armed otherwise?"

Mordecai turned to the man on his left. "Toby?"

The wiry little man said, "We got almost enough to go around. Priest and Jenkins and Handy Alf ain't got no side arms at all, and Forbush busted his all to hell a couple weeks ago tryin' to crack a walnut, but a few of the fellers got two."

When Mordecai furrowed his brow, Toby added, "Well, it were a piece'a-shit gun to begin with. Black powder and old as the hills. We got a couple men with two guns, like I said. They can share. Course, I got to tell you, Mr. McLean, it ain't gonna do much good. Most'a these fellers couldn't hit the side of a barn with a handful of gravel. Why, just last month Dutch Holstein had a rattler sneak up on him, and he emptied his pistol and didn't muss a scale on it. Finally had to hit it with a rock. Fanged the hit out of his boot, though . . ."

McLean sighed. "These are whores, Toby. Forty or fifty whores with only three men to guard them. I doubt if it will come to gunplay."

Mordecai said, "So it's Tom Malloy and who else? Skunky? He won't be much trouble."

McLean nodded. "Maybe Skunky, if they stopped to pick him up. They left town with a man named Slocum." That much, he had learned before he rode out here with Tiger and Harley.

Mordecai flinched, McLean thought. At least, Mordecai stood up straighter. "Slocum? John Slocum?"

Toby brightened. "Hey! That the feller in them

books we got in town a couple months back? You mean he's a real live person?"

"He's real, all right," Mordecai grumbled, and turned his back on the group, walking out into the darkness.

Now, that, McLean thought, *is very interesting.*

10

Slocum woke early. He lay there for a moment, thinking, while Jamaica slept on, curled beneath his arm. It was nearly dawn, and he figured that McLean might show up around nine or ten, depending on where he was riding from. Later if he came from town, sooner if he'd ridden out to his mine the night before. Either way, he'd get there.

McLean would most likely do nothing more than threaten and posture today, and he'd probably bring a few men to back him up. Slocum figured that they could put him off for a week, maybe longer, before McLean started applying serious pressure. Just how serious it was going to be would depend on just how irate—or how crazy—McLean was.

Frankly, Slocum didn't expect it to turn violent. After all, a fella would have to be plumb loco to open fire on forty-one women, especially unarmed women. He reminded himself that he, Big Tom, and Skunky might seem more like fair game to McLean, though, and without thinking, reached out to let his fingers brush the butts of his Colts.

Yes, McLean would come, but today's confrontation would be minor. The most important thing on today's agenda was the mine. Somehow, they had to get this mob of womenfolk organized into a group of miners.

He knew they could do it. Maybe they couldn't do the heavy work, but he'd seen women working in mines plenty of times before, and they were good at it. Once they knew what to look for, they had an eye for detail that was superior to most men's. They were better in small, dark places too, and willingly worked longer hours, all stakes being equal. He reckoned that the only reason more women didn't do it was because they were mostly smarter than that. Mining was dirty, grubby work, and he hadn't met a female yet that didn't prefer, if given her druthers, to stay clean and starched.

Now, he knew that these particular gals were definitely the powder-and-lace sort, but he also knew that most of them had come up hard, and were used to tough work. After all, whoring was no tiptoe through the daisies.

He disengaged himself from the still-sleeping Jamaica and sat up, his bones creaking. Old wounds gave their familiar early morning pangs and thuds, long-mended bones complained, then quieted. During these brief dawn pain spells, he often thought how much simpler life would have been if he'd just settled down someplace, and long ago. Just put down his guns and picked up the plow reins. But then he'd think about all the places he'd been and all the things he'd done and seen, and he'd forget all about those plow reins. He could only barely—

and briefly—imagine a life different from the one he'd led. So far anyway.

He and Jamaica had bedded down far away from the edge of the camp and above it, and he cast his gaze down over the sleeping throng. Here and there an arm or a foot stuck out from beneath the canvas of the tents. He and Big Tom had constructed only the basics—just the tented canvases for the roofs, with no sides, fronts, or backs.

A few of the girls were awake and stumbling around in the half-light. Farther down the slope, he could just make out the silhouette of the privy, and the forms of three—no, four—girls waiting in line. It crossed his mind that they'd best put Skunky to work digging a second privy. Maybe a third.

And then his eye settled on a lone form, seated in the soft glow of one of the dying fires. She was hunched near to it and scribbling away, dipping her pen over and over and writing like the Devil himself was after her. It was still far too dark to pick out the color of her dress, let alone her features.

"Funny," he muttered as he carefully stood and slowly stretched. "Why'd anybody want to write a letter all the way out here? Who's she think she's gonna get to mail it for her?"

Drummond McLean rode in sight of the camp at about nine in the morning, and halted his men while he sized it up. He hadn't brought the lot of them. He'd decided that thirty-some miners would be overdoing it. He'd brought along Harley and Tiger, of course, and Mordecai and Toby, plus two others.

Considering that there'd only be three armed men to go up against, the women being mostly like sheep, he'd figured that seven of them ought to do it.

Additionally, he'd discovered, much to his dismay, that there weren't enough horses to go around, most of the men having sold theirs months ago. They had wagons, but wagons would slow them down.

He hadn't expected, however, to find that the women had set up housekeeping at the Bum Nugget. This puzzled him, and it also made him angry enough to spit tacks. What nerve they had, and to top it off, that old bitch Rose was up there with them!

He scratched at his neck, running a finger between his skin and the collar, which felt for all the world like sandpaper. He'd slept in the bed of a wagon, for God's sake! How had more grit worked its way into him there?

"Boss?" said Tiger, who was sporting a black eye this morning, after McLean had taken his frustrations out on him last night. If any man was ill-named, it was Tiger Forbush.

"Shut up," McLean snapped. "I'm thinking."

Thinking how much more satisfying a target you are than Harley, he thought. Slugging Harley was like punching a gunnysack filled to bursting with half-melted lard. . . .

He stopped his mind from wandering with a small shake of his head, and turned his attention to the camp up the slope. He counted several big, crude tents, plus a sizable string of horses staked a good ways off to one side, and a line of seven empty wagons. The smoke of three fires drifted upward, and he could see a big iron pot hanging over one of them.

There were a handful of women outside, tending the fires or marching hither and yon with some unknown purpose, going in and out of the mine.

It seemed past strange to him that they'd be awake at this time of the morning, let alone ambulatory.

He looked again at Rose, and scowled. An unmistakable figure, she sat alone on a rock, fanning her chins with one hand while she shaded herself with that stupid little parasol. Whatever the rest of those whores were doing, she was having no part of it. But then, she hadn't left town as they had agreed, had she?

"Boss?" said Harley meekly. "What you want us to do?"

McLean was about to tell him to shut the hell up when one of the women at the cook fires looked up and spotted them. She began to shout something. He couldn't tell what it was, but the camp suddenly grew agitated. Women began to pour out of the mine.

"Judas Priest!" he muttered. "What the hell are they doing in there?"

But Mordecai had overheard. "Workin' it," he said flatly. "They're carryin' lanterns and picks, leastwise."

"Women?" McLean replied. "You've been in the

sun too long, Mordecai." Still, he didn't signal his
men to move forward. He simply sat there, watching
the hive of activity that the camp had become.

"I've known some women what were crack miners," Mordecai drawled. "Knew one gal what could
pinpoint-blast the wings off a fly."

"Aw, get stuffed," Toby said, and jerked at his
pinto's bridle in an effort to settle it down. It didn't
work.

McLean grunted.

And then Mordecai laughed. "No, sir, I believe
that Big Tom's got these gals workin' his claim for
him, all right!"

McLean felt the color drain from his face. He
snapped, "Shut up!" but he knew that Mordecai was
right. It was ludicrous, insane, but there it was. The
women emerging from the mine were covered in dirt
and grime, and as Mordecai had indicated, they carried picks and shovels and lanterns, or labored beneath the weight of heavy rocks, held either in their
hands or in buckets.

No self-respecting whore would ever get that dirty
unless there was money in it for her, and quite a bit
at that.

But how was Malloy paying them? McLean knew
that the man barely had two cents to rub together.
McLean had made certain of it, grinding him down
slowly and surely. He'd expected Malloy to give up
and go home any time now, but here he was, with
a full-tilt mining operation powered by the fancy
women of Twin Buttes!

His fancy women, by God! *His* whores, who were

surely breaking their nails and ruining their skin and getting so blasted filthy that it would take them weeks to get scrubbed clean and back into shape again. At least, into shape worth charging anything for.

He felt himself grinding his teeth, and willed himself to stop it. *Calm the hell down*. He had to appear in control and sure of himself.

But that sonofabitch! He'd see that bastard Tom Malloy tarred and feathered. Strung up by his balls!

And as for this Slocum character, this was all his fault, wasn't it? Malloy hadn't come up with this crud until Slocum came to town. The famous Slocum, the mighty hero of the penny dreadful. Ha!

"You gonna rip that saddle horn off?"

Mordecai had spoken, and McLean glanced over to see him smirking.

McLean let go of the saddle horn, and flexed his fingers to get the circulation going again. Up at the camp, it appeared that all the women were outside and grouped together. Skunky was nowhere to be seen, but Malloy and Slocum had moved out in front of the women, and were standing, waiting for him to make a move.

Behind him, Slocum heard Jamaica whisper, "Why don't they do something?"

"You in a hurry?" he asked without looking around. He kept his eyes on McLean's men. There were only seven of them, but they looked to be well armed. Nobody had cleared leather, though.

"Maybe they'll leave," Jamaica said hopefully.

"No," Slocum said. McLean had come this far, and Slocum knew that he wasn't about to just turn tail at the sight of them. Far from it. McLean might have been surprised to find them at the mine instead of a good piece down the road—in fact, Slocum was sure of that part—but he'd hardly shrug his shoulders and let them be. He wanted his girls back, and he wanted this mine, such as it was.

"Here they come," Big Tom said under his breath, although he hadn't reached for his holster yet. Slocum was a pretty fair judge of character, and he had determined through observation—and past experience, short though it was—that Tom was a good man: a good hand, and a steady one too. He was fairly certain that Big Tom Malloy would protect these girls—and this mine—with his life.

McLean came slowly toward them, the horses at a walk and the line of them spread out wide. McLean's men still hadn't drawn their weapons. It looked like this initial confrontation was going to be mostly peaceable, but Slocum still kept his hand near his gun leather nonetheless.

McLean halted his men a scant ten feet away from the two men and just sat there, leaning forward with his palms on his saddle horn. No one spoke. Even the girls had gone uncharacteristically quiet. For a long moment, the only sounds were the light wind whisking through the scrub and the occasional stamp or snort of an impatient horse.

And then Big Tom spoke. "If you've come by for breakfast, McLean, you're too late."

"Always said you had a sense of humor, Malloy,"

McLean replied, scowling. "Never said it was a good one, though." He looked past Slocum, whose eyes had never left his face, and said to someone in the crowd, "We've come to escort you ladies back to town."

Slocum heard scuffling feet as the crowd parted, and then Rose waddled up beside him. Red-faced from the effort, she still had enough energy to spit, "Fat chance, weasel's-dick."

"You sold out to me, Rose," McLean said, his tone condescending. "I can't see that you've got any say in this."

"Sold out against my will, Drum," she replied, and there was venom in her voice. "I know it and you know it. You fuddled me, and I signed them papers in a weak moment. I'll set up again, even if I have to kick your slimy ass outta town and start my business outta your goddamn newspaper office."

From atop his horse, McLean clucked his tongue and smiled patronizingly. "Rose, Rose, you big fat piece of shit. Whatever are we going to do with you?"

"*Fat?*" Rose shouted as she stepped forward. "Did you call me fat, you buzzard's backside?"

Slocum caught her by the shoulder and with some effort managed to get her stopped. The last thing he needed was Rose between himself and McLean.

She shrugged off his hand and moved back into the line, but not before she snarled, "You ain't much better than him, badger-butt."

Beside him, Tom whispered, "She's got a real way with words. . . ."

Slocum didn't look at him, but he snorted. "Looks like the ladies ain't budgin', McLean. 'Fraid I'll have to ask you to move on."

There was silence for a brief moment, and then a thin man on a flashy pinto horse quipped, "Hey, Big Tom! Looks like you got a hole in your hat!"

Tom stepped forward, and before Slocum had him stopped all the way, a new voice sounded. "This your property now, Slocum?"

For the first time, Slocum looked away from McLean and toward the man who had spoken. "Mordecai Jones," was all he said. He didn't let his expression or his tone betray any emotion.

"Been a long time," Mordecai replied. He too remained as expressionless as a rock. In fact, the brawny man's only movement was to lay two fingers flat on his thigh. It was a brief movement, only lasting a second or two, but Slocum saw it.

"It's my property, mister," Big Tom said with a scowl. "And you're trespassing."

Ignoring Big Tom entirely, McLean turned toward Mordecai and said, "Do you know him?"

"Long time ago," Mordecai replied, and then spat. "On the Salt Fork of the Brazos, wasn't it, Slocum?"

Slocum stiffened. "Sounds about right."

Mordecai said, "That sonofabitchin' bastard killed my brother."

"Jabez deserved killin'," Slocum said flatly. His fingers moved a little closer to his holster. "He stole my horse. Along with twenty head of Marc Scully's, as I remember. And then he tried to shove me over a cliff. I didn't take kindly to that."

"And so you shot him." Mordecai's brow furrowed dangerously. "Jabez was my brother, Slocum, and I freely admit he had his faults."

"There's nothin' lower than a horse thief," Slocum said, his eyes narrowed.

"Unless it's the man who murders him in cold blood and leaves him for the crows and coyotes to pick. They don't print that sorta crud in that book they wrote about you, do they?" Mordecai swung one arm wide. "Big hero, Slocum."

Slocum took a step forward. "Climb down from that horse, Mordecai."

"Glad to," Mordecai said.

The big blond man had his right foot free of the stirrup before a nervous McLean said, "Gentlemen, gentlemen!"

Mordecai paused for a moment, then eased down again and shoved his foot in the stirrup. He didn't look happy, though.

Slocum stood his ground, his right thumbnail tapping his holster rhythmically. His gaze shifted from Mordecai and back to McLean, though. "Get out," Slocum said. "Ride out while you can, and take this Reb trash with you."

11

Miranda slipped from the group the moment that McLean's men left the camp. Slocum had wandered off with Tom Malloy and Jamaica anyway, and there didn't seem much chance of Miranda getting close enough to eavesdrop. But my goodness, what a story this was turning into! Or at least, what a story she could *turn* this into.

She scribbled frantically for a good hour, squatting on her heels behind the cover of two low paloverde trees as her fingers grew darker and darker with ink stains, all the while hiding from anyone who might press her into service down the mine shaft.

Who is this Mordecai? she wrote in her notes. Obviously, there was a long-standing grievance between Mordecai and Slocum, but she thought it was something more than the one they'd spoken about, although that was certainly heinous enough. But she was sure that there must be more to it. After all, you didn't kill a man's brother and still call him by his first name, did you?

Well, Slocum might. The old rogue was full of surprises.

But still, she believed there was some story there that she either hadn't been told, or wasn't getting. She'd have to dig further. Additionally, she was bursting with questions, and just as quickly answering them for herself. After all, it was the novelist's prerogative, wasn't it?

Thoughtfully, she nibbled on the end of her pen.

For instance, McLean's men's horses were all wrong! There hadn't been more than three decent mounts among them, and the others had appeared to be cart or draft horses: nondescript, shaggy, and unaccustomed to the saddle. She'd surely have to do something about that! Perhaps she'd change them to black horses. Yes, a matched posse of gleaming ebony mounts, that was it. . . .

Pen dipped into ink once again, and she began to write anew.

"I don't know, Jamaica!" Slocum said for the third time, and added, "I'm not a goddamned mind reader!"

Jamaica crossed her arms and snorted.

"The main thing," Big Tom said quickly, "is that he's gone for now."

Jamaica opened her mouth, and Tom said, "And I don't know when he's coming back either, Jamaica, so don't ask."

She closed her mouth with an angry click.

"Right," said Slocum. He took off his hat and ran his sleeve over his forehead. It wasn't that hot, but it had been that close. It was a pure miracle that of all people, Mordecai had been there—and that he'd thought fast. From what Slocum had seen and heard of McLean, he liked to know well in advance exactly what would happen in any situation. Apparently Mordecai had sized him up the same way. When he'd signaled Slocum to go along with anything he said, then threw in a supposed old grudge—which Slocum embellished—and the expectation of imminent gunplay, McLean had panicked.

Actually, McLean would have been smart just to let them kill each other, and for just a moment, Slocum had been afraid that he would. But the promise of it came too unexpectedly for McLean. Mordecai had him pegged, all right. He'd played him like a fiddle.

It was just as well. Skunky, who had been hiding down behind the canvas drapes of the freshly dug outhouse, on his belly with his rifle aimed right at McLean's forehead, probably wouldn't have done them much good. He'd have taken out McLean, of course, but the rest of McLean's men would have been mad as a bag full of badgers.

Slocum figured that Mordecai had bought them at least a day or two, maybe more, although he didn't voice this to either Jamaica or Big Tom. He had inadvertently discovered, much to his surprise, that he had a friend in McLean's camp, but it was just as likely that McLean had a friend or two in *his*. Word traveled fast, especially among womenfolk. He'd keep this under his hat for the time being.

He settled the Stetson back on his head and stared out over the land, over the soft dust and sandy rocks and pale green of spring. "Well, if we've got some extra time, let's get to using it."

"Right," said Big Tom.

"Hmph!" snorted Jamaica, and turned on her heel.

"Women," muttered Big Tom.

"Well, what happened, consarn it?" called a cranky Skunky, who was just joining them, the rifle swinging from his hand.

"How's that privy coming?" Tom asked.

Skunky grimaced. "If I'd'a knowed I was gonna spend the rest of my life diggin' shitters on the desert, I would'a just stood right up durin' the War and let them Rebs shoot me."

Slocum grinned slyly. "Oh, I would've hated to do that, Skunky." He liked the old buzzard.

Skunky's brows hoisted an inch. "You too, Slocum? I swear, the world's fulla rapscallious sons of the South, and I do believe they've all come west." He turned toward Tom. "Next thing, you'll be tellin' me you're from Georgia or 'Bama or some heathen place!"

"Nope," Tom said, "you're safe. It's still Illinois."

"Lucky for you," Skunky grumbled, then turned toward Slocum again. "Well, why'd you call that big yeller-haired feller a damned Reb if you're one of 'em yourself?" He stopped and colored a little. "Aw, you know what I mean."

Because I was letting him know that I'd understood his signal, Slocum thought, but he shrugged and said, "Just somethin' to say, I guess."

The old man squinted at him as if he were about two brinks shy of a load, but had the sense to change the subject. "Did I see right?" Skunky asked. "Did McLean send two of his boys up the road?"

Slocum nodded thoughtfully. "Probably sent them to look for that crate of Winchesters you found." He didn't mention those godforsaken books. The girls were already fighting over the new ones.

Skunky smiled. "Well, they's gonna have them a long hunt."

Jamaica stood up straight and pressed her hands to the small of her back with a groan. They had received their orders from Big Tom, and now, all around her in the dimly lit shaft, women were swinging picks, gathering rocks, and scraping them into bags or buckets in preparation for hauling them to the surface.

Tom and Skunky had blasted and chipped their way deeper and farther into the earth than she could have imagined. Walking back up the shaft to daylight was like trudging from one end of town to the other, and all of it uphill.

No one spoke. She'd only been down here a couple of hours, and already the walls were closing in. How did men do this all day, every day?

Well, Tom had said that they'd probably blast tomorrow. Who knows what he'd have them doing after that?

But after this thing was finished, no matter how it turned out, she was going to give Slocum a piece of her mind. How on earth had he ever talked them into this?

Well, she thought, somewhat chagrined, *I sort of helped him. . . .*

No, she couldn't lay all the blame at his door. He was only trying to be of assistance. He was only trying to save her ass and her house and everything she'd worked for all these years. And when it had looked as if Slocum and that big, ugly blond brute were going to come to blows . . .

She shivered, despite the heat of the mine.

And once again, she managed to talk herself out of being angry. Not so much with Slocum, but with the situation. Although poor Slocum seemed to be the leading target for her anger.

Now, why in heaven's name was that? Last night, they had made slow, sweet love beneath a blanket of stars, and she had called out his name. She adored him. No other man had ever touched her in the same way that he had, both now and years ago, when they were both so much younger, when she wasn't all that far removed from innocent. Relatively speaking, that is.

She had often thought, over the years, that her memories of him had been tinged by time, colored by the passing years. She'd been young, she told herself. It was just that she'd been so impressed with him. He'd been older, a man with a reputation, even back then. He was world-weary and world-wise, and had known exactly what he wanted, both from a woman and from life.

She had thought that her recollections had half-created him: larger, bolder, and more virile than other mortals. But now that he was here with her, she realized that her memory had been better than she had credited it. He was older, true, but so was she. His body had suffered more insults and scars, and his brow carried the lines of time, and a life far fuller than most.

He was still the same man, though, no flight of a young girl's fancy, but real and human. He was rough but gentle, tough but soft, a man who could do what had to be done, who could kill another man without batting an eye if need be, but who held her in his arms as if she were weightless, as if she were made of soap bubbles, the most delicate of creatures.

Of course, that didn't stop him from getting a tad rough sometimes, she thought with a sudden grin. He always knew just what she wanted, even when she didn't know herself. He always knew how to make her cry out in the throes of her climax, each one better and more overwhelming than the one before. He knew how to make her hug him close and wish that he'd never, ever leave.

A sudden bump from the side wrenched her from her reverie, and she snarled, "Watch it!"

"Sorry," said the sweating blonde, and moved on beneath the weight of her bag of chipped rock.

Odd, thought Jamaica. She'd seen the girl before, but the first time had been at the meeting in town. Today, perspiration stains blotched her prim, school-marmish dress and her hair clung to her face in damp strings. She didn't dress like a whore, that was for sure. Nothing about her announced the sporting life. Yet here she was.

Jamaica raised her pick again. She brought it

crashing into stone three times, showering herself and those close to her with rock chips, before a thought struck her: What if the girl wasn't one of them after all? What if Drum McLean had put a spy in their midst?

By the time Drum McLean—and what men he hadn't sent down the road in search of his lost rifles—rode up to the Daisy Cutter, he was deeply regretting that he hadn't allowed Mordecai his head. It would have solved all their problems, wouldn't it? Mordecai would have killed Slocum, and surely one of the other men would have taken out Malloy. Of course, they might have lost a few town whores in the cross fire, but a man had to figure in some casualties, didn't he?

He stepped down from his mount and tossed his reins to Toby, who led the horses, hooves crunching fine gravel, across the camp to the picket line.

As he batted dust from his hat, McLean called, "Mordecai!" to the man who had been silent, but gnashing his teeth, for the whole of the long ride back.

Mordecai Jones, halfway to the mouth of the mine, turned toward him. He still looked angry enough to chew nails and spit out iron filings. "What?" he snapped.

McLean caught up with him. There was dust and grit in every crease of McLean's body. How he hated the great out-of-doors! "Are you really that mad at Slocum?" he asked.

Mordecai just looked at him.

"All right," McLean said, and pulled at his perspiration- and dust-soiled shirt. "Stupid question, what with him murdering your brother and everything. Terrible thing, just terrible," he added with a sad shake of his head. "How'd you like to get your revenge?"

Mordecai raised one sandy brow.

McLean had had a good long while to think it over, think about what an ass he'd been to stop that brewing altercation. He'd also been thinking about how he could remedy the situation with the least trouble possible. The least trouble for *him* anyway. As soon as he set things up with Mordecai, he was going back to town and have a nice, long bath. And put on fresh clothing. And sit in the barber's chair.

"Walk with me, Mordecai," McLean said, smiling.

Jamaica set down her plate. She'd just finished eating the midday meal, and Slocum was nowhere in sight. Big Tom was, however, and she made her way over to him through the lazing crowd that was spread out over the dusty campsite. Down the hill, she noticed Skunky digging away, and quite near him, a long line at the single outhouse.

"He'd better dig a few more," she muttered as she stepped over the legs and arms of countless women, women who were hot and dirty and tired and bringing up blisters, and didn't particularly like it.

Big Tom sat by himself, chewing thoughtfully on one of Mrs. Arnot's biscuits. "Tom?" Jamaica said. "Can you spare a minute?"

"For you?" he replied with a grin. "Any time. Pull up a rock."

She dusted off a flat stone and sat down. "It's about one of the girls."

"Somebody not pullin' her weight?" he asked. "Other than Rose, I mean."

When he smiled and stabbed his thumb up the hill, she saw Rose, sitting with a plate balanced on her lap, still shaded by that stupid little parasol. She appeared annoyed, as usual.

"Well, you can't exactly expect her to go down in the mine," Jamaica said kindly. "Some of that shaft is pretty damned steep."

"Aw, the exercise'd do her good," Big Tom said good-naturedly.

Jamaica considered this. "Maybe. But she isn't the one I wanted to talk to you about."

Tom swallowed the last of his biscuit, then took a long drink of coffee. "I'll bite," he said. "Which one?"

"I don't know her name," Jamaica began. "Never seen her before yesterday, but I've asked around. Nobody else seems to know her either. She's blond, and she's wearing the most gawd-awful drab dress, with buttons up to here." She held her hand under her chin.

"Oh, you mean Miranda," Tom said, just a tad more happily than Jamaica would have liked. "Nice little gal. Writes in her diary all the damn time, though."

Come to think of it, those blotches on the girl's

fingers might have been ink. Jamaica had taken them for dirt from the mine.

"You can vouch for her then?" she asked.

"Just said she seems like a real nice gal. Didn't say I went to church with her." He raised a hand and waved, and Jamaica looked up. Miranda, across the camp, waved back at him and started to make her way toward them.

"Wonderful," Jamaica whispered.

Tom hadn't heard. It was obvious to her, by his tone and by the besotted nature of his gaze, that he thought this Miranda was more than a "nice gal." He might not realize it yet, but it was plain as day that he thought she was something special, and Jamaica knew better than to voice her suspicions to him.

And maybe it was all in her head anyway. The Lord knows it had happened before.

She stood up and shook out her skirts. Decent bright emerald skirts, befitting her profession, not that horrible dead gray-green like Miranda's rig. What on earth was the girl thinking? And why was Big Tom suddenly stuck on her, even if he didn't yet know it?

There had been a brief time when Jamaica had considered Tom Malloy a good catch. It had even crossed her mind that he might be convinced to marry her and take her away from her profession. But that was long ago, and all of her wild and woolly fantasies had served, in the end, to convince her that she liked what she did and that she didn't need saving. She could make more money running her own house—and keeping the cash for herself, and running her own life—than she ever could as the wife of a mine owner. As the wife of anybody! She was fully committed to the house, to her girls, to taking pride in what they did. Prostitution was legal in Arizona Territory. She could hold her head up.

"Hold on a second," Tom said as she turned to leave. "I'll introduce you."

"Maybe some other time," Jamaica said as she continued to walk away, the brush underfoot crackling with the scrape of her skirts. "I need to find Slocum."

"He's down the shaft," Tom said, and then he stood up and took off his hat—not for her, but for Miranda. "Set a spell, Miss Miranda?" Jamaica heard him say as she walked toward the mine.

Jamaica shook her head. He was sweet, all right, but stupid. It was the male race's most fetching attribute—and biggest drawback.

12

Night had at last fallen over the hillside and the valley below, turning spring greens to moonlit tones of silvery gray, but the new crew at the Bum Nugget wasn't much interested in remarking over its beauty. Most of the women sat silently, massaging aching shoulders and throbbing feet. A few were on wash duty, trying to soak the soil from clothing meant only for city streets and boudoirs—and certainly not for physical labor in the depths of a mine—in what extra water was available.

Up the slope, Slocum sat quietly with his back against a rock. He checked his watch by the light of a lucifer. Almost time. He shook the match out. "Bet they've never been so quiet," he said, looking down at the slumped mob of women below.

"Don't talk to me," snapped Jamaica. "I hate you."

He stifled a smile. She was grimy and disheveled. From what had started as an elaborate coif, her hair hung down in strings and ringlets, and there was a smudge of dirt across her nose. She was still beautiful, though. At the moment, she was rubbing her neck with both hands. Her eyes were closed, and there was a grimace on her pretty face.

"Here," he said, and moved behind her, replacing her hands with his. He dug in with his thumbs and began to gently knead, working up her neck to that little soft point where the base of the skull met the spine, and back down again. She had a glorious neck, which she arched as she let out a little sigh of pleasure.

"Well, maybe I like you a little bit," she muttered. "To the left. Yes, that's it . . . oh, yes . . ."

Slocum found himself growing aroused, and remembered with reluctance that it was nearly time for him to be leaving. He stopped and pulled away.

"You rat," she murmured, and he could tell by the tone of it that she had fallen prey to the same stirrings that he was feeling.

"Honestly, Slocum," she said. "Just when I'm beginning to think about not murdering you, you quit rubbing. I could use a back rub too, you know. In fact," she said, tipping her head, "I could use a good all-over rub."

He grinned and stood up. "Gotta meet somebody. But when I get back . . ."

"Promises, promises," she said, and one more time, tried to pin up a stray strand of her hair. It was a futile attempt, but charming nonetheless. "Who the hell are you going to meet anyway? Big Tom?" She poked a finger down the hillside and sniffed. "He's right there. Huddled up with that Miranda. I asked Slow Nell about her. Says she calls herself Miranda the Minx."

Miranda the Minx? The name fit her about as well

as a dress fit a boar hog, but Tom was indeed huddled with some gal. He was real intent on her too.
He likely wouldn't notice when Slocum left.

Slocum shook his head. "No, gotta ride out. I'll
be back in a couple-three hours."

Jamaica opened her mouth, but quickly, Slocum
said, "Don't ask me any questions, Mudge," then
bent to kiss her.

Despite her dusty and bedraggled appearance, her
kiss was as sweet as nectar, and he was sorely
tempted to just stay put. But the signal had said eight
o'clock. He had to go.

He pulled away.

"I'll be back, darlin'," he said as he stood again.

"You'd better be," she grumbled as she struck a
match, then held it to the wick of a candle stub she'd
brought back from the mine. "And until you show
up again, I guess I'll just have to make do with
second best."

When Slocum looked at her quizzically, she produced the newest Slocum book and held the cover
toward him, a mischievous grin on her face. The
cover said, *John Slocum: Death Rides a Spotted
Stallion*.

"See you, Death," she said sweetly as she leaned
back and thumbed it open.

"Aw, hell," he grumbled, and made his way down
the slope, toward the remuda.

Miranda and Big Tom barely noticed when Slocum
walked past them, and by the time he'd saddled
Chaco and ridden out into the darkness, Tom (who

had at last noticed that he was leaving) only commented, "Wonder where he's going."

"Who?" asked Miranda.

"Oh, nothing," Tom said. In the short space of a day, he had become totally infatuated with this girl, a fact that he was just beginning to realize. He was very careful not to ask her anything that might pertain to the sporting life. He didn't want to know. He'd rather labor under the illusion that she was a nice girl.

She seemed relieved by his unspoken decision, and prattled on happily about growing up in San Francisco. He had nearly forgotten all about Miss Clementine Crockett. He found, in fact, that he could barely remember her face, and strangely, he wasn't ashamed that he couldn't.

But to think that he might have found the woman of his dreams and she had turned out to be a common cat! No, not common, not common at all. Still, it would take a lot of explaining to the relatives back home.

But then, maybe he wouldn't have to explain. Perhaps he could just avoid going home again, to Illinois, for the rest of his life.

He took one of her hands in his. It was so tiny and white, the fingers long and delicate. And ink-stained.

"You sure must do a lot of writing in that diary of yours, Miranda," he said.

She squirmed a little and tried to curl her fingers so that he couldn't see, but he held them out flat. She seemed to be considering something, although for the life of him he couldn't figure what would be so important about a diary that she'd have to squeeze up her face so prettily, and then she said, "I'm going to tell you a secret, Tom."

He waited.

"I'm not writing in my diary."

He almost said that it must sure be a hell of a shopping list, but he held his tongue. She seemed so earnest.

"I—I'm writing . . . a book."

Damned if he wasn't stuck for a thing to say! A sporting girl who had delusions of book-writing? It was a new one on him. He nearly barked out a laugh, but had the good sense to hold it back. At last, he said, "A book? What kind of a book, Miranda?"

She stared at her lap. "I can't believe that I'm telling you this, Tom."

He patted her hand. "Well, so far, you haven't told me much of anything."

"I mean, I've kept it a secret in every town I've been in. I haven't breathed a word. And now, here I am, telling you!"

He shook his head. "What?"

She looked up. "Promise you won't say a word? Especially to Slocum."

What does Slocum have to do with this? Tom thought, and realized with a start that he was jealous! Now, where had that come from?

But he said, "I promise, Miranda." And when she still stared at him, he held up one hand. "Word of honor."

She cleared her throat. "You know those Slocum books the girls are so crazy about?"

He nodded noncommittally. "Seen 'em."

Her eyebrows went up, just a tad. "Have you read them?"

He shrugged. "Not really," he lied, not wanting her to get the wrong opinion of him. "I don't read much of that sort of trash."

She sat up straight. *"Trash?"*

He blinked. "Well, I mean that I don't have time. And when I do, I like to read good books or newspapers. You know. I've got some Coleridge somewhere around here, and some Byron, and a couple books on mining, and some—"

She was already on her feet, although he didn't remember her standing up, and she had both arms folded across her chest.

"Never you mind, *Mister* Malloy," she said, her voice high and thin. "Just forget that I said anything at all."

"But honey . . ." he said plaintively, rising to his feet.

"Coleridge and mining indeed!" she snapped, and stalked off toward the main cook fire, which was, for the moment, a full-tilt laundry.

Tom thumbed his hat back and scratched his head. "Damn!" he said softly. "What'd I say?"

Slocum rode Chaco down across the desert at a slow jog. The moon was three quarters, the sky was cloudless, and the night was full of stars, illuminating the land with a ghostly, pewter glow. The eve-

ning had cooled things off some, and by the time
he'd rolled and smoked three quirlies and ridden
nearly an hour at this slow, rambling pace, he was
wishing that he'd thought to bring his jacket.

The chill had little more than set in, however,
when he spotted another rider coming toward him
in the distance, and it looked like the other man had
spotted him at just about the same time.

Silently, Slocum reined Chaco in. He waited.

The man in the distance, little more than a black
silhouette of horse and rider against the gray of the
moonlit desert, stopped too. He raised an arm slowly
to the side, then let it drop.

Slocum mirrored his gesture.

Both men started forward again.

They met in the middle, their horses' heads side
by side, and finally Mordecai said, "Slocum, you old
sonofabitch! What the hell's this 'Reb trash' business anyhow?"

Slocum grinned. "Takes one to know one, you
jackass."

Both men dismounted, and after a great deal of
backslapping and calling each other sonsofbitches
and rapscallions and such, kicked a place clear on
the desert floor and sat themselves down for a pa-
laver.

"Well, Slocum, it has surely been a while," Mordecai said as he pulled out his fixings and began to
roll himself a smoke. "When was the last time I seen
you? Fort Worth?"

Slocum nodded. "That was ten, eleven years back.
How you been keepin', Mordecai? And what brings

you to be workin' for such a worthless buzzard's backside as Drummond McLean?"

Mordecai poked his pouch back into a pocket, then struck a lucifer and held it to his quirlie. He took a draw and shook out the match before he answered.

"Money," he said. "Plain and simple. We don't get much news out to the Daisy Cutter, 'cept what McLean tells us. You want to explain just what the hell's goin' on?"

Slocum explained the situation as briefly as possible, which entailed him rolling and smoking a quirlie, and Mordecai smoking a second. When he was finished, Mordecai shook his head and muttered, "Well, I'll be jiggered. Always knew that McLean was a slippery, graspin' sonofabitch, but I never figured him for a whoremaster."

"You ask me," Slocum said, "it's just part of the problem. I think he's tryin' to take over Twin Buttes lock, stock, and barrel. Hell, he already owns the newspaper."

Mordecai nodded. "And the gun shop, and the biggest mercantile in town, and that outfitter store. Might be a few others he's got control of too what don't have his name plastered all over 'em on the outside. Looks to me like it's Bonny Flats all over again, pal."

This time, it was Slocum who nodded in agreement. Fifteen years ago, he and Mordecai had been in the employ of one Ernest Mayhew, Harvard graduate and entrepreneur, who had attempted to take sole ownership of the town of Bonny Flats, Nebraska. By force.

It had gone bad—as did most of these things, in Slocum's experience—and Slocum and Mordecai had ended up fighting against Mayhew. Of course, there had been the twin daughters of a sodbuster too. As Slocum recalled, the charms of Miss Lizette Frame had won him over quite a bit sooner than the strength of the townspeople's case.

Mordecai chuckled, as if he were reading Slocum's mind. "Them gals. Mine was Franny and yours was Lizette, as I recall. They was sure somethin', wasn't they? Blond as new corn . . ."

"Head to toe," said Slocum softly.

"Well," said Mordecai, shifting slightly, "I reckon we'd best figure somethin' out before it all goes to hell. Got any ideas?"

"Hoped you'd have one."

"Naw," said Mordecai, leaning back. "You go first."

Slocum chuckled and shook his head. "Gonna be the same old thing, isn't it, Mordecai?"

Mordecai grinned back at him. "Reckon it's too late to change us, ol' buddy."

They talked into the night, and as they were stepping up on their horses to go their separate ways, Mordecai said, "Y'know, Slocum, that was a dumb thing you did."

Slocum raised a brow. "What?"

"I know I opened the door for it and all," Mordecai went on as he gathered his reins, "but why'd you have to name my so-called brother Jabez? I'll be damned if I couldn't remember it when some-body asked. Had to stall for five minutes till I re-membered. Next time, why don't you pick somethin' easy? Joe, for instance. I could remember Joe."

Slocum leaned on his saddle horn. Grinning, he said, "Mordecai, why would the same folks that named you pick a common name like Joe for their second-born? Now, Jabez. That has a ring to it!"

Mordecai scowled. "I never thought I'd say it, Slocum, but I'm all of a sudden real happy that all I had was six sisters."

It was half past ten by the time that Slocum rode back into camp at the Bum Nugget, and he came in a good deal wiser than he had ridden out. Mordecai had told him that Big Tom's suspicions about Mc-Lean were correct—McLean was indeed digging and blasting his way right past the line where his mining rights ended and Tom Malloy's began. Mor-decai figured that the mother lode sat beneath Tom's property.

Of course, Slocum reminded himself that Mor-decai had no moral compunctions about this, Mor-decai's morals being largely formed by who had the most money to pay him. He'd admitted that he'd helped start the blaze that took out all of Big Tom's timbers, and that he'd sent men out, on McLean's orders, to take potshots at Tom and Skunky.

After all, McLean paid him, and McLean wanted it done. Mordecai asked no questions. He just did what he was told.

Until his old pal Slocum showed up, that is.

But now Mordecai seemed to be filled with the spirit of old-time camaraderie. Most of all, he loved turning situations ass over teakettle, just to see what would happen. Slocum knew that this could be a dangerous trait in a man, but so long as Mordecai was on his side, he was willing to use it.

Besides, amoral or not, he liked Mordecai Jones.

The two men had served together briefly during the War of Secession (where they'd worked out that little code of theirs), and fate had thrown them together two times since: once in Bonny Flats, where they fought for the townspeople and the sodbusters against the late land-grabber Ernest Mayhew, and once in Fort Worth, where mostly they were drunk for the better part of a week. As a matter of fact, he barely remembered leaving town.

Slocum vaguely recalled something in there about a pretty Mexican girl too, but frankly, he'd been so drunk that he didn't recollect most of it.

Well, it was probably a blessing.

This time, as in Bonny Flats, Mordecai seemed more than willing to swap horses in midstream and help Slocum out all he could. He'd even come up with a few good ideas. Well, a few bad ones too, such as simply putting a bullet in McLean's head and having done with it. Slocum had pretended to consider it for a moment before vetoing the idea.

He slipped the saddle from Chaco's back and slung it with the others, checked the horse's feed bag and rechecked the tie rope, then started up the slope toward the drowsing camp. He'd done all he could do for this evening.

And Jamaica was waiting.

He quickened his step.

13

The next morning, the men of the Bum Nugget blasted. The women, Miranda included, stayed well away from the mine's entrance as per Big Tom and Slocum's instructions. And when the two of them and Skunky came boiling out of the shaft, followed directly by an enormous belch of smoke and dust that seemed to last forever—and an earth-shaking rumble that Miranda felt as much as heard—she dropped to her knees, hands over her ears, certain that the world was ending.

She noticed—once she was capable of noticing anything but her own reaction, that is—that the other women had varying responses to the blast. Many reacted in the same way that she had, or close to it. Shock, surprise, or horror. Even Rose, up the hill, fell off her rock. But some had barely flinched, as if this was a common occurrence. It was only after she'd had a moment to think about it that she realized that some of these women were Wagon Girls.

She'd heard a couple of them talking about it on the morning when they first came to the Bum Nugget. Drum McLean apparently sent a wagon load of women out to the Daisy Cutter one day a month, just to keep the men happy. Those girls must be used to blasting.

And then she began to wonder why they'd be blasting on the one day in a month that they had women.

Shifts, she told herself. It must be that they work in shifts. Of course some men would be working the mine while the others were . . . were otherwise occupied.

And then she began to think of these women, trapped under frantically pumping male bodies while the earth shook all around them. Which set her to thinking about the sleeping arrangements at the Daisy Cutter. They had tents for privacy, didn't they? But if they were anything like the ones that Tom and Slocum had put up for the women, then they were communal, and . . .

Oh, dear! She found herself blushing hotly, and couldn't shake the imagined picture of all those naked bodies, those naked couples, all sweating and writhing and only inches apart, from her mind.

"You all right, honey?" Slow Nell's hand was on her arm. "Makes a hell of a boom, don't it? Say, you're red as a beet! C'mon down to the tents and sit in the shade for a spell."

"Yes," she said, tugging at her collar and feeling foolish, and then more foolish still when she found herself wondering if Slow Nell was one of the Wagon Girls. "Yes, I think I will."

•   •   •

By the time the clear, warm afternoon rolled around, most of the dust had settled. Big Tom and Skunky had assured everyone that the last of the rocks loosened by the blast had fallen—poor Skunky was nursing a bumped head, the result of one of the last to fall—and most of the women went down into the mine again.

It was a long trek down into the mine (or at least, the branching shaft that Tom and Skunky had chosen to blast), and a longer one coming back up. Although Tom and Skunky had laid some rails, the mine cart only went thirty feet down a shaft that now traveled better than 350 feet out beneath the desert floor, and gradually sloped downward a hundred more. Laden with blasted rock, the women toiled their way back up the mine in fifty-foot increments, handing off their burdens to the next women, who took it up another fifty feet or so. Eventually, the ore made its way to the girls working the outside, who deposited their burdens on the ever-growing pile beside the round, horse-powered ore grinder, then went back for more.

"Cain't carry half so much as a feller," Skunky had commented, "but they do sure make a mess of trips."

While the women hauled rock from the depths of the shaft, Slocum took a welcome break. He'd been going full tilt since dawn, and he was tired. They all were. The efforts of these women had pushed the shaft farther and deeper in just over a day than Big Tom and Skunky could have dug it in a month, a fact that Big Tom cheerfully admitted.

There were shirkers, of course, the mountainous Rose chief among them. To Slocum's knowledge, her only movements had been to lumber to her parasoled perch above, then down the hill to the tents, and back up again. And she cursed all the way.

"It's worth it," Big Tom had said. "Hell, if she hadn't come, I don't suppose her girls would have either."

If Big Tom was willing to cut Rose a share of the proceeds just for taking up space, then it was none of Slocum's business.

Slocum dug into his pocket for his fixings and rolled himself a quirlie, his first since eight o'clock that morning. It tasted past fine, and his first drag nearly burnt it down to half.

He barely noticed. His narrowed eyes were searching out over the desert floor, far away. There was nothing out of the ordinary, at least that he could see with his naked eye, and he wished he'd brought his spyglass up here with him. A coyote skulked through the pale green brush far to the south. Small animals—jackrabbits, pack rats, tortoises, and the like—set the sparse weeds to shivering. But nothing man-sized or man-made.

"There you are."

He looked up to find Jamaica, and grinned. "What?" he said, teasing. "You gonna shirk with Rose for a spell?"

"No, I thought I'd shirk with you," she said, and sat beside him, leaning into his shoulder.

He put his arm around her and gave her a hug. "Just a couple of slackers," he said. "That's us."

She laughed. "Skunky booted a few of us out to take a rest. He said that many skirts in that small an area made him nervous as hell. But look, Slocum." She leaned into him for a too-short moment and reached into the pocket of her skirts, then held her hand out toward him.

In it, she held a chunk of milky quartz. Thinly veined through it was a black substance that he knew was raw silver.

He whistled, long and drawn out.

"My feelings exactly," Jamaica said. "I ran into Big Tom on the way up the shaft, and he's practically dancing a jig already. Says that if we can get the mine cleared he'll blast again tomorrow. He said something about ore to the ton too, but . . . Slocum, do you think that he's actually going to hit something big?"

Slocum took the rock from her and turned it over in his hand. "Darlin', I believe you're all about to be rich."

Smiling, she said softly, "Then let's celebrate."

He knew that expression, and he quickly looked around. "Mudge, hadn't we best go on up the hill a piece?"

"Why?" she asked coyly, moving to straddle his lap. Her hands went to his belt buckle and unfastened it swiftly. "There's nobody for fifty feet in any direction," she murmured, and then she kissed him.

His arms went around her automatically. His hands traveled over the dusty silk of her bodice, feeling the soft curves that lay beneath, the outside swells of her breasts, the indentation of her waist, the heat of sun on silk.

"You're gonna ride me raw, Mudge," he said softly, teasingly.

She whispered, "Shut up, Slocum," as her hands began to push at his britches to free him.

He was already fully aroused—and deftly unbuttoning her bodice. If she wanted him out here, in front of God and everyone, far be it from him to stop her. But he wanted to see those gorgeous breasts again.

She didn't stop him. In fact, just as he freed her breasts and they spilled out into his waiting hands, plump and white, she drove herself down on his shaft, enveloping him completely as she purred out that sweet, slit-eyed sigh.

She leaned toward him again, and he craned his neck forward to catch one perfect nipple in his mouth. He rolled it between his teeth as she whispered, "Nobody's going to bother us, baby. Nobody at all . . ."

I can't help it, Miranda reasoned weakly as she bit her lip and stared. *I can't help it that Skunky sent me out of the mine too. I* could *help it that I was close enough to hear them talking, but I can't help it now that I can't even stand up without letting them and everyone in camp know that I was watching!*

She had secreted herself in her new writing place, the one she'd found last night. She was hidden from view by large boulders on two sides, and by low-growing, scrubby paloverde trees on the other two.

When she'd come across it, she'd thought it was a wonderful place for the secret novelist to ply her trade! Today, however, she'd snuck out here to be alone for a few seconds, not so much to write. Mostly, she wanted a moment alone to mull over her very confused feelings for Tom Malloy.

Trash indeed!

Except that thinking about it had only made her more confused, and she'd decided to get away from it by jotting down some notes on the indignities of hard, manual labor in a mine shaft.

And then Jamaica had shown up. Miranda hadn't realized Slocum was there until Jamaica had started talking to him.

Then the situation turned . . . embarrassing, and now Miranda found herself peering through the low brush, her ink spilled and soaking a large purple-black stain into her skirts. She didn't care. In fact, she barely noticed. She was utterly transfixed by the couple—and the coupling—on the other side of the paloverde.

I must stop, she told herself. *I must look away!* But she didn't, couldn't.

They were doing it so oddly, with Jamaica on the top, her emerald skirts spread back over Slocum's legs like a shroud. Slocum had eyes for no one but Jamaica, and his hands and mouth were busy with her breasts, kneading them, teasing the nipples, tugging on them, worrying them like a pup, and Miranda, watching, felt heat flood through her own breasts, her groin.

Jamaica's eyes were closed and her mouth was

open as she moved upon Slocum. She arched her back, as if to push her breasts closer to Slocum's greedy mouth, and Miranda, without thinking, touched her own breast.

The sensation was appalling and wonderful, all at once, and she quickly took her hand away. Why hadn't Cubby let her be on top on that one night long ago? She was ruined, and she only now realized that she'd been ruined in the most boring way possible. What Slocum and Jamaica were doing didn't look boring in the least, and Jamaica seemed to be deriving as much pleasure from it as Slocum!

The slow burning sensation that had begun between Miranda's legs had increased from a flicker to a full-blown blaze by this time, and her hand had crept back to her breast. Her breath was coming in shallow pants, and crouched behind the paloverde, she unconsciously wriggled her hips.

Strange fire shot through her veins, strange fire that warmed her and felt like ice and volcanoes all at once. Her supporting hand weakened suddenly and she fell the last few inches to the ground. A small gasp escaped her that had nothing to do with her stumble, and everything to do with the torrential feelings deep in her belly.

She slapped an ink-stained hand over her own mouth, pulled from the moment by that small burst of her sensation, her own sound, but she needn't have worried. Slocum and Jamaica were oblivious.

As Miranda hastily drew back, the last thing she saw was Jamaica craning her head backward as Slocum raised a hand to cover her mouth. Jamaica's muffled cry of delight came a half second later, when a flustered Miranda had backed up far enough that she could no longer see them. Within seconds, Slocum groaned long and slow, and the sounds of their movement stopped.

Miranda waited, quietly panting, her own body still in a bizarre sort of uproar.

She leaned back against the side of the big boulder, still quivering, still trying to catch her breath. But why should she be shaking? She hadn't done anything except watch something she had no business observing. Why should her insides be vibrating for all the world like harp strings?

That Slocum! she thought, trying to take her mind off her body. *I knew he was cavorting with whores, but in broad daylight as well? He has absolutely no business being a dime-novel hero!*

But her unspoken accusations were ineffective, and she knew it. How could she condemn him when she couldn't take her eyes off him, off the act? That was the size of it. She had come to Twin Buttes thinking Slocum was a paragon of virtue. She had unwittingly unmasked him for a mortal man, had cursed him, looked down upon him, and now she was wondering what it might be like to . . .

But it wasn't Slocum she wanted, she suddenly realized. Slocum was taken. Slocum was tainted somehow. No, the one she wanted was Tom. She wanted him to touch her like that, to make her cry out the way Jamaica had.

Miranda reasoned that she was already ruined by one sweaty, boring, embarrassing night all those years ago with Cubby. And if she was already ruined, she wanted, just once, to feel what Jamaica had felt minutes ago. What Slocum had felt. What Cubby had felt too. What everyone in the known universe felt from time to time, with, it would seem, the exception of herself.

What she had just experienced was so wonderful, so sweet. But the feelings one derived from just watching must be minuscule compared to the sensations of the participants. Suddenly, she wanted to participate in the worst way.

It wouldn't be so bad to burn in Hell if she had that one memory to cling to.

She pulled herself up to a sitting position and idly touched the large, fresh ink stain on her skirts, already clouded with dust. Her fingers trailed down then, and she picked up the empty ink bottle.

She turned it over in her hands. *Villiar's Premium Writing Ink,* read the label. *Blot for best results.* The loss was not a great one. She had more ink.

But she didn't believe she'd be doing much more writing for the moment. There was Tom to consider. He probably had his life mapped out, and he likely had a girl somewhere. But perhaps he wouldn't mind, just once . . . And she supposed she could hold her tongue and not tell him that she wrote "that trash."

She gritted her teeth just thinking about it, but told herself that he was good-looking and tall and certainly charming enough, and right up until he had said those words she'd even been sort of sweet on him! She could never be serious about a man who didn't respect her profession, her art. Why, she was practically famous, judging by the reactions around camp to her books! The girls were reading them aloud to each other, for heaven's sake!

But for a lover, a temporary lover to give her a sterling memory, Tom would do wonderfully.

Besides, what had she been thinking, nearly telling him about the books, and right out like that?

She squirmed, grinding her fanny down into the ground a bit. The sensations had stopped, and she was a little sad. Well, there was Tom, and there'd be later. She had no doubt that he'd be a good lover. The way he moved, the way he looked at her, the way he touched her arm or her hand while they were talking . . . Yes, Tom would be a much better lover than Cubby had been. Slocum obviously had no problems in that department, and even Slow Nell seemed wild about old Skunky.

It must just be Cubby who's bad at it, she thought. *Isn't that just my luck?*

She shook her head. Life was most assuredly strange.

14

In his office at the *Twin Buttes Telegraph,* Twin Buttes' leading (and only) newspaper, Drummond McLean paced back and forth in his office. News of the whores' strike had quickly spread all over town, and when he rode back into town yesterday, wanting nothing so much as to take a bath and change his clothes, he'd been waylaid three times by men who wanted to lynch him, punch him sideways, tie him to a horse and drag him out of town, or simply beat him to a bloody pulp.

The only thing that had saved him—aside from giving them Tiger and Harley upon which to take out their aggravations—was his reputation, but he had a feeling that was going to wear thin pretty soon. There was nothing so irritable as a man who needed a woman and couldn't find one. Except maybe a town full of men in the same circumstance.

The only bright spot in this was that once he got the girls back, he could double the prices. These boys would be in such a state by that time that they'd gladly pay anything.

He smiled, just a little.

Every cloud, as his aunt Maybelle used to say,

had a silver lining. Aunt Maybelle had been more correct than she knew. If Mordecai did his job right, McLean would come into a *real* silver lining. He'd have his Daisy Cutter, and the Bum Nugget too— and a bonanza in silver ore—because Big Tom Malloy and Slocum would be dead.

And Skunky, he reminded himself. *Don't forget that dried-up old fart.*

He checked the clock on the wall again, then checked his pocket watch. Both said three minutes past four.

Somebody should have been here by this time. Somebody should have reported in. Mordecai, or at least Tiger or Harley. He'd sent them both back out to the mine this morning, and they were glad to go, the spineless toads. They'd lit out of town at a gallop, while the men of the town chased them, shouting, "Cowards!" and hollering, "Where's our gals!" and pelting them with road apples and rocks.

McLean was antsy enough that he would have gone up front and looked out through the big, plateglass street window, had there still been one to look through. Somebody had put a brick through it at about ten that morning.

So he stayed in his office behind locked doors, nervously pacing the afternoon away and thinking very dark thoughts indeed about Slocum and Malloy and Skunky, and blacker ones about Harley and Tiger.

Far from town, Harley and Tiger sat beneath the meager shade of a tent flap at the Daisy Cutter Mine.

Around them was a flurry of activity. Men pushed a never-ending stream of ore carts up from the mine, mended equipment, hammered, pounded, swore, and sweated.

Tiger, who was nervous to begin with, and didn't feel one bit good about sitting there when they were supposed to be in town, said, "Where the hell's that Mordecai hombre?"

Harley looked up from the stick he'd been slowly whittling into a very long toothpick, and said, "That's the twenty-second time you asked me. I been keepin' count."

Tiger gritted his teeth. "And that's the twenty-second time you couldn't answer. Goddamn it! Where is he?"

"Twenty-three," muttered Harley.

"Shut up!" barked Tiger angrily. "You want another shiner to go with the one Rabbit Scruggs already gave you?"

Harley, who was indeed sporting one spectacular black eye, stopped whittling and pursed his lips for a moment. "Least I didn't get locked naked as the day I was born in some closet by a bunch'a damn whores."

Tiger punched him square in the nose.

It was dusk, and the day was ending at the Bum Nugget. With the long shadows had come the smells of beef stew bubbling and biscuits baking, and the sounds of women, too sore to shout and too tired to make a fuss, softly complaining.

In the fading light, Slocum walked through the

camp. Women who less than three days ago had
rested in feather beds, worn satins and silks, and
bathed daily, were clustered in somber knots. They
rubbed their feet, massaged each other's backs,
bandaged a multitude of blisters, and cleaned
scrapes and cuts.

Women were good workers, all right, but these
women were made for softer things. He hoped they
found the mother lode, and found it quick. They
were surely earning it. Tom was fairly giddy with
the progress they'd made; while some of the women
hauled rock, he and a few of the others slipped fresh
timbers into place. He'd told Slocum that the women
were allowing the mining effort to progress thirty
times as fast as what he and Skunky could have
done alone.

"Slocum!" barked a familiar voice. With a sigh,
he turned toward it to find Rose standing behind
him, a heaping dinner plate in her hand. As usual,
she was the first in the chow line. Most of the other
women were too tired to walk that far.

"Don't start with me, Rose," he said wearily.

Deep, vertical lines settled between her brows.
"The next time you go to town, you bring back some
peach preserves, you hear?"

He didn't quite know how to reply to that, and so
he just walked away. He heard her mutter,
"Monkey-butted asshole," but he just kept walking.
If he stayed to talk, he was liable to shoot her. It
would be a public service, by his reasoning.

He kept walking until he was down by the remuda. Skunky had tended all the horses, but he

stopped by Chaco and set to work with a curry comb and brush. The gelding's coat was already glossy, but Slocum figured that you could never groom a horse enough. Besides, he needed to think.

Several things had been tearing at him all day, and Mordecai was at the top of the list. He had seemed friendly enough, but with Mordecai, that didn't necessarily mean anything. He hadn't mentioned anything that had happened to him since Fort Worth, Slocum had realized later. That was ten years of nothing, just empty space. Just Fort Worth, and then working for McLean.

Slocum was beginning to wonder if maybe Mordecai had been in prison all that time. Braiding hackamores—that's what some men called it when they were in for a stretch. Of course, Mordecai was the type to run at cross-purposes with the law, and Slocum didn't fault him for it. But why hadn't Mordecai mentioned it?

Slocum shook his head as he circled the curry comb over Chaco's rump. "Just too much goin' on, old son," he murmured. "I'm makin' somethin' out of nothin'. Hell, he was probably just raisin' hell in Mexico or someplace."

Which got him to thinking about the pretty Mexican girl in Fort Worth, the one he could barely remember.

He flicked the brush after the curry comb, sending up little puffs of dust from the horse's coat. "Dammit, what was her name?" He could almost see her face. "Maria? Juanita? Ramona?"

"Slocum, you're going to brush that horse

bloody." It was Jamaica. She appeared at the Appaloosa's shoulder, and she was smiling. She took the curry comb and body brush from his hands. "Come and eat," she said. "And I'd appreciate it if you didn't bandy other women's names about, at least within my earshot."

He grinned sheepishly.

"How much longer do you think this will all take, Tom?" Miranda asked, and gave her eyelashes a little flutter. "How much longer will we have to be out here, I mean?"

She had managed to get him alone, which wasn't hard at all. And she was trying everything in her power—limited though her arsenal was—to seduce him. So far, she wasn't having much luck. She wished she'd paid more attention to this sort of thing when she was younger and had a chance, instead of always keeping her nose buried in a book.

"Hard to tell, Miranda," he said. He squinted at her. "Something wrong with your eyes?"

"No," she said with a sigh. When she'd tried sitting so close to him that their hips bumped, he'd colored, tipped his hat, and moved to the other side of the fire. And the eyelash thing wasn't working at all. He probably thought she had pinkeye.

She gave up. Maybe she'd think of something else later on. She said, "I'd like to apologize. About being so short with you last night."

"No need," he said, and smiled at her across their little fire of mesquite wood. She liked the smell.

"Yes, there is," she insisted, "and I'm sorry about

it. You're entitled to read what you *like* to read. Well, that was redundant, wasn't it?" she added with a roll of her eyes.

He chuckled. "Well, I guess I wasn't so truthful. Don't tell anybody, but I did read that first Slocum book. It gets sort of boring up here at night. Before you ladies came, that is."

Miranda snapped to attention. "You read it?" She couldn't bear it! What if he said that he'd hated it? She supposed that she'd just have to leave again, like she had the night before. Oh, if he hated it, she couldn't possibly sleep with him. She didn't believe she could ever say a civil word to him again!

But if he had liked it . . .

"D-did you . . . did you enjoy it?" she asked carefully. "Enjoy" seemed safer, somehow, than "like."

When he didn't answer right away, she had to remind herself to breathe. And then she chastised herself for putting so much weight on his answer. How silly! She'd likely never see this man again once this stupid strike was over. She'd go her way and he'd go his—men usually did, didn't they? After all, she'd led him to believe she was a common whore. Why cut herself off from what she trusted would be a memorable experience for the sake of an opinion over a book?

But when he finally opened his mouth to answer, her breath caught in her throat again.

"You know," he said thoughtfully, "all in all, it was a pretty fine story. Course, it was nothing like what Slocum's really like. But if I hadn't met him for real, I would've—"

He never finished the sentence, because Miranda was across the fire in a flash, blissfully covering his mouth with hers.

"Don't tell me you're leaving again tonight!" Jamaica said as Slocum stood up and stretched. "What in the devil are you doing out there anyway?" She looked awfully appealing, sitting in the center of his blanket with folded arms and tousled hair and a stern expression. But it was getting past seven, and he'd said that he'd meet Mordecai at eight again tonight, to decide what to do.

He bent to touch her face. "Trust me, Mudge," he said softly. "Be back in a few hours. Maybe less."

"Hmph," she snorted, and averted her eyes. "Just don't be surprised if I've found somebody else by the time you get back, Slocum."

He gave her a wink, then set off down the hill. He didn't think it wise to say what he was thinking, which was that Skunky would be thrilled to have a new bedmate. He liked his scalp better than that.

He was chuckling to himself when he nearly stumbled over Big Tom and some girl. They were tangled in a heated embrace, and it took him a second to recognize the girl. Actually, he only recognized her from her dress, her face being hidden at that moment. What was her name again? Jamaica had told him.

Miranda, that was it. The girl from his hotel in town, the one with the perpetually ink-stained fingers. As he walked on past, he was thinking that Tom had surely picked an odd one for loving. That

little gal was pretty, all right, but she hadn't looked
to him as if she'd ever let anybody into her knickers.

He was wondering once again what she was doing
up there when he passed the mouth of the mine,
where Skunky and Nell were sitting away from the
bulk of the tired crowd of women. They weren't
engaged in anything they needed privacy for,
though. Skunky was cleaning rifles, the rifles that
he'd found on the road.

Slocum stopped and asked, "How's it coming?"

"A dozen of these sonsabitches to go," Skunky
complained. "Why's they gotta pack 'em in grease?
That's what I want to know. Hell, I got grease
comin' out my ears."

"All over your pants too, sweetie," said Slow Nell
with a smile.

"If it ain't one thing, it's another," Skunky went
on. "You and Tom, Slocum. It's 'Skunky, dig me a
shitter. No, make it two.' Or 'Skunky, haul that ore.'
'Skunky, ride five miles out and pick up some decent firewood.' 'Skunky, clean them guns.' What's
it gonna be next? I ain't diggin' no wells or no more
outhouses, no, sir. And I ain't throwin' up no houses
so you boys can cat around in privacy."

While Slocum grinned, Slow Nell leaned over and
whispered something into Skunky's ear, and damned
if the old man didn't blush!

"Well, that'd be different," he said softly.

Slow Nell smiled, and winked at Slocum.

Slocum tipped his hat. "Evenin' then," he said.
Miranda forgotten, he made his way down past the
cook fires and the girls, and over to the remuda.

He saddled Chaco, talking softly to the horse as he did so. "Gonna have to cut into your drowsing time, ol' buddy," he said. "But it's just out to meet Mordecai and back again. 'Sides, you're gettin' lazy, what with standin' around all day."

With a creak of leather, he stepped up into the saddle and set out at a slow jog, riding over silvery desert between soft gray clumps of scrub. Soon, the camp at the Bum Nugget was long lost from sight, and before long, he could just make out the pinpoint of Mordecai's campfire ahead, at the place where they'd met before. A creature of habit, that was Mordecai Jones.

But when he rode closer, he didn't see Mordecai. He reined in Chaco well back from the ring of fire-light and sat, waiting in the darkness, one hand resting lightly on the butt of his Colt.

Finally, the silence was broken by Mordecai's call. "That you, Slocum?"

Slocum relaxed, but only a little. "Where the hell are you?" he replied.

"Takin' me a shit." The answer came from a spot off to the left, beyond the fire, and was followed by an embarrassed laugh. "I swan, them biscuits of Cookie's binds me up somethin' terrible. C'mon in and pull up a rock. Be with you shortly."

Slocum's hand left the butt of his gun, and he eased his way toward the firelight, dismounting at its edge and looping Chaco's reins through a hop-seed bush. He heard Mordecai grunt in the distance as he walked into the ring of light.

Into the darkness, he said, "Mordecai, you tell McLean what you were supposed to?"

"If'n you mean about how I was gonna come out here and kill you, then yes, I surely did. Told him that yesterday, come to think of it. Course, I said as how I was gonna do it by this afternoon." He gave a little laugh.

Mordecai's tone had changed, just slightly, and the skin on the back of Slocum's neck began to crawl. Not a good sign. He never should have trusted Mordecai, dammit, but it had just been too good a thing, finding him among McLean's men. Too good to be true, as it was turning out.

Slocum took a step back, away from the fire.

He heard the unmistakable *click* of a gun's hammer at the same time Mordecai said, "I wouldn't move no more if'n I was you, ol' buddy."

Slocum froze.

"Unbuckle the Colt and let 'er drop real easy."

Slocum began to work at the buckle.

"Suppose you'd like to know why I'm gonna kill you," Mordecai said. His voice had moved to a new location beyond the firelight. He was moving to Slocum's left.

Slocum dropped the Colt. It landed in a small puff of dust at his feet, the firelight coloring the barrel orange.

"Cross-draw rig too."

Slocum muttered a curse, but he unbuckled the cross-draw rig and let it drop.

He said, "Now that you got me naked, you want to tell me why?"

Bitterly, Mordecai laughed. He'd moved again, always going to his right. "You remember that time in Fort Worth, Slocum?"

"Barely."

"You remember a little Mex gal name of Lola?"

"*That* was her name!" Slocum said. "Hadn't thought of her in years. I been tryin' to think of what we called her."

"You remember her brother, Eduardo?" He was almost even with Slocum's left shoulder, out there in the dark. Why was he working his way around? Slocum tried to calculate how quickly he could drop, grab a gun, and fire. Mordecai had been fast back in the old days. Fast enough that Slocum knew he only had a fifty-fifty chance of making it to the ground alive.

"Nope," he said in all honesty. "Don't remember him. Barely remember Lola."

"Well, Eduardo got sorta pissed after he found out what you'd been doin' with his sister all that week." Mordecai had stopped moving. For the moment.

"My recollection's fuzzy," Slocum said slowly, "but I seem to recall that she was real headstrong about askin' for it. Several times a day."

"You was like a pair of goddamned rabbits," Mordecai said. "Step yourself back from them guns."

Dammit! Slocum took a step back.

"Farther."

Slocum obliged, although grudgingly. Now he was too far away. Mordecai would nail him before he got halfway to his guns. It would have to be the boot knife. But his chances with the blade were slim to none in these circumstances, because he'd not only have to reach down, but pull up his pants cuff to get at it.

Damn!

"Mordecai, I'm real confused about this whole thing," he said, playing for time.

"I'm about to enthrall you with the details," Mordecai said grandly. He'd moved again. Now he was behind Slocum, and Slocum turned toward the voice, giving up what meager chance he had to get at his guns.

"Ol' Eduardo got real pissed, like I said," Mordecai went on. "And you know, seems to me you'd already left town by the time he showed up. But anyhow, he was mad enough to spit nails, and the first thing he did when he found out I'd been with you—guess he figured I was guilty by association— was to go on down to the livery and kill my horse."

Something inside Slocum froze. Now he realized why Mordecai had been working his way around the ring of firelight. The lunatic was within ten paces of Chaco right now.

"Next thing, he come up to the hotel and pulled me outta bed, hungover as sin, and beat the livin' shit outta me," Mordecai continued matter-of-factly. "Well, I was hungover, and he was a big feller, near six-foot-four and muscled up. Whomped me so bad that I couldn't figure out which of the fellas I was seein' was him, so when I got hold of my pistol, I just aimed for the one in the middle. Turned out I killed him, all right, and they threw me in jail. Nine years I did. Would'a been more, but he was only a Mex."

Slocum's hands tightened into fists at his sides. "Tough break, Mordecai," he said as evenly as he was able. The sonofabitch was now within five feet of the hopseed bush where he'd tied Chaco.

"Yeah," Mordecai said, "that's what I thought. Really got to hating you while I was in there, Slocum. Now, don't get me wrong. When we was out here last night, I thought about going along with you, I really did. Old times, and like that. It held a strong pull, 'cause I don't much like Mr. Drummond McLean either, the Yankee asshole. But I thought it over, and I decided that killin' your horse while you watched, then killin' you, you would make me feel a whole lot better than just ruinin' *him*."

He paused. "You was always real crazy about your horses, wasn't you, Slocum? This little Appy you been ridin' looks right nice."

Mordecai's gun went off.

In the instant that the powder flared, Slocum threw himself backward. He landed on the cross-draw rig and barely noticed the buckle stabbing him in the back, because he was within reach of the Colt. He whipped it off the ground, holster and all, and began firing blindly toward the spot where Mordecai had last been standing, fired until the gun's hammer clicked on an empty chamber, then rolled over and brought up the cross-draw harness, a pistol in each hand.

He didn't fire, though. He waited, listening over the sound of his own shallow breathing for the slightest break of a twig, the tiniest shiver of weed against boot.

There was nothing.

Warily, he climbed to his feet. Still aiming the pistols out into the darkness, he backed slowly toward the fire, letting one pistol drop down to dangle from its harness when he picked up a flaming brand from the fire. Then slowly, he walked forward again.

Mordecai was dead. Five slug holes peppered the spreading bloodstain on his shirt. A sixth went through his throat.

The Appy was dead too. It looked to Slocum as if he must have been killed instantly, for Mordecai had put a single bullet just behind his eye. Blood, glistening black in the moonlight, pooled around the horse's head, soaked into the desert floor.

"Aw, Chaco," Slocum whispered, sinking to his knees. "Aw, Chaco." He let the gun slip from his fingers and gently lifted the horse's head into his lap. "I'm sorry, old son. . . ."

15

Slow Nell, smoking a post-coital cheroot while Skunky drowsed happily beside her, sat up abruptly and poked an elbow into Skunky's side.

"Not again, darlin'," he muttered teasingly, his eyes closed. "I'm an old man, remember?"

But she hissed, "Did you hear that?" and poked him again.

Skunky groaned. "Aw, just go to sleep, puddin'."

She stared out over the desert, listening, waiting. It didn't come again, and it had been very far away, but she knew what she'd heard. "Sounded like shots, Elroy."

He opened one eye. "Drat it, woman, I told you not to call me by my true name! Suppose somebody was to hear?" He paused, and then the other eye popped open. "You say shots?"

"Slow down, Skunky," Big Tom cautioned the older man. "We're not going to do anybody any good if your horse steps in a hole and busts a leg."

Skunky mumbled a curse, but he slowed back down to the lazy jog to which Tom was keeping. Tom was a little worried about Slocum, who by his reckoning had left camp an hour and a half before, although he honestly figured that Slocum had just shot at a snake or coyote or some such. He was relieved to have an excuse to ride out, though. That Miranda! She'd been all over him, and it took every ounce of self-control he owned not to take her up on what she was offering.

What *was* it with women anyway? Some of them threw themselves at you, some of them turned to ice if a man so much as glanced at them, and some would go either way at the drop of a hat. He'd never understand them as long as he lived.

When Skunky had come running up the hill to fetch him, he'd been pinned down and was losing his resolve in a hurry. Four times he'd slipped free of her, calmed her down, told her he wanted to take it slow, but every damn time she'd managed to work in close to him again and start kissing and hugging.

Didn't she understand that he was serious about her? A man didn't want to just throw a girl—a girl he was serious about anyhow—to the ground and take her without so much as a fare-thee-well!

And most of all, didn't she understand that she'd got his balls as blue as cornflowers? It was the worst kind of torture!

It had been all he could do not to tell her that he'd figured her out, that he knew she wasn't a whore, although she'd surely been acting the part tonight. He thought it best that she told him herself, told him about what she was really writing in those so-called diaries of hers.

Well, a man couldn't help it if he just happened

to be passing by her pack, could he? He couldn't help it if her valise just sort of happened to fall open, and one of those diaries just happened to fall open, right to the middle of a new Slocum adventure. There was a half-finished letter to somebody called Cubby, who he took to be her editor or publisher or some such, and pages and pages of notes on everything from the interior of a café in town to how to pick a horse's hoof clean.

He wanted to give himself a good sound kick for making light of that Slocum book the night before. He could sure make a mess of things, couldn't he? Because she was writing them as sure as he was sitting this horse.

He smiled, just a little, which was something that he'd been doing off and on ever since he found her diaries. That little bit of a gal, writing those Slocum books! Published and everything. Imagine that!

Of course, the diaries had been deep down inside her belongings, and he didn't exactly want her to know that he'd been snooping. . . .

But still, didn't she trust him?

The smile turned into a sheepish grin. He guessed that they were both equally guilty of deception. It was only fair.

"Light," Skunky said, pointing up ahead and breaking into Tom's reverie.

Far ahead, the light of a campfire flickered. No, two campfires, for as they rode closer, he began to make out that there were two, one big and one small. The bigger one was roaring. And then he saw something coming toward him, something intermittently backlit by the big fire's blaze.

"Rider," said Skunky before Tom had a chance to form the word. Tom saw Skunky slip his old Remington free of its holster and rein his horse wide of Tom's.

Skunky had gone twenty yards to the side, and Tom had his gun drawn too, when the rider, now perhaps a hundred yards distant, halted and waved slowly.

"Who goes there?" shouted Tom.

"Me, you pair of idiots!" came the reply.

Tom relaxed. It was Slocum.

He jogged forward, Skunky easing in at an angle to meet him, and they reached Slocum within seconds.

Right off, Tom knew something was very wrong.

For one thing, Slocum was covered in something black and wet that could only be blood. For another, he looked like hell.

"Good God, man!" he whispered. "Where are you shot?"

"I'm fine," Slocum said, and fell in between them.

"What happened to that Palouse horse'a yours?" Skunky asked, and for the first time, Tom noticed that Slocum was riding a jug-headed bay. He'd previously been too intent on the man himself to notice.

"Dead," Slocum said tersely.

"Dead!" said Skunky, and Tom felt his heart sink. He knew Slocum was crazy about that damn horse. He'd spent more time down at the picket line than

he had in Jamaica's arms. He knew, now, what was
burning in that bonfire.

But old Skunky didn't know when to keep quiet.
"What in tarnation happened? You tangle with
some'a McLean's men? What was you doin' out
here? Did they come up on you all in a rush? How
many was there anyways?"

Slocum didn't answer. Tom hadn't known him
long, but he knew him well enough that he didn't
expect him to respond. Slocum simply showed the
bay his heels and rode out about twenty feet ahead
before he slowed to a jog again.

"What the Sam Hill's got his butternuts in a
bunch?" Skunky carped.

"Just leave him alone for now," Tom said. "He'll
tell us in good time."

"But what if McLean's men come upon him?"
Skunky said crankily. "What if they's fixin' to ride
down on us now?"

"They're not," Tom said firmly.

"Well, I ain't so sure," Skunky grumbled, but he
said no more after that.

As they rode slowly back to the Bum Nugget,
Slocum far in the lead, Tom took a last glance over
his shoulder at the funeral pyre fading into the distance.

At the Daisy Cutter, a single man on guard duty had
just made out the distant shots, and he'd alerted the
rest. They had gathered together and decided to send
a party of five men out to reconnoiter, and a reluc-
tant Tiger and Harley were among them. Toby, who

was in charge now that Mordecai had left the camp, led them on his flashy pinto.

Tiger had no time for Toby. He believed that the little man was a spineless show-off who would do them absolutely no good if things got bad. He firmly believed that Toby was a weasel and a coward who was out for himself, period. If the truth were told, Tiger recognized a kindred spirit in Toby, and hated him for it.

But Toby was in charge—temporarily anyhow—and so they followed.

I'll quit, Tiger thought as they rode along through the moonlight. *I'll quit and get shed of Mr. Drummond McLean. But I'll get my damned knife back first.* He had a happy vision of sticking the knife into McLean's belly and twisting.

McLean hadn't panned out at all. He'd promised Tiger—Harley too, the idiot—lots of money and lots of power. But when Tiger had cut up just a few gals, gals that nobody cared about or would miss, McLean had gone loony on him. The stupid bastard. Didn't he realize that out here a man had to be tough and get his point across quick and hard? If Tiger could have sliced up just a few more whores, they would have started paying attention, goddamnit! Hell, they were starting to already!

But no, Mr. Drummond Gotta-Have-a-Bath-and-a-Shave-Every-Damned-Day McLean had taken Tiger's knife and pushed him around and made him feel like a worm under a boot. It wasn't natural, a man being so clean and kept-up as the boss was.

Tiger felt it pointed to grievous underlying faults.

"Up there!" shouted Harley, and the others all shushed him at once. They'd all seen it. Fires.

Frankly, Tiger didn't understand how Harley could see much of anything, what with both his eyes black and blue and swollen nearly shut, and his nose swollen to the size of a turnip.

"Jeez!" hissed Harley, who was having to breathe through his mouth. "I was only sayin'."

Toby said, "Spread out," and they did, riding cautiously toward the fires.

By the time he was fifty feet out, Tiger decided that there was nobody there, but something was surely burning, something that smelled like hair and meat. He found out quick enough what it was.

"Who'd trouble to burn up a horse?" he asked softly as he leaned on his saddle horn. A charred hoof stuck out of the mound of burning debris, and the stench was overpowering. No one heard him, though. They were off scouting.

"Over here!" shouted one of the men at the edge of the firelight, a sandy-haired fellow. Tiger didn't know his name. He didn't care to know any of their names. He just wanted to get back to town, and then out of it on the first stage. He was having second thoughts about killing McLean. Sticking a feller was a whole different proposition than sticking a scared whore. Unless you could sneak up on him, that is . . .

The sandy-haired fellow stood up. "Found a saddle and bridle!"

There came the sounds of brush being jostled, although Tiger didn't know how. It seemed that somebody had ripped up all the brush as far as he could

see and set it afire on top of this stupid horse. Somebody was a real bonfire-fancier or a real horse-hater,
that was all he could figure.

"Hey," the man shouted again. "It's Mordecai's
rig!"

Before Tiger quite had time to take in the gravity
of this statement, Toby, who was off a ways, out in
the darkness, called, "Shit! Get over here!"

Tiger followed the others off into the shadows,
leaving the fire's light behind. And then, in the
moonlight, he began to pick out a rock jutting up
from the desert floor like a single, worn tooth. Men
were clustering around its base. And as he rode
closer, he saw why their heads were craned up and
their hats were in their hands.

Somebody was lashed to the rock. Lashed upside
down, with his knees bent over the very top of it
and his head at a sick angle, scraping the desert
floor. His chest, neck, and head were obscured by
dark, drying blood, and on the stone between his
splayed legs, somebody had scrawled "Horse
Killer." In blood.

"Holy cow," breathed Harley.

Toby, who was kneeling by the man's face, said,
"It's Mordecai. Dang!"

Tiger, in his infinite wisdom, simply muttered,
"McLean ain't payin' us enough."

16

How did he get into these things?

That's what Slocum was asking himself as he rode back toward the Bum Nugget, ahead of the others. Poor old Chaco! All he'd wanted was to pick up a little easy cash by delivering that letter for Mad Hat Crockett, a letter that Tom Malloy didn't seem in much of a hurry to answer. Then somehow, he'd gotten himself embroiled with a whole townful of whores and a nasty land dispute, which was annoying in a way, but had still looked like a cake walk.

But then it had gone nasty. An old friend had turned enemy, and now that nice little Appy gelding he'd borrowed to get himself down here had been willfully murdered.

That was the worst thing. Slocum couldn't abide waste, and especially couldn't abide the senseless waste of a good horse. And if the truth be told, he was real fond of that copper-colored gelding with the butt full of ticking and spots.

Slocum shook his head. Chaco had been fast, that was for sure. He'd been surefooted over treacherous ground, could spin on a bottle-stopper, didn't spook, and reined at a feather's touch. And he'd been as good-natured a horse as Slocum had ever had the pleasure to ride.

Mordecai had died too quickly, if you asked him.

He heard a horse quicken its trot just a little, and shortly found Big Tom riding at his elbow. The two men rode in silence for a spell, their saddle leathers creaking in time, before Big Tom said, "Sorry to break in on your thoughts, Slocum, but we're coming close to camp. I've got to know what happened back there."

Slocum ground his teeth, but Big Tom had a right to know. He'd have plenty of time to fester over Chaco later.

"You remember Mordecai?"

Big Tom nodded. "The one whose brother you killed."

Slocum had nearly forgotten the story they'd made up. He said, "Bunch of lies. I've known Mordecai, off and on, since the War. The day McLean and his men rode in, Mordecai signaled me to meet him that night. I did, and we hatched us a plan. Mordecai was gonna double-cross McLean."

Big Tom scratched the back of his neck. "He was? How?"

Slocum thought about telling him, but it was too involved, and besides, it didn't matter anyway, did it? So he skipped over the how of it, and simply said, "Doesn't matter. He didn't turn out to be a friend after all. He shot my horse and was gonna shoot me, except I got him first. I suppose you already figured that it was my horse burnin' in the bonfire. Got my tack off him before I started the fire, though." He smacked his saddle horn with a cupped hand.

"Figured," Big Tom said. "And I'm real sorry, Slocum. That was a real handy colt, from what I saw of him."

"Goddamn shame, if you was to ask me," said Skunky, who had ridden up next to them as they talked. "That horse'a yours were right nice. I said so, didn't I, Tom? I said he were a right nice one the first time I seen him."

Slocum simply nodded.

"Were that Mordecai feller all by his lonesome when you killed him?" Skunky went on. "Nell said she heard a bunch'a shots."

"He was alone," Slocum replied.

"Well, you think them fellas is gonna come pourin' down on us?" Skunky asked in a more urgent tone.

"Not tonight," Big Tom replied.

Skunky huffed. "An' how the hell do you know that, Tom?"

"He's right," said Slocum, and before Skunky had the chance to interject another comment, he added, "If they were, they'd already be here. Sound carries both ways, you know. Besides, I don't think they'd want to take a chance at night. They wouldn't take the chance of galloping over the desert at night, and they won't take the chance of riding in on our camp with their guns drawn. They'd shoot too many whores by accident."

He reined the late Mordecai's jug-headed bay around a clump of brush. He reined like a plow horse. Slocum said, "They likely only sent out a handful of men to investigate anyhow. No, they'll find Mordecai and puzzle over that for a while, then go on back home and think about what to do next. Probably have to check in with McLean. And if I haven't missed my guess, he's back in town."

Big Tom said, "Why puzzle over Mordecai?"

Slocum was silent for a moment, then said, "I left a message with him."

"What?" Skunky piped up. "What'd you say?"

The lights of the Bum Nugget's campfires were just coming into view, and Slocum gathered the bay's reins. "Skunky," he said, "you ask too many questions."

He kicked the bay into a slow lope.

Jamaica nearly swooned when she first saw Slocum, for he was covered in blood from his chest down to his toes. But when he stepped down off the horse and she saw that he wasn't limping or staggering or cradling an arm—and when she realized that his horse wasn't his horse at all—she immediately took charge of the situation.

"Out of those clothes this instant," she demanded, setting aside the Winchester that Skunky had hurriedly handed her before he set off with Big Tom. Actually, he'd shoved two dozen shiny new rifles into her arms and hollered, "Give 'em to those what knows how to use 'em!" before he'd headed out.

She'd had plenty of takers, all right. Slow Nell had doled out the ammunition, and when Skunky, Big Tom, and Slocum had ridden back into camp alone, she'd heard a few grumbles of disappointment.

She picked up a torch to light their way. Slocum was a mess, but she knew better than to ask him any questions. He'd tell her when he was ready. In silence he followed her up the gentle hill, but halfway up they came upon Rose.

The big woman clambered gracelessly off the rock she'd been perched upon, and snorted derisively at the sight of him. "Whose blood, Slocum?" she asked.

He pushed on past her without speaking, but Rose called, "Them books are wrong about you, Slocum. What'd you do, shoot a coyote just to show off? Or maybe to pretend you was protectin' us?"

He wheeled to face the fat woman, and Jamaica held her breath.

"I don't cotton to men who hit women, Rose," Slocum said, and his steely voice was pitched low and deadly serious. "But in your case, I'm about to make an exception."

Rose didn't flinch. She barked out a scornful laugh. "You wouldn't dare, you monkey's whacker."

Jamaica found herself wishing that Slocum would just haul off and pound Rose into the ground. Jamaica had never been able to stand the evil old biddy, not really, and for the life of her couldn't figure out why Rose's girls stayed with her. Jamaica was more than tempted to haul off and slug the cow herself!

But Slocum was made of sterner stuff. He turned

away, as if to leave, then stopped. "Aw, hell," he muttered, then turned back, spread his hand over Rose's wide face, and shoved hard.

She went down in a sputtering heap, shouting that she was murdered and shrieking for help, but by then he'd already walked away from her and joined Jamaica. She noticed that a couple of Rose's girls were slowly making their way up the hill to see what was the matter, but that nobody was in too much of an all-fired rush.

"Such a gentleman," Jamaica said to him over Rose's cries and catcalls. It was all she could do to contain her laughter, and in the end she failed.

"I do my best," he muttered, and they walked the rest of the way up the hill.

During the time that Tom had been gone, Miranda's insides had slowly come unknotted. *What on earth is wrong with him?* she kept asking herself.

Or what was wrong with her? Perhaps that was more to the point. She didn't believe it could be the way she looked. She wasn't ugly. She'd been told she was pretty, in fact. Although, looking down at herself, she had to admit it might be something about the way she was dressed.

Her apparel was sadly lacking—or more to the point, much too much—from a sporting girl's perspective. But she couldn't change that, now could she? The rest of her luggage was back at the hotel. And besides, all her other dresses were just as prim and proper as this one.

I look like a Sunday school teacher! she inwardly

moaned. *That's why he won't do anything!*

Or was it? Perhaps men just knew when women couldn't do it right, and she had to consider that perhaps it hadn't been Cubby, all those years ago, who'd been clumsy or inept. Maybe it had been her, she thought with a horrid sinking feeling. Maybe she just wasn't meant for this mating dance.

"Maybe I just should have joined a nunnery," she muttered.

"What's that, darlin?" asked the tall, elegant black woman perched on the cot at her side. They were down in the open-sided tents, and all around her women were sipping coffee or snoring, or talking softly in twos and threes. Everything had relaxed again, now that the men were back, although she had noticed that nobody had given their rifles back. She hadn't taken one when it was offered. She doubted that she could hit a draft mare's butt from five feet with a scattergun.

"Nothing, Sassafras," she said, then took a close look at the woman. "How do you do it?"

Sassafras set down her coffee cup. "Do what, child?"

"How do you manage to look so . . ." Miranda sighed. "Clean, I guess. I feel like I've been dragged through the dirt for three days." She smiled. "Well, I guess I have. But you've been down working in the mines too!"

Sassafras shrugged. "It's not much. I brought three outfits, you see. One, I wear. One is in the wash, and the other one is drying. When I finish in the mines, I have a little sponge bath, and I always have something fresh to wear." She looked up the hill, at the mine entrance. "That mine, it's a dirty one. Puts the filth into your very pores. But I have been watching the rock. Very soon, we'll hit."

"The mother lode?" Miranda asked. "I thought that we were already bringing up good ore. Tom said so. He seemed very happy about it." Ah, Tom . . . She wished she'd thought to bring three dresses!

"Good, yes. But I think that soon we will reach the mother of them all," Sassafras said thoughtfully, before shifting her gaze once again to Miranda. "Do you know where the boundary's marked between this mine and McLean's?"

Miranda shook her head.

"I wish I knew for certain," Sassafras said. "We've tunneled far to the east." She tipped her head toward the darkness from which Slocum and the others had emerged.

"Are you sure?" Miranda asked somewhat dubiously. "I get awfully turned around down there."

But the reply was firm. "I am sure." And then Sassafras cocked her head. "Miranda," she said, "I hope you don't mind my asking, but why are you here?"

Miranda blinked. "Well . . . well, we were going on strike!"

But Sassafras shook her head. "Child, if there's one thing I know, it's whores. And you are not of the sisterhood."

Sassafras's smile was kindly, but Miranda was stuck for a reply. If they found her out, would they banish her from camp? She didn't think she'd like

town one bit at the moment. She could just guess
what the men would do if a lone women showed up
in their midst.

But Jamaica patted her hand comfortingly. "You
must have your reasons. You may keep them to
yourself if you wish."

She picked up her coffee again and started to rise,
but as an afterthought, Miranda touched her arm and
said, "Please wait."

Sassafras arched a brow.

"How do you make a man . . ." Miranda began.
"That is, how do I . . . ?"

The black woman laughed softly. "You want to
know how to make Big Tom fall in love with you?"

Miranda's mouth fell open. Actually, she'd want
to know only enough to make him take her in the
throes of passion, so to speak, but now that Sassafras
had said it right out, she knew that his love was what
she wanted. Sassafras must be part Gypsy. Or part
Obeah woman.

Miranda swallowed. "How . . . how did you know
that?"

"My dear child, it's obvious to anyone who takes
the time to look," Sassafras said. She set her coffee
aside again and took both of Miranda's hands in
hers. "I will tell you something about Tom Malloy,
all right? First of all, he doesn't come to town to
look for women. Never. He used to come to talk to
Jamaica, but I believe it was because he enjoyed the
company of an educated woman. Jamaica is quite
bright, you know. And don't look so dismayed, pet.
Her company and her coffee was all he sought. And

secondly, I believe that you have already succeeded in your venture."

Miranda blinked rapidly. "W-what?"

"I believe that he is already in love with you."

Miranda tucked her chin. "No!"

Sassafras chuckled. "A man who will not sleep with a woman who offers herself so freely?" She clucked her tongue. "And put away that look you have on your face. I saw you earlier tonight, but I don't believe that anyone else did, so have no fear. He was most adamant, yet most tempted. Heartily tempted, one would say. Take my advice and let him come to you. He will, and sooner than you think."

With that, Sassafras rose, retrieved her coffee cup, and walked away, leaving a flummoxed—and speechless—Miranda to stare blankly after her.

It was nearly three o'clock in the morning by the time Tiger and Harley rode into town, which was just fine as far as the two of them were concerned. They came in the back way, and the streets they rode were empty of potential assailants, most of the waking population being up on Main Street. Tiger was glad. He figured that anything McLean would do to them for waking him up was a sight better than what the men of the town would do if they spotted them.

Tiger and Harley rode over to Third Street, their horses' hooves sounding loud and echoing in the empty streets, and Tiger breathed a sigh of relief as he dismounted and tied his horse to the neat, white-washed picket fence that surrounded McLean's front yard.

"Gives me the spooks," Harley commented. What with his nose being swollen shut, his voice sounded odd and boxy. "They's usually a bunch'a whores hanging round, you know? Wonder what the boys is doing for entertainment." He tittered, and Tiger was tempted to slug him again.

He refrained, however, and opened McLean's front gate. He let it slap shut behind him, and heard Harley's complaining, "Hey!" as it struck him.

Tiger didn't look back, though. He just went up the walk and climbed the steps. He rapped on the front door, and it was only then that he noticed the tomatoes.

Somebody had been throwing ripe tomatoes at McLean's house. A whole lot of them. They were smeared on the clapboards, drying in seedy streaks on the windows. He looked down at his feet, and sure enough, he was standing in squashed tomatoes. Eggshells too. In fact, there were eggshells and smeary egg yolks and tomatoes all along the front porch.

He didn't want to be around tomorrow when those eggs started to stink. In fact, he didn't want to be around tomorrow, period.

He paused his fist in mid-knock, then dropped his hand to his side.

"What you doin', Tiger?" Harley asked.

"Shut up and let me think," Tiger snapped. The town was a real bad place for him to be right now, although if he managed to bring the whores back, he'd be a hero. Sort of. Come to think of it, it didn't seem to him that the men in town were all that friendly to begin with. And the boss was always cranky. McLean wouldn't let a man do his work, dammit, and confiscated his blade to boot! And the men from Big Tom's camp—for he could figure it was no one else but them—had done a bad piece of work on Mordecai tonight. A very bad piece of work indeed.

Did he want to hang on and let McLean kick him around, and maybe end up roped dead and upside down to a rock?

"Hell, no!" he said aloud.

A startled Harley said, "I didn't do nothin'!"

"Not you," Tiger said, and turned his back on the tomato-smeared door. "Harley, you can go ahead and bang on that door all you want, but I'm—"

Behind him, the door swung open.

A groggy McLean leaned out and hissed, "About goddamn time you jackasses showed up! Get the hell in here and tell me what's going on!"

With a sigh, a frustrated Tiger turned back and walked through the door, Harley on his heels.

Tomorrow, Tiger was thinking. *Tomorrow, I'll just hie out.*

17

Dawn at the Bum Nugget came too early.

Skunky was up on top of the hill with a pair of battered binoculars, keeping watch and undoubtedly carping nonstop about lack of sleep and how these young scamps had no respect for an old man.

Big Tom, who Slocum figured to have a mind for silver and little else, and who was dead set on blasting no matter what, was deep in the mine shaft, rigging charges with a little help from two of the crib gals. Their daddies had been miners and they therefore knew what they were doing.

And Slocum himself, who had changed into clean clothes at Jamaica's insistence, and who had managed to get a grand total of four hours of sleep, give or take, was standing halfway up the hill between the mine opening and Skunky's roost, right along that banding ribbon of rock. With a spyglass, he searched the distance. It wasn't that he didn't trust Skunky. He just didn't want any surprises today, that was all.

The distance was clear for the moment anyway, and he lowered the glass to the camp. Everything sprang into sharp detail.

He picked out a few of Jamaica's girls. There was the darkly beautiful Sassafras, her earrings glinting in the morning sun and her turban piled high as she leaned against a tent pole and smoked a slim black cigarillo. She nervously glanced out toward the east every few seconds too. The girl by her side was Abra, if Slocum remembered correctly, a wispy little blond thing who favored feathers. She wasn't wearing any now, though. She looked bedraggled and tired, and she was reading a copy of *John Slocum: Death Rides a Spotted Stallion*.

He growled. He couldn't read the words on the cover from here, but he recognized the cover art. A big blob of yellow, which when you looked closer, would turn out to be the giant sun that Slocum was riding off into. Damn books anyway!

Testily, he shifted his gaze lower down the hill. The women had formed a sort of sentry line and they were spread out every few yards, sitting or standing, those gleaming new Winchesters cradled in their arms. He recognized a few of them, although not many.

The cherubic girl with honey-brown hair caught back with a scrap of cloth and hanging nearly to her knees was Susan, he thought.

The tall, strawberry blonde was Cindy. Or was it Cindy Lou?

The beautiful mulatto girl with the skin like cinnamon and bleached blond hair was Faith.

He saw Jamaica then, walking slowly along the line, stopping at each girl to chat for a moment. That was his Jamaica, he thought with a sudden grin. Always making everything a party, always putting everyone at ease.

Reluctantly, he lifted the spyglass from Jamaica to check the distance once again. Nothing, not even a lonely coyote. He slowly swung the glass nearer in, to the south and the remuda, and felt something go tight in his chest when he remembered, all over again, that Chaco wasn't there.

He dropped the glass from his eye for a moment and cleared his throat roughly. This was no time to be mourning horses. No time, he suddenly remembered, to be mourning people either.

Still, he felt ashamed of himself. Flossie. Jamaica had mentioned that she'd been killed, stabbed to death, the night before they'd all left town. And that the killer was likely one of McLean's toadies, either Tiger or Harley. He hadn't given it much more than a thought at the time. There had been a whole heap of other things to think about. But at the moment, he was wondering why he should be saddened so much more by the death of a horse than a girl.

There was nothing to do about it, though, nothing but to take revenge for Flossie, poor little Flossie with the pillowy breasts and the sweet, languorous smile. He'd already had his revenge for Chaco.

He lifted the glass again. The horizon was still clear, although he didn't expect it to be anything else at this hour. The men from the Daisy Cutter wouldn't ride out before dawn, and it would take them at least an hour to get here, riding hard. If they came, that is. He kept checking anyway.

Nearer in, he took a peek at the cook fires. Rose's

cook, Edna Merle, a thin woman with her thick, gray hair wadded up into a tight knot on top of her head, appeared to be baking pan after pan of biscuits. Jamaica's cook, Mrs. Arnot, was at a second fire some fifteen feet away, cracking eggs into one oversized skillet while ham sizzled in another.

Slocum felt his mouth release a sudden gush of saliva. He hadn't realized how hungry he was.

And about fifty feet up the hill from the fires, sitting all alone, was that odd girl Miranda. He could see that her dusty skirts were blotched with big ink stains, and that she was hunched over a book, a pen in her hand. He could just make out that it wasn't a printed book, but something filled with handwriting. The glass wasn't good enough to read it, but she wasn't writing anything anyway. She just sat there, blankly staring off into the distance and chewing on the end of her pen.

She was sure an odd duck, he thought. She didn't fit. Didn't act right, didn't talk right, didn't even move right. At least, he hadn't thought she did until he'd seen her practically attacking Big Tom last night. But still, she just didn't fit in. And it still bothered him that she'd known his name back in town.

A yell sounded, and Slocum swung his spyglass toward the ruckus.

Big Tom, along with the two girls who'd been helping him, burst from the mouth of the mine and threw themselves to the side. It was Tom who had shouted. The girls were yelping and laughing with excitement.

Moments later, the mine belched out a thin cloud of dust that lasted for several minutes and coated everything before it, Rose included. The massive woman was seated on that damned boulder she'd staked out for herself. She was roughly as high up the hill as Slocum, but much closer to the mine's entrance. She wasn't speaking to him this morning, which was just dandy so far as he was concerned, and the dust turned her dress a shade lighter inside of three seconds.

The ground under his feet didn't rumble, though, as it had with the blast yesterday, and while the distant Rose coughed and sputtered, Slocum swung his spyglass out toward the east and the valley floor. Sure enough, weeds shivered and cactus shook. They were making fast progress, but he reminded himself, once again, to have Big Tom check the boundary lines. It wouldn't do if they were to tunnel right underneath McLean's land.

Well, actually, it would be just fine with him, but he didn't figure the local constabulary would see it that way.

He took one last scan of the eastern horizon and saw nothing. The entrance to McLean's mine, and therefore his campsite, was at the far end of his property, Slocum reminded himself. He'd actually been on McLean's land when he met Mordecai on both nights. McLean and his crew would have to gallop most of the way here before they left Daisy Cutter land.

Which was really neither here nor there. They'd come, and that was all he was interested in.

He collapsed the spyglass and started down the hill.

"What do you mean, you didn't find the rifles?" McLean demanded.

The little man standing before him in the shade of a tent—what was the man's name? Eddie? Teddy? Freddy? He rolled his hat in his hands. "They wasn't nowhere, Mr. McLean, sir. We rode all the way to Hoople Flats and couldn't turn up no sign of 'em."

McLean was already testy, having ridden the back way out of town at four in the morning to avoid a new onslaught of eggs and tomatoes and bricks, after having been apprised that his chief (and only) hired gun, Mordecai Jones, had been found dead under appalling circumstances. That was hard to take. And now, no rifles. He said, "Well, you didn't look good enough, did you, you idiot?"

The little man took a step back. "N-no, sir, I guess we didn't. Sorry, sir. But—"

"Boss!" It was Tiger, sticking his head through the tent flap. He looked more agitated than usual.

"What!" McLean snapped. "Can't you see that I'm busy?"

But Tiger seemed to have bigger things on his mind, and said, "You gotta come quick!"

McLean muttered, "Idiots!" between clenched teeth, told Eddie—or Teddy or Freddy—to get out of his sight, and followed him through the flap out into the morning sunshine.

Tiger, shifting nervously from boot to boot,

grabbed McLean's coat sleeve. "C'mon, c'mon! Something happened!"

"Let go of me, you scarecrow," McLean said, shaking him off and pausing to inspect his sleeve. "I just had this jacket brushed and pressed."

"But, Boss, you've gotta come right now! They're hurt!"

McLean's features twisted. "Who's hurt?" And then his eyes widened. "Have they found another one?" He was still upset about Mordecai's demise, not so much because he really liked the man or even knew him, but because it came as a slap in the face to him personally.

What was wrong with people anyway! Why hadn't Tom Malloy just moved off that land months ago, when they'd burnt out his timbers? They'd shot at him and run off his hired men. Any sane man would have just packed up and moved on. And why had McLean's whores all of a goddamn sudden just up and left town?

Somehow, McLean had a feeling that it was all this Slocum's fault. Slocum the brave, Slocum the champion of the weak, if you believed that goddamn book. The whores, Malloy's continued tenancy on the Bum Nugget, Mordecai's death, and very likely those eggs and tomatoes too: all Slocum's doing. These upstarts were going to pay!

Slocum was going to pay!

"No, it's the mine," Tiger was insisting. "Somebody's blew up the mine!" Once again Tiger grabbed his sleeve and dragged him around the tent.

A thin layer of dust hung in the air just outside

the mouth of the Daisy Cutter, and three men—the last of whom was just emerging from the mine on the arm of a compatriot—were bloodied. One cradled his arm, as if it were broken.

McLean stood speechless for a moment, possible explanations flitting through his head. None of them took root. His fists propped on his hips, he said, "Jesus Christ! What was it? A cave-in?"

Toby came forward. He was unharmed, and didn't look as though he'd been in the mine at all that morning. He had taken on airs since Mordecai's recent demise, McLean thought, and looked as though he could use being taken down a peg or two.

"Somebody blasted, Mr. McLean," Toby said angrily, without bothering to take off his hat. "Some sonofabitch set off a charge down there. Several of 'em, to shake the shaft that hard. These boys wasn't all the way down, or they would'a been kilt for sure."

McLean slapped the hat off Toby's head. "Show some respect, boy!" he fumed. While a surprised Toby bent to retrieve his Stetson, McLean thought fast. "Who could have gone down the shaft and planted charges?" he asked curtly. "Did you see anybody? Did anybody run up the tunnel?"

Around him, men's heads slowly shook.

"Weren't none of us," said a dust-caked miner.

Another agreed with the first. "It was like it was coming from the other side."

"*What* other side?" McLean shouted.

The man with the broken arm looked up. "The other side'a the rock, Boss."

A chill raced up McLean's spine, a thousand icy fingers. They couldn't have made it that far, could they? But if they'd been blasting before, and if those whores were helping . . .

No, it would be too great a coincidence.

But still, if Malloy was following the vein . . .

"Which tunnel was it?" he asked.

"B-12," replied Toby, who was still dusting his hat off.

B-12 was the shaft that went to the west, the shaft that had been the most promising. The shaft that McLean knew snaked all the way to his property line and beyond. He had already mined several hundred yards beneath Big Tom Malloy's land.

"You all right, Boss?" asked Harley. The racoon-eyed idiot had been standing over to the side the whole time. He ducked his head and squinted. "You look kinda pale."

McLean thought he heard Tiger snicker, and wheeled toward him. The ferrety little man was as straight-faced as could be, though.

"Take care of these men," McLean said curtly. "You do it." He pointed to an old geezer at the edge of the crowd. He'd be the least use to them. "The rest of you, mount up."

Tiger said, "Boss?"

"You heard me," McLean growled. It would be better if the law had been along, but Sheriff Joe Doolin had been out there throwing tomatoes too, the bastard. Why couldn't those egg-lobbing cowards from town come out here and give him some help instead of giving him grief? "Everybody had better be armed too."

And then he remembered the sorry state of their armaments—not to mention their remuda—and added, "Hitch up a couple of wagons, and bring along a case of dynamite."

If these idiots couldn't shoot the men on the Bum Nugget—and he doubted that most of the fools knew which end of a gun to aim—maybe they could blow them up. He supposed he'd lose a few whores in the process, but it couldn't be helped.

Most of the men stood up and wandered down toward the remuda, but a "Hurry up, dammit!" from him quickened their steps. Harley, Tiger, and Toby remained. "Well?" McLean demanded. "What is it?"

"But where're we goin'?" Harley asked. The fool hadn't a clue. McLean asked himself, for the hundredth time, what on earth he had ever seen in Harley—or Tiger, or this little shit-heel Toby, for that matter—to have hired them in the first place.

"Yeah, where?" asked Tiger, who didn't appear to be at all enthusiastic. "Seems to me we oughta wait till the tunnel settles down, Boss, then start movin' rock. You know, see where that blast came from. Maybe we could go right on through the tunnel, and—"

"Move!" McLean shouted. "We're going to the Bum Nugget, and we're going to shoot it out with Malloy and that goddamn Slocum and Skunky too. We should have done it right from the start."

Toby shook his head. "If you'd seen what I did last night, mayhap you wouldn't be so quick to—"

"Move!" McLean shouted once again.

Toby slapped his hat back on his head. "Sure, Mr. McLean. Anything you say, Mr. McLean."

And McLean was thinking, as he followed them, stiff-legged, down to the remuda, that the minute this thing was over, he was going to fire Toby and Tiger and Harley so fast and hard that they'd have their butts soaking in a bucket for weeks.

18

Big Tom Malloy was beside himself with excitement. He had shoved all but one thing to the back of his mind, and could think of nothing else but silver, bright silver.

The fact that the men of the Daisy Cutter would likely very soon take their revenge for Mordecai was momentarily forgotten, and even thoughts of Miranda—sweet Miranda—were banished from his fevered mind. Such was the hold that the promise of bright metal held over men.

Before the dust of the blast had settled, he tied a bandanna over his mouth and nose, grabbed a lantern, and started back down the tunnel.

But before he had a chance to leave the sunlight behind, a hand grabbed his shoulder and spun him around.

"You crazy?" Slocum barked angrily. "You know damn well there's gonna be rock fallin' back there for a good bit. Wait a while."

Shaking his head, Tom brushed Slocum's hand away. "I'll be careful. But I've gotta see, Slocum. I've gotta see what we brought down."

Slocum worked his jaw muscles, and Tom was

wondering if he was going to have to hit him—and just how hard Slocum would hit him back. But then Slocum said, "Jesus, Tom, you're one mule-stubborn sonofabitch! All right, hang on while I grab a lantern. Somebody's gotta go with you and see that you don't break your fool neck."

Tom waited, shifting giddily from foot to foot, and he thought about Miranda twice—for a total of three seconds—and not at all about the men from the Daisy Cutter in the whole of the time it took Slocum to fetch a second light and rejoin him.

Slocum too pulled his neckerchief up over his nose, and the two men, both tall as trees, started carefully down the tunnel.

It wasn't too bad for the first thousand feet or so. The air was thick with hanging dust that seeped through their bandannas and clogged their noses, but they didn't start hitting the falling rock until they'd walked nearly a quarter mile down.

A hundred yards after that, Tom had dodged a shower of pebbles, then failed to dodge a fist-sized stone that left a jagged little line of blood down the back of his neck.

"Will you watch where you're goin'?" Slocum growled behind him. "Y'know, you oughta put in a second access shaft about here. Dig it straight down. Save a lot of time. Jesus!" he grumbled as he pushed Tom to the side again, both men narrowly avoiding the loose rock that came pelting down. "You got enough timbers left to shore this thing up?"

Tom was grateful, but if the truth were known, he barely noticed Slocum's shoves or Slocum's curs-

ing. In fact, Tom barely noticed when the occasional
rock hit him.

He was too busy staring in wonder at the fallen
rocks and the walls of the shaft. It was the mother
lode, the leading edge of it anyway.

All around, he saw jagged chunks of quartz,
freshly dislodged and turned nearly black by heavy
veining. He'd never seen rock like this! He'd never
imagined that he would!

With every step he took, his excitement grew
more fevered, and with every rock he picked up and
turned over in his hands, the heated buzzing in his
belly grew stronger. He saw that they'd gone wrong.
He saw that they were going to have to blast again
and again and turn the shaft to the left. Go deeper
still into the earth. But he saw that they were all
going to be very rich.

They already were.

And out of nothing but habit, he thought that now
Clementine Crockett could finally be his.

"Aw, crud," he said in disgust.

"Look out!" hissed Slocum.

The shower of rocks came down before Slocum had
called out the rest of his warning—which was to
consist of "Look out, you jackass!"—and Big Tom
Malloy folded up and went down under a blanket of
stones. Slocum knelt beside him and checked the
pulse in his neck. He was alive, all right, but
knocked cold. And on top of that, his lantern had
smashed on the rocky tunnel floor. A small, spreading pool of kerosene blazed brightly.

Cursing and thinking that he didn't exactly want to haul Big Tom all the way up a half mile of tunnel or more, he stood up again and made ready to stamp out the fire. First things first.

But he paused before his boot struck once. Something was odd. Something was wrong. He couldn't figure out what it was at first. They'd walked nearly to the edge of the biggest rockfall, and ten feet ahead the tunnel was filled nearly to the ceiling with loose stone and gravel. And ore, don't forget that. He didn't rightly blame Big Tom for not giving his safety his full attention.

Then he saw it. The smoke from the kerosene fire wasn't behaving. Instead of going straight up, it was wafting slowly up-tunnel. It shouldn't be doing that. Not unless . . .

He shook his head. That was crazy! Could Big Tom have been right back in town? He'd voiced his suspicions then, but not since. Out of all this land, all these wide-open spaces to dig under, it was just too big a coincidence. Unless, of course, McLean's men had been following the very same vein.

In all of Slocum's years, he'd worked more mines than he could shake a stick at. He'd seen veins that rose up like the letter Y or the letter T, veins that traveled parallel to the surface, veins that zigzagged along, then came straight up to the light of day. Some places, ore ran in spiral patterns deep into the earth. Occasionally, ore was deposited in giant caves, like big bubbles in the rock far below the surface, where the walls gleamed like smoky mirrors.

Ore had a mind of its own. It went where it wanted.

Through clenched teeth, he swore a curt "Shit!" then quickly kicked out the little blaze. He jammed the remaining lantern's handle between his teeth, grabbed Big Tom under the armpits, and in this ungainly position, started backing up and dragging Tom for all he was worth.

"Slow down!" Harley called.

Drummond McLean, who had been lost in thoughts of just exactly what he was going to do to these upstarts, looked over to find the fat little man cantering on his off shoulder.

"The wagons, Boss!" he shouted again, poking a thumb to the rear.

McLean glanced back, and immediately reined his horse down to a trot, then a walk, and finally a full stop. The other men followed suit gratefully, but Harley cantered on a bit before he could get his horse reined in. *Corn-holing idiot,* McLean thought in disgust. It was a wonder that Harley hadn't gone blind as well as stupid.

The wagons were indeed in something of a mess. McLean had had to bring three to accommodate all the men with no horses, but they were ore wagons, built stout to haul the heaviest of loads and not fit for racing across the countryside. Two of them were far back, and the third had stopped entirely, so far back down the road that he could barely see it.

"Tiger!" he bellowed.

"Went back to the far wagon, Mr. McLean, sir,"

called Toby, fifty feet distant. His fancy pinto danced beneath him. At least one of these bastards was eager to get to the Bum Nugget, McLean thought, even if it was only a horse.

Harley had returned to his side. "You want I should go and get him, Mr. McLean?" he asked, breathing heavily through his mouth. Sweat dripped down his discolored, swollen nose.

McLean glanced over at Harley's horse, which he had rented from the livery in town. It was a dust-caked, Roman-nosed black, fit for little more than dog food, and why Harley had picked it was beyond him. Harley didn't own a horse, and for good reason. He rode like a plump duck, with his elbows flapping like wings and his backside out of the saddle more often than in it.

"No," McLean said. "Send Toby."

A moment later, Harley had hollered to Toby, and Toby was racing away from them and toward the wagon.

"I meant for you to go over there and tell him, you idiot," McLean said tersely. He gave his ear a rub.

"Sorry, Boss," Harley said nasally.

Toby galloped back to them in no time, but McLean already knew what was going on. Men had already climbed down and unhitched the horses from the wagon, and as Toby slid his pinto to a stop, McLean could see that the men were clambering onto the heavy cart horses, two and three at a time. Nearer, the men crouched in wagons or sat their horses with expressions ranging from boredom to fright. Not one sonofabitch looked the least bit eager for a fight.

Except perhaps Toby. Maybe he wouldn't fire him after all.

"Axle's busted, Mr. McLean," Toby said once the dust from his sliding stop had settled. "You just can't run them carts like that. Ain't built for it."

McLean nodded, but didn't speak. Tiger was down there too, starting forward with the rest of them at a slow jog. Wonderful, just wonderful. Their assault on the Bum Nugget was turning into a Sunday picnic whose unwilling participants would rather have been asleep under a tree, with their bellies full of fried chicken and potato salad.

He took out his handkerchief and ran it over his neck and face. It came away gray.

Dirty, he thought with a resigned frown. *Dirty and sweaty and already losing the battle.* He'd have to have this suit brushed and pressed again.

Then he sat up straighter in the saddle. "Damn it," he muttered.

"Beg pardon, sir?" said Harley, cringing back a little.

The stupid toad. McLean had come too far, worked too hard to see it all collapse now because of this spineless crew. He'd get to the Bum Nugget by hook or by crook. He'd crush those bastards, if he had to roll around in the dirt to do it. If he had to kill off every last whore in a twenty-mile radius. If he had to throttle Big Tom Malloy and his cohorts with his bare hands.

He'd do it.

He'd just have to do it differently than originally planned.

He held up his hand, waving it for attention.

"A fifty-dollar bonus to the men who bring down Slocum, Malloy, and Skunky!"

There was no reaction.

"And a week's paid vacation with all the free whores you can handle!" he added.

This time, several heads came up. One man even licked his lips.

It was a start.

"Let's go!" he cried, and started up the road again at a slow trot, his men trailing behind him.

Slocum emerged from the mine alone, having left Big Tom halfway down the shaft. He'd pulled him as far as he could, and he was resting comfortably—or maybe not so comfortably, but at this point Slocum didn't really care—well up into the timbered portion of the shaft.

Jamaica and Miranda greeted him, but Miranda was the first to speak. "Where's Tom?" she asked nervously.

He stabbed his thumb back over his shoulder. "Down there," he said. "Out cold."

"Oh, my God!" she yelped. "He's hurt?" She grabbed the lantern from his hand and raced into the mine before Slocum could stop her.

Slocum scratched the back of his neck. "Do you know her?" he asked Jamaica.

"Not really," Jamaica replied with a quizzical shake of her head. She laid the flat of her hand on

Slocum's chest. "What did you find down there, dar-lin'?" Then, as an afterthought, she added, "Big Tom's all right, isn't he?"

"He is, and we found silver. Lots of it."

Her mouth widened into an avaricious grin, and her hand began to slide down his chest, toward his belt buckle. "Let's celebrate, Slocum," she purred. "I'm a rich woman now."

He grabbed her hand. "Jesus, Jamaica!"

She tipped her head. "Well, we could go up to 'our place' first, sugar." Her fingers hooked around his belt and gave it a little tug. "I never thought any different."

He sighed. Women. They had no sense of prior-ities. And neither, it seemed, did his cock, which was already rising to the occasion.

But he gently took her hand from his belt and said quickly, "Jamaica, do you realize that there are gonna be over two dozen of McLean's boys boilin' up the road any minute now?"

Jamaica rolled her eyes. "I forgot. All right. Heat of the moment and all . . ."

Slocum continued. "Well, me and Big Tom found more than silver down there. I'm pretty sure that last blast of ours ran us straight into the Daisy Cutter shaft."

She scowled prettily. "Oh, Slocum! That's im-possible! We couldn't have tunneled that far in just these few days. And besides, what are the chances that we'd run smack dab into . . ."

She paused, and Slocum added, "Unless they were following the same vein as Big Tom. Ore's been known to vent up in a Y pattern before, honey."

A look of realization slowly spread over Jamaica's features. "Drummond McLean!" she said. "That slimy good-for-nothing snake! No wonder he wanted Big Tom off this land in such an all-fired hurry! He's on Tom's land—*our* land!" And then the realization turned to anger. "Hey! Just how much of our silver you think he's already mined out of there anyhow?"

"Hey!" came a yelp from the top of the hill. They both looked up to see Skunky, a pinpoint atop the hill, jumping up and down and waving his arms. Slocum strained to hear him over the thin whistle of the wind through the brush. "For the fourth time, they's comin', goddamn it! Don't you folks listen when a feller's shoutin'?"

19

Slocum raced up the slope, pulling his spyglass from his pocket as he went. He stopped halfway and trained the glass on the road. Sure enough, somebody was coming, and about two dozen somebodies at that. At second glance, they didn't appear to be coming too fast, but fast or slow, they were going to be on his doorstep in just a few minutes. He skidded down the hill again.

"Jamaica! Sassafras! Get those gals with the guns up here." He pointed uphill, to the skirt of rock. Then, as an afterthought, he called, "Have somebody bring that extra ammo up too!" Then he raced farther down the hill, grabbing a couple of girls at random as he went.

They skittered down the slope, the girls shrieking and giggling at the surprise of it, until they came to a cloth-covered mound. Quickly, he threw the tarp aside to reveal three cases of dynamite. He picked up the first crate and handed it to one of the girls, a buxom, curly-haired redhead clad in a low-cut but ripped velveteen gown.

"Here," he said. "Get this up top."

She blinked rapidly, and a tendril of hair fell before her eyes. It bounced like a spring. "Y-you're askin' me to carry dynamite, Slocum? Is that safe? Skunky and Big Tom ain't let us come near it once!"

"Move your butt, and *now*!" he roared, and fairly threw the next crate at the second girl. Both girls were already lumbering up the hill beneath heavy boxes when he picked up the third—along with a fistful of fuses—and started up after them.

Jamaica was moving their infantry—or at least, what passed for it—up the hillside. The girls walked quickly but nervously, peeking back over their shoulders every few paces, and whispering among themselves. Identical Winchesters hung from their hands or were propped over bare, sunburnt shoulders.

Proud and regal or cheap and tawdry, they knew how to handle guns, and had the knowledge that they were protecting their own property. He doubted that many of them had been granted that privilege before, and he began to see something else in their ascent. They were scared, yes, but they were willing to fight.

It was all that he could ask.

And scared could be a good thing, so long as nobody panicked.

He trotted up the hill and placed his box of dynamite with the others, along with the fuses. The girls that had carried them were nowhere in sight. Likely they had gone as far away from that dynamite as humanly possible.

He allowed himself a smile, just a little one. Skunky and Big Tom must have scared the pee-

wadding right out of these girls about getting too
near the blasting supplies.

He looked down the hill, past the cook fires and
the laundry kettles, past the lines of gently fluttering
petticoats and unmentionables on the clotheslines,
past the deserted tents, and out across the vast valley. He didn't need the glass to see the line of men
in the distance. They approached with what seemed
a grim steadiness, which was more ominous somehow than if they'd just galloped in and started shooting.

He signaled to the women to spread out in a line
along the hillside, and he only had to motion to three
of them to get down. The rest dropped behind the
rock barricade without being told and sighted their
rifles, propping them on elbows or knees. They'd be
able to shoot, all right.

"Hold off till I tell you," he called, and then he
remembered Tom. He and Miss Ink Stain were still
somewhere down in the mine.

He sprinted down the hill again, yelling, "Get up
the hill, dammit!" at Rose as he passed. She was
still sitting exactly where she had been when the
blast went off, with her parasol cocked over one
shoulder and her fat legs straining the fabric of her
dust-caked skirts.

"Screw you, Slocum!" she shouted back. She
didn't budge an inch.

He didn't stop to argue. If you asked him, it
would serve the old cow right if she took a slug or
two, and he couldn't exactly say that he'd weep at
the funeral.

He skidded to a stop near the mine's entrance, picked up a lantern and lit it, then started back into the darkness. He hadn't gone far before he made out the light of the girl's lantern, moving slowly toward him. Tom was beside her and they were walking leisurely, holding hands!

"This ain't no church social, goddamn it," Slocum barked as loud as he dared. There were timbers in this portion of the mine, but you never knew how much that last blast had unsettled the surrounding ground. "McLean's comin'."

When they didn't pick up their pace, he added, "He's comin' *now!*"

The girl, Miranda, made calf eyes up at Tom, who blushed. Blushed! What was the world coming to?

Slocum shoved back his hat, and said, "Well, I reckon I'll just leave the pair of you to it. Don't mind me none. I'll just go back up top and get shot at."

Then he turned on his heel and started marching back up the tunnel. He had gone nearly twenty feet—and was thinking some very evil thoughts about his situation in general and Big Tom Malloy in particular—when he heard Tom call, "Wait up, Slocum!"

He stopped and waited until Tom and Miranda caught up with him.

"Sorry," Tom said, and his arm was around Miranda's shoulders. Slocum didn't know what had transpired down in the mine, but she was nearly glassy-eyed, and he'd have bet that he wouldn't've been able to scrub the smile off her face with a wire brush.

There wasn't time to ask questions, though, even if he was inclined, which he wasn't.

Quickly, the three moved up-tunnel, with Slocum filling in Big Tom as they went. By the time they came, blinking, into the sunlight, McLean and his men had reached the foot of the hill and Tom was mad as hell.

"I was right," he kept muttering. "I was right all along." Tom smacked Miranda's behind and said, "Get up behind those boulders, honey." As she scurried away, he turned to Slocum. "What the hell are they gonna do with those wagons? Haul our rock off too?"

Slocum shook his head. McLean's crew, down beyond the tents and the fluttering laundry, was certainly ragtag. They had arrived with only a few of the men mounted and the rest in two ore wagons. They must have lost a third wagon somewhere along the way, because four of the horses tethered with their saddle mounts were still in their harness.

Slocum opened his mouth to answer, but he never had the chance. Two shots sang off the rock behind him, and both he and Big Tom fairly threw themselves back into the mine.

"That answer your question?" Slocum asked. His gun drawn, he peeked around the rock and down the hill. Somebody was a better shot than he'd expected. Or a lot luckier.

He hoped it was the latter.

McLean's voice, unmistakable, hollered, "Malloy! Slocum! C'mon out!"

Big Tom replied, "So you can shoot at us again? Fat chance!"

"One of my men got a little antsy, Malloy," came the reply.

From higher up the slope, a girl clad in bright blue called, "Now, Slocum?"

Bless the eager little darlings.

But he shouted back, "Not yet," then turned toward Tom. "You mind?" he asked, and when Tom shrugged, he called to McLean, "This is Slocum, McLean. You're on private property. In fact, you've been trespassin' for a good long time now. How much ore have you already pulled outta Tom Malloy's land?"

"My land too, dad blast it!" came Skunky's insulted cry from atop the hill.

But McLean didn't appear to have heard him. Or he was ignoring him, which Slocum thought was a great deal more likely. McLean called, "We want the girls back, Slocum."

From her rock perch, Rose bellowed, "Eat horse shit, Drum!"

Slocum couldn't stop one corner of his mouth from crooking up. At least she hated everybody.

And then somebody fired a single shot that took Rose's parasol: simply snapped its handle in two and sent it sailing.

And despite the fact that McLean's men looked as if he'd just yanked them off the farm and mustered them into service, Slocum ground his teeth.

McLean had at least one sharpshooter down there, and if there was one, there might be quite a few more.

He held his hand up and signaled to the girls to calm down, to wait, and while Rose fumed and shouted further obscenities to the crew down the hill, he said, "Tom, we've got trouble."

McLean stared at Harley in utter shock. "Where the *hell* did you learn to shoot like that?"

Harley shrugged and ran a wet thumb over his gunsight again. "Just good at it, I guess," he said. He sighted his old rifle again through swollen and bruised eyes. "You want I should take her down, Boss? The next time the wind lifts up that pair'a bloomers there on the end of the line, I reckon I'll have me a good—"

"Who!"

Harley looked up, blinking. "That old sow Rose."

She was still blustering away, although McLean let the wind blur her words.

"No! Just wait!" McLean shook his head. He'd been positive—absolutely *positive*—that Harley wouldn't be able to hit the side of the livery with a handful of beans, and now this. "Tiger?" he asked.

But Tiger, to his right, just shrugged his shoulders. "Didn't have me any idea, Mr. McLean."

"But you said as how you didn't care if'n we shot the whores," Harley went on, a whine riding his voice. "That Rose, she's been a thorn in my side since the day I hit town. And she's standin' right out there shoutin' evil things and wavin' her fists at us!"

"Just wait," McLean said. He'd been the next thing to cracking Harley over the skull with a two-by-four and leaving him for dead in the nearest ditch, but now . . . Well, Harley had saved himself, all right, even if the fat little bastard didn't know it. Maybe even gotten himself a little raise in pay.

Suddenly, McLean began to feel almost chipper.

He said, "Harley, you just stand by until I tell you. I've got something special planned for you to do."

Harley leaned back and looked over with those purple racoon eyes. "Sure thing, Mr. McLean," he said, as if he hadn't done anything at all out of the ordinary.

McLean had been looking up the hill, although it was difficult with the tents and all that goddamn flapping laundry in the way. He'd never seen so much female underwear in all of his life!

Well, they'd best get this under way.

Rose had finally stopped her screeching, and he holstered his pistol. Slowly, he stood up in full view of the crew from the Bum Nugget, his arms held wide, his hands empty. The three men up there wouldn't take a shot at him, he was certain. And as for the women, they were just hiding in the brush. They didn't even have guns, for God's sake!

Well, there might be a derringer or two hidden up their sleeves, but certainly nothing that could fire a slug that would hit him at this distance!

"Who's doing the talking for the Bum Nugget and these whores?" he shouted.

Slocum, the dime-novel hero, stepped clear of the Bum Nugget's mouth. His hands were also empty.

"Don't shoot, Harley," McLean whispered. "I'll tell you when." And then he called out, "Who put you in charge?"

"There was a vote," Slocum hollered back. "I won."

McLean wasn't too happy. He would have preferred talking to Big Tom, or even Skunky. At least he knew something about them! All he knew about Slocum was what he'd read in that scrofulous book. And also what Slocum had done in town. The man was tough, and he was a question mark.

"I supposed they elected you to kill my head man," he shouted.

"Nope," Slocum replied through the thin whine of wind. "Did that all on my own. We had bad blood from way back."

"His brother," shouted McLean.

"Something like," answered Slocum.

"That your horse or Mordecai's that we found out there?"

"Mine, and stop makin' small talk," Slocum replied. "Move your men off."

McLean shook his head. "Not yet," he shouted. "You're an interloper here, Slocum. Suppose I get you a new horse, better than the one you had. Suppose I forget all about what you did to old Mordecai. Will you ride out? Will you let Tom and me settle this, citizen to citizen?"

It was Slocum's turn to shake his head. "Seems to me that I'm already deep into it, McLean. I was in it the minute I heard how you'd been stomping all over these ladies. That ain't nice, McLean. And now I've kind of got to liking Big Tom and Skunky."

From the very top of the hill came Skunky's thin shout of, "You tell him, Slocum!"

"You're walking on my friends," Slocum continued. "Looks to me like you've been walking over them for a long time. Not only are *you* the one who's gonna be leaving, but you're gonna sign over your mine to Tom and Skunky before you go."

McLean felt his face turn red and his hands ball into fists. "What?" he railed. "Are you mad?"

"Ain't as crazy as you," came Slocum's reply. "You been stealing their ore for a long time, McLean. Big Tom's willin' to let you keep what you already stole in exchange for your deed. And you gettin' out of town, of course."

McLean's jaw muscles worked back and forth, and his face got hotter. This sonofabitch, this goddamned dime-novel hero, had some kind of balls, all right. Just who the hell did he think he was!

Well, McLean would take him down a peg or two. He'd take him down to the bottom of a goddamned well! "Harley?" he hissed through clenched teeth.

"What, Boss?"

"As soon as you get a clear shot, take it."

Harley seated the rifle against a plump shoulder, cheek to the stock and a swollen eye to the sights. "Sure thing, Mr. McLean."

20

Miranda huddled behind a small clump of boulders, her ink-blotched fingers pressed hard to the rock, her eyes peering over the rim of the shortest one. A person could say a lot of bad things about Slocum—and since first making his acquaintance, she had said or thought most of them herself—but Lord, you had to admit he was masterful.

Why, if she'd been Drummond McLean, she would have given in right then and there!

What a speech, and he'd given it in such a rousing timbre of voice too. Maybe the books she'd written to date hadn't been so far off the mark after all. She'd have to add "rousing orator" to his list of finer qualities.

And as for his baser qualities, well, she was re-thinking that too. After all, she supposed it was really none of her business if he liked to drop in on prostitutes every now and again and avail himself of their services.

He was human, after all. He had appetites.

The same kind that she did, she thought with a guilty flush. Why, when she'd been down in the mine, cradling poor unconscious Tom's head in her lap and weeping, he'd fluttered his eyes open and the first thing he'd done was to kiss her. The very first thing!

It wasn't her kissing him, no siree-bob. He'd made the move, pulled her head right down to his, and she'd remembered Sassafras's advice and didn't push it, didn't ask for more.

She'd sure enjoyed it, though.

And then he'd said, "By God, Miranda, I'll be danged if I don't think that I love you."

Her belly was full of butterflies again, just from remembering it.

Of course, he'd just been hit on the head.

She'd worry about that part later.

Jamaica and Sassafras crouched behind a few stunted paloverdes, just above the line of armed women. Looking down the hill, Jamaica couldn't see McLean's men too well, what with the tents and laundry being in the way, but she could see Slocum standing out there, big as you please, and she could hear every word that he exchanged with McLean.

"That great big green-eyed man of yours has got some kind of bark on him, I'll say that, sugar," Sassafras remarked, idly brushing paloverde needles away from her face. "But Drum McLean willingly giving up his mine? That'll be the day."

Jamaica eyed her, and settled her gaze on Sassafras's tall red turban. "You'd make a very good target, you know."

"Not as good as that old bat Rose," Sassafras replied.

"Not so appealing either," Jamaica admitted. Rose was still on her rock, muttering to herself. "Why doesn't somebody just shoot her? Either side, I don't care. They wouldn't have to kill her, just wound her bad enough that she couldn't talk for a while."

Sassafras grinned. "Now, Jamaica, this is a serious situation we've got here. No use dreaming about what you can't have."

"I'd still take off that turban if I were you."

"Anybody dumb enough to aim for it would miss me by a mile, love."

"Well, still, I—"

Jamaica's reply was cut short by the sing of a bullet, and she shot to her feet, crying, "Slocum!"

If Slocum had turned an instant later, the slug would have taken him through the lung. As it was, it blasted into his left arm and knocked him sprawling.

On his knees, he scrambled for the mine's entrance, and Big Tom risked his own hide to come halfway out and drag him to safety while Skunky fired covering shots from atop the hill.

"Jesus," Tom muttered as he ripped off his own bandanna and tied a makeshift tourniquet around Slocum's arm. "Jesus H."

"They've got somebody out there that can shoot, all right," Slocum said. He reached over to feel his left side, and sucked air through his teeth. There was blood there too, and it hurt like hell. The slug must have gone all the way through his arm and stopped against a rib. He could feel it there, a small lump grating against the bone. It felt like it was on fire.

He moved his left arm a bit. At least it wasn't broken. Fingers worked and everything.

"Stop wiggling around," Big Tom warned when Slocum went to stand up.

"It ain't that bad," Slocum grumbled. "And you've got bigger problems. Give me a hand."

Big Tom did, although judging by the look on his face, he thought Slocum was crazy.

Slocum peeked around the rock of the opening. "That Skunky up there, firing?" And before Big Tom could answer, Slocum signaled to Skunky to stop. It was suddenly quiet. Only the sounds of the wind seeping through the rocks and rustling the brush and the clothes on the lines remained.

McLean was relying on his sniper. That was good, because it likely meant he had only the one instead of the two or three that Slocum had imagined before. If he'd had more than one, Slocum would have been dead.

"McLean!" he called. "That the best you can do?"

"That was just a taste of it, Slocum!" came the reply.

Slocum shook his head. Softly he said, "This idiot doesn't know when he's beat."

"When *he's* beat?" Tom exclaimed, his eyes wide. "You're the one that's shot up!"

Slocum regarded him for a moment. "You've never been in a war or fought Indians, have you?"

Tom shook his head.

"I didn't think so," said Slocum. He turned back toward the light, toward the mine's opening. "I'm warning you, McLean," he called out. "This is your last chance."

"*His* last chance?" Big Tom said incredulously. "Did you get hit in the head too?"

Slocum ignored him. He shouted, "You can't win, McLean. We've got the high ground. We've got plenty of water and food. If nothing else, we'll outlast your sorry carcasses."

He heard McLean laugh, and at the same time Big Tom hissed, "We don't have any food, Slocum."

"Well, he doesn't know that, does he?" Slocum replied crankily. His arm hurt like a bastard. "We've got plenty of springwater, though. Remind me to send Skunky over the hill to guard it if this thing doesn't get settled right away."

"But the women!" Tom insisted. "Somebody's going to get killed!"

Suddenly, Slocum shoved him back against a rock wall. "What'd you think when we all came out here? Huh? What'd you think would happen, you jackass?"

Big Tom didn't come at him, which was a very good move on his part, all things considered. He simply said, "I . . . I . . . didn't think that far, I guess. I suppose I just thought that it'd be all right somehow."

Slocum backed off and checked his pistol. "Well, this is the 'somehow' that it's turning out to be."

McLean was hollering something, and Slocum leaned out just far enough to shout, "What's that, McLean? Didn't hear you!"

"I said, why don't you just come on down. You're shot. I saw it. You've only got two good men up there now, Slocum. Why don't you do the sensible thing? And why don't you let Big Tom Malloy talk for himself! Big Tom, what do you say?"

Tom took a deep breath. "I reckon you're right, Slocum," he said. He stepped forward into the light beaming in from the outside—although not far enough, Slocum noticed, that McLean's sniper could get a bead on him—and called, "Ladies? One round, in the air!"

A long line of glinting rifle barrels, heretofore hidden from McLean's line of sight, poked up from the brush and rocks on the hillside, and Slocum thought he heard somebody—most likely McLean—say, "Shit!" just before they boomed in one glorious volley. Smoke drifted in thin tatters, and he heard Jamaica's bawdy laugh.

"My rifles, you sonsofbitches," shouted McLean. "Thieves! Robbers!"

"Take that, you shit-sniffers!" shouted Rose, who Slocum had nearly forgotten was out there.

"Finders keepers!" came Skunky's shout, followed by a cackle of laughter.

McLean was a fastidious man, a methodical man, a proud man. He hung his suits in the chifforobe by the days of the week he planned to wear them. His toiletries were always arranged just so on his dresser top: his razor to the right, his soap and shaving brush to the left, his comb and hairbrush to the middle. He always walked the same route to work, always sat in the barber's chair at exactly the same time each morning, always drank exactly three cups of coffee—

no more, no less, and each with precisely two sugars—before he took a break for lunch.

But under pressure—something that he ordinarily
avoided—he became unsettled. And like many men
of his ilk, when he got angry, he lost all common
sense.

So when he heard Rose's shout and Skunky
laughing—laughing at *him!*—he didn't think. He
simply shouted, "Fire!"

All hell broke loose.

His men, hampered by the small fact that they
couldn't see what they were shooting at, simply
started peppering the empty tents and blowing random holes through the bloomers and petticoats on
the laundry lines.

By the time McLean realized that nobody was
shooting back, his men had laid waste to probably
sixty yards of canvas, and riddled enough underwear
to make up a trousseau for a three-month honey-
moon. Only a few shots had made it up to the place
where the women were hiding, and those had hit
nothing but rock.

"Stop!" he cried. "Stop it! Stop firing!"

Gradually, they did.

From up the hill, a woman he couldn't see
shouted, "Them was my best goddamn pantaloons,
Drummond! You gonna pay for those?"

"Give up, dammit!" he shouted helplessly.

"Go screw yourself!" called Rose.

He couldn't stop clenching and unclenching his
jaw. Damn these women! Damn those three men up
there with them! Didn't they realize who they were

dealing with? Didn't they know who owned this whole damn town, practically the whole damn county? Just who the hell did they think they were anyhow?

He aimed a kick at Tiger, who was slapping his pockets for more ammunition but coming up empty, and had the satisfaction of hearing a *thump* when his boot struck. Tiger rolled down the hill, clutching his side, and Harley, who had been occupied much the same as Tiger on McLean's other side, scuttled out of range.

"Toby!" he snapped, and when Toby came running, McLean was a little calmer. But only a little. Still looking up the hill at the tattered lines of clothes and the lead-shredded tents, he said tersely, "Bring up the dynamite."

"What are they doing now?" Big Tom asked.

Slocum had signaled the girls to get down and hold their fire while McLean's men made colanders of the laundry and tents. He'd situated the women far enough up the slope and behind that long, low, uneven upthrust of rock. He didn't figure they'd have much chance of getting shot so long as they kept down. He'd figured to let McLean use up all his ammunition firing blind through the clotheslines. He figured they must be about down to scratch by now.

Slocum peered from the mouth of the mine, leaning out as far as he dared. They likely had a few shots left, and he didn't particularly want them deposited in his hide.

"Well, I'd like to tell you that they're goin' home, Tom, but I don't think so," he said.

Big Tom leaned past him, blinking in the sun, and looked down the hill. "Aw, crud. They doing what I think they're doing?"

Slocum nodded. "Yup."

Panicked, Big Tom asked, "Should we get the gals out of there?"

Slocum leaned back in and dug into his pocket for his fixings. His left arm was thumping right in time to his heartbeat, and he wanted to get this over with and avail himself of a little female nursing. "You ever see a baseball game?"

"What does that have to do with anything?" Tom demanded. "That's dynamite they're carrying back to their lines! Dynamite, Slocum! Shouldn't we shoot or something?"

One-handed, Slocum began to roll himself a quirlie. "You ever pace off the distance between home plate and the outfield?"

When Big Tom didn't answer, but only grew more red-faced and angry, Slocum continued solemnly, "Well, I have, and I'm willin' to bet that those gals are at least that far, plus twenty paces or so, from McLean. His boys ain't hitting that dynamite with no bat, not unless they're owlshit crazy, and they're throwin' it uphill to boot. I'm willin' to bet good money that—here they come!"

Three sticks of dynamite, their blazing fuses barely visible against the bright desert sun, sailed through the air.

"Might want to duck," said Slocum, although he stood his ground.

The first sticks to hit the ground fell short, as he

had imagined they would, and began to roll backward, toward the tents. The third exploded on impact
and took out one cook fire and half of the laundry.
The other two exploded only a half second later, and
Slocum watched as one of the tents sailed into the
air in flames, McLean's men scattering before it.

A cheer rose up from the women—although there
were a few wails too, likely in mourning for those
possessions that had been blown to pieces in the
tent—and Tom breathed, "Well, I'll be jiggered!"

He didn't have much time to be awed, though,
because two more sticks followed the first three.
One of these was tossed by a man with a less than
admirable arm, because it only went as far as the
burning tent, which caught it on its way back to
earth, and exploded it prematurely.

The second stick, being thrown a bit farther to the
south than the others, went higher up the hill and
landed at Rose's feet. Scowling, she gave it a kick.
It bounced back down the slope, blowing up the rest
of the clotheslines.

Unfortunately, she had kicked it just a little too
close to the mouth of the Bum Nugget. The blast
shivered the surrounding rocks, and Slocum dropped
his fixings, grabbed hold of Tom, and pulled him as
far back into the mine as he could.

He landed on his bad arm—with Tom on top of
him—just as a shower of rock closed down the tunnel's opening and effectively shut off the light.

"The old biddy did that on purpose," Tom muttered in the darkness.

"Get the hell off me," growled Slocum.

21

Miranda couldn't see the mine's entrance from where she was secreted, but she heard the rock slide and felt her stomach give a sick twist. Before she knew what she was doing, she was on her feet and racing around the boulders, down the slope. "Tom!" she cried. "Tom!"

Mindless of airborne sparks, she half-skidded, half-fell onward, toward the roiling cloud of dust raised by the slide. She barely saw Rose, covered in fine grit, slowly rising from her perch on the big boulder, but she saw the fist in front of her face, saw it coming suddenly closer as she ran right into it.

Jamaica popped up from her cover behind the palo-verdes. "Slocum!" she shouted as rock rumbled and slid downward, covering the Bum Nugget's opening. And then she saw Miranda through the cloud of dust and smoke, saw her dart from behind the rocks above the mine, saw her dash down the slope.

And collide with Rose's outstretched fist.

Miranda slithered to the ground and rolled to a halt, out cold. Jamaica was about to run down there too, to go to her or go to Slocum, she wasn't sure which. But Sassafras caught her arm.

"Stop it, Jamaica!" she hissed. "You can't do a thing. But Rose, she's going to." She pointed as Rose, mad as a bag of wet bobcats and just as mean, began to lumber slowly down the hill, the top of her broken parasol in her fist.

"What else can go wrong?" Jamaica groaned as she covered her eyes with weary hands.

Sassafras, however, was cool as a cucumber and shouted, "Easy, there, you girls! Back off, Susan. Sit down, Cindy. Everybody, just hold your fire."

Slocum and Big Tom had managed to get untangled and relight a lantern, and were busy moving rock. Big Tom worked like a man possessed, and Slocum did his part, although he was hampered by only having the use of one arm.

The slide wasn't as bad as they had at first thought, and within just a few moments they had cleared a small space that let in the daylight, then widened it enough that one man could poke his head out.

Slocum did, only to discover that Rose was on the move, and she looked deadly determined. He didn't know what she was up to, but it was bound to be ugly.

"Hurry!" he said to Tom, and they both began to shove rocks again.

Rose was talking now, shouting, and it made Slocum nervous at hell. She was giving Drummond McLean a very large piece of her mind, and in no uncertain terms. Slocum himself had been the target of her poisonous tongue, and it wouldn't have surprised him if McLean just sicced his sniper on the old bitch to shut her up. Or tossed up another stick of dynamite.

But McLean's men had scattered in the face of one of the first blasts, as he recalled. He didn't know if the sniper was still alive, or if he was close enough to get a clear shot. Furthermore, despite Big Tom's tourniquet, Slocum had lost a lot of blood and he knew it. He was feeling woozy and faint, and had to brace himself on the mine wall every blasted time he lobbed another stone from the pile.

"Sonofabitch," he muttered under his breath as he hefted the weight of yet another rock.

McLean heard Rose coming before he saw her.

"Drummond!" she shouted, and her disembodied voice came to him through a haze of dust and grit, and sparks thrown up by the flapping, burning tarps.

"Drummond McLean! Get your straw-walkin', fancy-boy butt out here where I can see it!"

And then he saw her emerging from the cloud of smoke and dust, like a mad hippopotamus dressed in tattered pink and purple and carrying a sawed-off parasol that she waved at him like a weapon.

"You scummy little sonofabitch!" she railed as she lumbered closer. Her round face was grimy with dirt, and the perpetual scowl marks looked even deeper. "This is enough! I've had it with you!"

Harley—who was far to the rear, having taken flight at the first blast—called, "Mr. McLean? You

want I should kill the bitch?" His rifle was poised
halfway to his shoulder.

"No!" shouted McLean. That would be all he
needed. "Stand down, Harley!"

Harley shrugged, but he dropped the rifle and let
it dangle from his fingers.

Toby, ten paces to his left, said, "Mr. McLean?
We could rush 'em. If we could work a way to get
around them tents and the fire, I mean."

McLean shook his head. She was getting closer.

"It was bad enough when you come to Twin
Buttes," Rose continued, and each step closer was
like a cold knife in his belly. He couldn't move.
"Worse when you started buyin' out half the folks
in town," she continued. "And what you done to Big
Tom here was a scandal. But did I say anythin'? No,
sir, you bet your butt I didn't. I didn't make a peep.
But when you threw your own sweet mama outta
town, that was the goddamn clincher. I oughta throw
you over my knee and paddle the holy Jesus outta
you, you skinny-assed, sorry little whelp."

McLean backed up a step. "Now, Rose . . ."

"I let you have all the free rides you wanted up
to my house," she continued, oblivious to his plea.
"I paid for your room and board for years, paid for
your highfalutin schoolin', which, I might add,
you've wasted entirely. And I didn't say nothin'
when them girls was killed, did I? But goddamn it,
Drummond!" She stopped only ten feet from him
and propped chubby, beringed hands on her massive
hips. "You're a real bad boy."

"What's she talking about, Boss?" hissed Tiger, behind him.

"Shut up," McLean whispered without taking his eyes off Rose.

"Why'd I do what I done, huh?" she went on. There didn't seem to be anything he could do to stop her. His feet seemed frozen to the ground. "Why'd I send you back East and fork over the cash for all them expensive schools? So's you could grow up to be a murderer? So's you could wait until you was thirty-five goddamn years old to traipse out here like Mr. Bigwig and make my life a livin' hell?"

"But Mama . . ." The words came out of him in a little squeak, and he heard Tiger muttering something as he inched away.

"Don't 'Mama' me, you little candy-ass twit!" she spat. "Twin Buttes was *my* town, you understand? If you'd been anybody else, I would'a run your skinny butt outta the damn place—or at least give you a visit to the woodshed you wouldn't forget— when you first started tryin' to take over. Hell, I only let you talk me outta my house 'cause I had a moment of whatchacall. Sentiment." Smoke and fire billowed behind her like the coming of Judgment, McLean thought with a shiver.

"Are you listenin' to me, boy?"

McLean gulped. "Yes, Rose."

"I want you outta here," she said, and she began to walk toward him again. "I want you outta here and gone for good and all."

He couldn't move. All the starch had gone straight out of him, and he meekly waited until

Rose, cursing and swearing, had come belly to belly with him.

She jabbed his chest with her broken parasol, and it nearly knocked him over. "I want you to sign over them businesses to me, you marmalade-dipped little bastard." She turned just long enough to shout, "Paper and a pen, goddamn it!" over her shoulder. Her head whipped back toward him. "You're gonna sign the Daisy Cutter over to Big Tom, if'n those fools of yours ain't already killed him. And you're gonna get your sorry butt back on the other side of the Mississippi. Leave the West to me!"

He made one final attempt to salvage his manhood, his reputation. "You can't tell me to—"

She whacked him over the head with her parasol, and he cringed.

"Goddamn it, you insolent whelp!" Rose shouted. "Do what your mama tells you!"

He heard the sounds of men trying to quietly step into leather and slink away, and the sound of a wagon easing out. It was too late. He'd been humiliated in front of his men as well as the whores of the town, and all because of his mother, this obese, triple-chinned, foolish cow, who had never done more for him than whelp him in a field. She'd birthed him like a cow drops a calf or a bitch drops a pup, then bundled him off to the East. Well, she had sent money, but still . . . Numbly, he felt his hands balling into fists at his sides.

"Us McLeans is all fools or outlaws or worse," she muttered, staring at him as if he wasn't there, as if he wasn't a living man at all, but a badly made statue at which she was turning up her nose. "We're no good. I thought that once Pappy was gone, I'd be the last. But no, you had to slip through the French letter or dodge the vinegar or whatever it was you done to take root. Why the hell couldn't you stay back East?"

"I suppose I had some of my father in me," he said, in an attempt to salvage what little was left of his pride, but the words came out clipped and hard and sounding foreign, as if someone else had said them.

Rose snorted and tucked her chins. "Whoever he was, the rat bastard."

"I could kill you," McLean whispered.

She smiled nastily. "But you won't."

"Paper, Miss Rose," said a voice, and he looked over to see Sassafras standing behind Rose. She held a few scraps of partially burnt paper in one hand, and a pen and ink bottle in the other. Somehow she'd come all the way down the hill and he hadn't noticed.

He also hadn't noticed that there were at least a dozen women standing fifteen feet behind her, most of them holding rifles. His rifles, goddamn it. The rest had clustered just up the hill, right behind Slocum. Big Tom Malloy was just crawling out of the mine.

Quickly, McLean checked over his shoulder. The horses were gone, along with his men. Even Toby had fled on that lousy pinto of his.

Just one wagon and his saddle horse remained. Harley stood by the lead horse, and Tiger waited up on the seat. They both looked more than embarrassed.

"Do it now," Rose said softly, although her pitch was the only thing remotely soft about it. "Do it. One way or the other."

"Goddamn you, Rose," he said between gritted teeth. But he took the pen and paper.

"I'll be damned," Slocum said, scratching at the back of his neck.

"Probably," replied Jamaica, who was fussing at his arm. It was still bleeding, despite the tourniquet.

Slocum had heard most of the interchange between Rose and McLean, but he asked, "Did anybody know they were kin?"

Edna Merle, Rose's reed-thin cook, piped up. "I worked for her these last twenty years, from Kansas City to Dodge to sixteen other places, and finally here. I ain't never heard her mention it." She shook her head, her iron-gray bun bobbling. "Never a word. Course, as I remember, up till 'bout ten, fifteen years back, she was always havin' me mail letters to someplace in Massachusetts. Went out like clockwork, one a month."

Incredulously, Slocum turned toward her. "Twenty *years*?" He couldn't imagine anybody spending twenty minutes in a room with Rose, let alone working for her, if there was a window handy. Even a third-floor window.

Edna Merle shrugged. "Oh, she ain't that bad," she said philosophically. "I worked for worse."

Slocum was just mulling over who she might have worked for when he heard Tom shout, "Miranda! Help, Miranda!"

He turned sharply, and was rewarded by a quick surge of dizziness—and Jamaica's arm was suddenly the only thing between him and the ground.

"Sit," she demanded.

He didn't have much choice. He folded like a licorice stick on a hot day.

"Miranda's all right," Jamaica said as she sat beside him. "Rose just knocked her out, that's all. Susan," she said to one of the girls above them, "fetch me some clean water and rip up some bandages, would you?" She began to remove Tom's tourniquet, muttering, "My God, Slocum, this is a lot of blood!" Then Slocum heard her mutter, "Her town, my ass! I was here before that old sow was!"

Slocum looked over at her, and she added, "By at least a day or two, Slocum! Oh, she's going to be impossible now! She'll have the paper and the dry goods and the outfitters and everything else."

Slocum looked down the hill. Rose was standing over Drummond McLean, dictating while he scribbled, and for a lingering second, Slocum felt sorry for him: not so much for the fact that Rose had browbeaten him in front of everybody, but because it must be pure hell to have Rose for a mama.

That any son of Rose's would have wished to find her was one thing. Slocum could fathom that. But the fact that McLean had stuck around afterward—and tried to take the town out from under her, even if she had it only in her mind—was another entirely. They were both as crazy as a pair of colts that had been too long in the locoweed.

No, Slocum decided. He wasn't going to feel a

bit bad for McLean. He had stayed. He deserved everything that Rose was slinging at him.

At 6:15 that evening, Drummond McLean was on the stage, heading west toward Hoople Flats. That was as far as he'd make it that night. He'd bed there and have a bath—Lord, how he needed a bath!— then take the stage north in the morning, eventually catching the train at Flagstaff to head back East.

As he passed the Bum Nugget, he turned his head in the opposite direction. He couldn't stand to look at it, couldn't stand to think about it. They were probably still up there celebrating, goddamn it.

Well, he had fooled all of them. He'd sent Tiger and Harley back to the mine to tell the boys to clear out, and then he'd cut across country at a hard gallop, going directly back to town. He'd somehow managed to dodge the tomato-tossers and the egg-lobbers entirely, and emptied out the petty-cash drawers of each and every business he owned, then gone to the bank and emptied his personal savings account as well as his business accounts.

Ron Gleason, the banker, was probably still pitching a holy fit, but McLean now had roughly $22,000 secreted up on top of the coach in his valise, between clean shirts and a spanking-fresh suit and nice, fresh underwear.

The hell with Rose, he thought, rubbing the back of his head. A frustrated cowpoke with a rock had nailed him as he was boarding the stage, and he grimaced when he felt the rising lump. *That's what you get for trying to ease your aging mother into*

*genteel retirement, Drummond. Well, the hell with
all of them. I'm going someplace clean, by God,
someplace where a man can be tidy without everybody sneering at him. Someplace where a man can
do business!*

They were finally past the Bum Nugget, and he
allowed himself to look out the window again. He
leaned an elbow on the window casing and took a
deep breath.

He'd been foolish to come out here in the first
place, and more foolish still to try to edge in on
Rose's town. He'd been raised by acquaintances—
the woman he called "Aunt Maybelle" had been a
friend of a friend of Rose's, motivated entirely by the
money Rose sent each month. He'd been fostered by
dry and preachy schoolmasters, and once on his own,
had fallen back to his natural proclivities and been
enthusiastically tutored on the streets. He'd been a
con man once, by God, and he could be one again, although certainly more successful than he'd been before.

Hell, now he had business experience!

The stage hit a big bump, and he lost his balance
for a moment, falling back in the seat. "Sorry," said
the drummer beside him, who had also been tossed
around, and now scooted back over. McLean
scowled at him.

So what if when push came to shove he couldn't
put a bullet in his mother, vile as she was? He had
played her, and the old bat had won fair and square.
Well, except for his rifles. How'd they get their
hands on his rifles in the first place?

He muttered a curse.

"You say somethin', mister?" asked the drummer.

"Shut up," growled McLean without looking at him.

Things were going to get better. Things would be fine, just fine. He'd left his pride back there on the desert, but he could get it back again. He was getting it back already. Rose was going to be in for a surprise when she checked the bank accounts. And Tiger and Harley were going to be in for a bigger one when they came back to town and found him gone. He was keeping Tiger's knife for a souvenir.

Hell, maybe the town would lynch the weaselly little sonofabitch!

He smiled.

The stage pulled into Hoople Flats just past dark. With cramped legs, McLean got down from the coach, brushing aside his traveling companion. He was eager for a bath and a shave and clean clothes, and he waited impatiently for his valise and trunk to be tossed down. The trunk came, but not the all-important valise.

When the driver climbed down from the top, McLean grabbed him by the throat and shoved him up against the stage's rear wheel.

"Where's my case!" he demanded. "Where's my valise? Small. Moroccan leather. I saw you put it up there and strap it down with my own eyes!"

The driver, a lean kid little more than half McLean's age, shoved back. McLean went sprawling on the boardwalk.

"Mister," the driver said, "you got any notion of

how many bags and crates and trunks and boxes I
hoist every day? If I did strap down your valise and
if it ain't up there now, which I can promise you it
isn't, it's probably back on the road somewheres.
We hit us a passel of chuckholes on the way in.
Dang stage company oughta do somethin' about that
road, if you ask me. Complain to them."

And then he walked off, leaving McLean sitting
in the street, his face cradled in his arms.

Skunky crouched on the road, smiling wide. He'd
seen the stage, seen the leather bag arc through the
air and drop, and while most of the gals—along with
that shot-up Slocum fellow and Tom Malloy—were
either stamping out the last of the fires or setting out
for town, he'd come down here. His old mare,
Whisk, was waiting patiently off the side of the
road, tied to a thornbush.

"I'd just like to thank you, Lord," he said, still on
his knees and fingering the cash he'd found between
the pressed shirts and the toiletries. "Now, I reckon
I complained a good bit about diggin' them privies
and such, and I'm right sorry. I guess that's what
you wanted me to do, else you wouldn't have rewarded me so fine."

He paused, then added, "Course, you could'a put
some sweets in the mix, Lord, but I ain't holdin' no
grudges, no, sir. Well, amen."

Whistling, he carefully repacked the case, stood
up, and began meticulously brushing away his foot-
prints.

22

"Tom," Miranda said, "this is all going far too fast for me."

He grinned at her, and the morning sun glinted white on his teeth. "Stop putting on the brakes, honey. Here you are, dressed in white and balking in the middle of Main Street! I love you and you love me. Isn't that enough?" He paused for a second, then added, "And if it isn't, did I mention that I'm rich?"

"But I can't!" Miranda insisted. She was in her wedding dress—Tom had insisted on a white one, despite the fact that she knew he thought she was the rankest sort of prostitute. That he didn't care was so sweet that it gave her chills, but still . . .

The bouquet of wild roses was in her hand, and Tom was wearing his boutonniere and about to bust his buttons, and she wanted to go in to the justice of the peace, wanted it like she had never wanted anything before in her life. But yet, she said, "I can't until I . . . Tom, I have to tell you something."

"Tell it fast, darlin'," he said with an infatuated grin. "Slocum and Jamaica are waiting."

She slid a glance across the street, toward the

town hall. She could just see Slocum through the open door. He had his arm in a sling, and was engaged in conversation with somebody hidden in the shadows.

"Come here," she said, grabbing Tom by his sleeve and pulling him back underneath the overhang. She pointed to a barrel. "Sit down."

Tom grinned again. Lord, but he was a handsome man! So kind and so good-tempered and smart and warm and . . . just so *everything*! She'd never find another like him, not ever in a million years. Why, oh, why was she about to ruin it?

"Yes, ma'am," he said, still smiling, and sat down. "Talk quick, honey."

"Tom," she began, shifting nervously from foot to foot, "there's no other way to put this. I . . . I'm not a prostitute."

He stared at her, waiting, with no change of expression.

"Doesn't that surprise you?" she asked with a hike of her brows. What was wrong with him? Why wasn't he overjoyed—or even mad?

Finally, he said, "Nope, it doesn't. That all, sweetheart?" He started to stand up, but she pushed him back down.

"Well . . . well, why do you think I went out to the mine with you if I wasn't one of the . . . them?"

Patiently, he said, "Because you were following Slocum."

Her mouth fell open. "How did you know that?" she demanded.

He sighed, although good-naturedly, and reached

around to pull something from his back pocket. He held it out to her.

"Death Rides a Spotted Stallion," she whispered, touching the cover. "But how did you know? I was so careful!" And then it occurred to her that maybe he didn't know she was "Dusty Rhodes." Maybe he thought that she was just a camp follower, trailing some dime-novel hero from pillar to post!

But he put his arms around her waist and said, "Honey, I'll tell you later how I figured you were writing those things. But not till after we're hitched and you can't run out on me!" He winked, then stood up. "Let's go get married."

He took her hand and studied it for a minute. "Remind me to find you a pen that doesn't leave ink stains all over your pretty little fingers."

"Oh, Tom," she cried, and stood on tiptoes to throw her arms about his neck.

Slocum and Jamaica walked back up to the Pleasure Barge after the ceremony, arms linked. Jamaica had seemed touched by the wedding vows. Slocum was just glad he wasn't the one saying them.

"You seem to be feeling some better," Jamaica said as they went through the open front door. It was business as usual, although a bit more frantic. The single men of Twin Buttes seemed intent on making up for lost time, and there was a steady stream of traffic going up and down the stairs.

"You keep saying that," Slocum said, and moved aside to let an overeager businessman slip past him to the parlor. "You tryin' to tell me something, Mudge?"

Jamaica folded her arms over her ample bosom, and the tops of her breasts plumped out, straining against the fabric of her bodice. "Upstairs, mister. I didn't nurse you all night for nothing. Now it's time to pay for all those cold compresses."

His mouth crooked up in a grin. "So that's the way it is, is it? That the way a fella has to pay his doctor bills in Twin Buttes?" He cupped one hand over the top of a flawless breast, then slid his fingers up her neck, cradling it with his thumb under her chin.

Sassafras, who was just coming up the hall, stopped dead in her tracks with a little jangle of earrings. "You two going to do it right here on the steps?" she asked.

Never taking her eyes from Slocum's, Jamaica purred, "May have to, if I can't get this big galoot upstairs."

"Well, don't mind me," Sassafras said, and went on her way, stopping only to say, "Earl, get back in that parlor and wait your turn, damn it!"

Slocum didn't see who she was talking to. He only had eyes for Jamaica. "All right, kitten," he allowed. "You talked me into it."

"Golly. And I had to work so hard to do it," Jamaica said impishly. She started up the steps, and Slocum gave her a swat on her fanny.

When they were halfway up, stopping every few steps to make way for giggling couples going up or sated cowboys and miners—and happy girls who were just a tad richer—going down, a voice rose up from the hallway below.

"Miss Jamaica?" said a bowlered gentleman, his head craned up. "I don't suppose there's any chance in the world that, well, what with there bein' a two-hour wait and all . . . that you'd personally, that is—"

"Hang your hat on it, Harry," Jamaica said firmly.

Slocum tossed his Stetson down to the bemused businessman and said, "Mine too," before he put his good hand in the small of Jamaica's back and hurried her, giggling, up the rest of the stairs.

When they arrived in her room, it looked a good bit different than when they left it. Gone were the pans of water and the bloody bandages. The bedclothes had been changed. Someone had aired out the room, and gone too was that particular stink that comes when men are wounded and feverish.

Everything was back to normal, with the exception of a bottle of champagne, resting in a bucket of that rarest of commodities, ice. He thought he caught a glimpse of a box of Cuban cigars on the far table too.

"Doc said he never saw anybody recover as fast as you, Slocum," Jamaica said as he crossed the room and sat on the edge of the bed, waiting for her. "Said it was a miracle. Of course, once he got a good look at you, he said it was a miracle you were still alive at all."

Slocum arched a brow.

"All those scars," Jamaica explained. "He said you should have been dead twenty years ago." Her fingers went to the buttons of her bodice. "Course, I told him you were too plain mean to die."

"C'mere," Slocum said, and held out his arm.

She didn't budge, though. She stayed right beside that door, slowly unbuttoning her dress. "Now, Doc told me that you were supposed to take it easy." The dress slipped over her hips and puddled about her ankles on the floor. "He winked when he said it, though." She untied her first petticoat, and it joined the dress. "Wonder where he could have got the idea that you were planning a few heavy activities."

"Jamaica . . ."

She had dropped the second petticoat and the third, and she coyly stepped from the pile of clothing in nothing but her shoes, stockings, pantaloons, and chemise.

Slocum had an erection that was just about to split his trousers, and he started to get up to bring her to the bed. But she held up a hand. "You just stay put, boy. You've already had enough exertion for today, what with walking down for the wedding and all, and I'm not about to go against Doc's orders."

Sideways, she slid into a chair—the same chair that Slocum had screwed her in on the first morning he'd come to town. She kicked off her shoes and stuck out one of those long, slender legs that Slocum wanted wrapped round his waist in the worst way. Carefully, she began to roll down the stocking. "You're not gonna push yourself at all today, my dear." She tossed the stocking aside and started peeling down the other one.

Slocum was still sitting on the edge of the bed.

One-handed, he unbuckled his belt, then unbuttoned his pants to make room for his swollen cock. Making love to Jamaica under the stars was all well and good, but doing it on clean sheets behind a locked door had myriad advantages.

"Get over here, Mudge," he coaxed. "Don't make me come and get you."

She tossed aside the second stocking, then languorously stood up. She didn't come forward, though. She just started her fingers working on the ribbon of her chemise. "Patience, darlin'," she cooed, and deftly pulled the chemise over her head.

She stood there nude to the waist, the filtered sunlight caressing her bare breasts, warming skin that he wanted to get his mouth around in the worst way. Her pale pink nipples were already peaked and hard, but still she didn't move toward him. Her hands went to her waist, and she began to slowly untie her pantaloons.

"My goodness, Slocum," she said after she slid him a glance that lingered on his crotch. "Is that all for little ol' me? No, don't you move!" she added sternly when he lurched forward.

He sat back down. "Jamaica, you're killin' me," he said, just as her pantaloons slid to the floor.

She stepped out of them gracefully. She was all long legs and firm flesh. Her breasts were high and proud, her waist tiny, and her hips smoothly curved. She ran a hand slowly over one breast, down her rib cage, then lower to let it trail off her hip.

"Pretty nice for an old bat who's been camping on the desert, don't you think?" she asked playfully.

"Mudge!"

"Oh, all right," she said with a cluck of her tongue. "Honestly. You men!" She came slowly forward, letting him drink her in with his eyes, and when she was within grabbing distance, he reached for her waist.

But she backed off a step and shook her finger at him. "Bad boy. You let me do all the work." She stepped forward again, and it took every ounce of Slocum's self-control not to pull her off her feet and just burrow into her.

"That last thing we need," she said as she helped him off with his boots, "is for you to pass out and stay that way for a day or two."

With her back to him, she straddled his leg and bent over, and he put the other foot on that beautiful backside, and after a moment, pushed. In her present position, he could see just an inviting hint of that soft, Titian-haired delta between her legs.

He wanted to take her from behind. He wanted to take her any way he could.

The boot came off, and she repeated the process on the second.

"There," she said, tossing the boot aside. "How's that arm?"

"What arm?" he answered gruffly.

She smiled. "Lay back," she said softly, and tossed his hat to the dresser. "Here, put a pillow under your arm. Careful! Now, let's get your britches off."

He knew by now that it was best to follow instructions, to just grin and bear it. Jamaica'd be the death of him yet, but he had a feeling he'd go with a smile on his face.

Sighing, he lay back and propped his arm on a pillow, and slowly, she pulled off his britches. On her way back up from his feet, a motion accomplished by dragging the hard tips of her nipples up his thighs, she stopped to leisurely lick his shaft from base to tip, then circle the throbbing head with her lips.

"Goddamn it, Mudge," he heard himself murmur. "If I wasn't banged up . . ."

She kissed his belly, stuck her tongue into his navel. "Mmm," she purred softly. "You have a taste like no other man, Slocum."

His good hand went to her shoulder and gripped it, urging her head forward, coaxing her along his body, toward his face. He wanted to simply take her, but he had to grudgingly admit that she was right. Every time he so much as thought about moving his left arm, the pain told him otherwise.

"Your shirt," she whispered as she crouched over him, her thighs hugging either side of his hips, the wet, sweet, center of her hovering just above him, her nipples pressing against his chest. "I haven't taken off your shirt."

He ran his hand down her back, following the silky curve to her hip, down to her knee, and up again. "*Now,* Mudge," he whispered.

"Anything for you, Slocum," she said, and reached between their bodies to position his aching shaft. Gratefully, he felt just the tip enter her, and he groaned.

"Anything at all," she repeated. And with a kiss, she sank slowly down upon him.

In the bridal suite of the Silver Cartwheel Hotel, Miranda, now officially Mrs. Thomas Malloy, lolled happily against the pillows. Men were wonderful. Life was wonderful. And Tom had been superb. Both times!

He dozed beside her now, and she turned on her side so that she could study him. So sweet. So handsome.

Does he have any idea? she wondered. *Does he know at all how he makes me feel?*

That little "thing" she had felt while she was spying on Slocum and Jamaica? She had thought it was strong at the time. She'd thought it was a powerful explosion. It had nearly overwhelmed her. But after having experienced her first two carnal acts as Mrs. Tom Malloy, she could say in all honesty that it had been, well, nothing.

No, not nothing exactly.

It got me stirred up enough that I went after Tom, she thought with a smile. *And then he caught me.*

"Law, did you ever," she whispered to his sleeping profile. The late afternoon sun slanted across it, picking out his full lips, his straight nose, his clean brow, his strong jaw. His nostrils flared softly as his slept.

Even in her wildest dreams—and there had been quite a few of those lately—she'd never been able to imagine what it would really feel like to be loved so perfectly. She shivered, and hugged herself at just

the thought of it. He had tenderly explored her
body's every secret place with his fingers and lips
and tongue, and she had climaxed twice—wildly,
madly, wonderfully—before he ever entered her.
The man was a poet of the flesh. And he was hers,
all hers, until the end of time.

She smiled happily. She couldn't seem to stop
smiling.

The only thing niggling at the back of her brain
was the thought that her work in progress, *John Slocum: The Death Mongers,* had gone up in flames.
Silly of her to have left it in the tent, but then, where
else could she have left it? At least Tom had told
her that Mr. Drummond McLean, the openmouthed
chewer, had written out his quit-claim deeds on the
backs of the remaining pages. She supposed there
was some justice in that.

And she had two more novels "in the pipe," so to
speak. *John Slocum: Death Comes Running* and
John Slocum: Death Carries a Colt Pistol would
come out in due course. She wasn't exactly sure if
she really wanted to write another. Oh, Tom didn't
mind. He was actually enthusiastic about it. He said
he never imagined he'd have a famous wife.

She giggled, and covered her mouth. Tom stirred,
but didn't wake.

Famous, my foot, she thought. Dusty Rhodes was
just a little bit famous perhaps, but not she. Perhaps
she'd write another book, but under her real name
this time. Maybe she'd write about what it was like
to be a miner's wife in Arizona.

She was staring at the ceiling, mulling this over,

when she felt movement on the other side of the
bed. Tom rolled toward her and stroked her hair.

"It's almost dark," he said.

"Let's bring on the night," she whispered.

He kissed a line down her throat, her chest, then
softly sucked one waiting nipple into his mouth.

Epilogue

Six days later, Slocum was sufficiently recovered to ride north again. Actually, he'd been ready two days before, but he was having such a high old time with Jamaica that he lingered.

But his feet were getting itchy again, as his daddy used to say, and he finally threw his saddle on that jug-headed bay of Mordecai's. He'd said good-bye to Jamaica up at the Pleasure Barge. She'd cried, but she hadn't tried to hold him. She'd said she knew he couldn't be held.

He jogged out of town past the Twin Buttes jail, and saw Tiger glaring at him from behind his barred window. A gleeful kid tossing rotten eggs forced Tiger's head back down, though. Judging from the smears that covered McLean's—now Rose's—house and businesses, the folks of Twin Buttes had a real fancy for tossing eggs and tomatoes, Slocum thought. Tiger wouldn't be around to be the target for many more of them, though. He'd already been tried and convicted for the murder of soft, blond, little Flossie.

It had been a kangaroo court if Slocum had ever seen one, and the world's shortest trial. The sheriff, who was more than eager to placate the crowd and keep his job now that McLean was gone, had nervously led Tiger into the Thirsty Dog Saloon, which was crammed with waiting townsmen.

"Well?" asked the sheriff, his voice breaking.

"Guilty," said the men as one.

"Hang the whore-killin' sonofabitch," said the bartender, and then everybody had cheered.

Except Tiger, of course.

Nobody had seen hide nor hair of Harley, and it was assumed that he had bounced and jolted his way in the opposite direction from town. At least, the rental horse never came back. The stable man had mentioned that it was worth the price of the nag to have Harley gone.

All in all, Slocum supposed Tiger had got better than he deserved. He was lucky they were planning to hang him formal-like, and hadn't stretched him from the first available tree.

Slocum didn't ride immediately north when he left town. He went south of town, then to the west, until he found the place where Chaco had met his fate. He stepped down off the jug-head and ground-tied him, and then, with the shovel he'd brought from town, he buried what was left of the burnt corpse. The coyotes had been at it, but he gathered up what bones and hooves and hair he could find and buried them all beneath a mound of desert, topped off by rocks.

He didn't say any words. What could you say about a horse anyway, except that he'd been a good keeper, been easy to handle, and had a kind way about him? In the end, Slocum just jammed that shovel down in the ground, handle first, and let it stand as a marker.

He made a final swing past the Bum Nugget. He didn't ride in, just glassed the camp from a distance. Things seemed to be booming. There was no remaining sign of the uproar that had put his arm into a sling, and he could see that they were just starting in on a new shaft, digging straight down into the valley floor. It was just about in the place where he'd figured Tom would put it.

The mining crew had changed a little, though. Some of the sporting girls had gone back to working on their back, and some had left town clutching their shares to their bosoms, but several had decided to guard their investment a little closer, and had given up whoring entirely for rock-breaking, and a little larger piece of the silver pie. He could see a number of females lugging rocks away from the new shaft, and others piling ore into one of the big wagons.

A few of the Daisy Cutter boys were down there too. They'd come over once they'd lost their jobs with McLean, and Tom had said he was going to give them a chance. Slocum spied Skunky, sitting atop an ore wagon and gleefully overseeing the proceedings.

Without thinking, Slocum touched his pocket. The letter Tom had given him for Mad Hat Crockett was still there. He collapsed his spyglass and put it away. Time to move on.

• • •

Better than a week later, he was back up in Bent
Elbow, Nevada. He'd seen Esteban Vargas, picked
up his leopard mare, and explained about Chaco.
And when Vargas demanded a king's ransom in
damages, Slocum didn't quibble. He still felt damn
bad about that little sorrel Appy. He paid Vargas
nearly every cent he had on him, and tossed in the
jug-headed bay to boot.

He rode Cheyenne—now fully recovered and
rested and a sheer pleasure to sit after a week on
that damned jug-head—over to where he'd heard
Mad Hat was at, namely the Big Pepper Tree Saloon. The Big Pepper Tree was badly named, for
there were no pepper trees in sight, and it was barely
large enough to seat six people.

Mad Hat was waiting for him. "Heard you was
back," the old man said, and rocked his chair back
against the thin wall. Sun came through the cracks
between the boards in dusty knives of light. "Took
you long enough. You get there in time?"

"Yup," Slocum said with a nod, and ordered a
whiskey from the board-and-keg bar. "Couple of
days early. Got you a letter in reply too," he said,
sitting down. He and Mad Hat and the bartender
were the only souls in the joint.

Mad Hat took the envelope and tore off the end.
Slocum sipped his whiskey and watched the old
miner's face as he read.

Mad Hat's face grew dark right off, which was
not the best sign. What the hell had Big Tom written
to get Mad Hat's small clothes in that tight a knot
anyhow? But as the old man read on in silence, his

face softened, and at long last, he laughed right out loud. He kept on laughing while he stuffed the letter in his pocket.

"Pour me up another beer, Carlos," he said to the barkeep. He seemed in a jovial mood for somebody who'd looked like he could spit nails just a few minutes earlier.

"You satisfied?" Slocum asked leerily.

"That I am," Mad Hat replied as the barkeep slid his beer across the rough-hewn table. He lifted it and took along gulp. "I'm disappointed, howsom-ever," he said as he wiped the foam from his mus-tache. "Right disappointed, But I s'pose it cain't be helped." He paused and eyed Slocum. "Tom tell you what was in the letter?"

"Neither comin' nor goin'," Slocum said.

Mad Hat nodded curtly. "Just as well, just as well. 'Tweren't none'a your business no how. Just some-thin' betwixt me an' Tom. And my lazy-assed daughter," he added in a grumble. He reached into his back pocket, pulled out a purse, and tossed it across the table. "You done your job. This makes us even."

Slocum hefted the leather bag and felt the heavy weight of gold coins. Without opening it, he stuck it in his pocket. "Thanks."

Mad Hat leaned across the table. "I'll tell you somethin', Slocum. Tell you somethin' of what Tom said."

"No need."

"Oh, this here concerns you."

Slocum arched a brow.

"Tom says as how there's only gonna be two more'a them books about you. He says as how his new wife's temporarily retired from the writin' game."

Slocum sat bolt upright.

"Now, don't get riled," Mad Hat said, and it made matters worse that Slocum could tell the old man was barely holding back a chuckle. "Tom says that 'Dusty Rhodes' ain't gonna write no more books. Them two others, the ones what ain't been printed yet, was already turned in to the company what makes 'em."

"His *wife*?" Slocum roared. "*Miranda* is Dusty Rhodes?"

"That's the size of it."

Slocum stood up so fast that he knocked his chair over in the process. "Son of a *bitch*!" That pretty little blond bit of nothing, acting like she was . . .

"Sonofabitch," he said again, although this time he muttered it.

"Carlos," Mad Hat said, "send somebody to wake up that lawyer fella and bring him on down here. Feel like changin' my will. Goddamn that fool gal Clementine anyhow."

Slocum, who had barely heard him, marched out through the bat-wing doors, leaving them swinging furiously.

"Just take it from me, Slocum," Mad Hat called out after him. "Never have you no daughters!"

Slocum rode eleven miles toward Carson City before the last of the mad leaked out of him.

"Sonofabitch," he muttered with a shake of his head. And then he actually smiled.

Well, what the hell. He'd lived through two of those blasted books, and he guessed he could live through two more.

Besides, he knew a woman in Carson City, and a woman was what he needed right know.

Sinking his heels into Cheyenne's sleek flanks, he cantered into the west.

LONGARM

Explore the exciting Old West with one of the men who made it wild!